Praise for *New York Times* bestselling author Brenda Jackson

"Brenda Jackson writes romance that sizzles and characters you fall in love with."
—*New York Times* bestselling author Lori Foster

"Jackson's trademark ability to weave multiple characters and side stories together makes shocking truths all the more exciting."
—*Publishers Weekly*

"There is no getting away from the sex appeal and charm of Jackson's Westmoreland family."
—*RT Book Reviews* on *Feeling the Heat*

"Jackson's characters are wonderful, strong, colorful and hot enough to burn the pages."
—*RT Book Reviews* on *Westmoreland's Way*

"Jackson is a master at writing."
—*Publishers Weekly* on *Sensual Confessions*

"Brenda Jackson is the queen of newly discovered love.… If there's one thing Jackson knows how to do, it's how to pluck those heartstrings and stir up some seriously saucy drama."
—*BookPage* on *Inseparable*

D1310976

BRENDA JACKSON

is a die "heart" romantic who married her childhood sweetheart, Gerald, and still proudly wears the "going steady" ring he gave her when she was fifteen. Their marriage of forty-one years produced two sons, Gerald Jr., and Brandon, of whom Brenda is extremely proud. Because she's always believed in the power of love, Brenda's stories always have happy endings, and she credits Gerald for being her inspiration.

A *New York Times* and *USA TODAY* bestselling author of over one hundred romance titles, Brenda is a retiree from a major insurance company and now divides her time between family, writing and travel. You may write Brenda at P.O Box 28267, Jacksonville, Florida 32226, by email at authorbrendajackson@gmail.com or visit her website at www.brendajackson.net.

New York Times Bestselling Author

BRENDA JACKSON

Delaney's Desert Sheikh

and

A Little Dare

Recycling programs
for this product may
not exist in your area.

ISBN-13: 978-0-373-60652-8

DELANEY'S DESERT SHEIKH AND A LITTLE DARE
Copyright © 2014 by Harlequin Books S.A.

The publisher acknowledges the copyright holder
of the individual works as follows:

DELANEY'S DESERT SHEIKH
Copyright © 2002 by Brenda Jackson

A LITTLE DARE
Copyright © 2003 by Brenda Jackson

Printed in U.S.A.

www.Harlequin.com

CONTENTS

DELANEY'S
DESERT SHEIKH

Ponder the path of thy feet,
and let all thy ways be established.
—*Proverbs* 4:26

Acknowledgments

To the love of my life, Gerald Jackson, Sr.

To fellow author Olivia Gates, whose help was immeasurable. Thanks for sharing information about your homeland in the Middle East and for giving me a better understanding of your culture.

Chapter 1

This was the first time he had been between a pair of legs and not gotten the satisfaction he wanted.

Jamal Ari Yasir drew in a deep, calming breath as he slid his body from underneath the table. Standing, he wiped the sweat from his brow. After an entire hour he still hadn't been able to stop the table from wobbling.

"I'm a sheikh and not a repairman, after all," he said with a degree of frustration, tossing the handyman tools back in the box where they belonged. He had come to the cabin to get some rest, but the only thing he was getting was bored.

And it was only the second day. He had twenty-eight to go.

He wasn't used to doing nothing. In his country a man's worth was measured by what he accomplished each day. Most of his people worked from sunup to sundown, not because they had to, but because they were accustomed to doing so for the good of Tahran. And although he was the son of one of the most influential sheikhs in the world, he had been required from birth to work just as hard as the people he served.

Over the past three months he had represented his country as a negotiator in a crucial business deal that also involved other nations surrounding Tahran. When the proceedings ended with all parties satisfied, he had felt the need to escape and find solitude to rest his world-weary mind and body.

The sound of a slamming car door caught Jamal's attention, and he immediately wondered who it could be. He knew it wasn't Philip, his former college roommate from Harvard, who had graciously offered him the use of the cabin. Philip had recently married and was somewhere in the Caribbean enjoying a two-week honeymoon.

Jamal headed toward the living room, his curiosity piqued. No one would make the turnoff from the major highway unless they knew a cabin was there—five miles back, deep in the woods. Walking over to the window, he looked out, drawing in a deep breath. Mesmerized. Hypnotized. Suddenly consumed with lust of the worst kind.

An African-American woman had gotten out of a late-model car and was bending over, taking something out of the trunk. All he could see was her backside but that was enough. He doubted he could handle anything else right now.

The pair of shorts she wore stretched tightly across the sexiest bottom he had ever seen—and during his thirty-four years he had seen plenty. But never like this and never this generous. And definitely never this well-defined and proportioned. What he was looking at was a great piece of art with all the right curves and angles.

Without very much effort, he could imagine her backside pressed against his front as they slept in a spoon position. A smile curved his lips. But who would be able to sleep cuddled next to a body like hers? His gaze moved to her thighs. They were shapely, firm and perfectly contoured.

For an unconscious moment he stood rooted in place, gazing at her through the window. Reason jolted his lust-filled mind when she pulled out one large piece of luggage and a smaller piece. He frowned, then decided he would worry about the implications of the luggage later. He wanted to see the rest of her for now.

No sooner had that thought crossed his mind than she closed the trunk and turned around. It took only a split second for heat to course through his body, and he registered that she was simply gorgeous. Strikingly beautiful.

As she continued to toy with her luggage, his gaze began toying with her, starting at the top. She had curly, dark brown hair that tumbled around her honey-brown face and shoulders, giving her a brazenly sexy look. She had a nicely rounded chin and a beautifully shaped mouth.

He reluctantly moved his gaze away from her mouth and forged a path downward past the smooth column of her throat to her high round breasts, then lower, settling on her great-looking legs.

The woman was one alluring package.

Jamal shook his head, feeling a deep surge of regret that she had obviously come to the wrong cabin. Deciding he had seen enough for one day—not sure his hormones could handle seeing much more—he moved away from the window.

Opening the door, he stepped outside onto the porch. He was tempted to ask if he could have his way with her—once, maybe twice—before she left. Instead he leaned in the doorway and inquired in a friendly yet hot-and-bothered voice, "May I help you?"

Delaney Westmoreland jerked up her head, startled. Her heart began racing as she stared at the man standing on the porch, casually leaning in the doorway. And what a man he was. If any man could be described as beautiful, it would be him. The late-afternoon sun brought out the rich caramel coloring of his skin, giving true meaning to the description of tall, dark and handsome. Her experience was limited when it came to men, but it didn't take a rocket scientist to know this man was sexy as sin. This man would cause a girl to drool even with a dry mouth.

Amazing.

He was tall, probably six foot three, and was wearing a pair of European-tailored trousers and an expensive-looking white shirt. To her way of thinking he was dressed completely out of sync with his surroundings.

Not that she was complaining, mind you.

His hair, straight black and thick, barely touched the collar of his shirt, and dark piercing eyes that appeared alert and intelligent were trained on her, just as her gaze was trained on him. She blinked once, twice, to make sure he was real. When she was certain that he was, she forced her sanity to return and asked in a level yet slightly strained voice, "Who are you?"

A moment of silence passed between them before he responded. "I should be asking you that question." He moved away from the doorway and stepped off the porch.

Feeling breathless but trying like hell not to show it, Delaney kept her eyes steady as he approached. After all, he was a stranger, and there was a good chance the two of them were all alone in the middle of nowhere. She ignored the foolish part of her mind that said, There's nothing worse than not taking advantage of a good-looking opportunity.

Instead, she gave in to the more cautious side of her mind and said, "I'm Delaney Westmoreland and you're trespassing on private property."

The sexy-as-sin, make-you-drool man came to a stop in front of her, and when she tipped her head back to look up at him, a warm feeling coiled deep in her stomach. Up close he was even more beautiful.

"And I'm Jamal Ari Yasir. This place is owned by a good friend of mine, and I believe *you're* the one who's trespassing."

Delaney's eyes narrowed. She wondered if he really was a friend of Reggie as he claimed. Had her cousin forgotten he'd loaned this man the cabin when he'd offered it to her? "What's your friend's name?"

"Philip Dunbar."

"Philip Dunbar?" she asked, her voice dropping to a low, sexy timbre.

"Yes, you know him?"

She nodded. "Yes. Philip and my cousin, Reggie, were business partners at one time. Reggie is the one who offered me the use of the cabin. I'd forgotten he and Philip had joint ownership to this place."

"You've been here before?"

"Yes, once before. What about you?"

Jamal shook his head and smiled. "This is my first visit."

His smile made Delaney's breath catch in her throat. And his eyes were trained on her again, watching her closely. She didn't like being under the scope of his penetrating stare. "Do you have to stare at me like that?" she snapped.

His right eyebrow went up. "I wasn't aware I was staring."

"Well, you are." Her eyes narrowed at him. "And where are you from, anyway? You don't look American."

His lips lifted into a grin. "I'm not. I'm from the Middle East. A small country called Tahran. Ever heard of it?"

"No, but then geography wasn't my best subject. You speak our language quite well for a foreigner."

He shrugged. "English was one of the subjects I was taught at an early age, and then I came to this country at eighteen to attend Harvard."

"You're a graduate of Harvard?" she asked.

"Yes."

"And what do you do for a living?" she asked, wondering if perhaps he worked in some capacity for the federal government.

Jamal crossed his arms over his chest, thinking that Western women enjoyed asking a lot of questions. "I help my father take care of my people."

"*Your* people?"

"Yes, *my* people. I'm a sheikh, and the prince of Tahran. My father is the amir."

Delaney knew amir was just another way of referring to a king. "If you're the son of a king then what are you doing here? Although this is a nice place, I'd think as a prince you could do better."

Jamal frowned. "I could if I chose to do so, but Philip offered me the use of this cabin in friendship. It would have been rude of me not to accept, especially since he knew I wanted to be in seclusion for a while. Whenever it's known that I'm in your country, the press usually hounds me. He thought a month here is just what I needed."

"A month?"

"Yes. And how long had you planned to stay?"

"A month, too."

His eyebrow arched. "Well, we both know that being here together is impossible, so I'll be glad to put your luggage back in your car."

Delaney placed her hands on her hips. "And why should I be the one who has to leave?"

"Because I was here first."

He had a point, though it was one she decided not to give him. "But you can afford to go someplace else. I can't. Reggie gave me a month of rest and relaxation here as a graduation present."

"A graduation present?"

"Yes. I graduated from medical school last Friday. After eight years of nonstop studying, he thought a month here would do me good."

"Yes, I'm sure that it would have."

Delaney breathed a not-so-quiet sigh when she saw he was going to be difficult. "There's a democratic way to settle this."

"Is there?"

"Yes. Which do you prefer, flipping a coin or pulling straws?"

Her options made his lips twitch into an involuntary smile. "Neither. I suggest that you let me help you put your luggage back in the car."

Delaney drew in a deep, infuriated breath. How dare he think he could tell her what to do? She'd been the only girl with five older brothers and had discovered fairly early in life not to let anyone from the opposite sex push her around. She would handle him the same way she handled them. With complete stubbornness.

Placing her hands on her hips she met his gaze with the Westmoreland glare. "I am not leaving."

He didn't seem at all affected when he said, "Yes, you are."

"No, I'm not."

His jaw suddenly had the look of being chiseled from stone. "In my country women do what they are told."

Delaney flashed him a look of sheer irritation. "Well, welcome to America, *Your Highness.* In this country women have the right to speak their minds. We can even tell a man where to go."

Jamal's eyebrows shot up in confusion. "Where to go?"

"Yes, like go fly a kite, go take a leap or go to hell."

Jamal couldn't help but chuckle. It was apparent Delaney Westmoreland was potently sassy. He had learned that American women didn't hesitate to let you know when they were upset about something. In his country women learned very early in life not to show their emotions. He decided to try another approach, one that would possibly appeal to her intelligence. "Be reasonable."

She glared at him, letting him know that approach wasn't going to work. "I *am* being reasonable, and right now a cabin on a lake for a month, rent free, is more than reasonable. It's a steal, a dream come true, a must have. Besides, you aren't the only one who needs to be in seclusion for a while."

Delaney immediately thought of her rather large family. Now that she had completed medical school, they assumed she was qualified to diagnose every ache and pain they had. She would never get any rest if they knew where to find her. Her parents knew how to reach her in case of an emergency and that was good enough. She loved her relations dearly but she was due for a break.

"Why are you in seclusion?"

She frowned. "It's personal."

Jamal couldn't help wondering if perhaps she was hiding from a jealous lover or even a husband. She wasn't wearing a wedding band, but then he knew from firsthand experience that some American women took off their rings when it suited them. "Are you married?"

"No, are you?" she responded crisply.

"Not yet," he murmured softly. "I'm expected to marry before my next birthday."

"Good for you, now please be a nice prince and take my luggage into the house. If I'm not mistaken, there are three bedrooms and all with connecting bathrooms, so it's plenty big enough and private enough for the both of us. I plan to do a lot of sleeping, so there will be days when you probably won't see me at all."

He stared at her. "And on those days when I do see you?"

Delaney shrugged. "Just pretend that you don't. However, if you find that difficult to do and feel things are getting a little bit too crowded around here to suit you, I'd completely understand if you left." She glanced around the yard. "By the way, where's your car?"

Jamal sighed, wondering how he could get her to leave. "My secretary has it," he responded drily. "He checked into a motel a few miles away from here, preferring to be close by just in case I needed anything."

Delaney lifted a cool eyebrow. "Must be nice getting the royal treatment."

He ignored her chill and responded, "It has its advantages. Asalum has been with me since the day I was born."

Delaney couldn't help but hear the deep affection in his voice. "Like I said, it must be nice."

"Are you sure you want to stay here?" His tone was slightly challenging as his black eyes held her dark brown ones.

The question, spoken in a deep, sexy voice, gave Delaney pause. No, she wasn't sure, but she knew for certain that she wasn't ready to leave; especially not after driving seven hours straight to get there. Maybe she would feel different after taking a shower and a very long nap.

She met Jamal's dark gaze and almost shuddered under its intensity. A shiver of desire rippled through her. She felt it now, just as she had when she'd first seen him standing on the porch. At twenty-five, she was mature enough to recognize there was such a thing as overactive hormones. But then, she was also mature enough to know how to control them and not yield to temptation. Getting involved with a male chauvinist prince was the last thing she wanted, and she hoped getting involved with her was the last thing he wanted, as well.

She met his gaze and lifted her chin in a defiant stance and said, "I'm staying."

The woman was as stubborn as they came, Jamal thought as he leaned against the doorjamb in the kitchen. He watched Delaney as she unpacked the groceries she had brought with her. When she finished she turned around. "Thanks for bringing in my luggage and those boxes."

He nodded as his gaze held hers. Once again he felt that sudden surge of lust that made his body tighten and knew she had noticed his reaction. Nervously she licked her lips as she dragged her eyes away from his. It was obvious that she was also aware of the strong sexual chemistry arcing between them.

"If you're having second thoughts about staying…"

Her eyes filled with the fire he was getting used to. "Forget it."

"Remember it was your decision," he said evenly.

"I'll remember." She walked over to him and glared up at him. "And I would suggest that you don't get any ideas about trying to do anything underhanded to run me off. I'll leave when I get ready to leave and not before."

Jamal thought that the angrier she got the more beautiful she became. "I'm too much of a gentleman to behave in such a manner."

"Good. I'll take your word on that." She turned to leave the room.

He watched the sway of Delaney's hips until she was no longer in sight. His nostrils flared in response to the enticing feminine scent she had left behind, and the primitive sultan male in him released a low growl.

One thing was for certain; he would not be getting bored again anytime soon.

With a soul-weary sigh, Delaney ran her fingers through her hair and leaned against the closed bedroom door. A jolt of heat ripped from the tip of her painted toes all the way to the crown of her head. Jamal's gaze had been hot and hungry.

What had she gotten herself into?

The thought that she was actually willing to share a cabin with a man she didn't know was plain ludicrous. The only thing to her credit was the fact that while he had been outside getting the boxes out of the car, she had used her cell phone to call Reggie.

Born the same year, she and Reggie had forged a closeness from the time they had been babies, and over the years he had become more than just a cousin. He was sort of like her best buddy.

He had always kept her secrets, and she had always kept his. Since his interest had been in working with numbers, no one was surprised when he had established an accounting firm a few years ago after earning a graduate degree in Business Administration from Morehouse College.

After apologizing for the mix-up, Reggie had assured her that Jamal was legit. He had met him through Philip a few years ago. Reggie further verified Jamal's claim that he was a prince and had gone on to warn her that according to Philip, Jamal had very little tolerance for Western women.

She had ended the conversation with Reggie, thinking that she couldn't care less about the man's tolerance level, and had no intention of letting him dictate whether or not she would stay. She deserved thirty days to rest and do nothing, and by golly, come hell or high water, she planned to enjoy her vacation.

Crossing the room, she plopped down onto a reclining chair. She glanced at the luggage on her bed, too tired to unpack just yet. Putting up the groceries had taken everything out of her. Jamal had stood there the entire time watching her.

Although he hadn't said anything, she had felt his gaze as if it had been a personal caress. And a few times she had actually looked across the room and caught him staring. No, *glaring* was more like it.

She knew his intent had been to try to unnerve her. But as far as she was concerned, he had a long way to go to ruffle her feathers. The Westmoreland brothers—Dare, Thorn, Stone, Chase and Storm—made dealing with someone like Jamal a piece of cake.

Her cheeks grew warm when she imagined that he was probably just as tasty as a piece of cake. Utterly delicious. A mouthwatering delight. Even now her body felt the heat. He had evoked within her the most intense physical reaction and attraction to a man she had ever experienced.

She shook her head, deciding she definitely needed to take a cool shower and not get tempted.

No matter how crazy her body was acting, she didn't need a man. What she needed was sleep.

Chapter 2

Delaney stood in the kitchen doorway and stared for a long moment at the masculine legs sticking out from underneath the kitchen table. Nice, she thought, studying the firmness of male thighs clad in a pair of immaculately pressed jeans.

Since arriving four days ago, this was only her third time seeing Jamal. Just as she'd told him that first day, she intended to get the sleep she deserved. Other than waking up occasionally to grab something to eat, she had remained in her bedroom sleeping like a baby.

Except for that one time he had awakened her, making a racket outside her bedroom window while practicing some type of martial art. She had forced her body from the bed and gone to the window to see what the heck was going on.

Through the clear pane she'd watched him. He'd been

wearing a sweat top and a pair of satin boxing trunks that were expertly tailored for a snug fit.

She'd watched, mesmerized, as he put his body through a series of strenuous standing-jump kicks and punches. She admired such tremendous vitality, discipline and power. She had also admired his body, which showed an abundance of masculine strength. For the longest time she had stood at the window rooted in place, undetected, while she ogled him. A woman could only take a man like Jamal in slow degrees.

Deciding that if she didn't move away from the window she would surely die a slow and painful death from lust overload, she had made her way back to the bed and nearly collapsed.

"Dammit!"

Jamal's outburst got her attention and brought her thoughts back to the present. She couldn't help but smile. No matter how well he mastered the English language, a curse word coming from him didn't sound quite the same as it did coming from an American. Her brothers had a tendency to use that particular word with a lot more flair.

She walked over to the table and glanced down. "Need help?"

At first he froze in place, evidently surprised by her presence. "No, I can manage," was his tart reply.

"You're sure?"

"Positive," he all but snapped.

"Suit yourself," she snapped back. She turned and walked over to the kitchen cabinet to get a bowl for the cereal she had brought with her, ignoring the fact that he had slid from underneath the table and was standing up.

"So, what got you up this morning?" he asked, tossing the tools he'd been using in a box.

"Hunger." She put cereal into her bowl, then poured

on the milk. Seeing the kitchen table was not available for her to use, she grabbed the cereal box and a spoon and went outside onto the porch.

Already the morning was hot and she knew it would get hotter, typical for a North Carolina summer. She was glad the inside of the cabin had air-conditioning. This was sweaty, sticky heat, the kind that made you want to walk around naked.

Her brothers would be scandalized if they knew she'd done that on occasion when it got hot enough at her home, which was one of the advantages of living alone. She released a deep sigh as she sat down on the steps thinking that with Jamal sharing the cabin walking around naked wasn't an option.

She had taken a mouthful of her cereal when she heard the screen door opening behind her. The knowledge that Jamal was out on the porch and standing just a few feet behind her sent every instinct and conscious thought she had into overdrive. Out of the corner of her eye she saw him lean against the porch rail with a cup of coffee in his hand.

"You've given up moonlighting as a repairman already, *Your Highness?*" she asked in a snippy voice, dripping with sarcasm.

He evidently decided to take her taunt in stride and replied, "For now, yes, but I intend to find out what's wrong with that table and fix it before I leave here. I would hate to leave behind anything broken."

Delaney glanced over at him then wished she hadn't. It seemed his entire face, dark and stunning, shone in the morning sunlight. If she thought he'd been classically beautiful and had dressed out of sync four days ago, then today he had done a complete turnaround. Shirtless, unshaven and wearing jeans, he looked untamed and rugged and no longer like a wolf in sheep's clothing. He looked every bit a wolf, wild and rapacious and on the prowl. If given the chance he would probably eat her alive and lick his chops afterward.

There was nothing in the way he looked to denote he was connected to royalty, a prince, a sheikh. Instead what she saw was an extremely handsome man with solid muscles and a body that exuded sheer masculinity.

He lowered his head to take a sip of his coffee, and she used that time to continue to study him undetected. Now that he was standing, she could see the full frontal view. His jeans were a tight fit and seemed to have been made just for his body. Probably had since he could afford a private tailor. And even if she hadn't seen him doing kickboxing, it would be quite obvious that he kept in shape with his wide, muscular shoulders, trim waistline and narrow hips.

She imagined having the opportunity to peel those jeans off him just long enough to wrap her legs tight around his waist. And then there was his naked chest. A chest her hand was just itching to touch. She was dying to feel whether his muscles were as hard as they looked.

Delaney's heart began pounding. She couldn't believe she was thinking such things. She was really beginning to lose it. Incredible. Nothing like this had ever happened to her before. She couldn't think of one single man in all her twenty-five years who had made her feel so wanton, so greedy, so…needy.

The only need she had experienced with the guys she had taken the time to date in college and medical school had been the need to bring the date to a quick end. And her only greed had been for food, especially her mother's mouthwatering strawberry pie.

No longer wanting to dwell on her sex life—or lack

thereof—she racked her brain, trying to remember the question she had intended to ask Jamal a few minutes earlier. The same brain that had helped her to graduate at the top of her class just last week had turned to mush. She collected her scattered thoughts and remembered the question. "What's wrong with the table?"

He raised his head and looked at her as if she was dense. "It's broken."

She glared at him. "That much is obvious. How is it broken?"

He shrugged. "I have no idea. It wobbles."

Delaney raised her eyes heavenward. "Is that all?"

"A table is not supposed to wobble, Delaney."

And I shouldn't be getting turned on from the way you just said my name, she thought, turning her attention away from him and back to her food. That was the first time he had called her by name, and her body was experiencing an intense reaction to it. His tone of voice had been low and husky.

Her eyes stayed glued to her cereal box as she ate, thinking that her fixation with Tony the Tiger was a lot safer than her fascination with Jamal the Wolf. The last thing she needed was a complication in her life, and she had a feeling that getting involved with Jamal would definitely rank high on the Don't Do list. She had no doubt he was a master at seduction. He looked the part and she was smart enough to know he was way out of her league.

Satisfied that she was still in control of her tumultuous emotions, at least for the time being, Delaney smiled to herself as she continued to eat her cereal.

Releasing a deep sigh, Jamal commanded his body to take control of the desire racing through it. Ever since he had begun business negotiations with the country surrounding Tahran for a vital piece of land lying between them, he had been celibate, denying his body and freeing his mind to totally concentrate on doing what was in the best interest of his country. But now that the negotiations were over, his body was reminding him it had a need that was long overdue.

He scolded himself for his weakness and tried to ignore the sexual urges gripping him. If he had returned home after Philip's wedding instead of taking his friend up on his offer to spend an entire month at this cabin, he would not be going through this torment.

In Tahran there were women readily available for him—women who thought it a privilege as well as an honor to take care of their prince's needs. They would come to his apartment, which was located in his own private section of the palace, and pleasure him any way he wanted. It had always been that way since his eighteenth birthday.

There was also Najeen, the woman who had been his mistress for the past three years. She was trained in the art of pleasing only him and did an excellent job of it. He had provided her with her own lavish cottage on the grounds not far from the palace, as well as personal servants to see to her every need. At no time had he ever craved a woman.

Until now.

"Tell me about your homeland, Jamal."

Jamal arched a brow, surprised at Delaney's request. He shifted his gaze from his cup of coffee and back to her. Her honey-brown face glowed in the sunlight, making her appear radiant, golden. She wasn't wearing any makeup, so her beauty was natural, awe-inspiring. He swallowed hard and tried once again to ignore the urgent need pounding inside him, signals of desire racing through his body.

"What do you want to know?" he asked with a huskiness he almost didn't recognize.

Delaney placed her empty bowl aside and leaned back on both hands as she looked at him. "Anything you want to tell me. It must be an interesting place to live."

He chuckled at the curiosity in her voice, then stared down at her for several moments before he began speaking. "Yes, interesting," he said slowly, "and quite beautiful." She couldn't know that he had just referred to his country...as well as to her.

Fighting for total control, he continued. "Tahran is located not far from Saudi Arabia, close to the Persian Gulf. It's a relatively small country compared to others close to it like Kuwait and Oman. Our summers are intensely hot and our winters are cool and short. And unlike most places in the Middle East, we get our share of rain. Our natural resources in addition to oil are fish, shrimp and natural gas. For the past few years my people have lived in peace and harmony with our neighbors. Once in a while disagreements flare up, but when that happens a special regional coalition resolves any disputed issues. I am one of the youngest members of that coalition."

"Are both your parents still living?"

Jamal took another sip of his coffee before answering. "My mother died when I was born and for many years my father and I lived alone with just the servants. Then Fatimah entered our lives."

"Fatimah?"

"Yes, my stepmother. She married my father when I was twelve." Jamal decided not to mention that his parents' marriage had been prearranged by their families to bring peace to two warring nations. His mother had been an African princess of Berber descent, and his father, an Arab prince. There had been no love between them, just duty, and he had been the only child born from that union. Then one day his father brought Fatimah home and their lives hadn't been the same.

His father's marriage to Fatimah was supposed to have been like his first marriage, one of duty and not love. But it had been evident with everyone from the start that the twenty-two-year-old Egyptian beauty had other plans for her forty-six-year-old husband. And it also became apparent to everyone in the palace that Fatimah was doing more for King Yasir than satisfying his loneliness and his physical needs in the bedroom. Their king was smiling. He was happy and he didn't travel outside his sheikhdom as often.

King Yasir no longer sent for other women to pleasure him, bestowing that task solely upon his wife. Then, within a year of their marriage, they had a child, a daughter they named Arielle. Three years later another daughter was born. They named her Johari.

Arielle, at nineteen, was now married to Prince Shudoya, a man she had been promised to since birth. Johari, at sixteen, was a handful after having been spoiled and pampered by their father. Jamal smiled, inwardly admitting that he'd had a hand in spoiling and pampering her, as well.

He simply adored his stepmother. More than once during his teen years, she had gone to his father on his behalf about issues that had been important to him.

"Do the two of you get along? You and your stepmother?"

Delaney's question invaded his thoughts. "Yes, Fatimah and I are very close."

Delaney stared at him. For some reason she found it

hard to imagine him having a "very close" relationship with anyone. "Any siblings?" she decided to ask.

He nodded. "Yes, I have two sisters, Arielle and Johari. Arielle is nineteen and is married to a sheikh in a neighboring sheikhdom, and Johari is sixteen and has just completed her schooling in my country. She wants to come to America to further her studies."

"Will she?"

He looked at her like she had gone stone mad. "Of course not!"

Delaney stared at him, dumbfounded, wondering what he had against his sister being educated in the United States. "Why? You did."

Jamal clenched his jaw. "Yes, but my situation was different."

Delaney lifted her brow. "Different in what way?"

"I'm a man."

"So? What's that supposed to mean?"

"Evidently it means nothing in this country. I have observed more times than I care to count how the men let the women have control."

Delaney narrowed her eyes. "You consider having equal rights as having control?"

"Yes, in a way. Men are supposed to take care of the women. In your country more and more women are being educated to take care of themselves."

"And you see that as a bad thing?"

He gazed at her and remembered her sassiness from the first day and decided the last thing he wanted was to get embroiled in a bitter confrontation with her. He had his beliefs and she had hers. But since she had asked his opinion he would give it to her. "I see it as something that would not be tolerated in my country."

What he didn't add was that the alternative—the one

his stepmother used so often and had perfected to an art—was for a woman to wrap herself around her husband's heart so tightly that he would give her the moon if she asked for it.

Taking another sip of coffee, Jamal decided to change the subject and shift the conversation to her. "Tell me about your family," he said, thinking that was a safer topic.

Evidently it's not, he thought when she glared at him.

"My family lives in Atlanta, and I'm the only girl as well as the youngest in the third generation of Westmorelands. And for the longest time my five brothers thought I needed protecting. They gave any guy who came within two feet of me pure hell. By my eighteenth birthday I had yet to have a date, so I finally put a stop to their foolishness."

He smiled. "And how did you do that?"

A wicked grin crossed her face. "Since I never had a social life I ended up with a lot of free time on my hands. So I started doing to them what they were doing to me—interfering in their lives. I suddenly became the nosy, busybody sister. I would deliberately monitor their calls, intentionally call their girlfriends by the wrong name and, more times than I care to count, I would conveniently drop by their places when I knew they had company and were probably right smack in the middle of something immoral."

She chuckled. "In other words, I became the kid sister from hell. It didn't take long for them to stop meddling in my affairs and back off. However, every once in a while they go brain dead and start sticking their noses into my business again. But it doesn't take much for me to remind them to butt out or suffer the consequences if they don't."

Jamal shook his head, having the deepest sympathy for her brothers. "Are any of your brothers married?"

She stared at him, her eyes full of amusement at his question. "Are you kidding? They have too much fun being single. They are players, the card-carrying kind. Alisdare, whom we call Dare, is thirty-five, and the sheriff of College Park, a suburb of Atlanta. Thorn is thirty-four and builds motorcycles as well as races them. Last year he was the only African-American on the circuit. Stone will be celebrating his thirty-second birthday next month. He's an author of action-thriller novels and writes under the pen name of Rock Mason."

She shifted in her seat as she continued. "Chase and Storm are twins but look nothing alike. They are thirty-one. Chase owns a soul-food restaurant and Storm is a fireman."

"With such busy professions, how can they find the time to keep tabs on you?"

She chuckled. "Oh, you would be surprised. They somehow seem to manage."

"Are your parents still living?"

"Yes. They have been together for over thirty-seven years and have a good marriage. However, my mother bought into my father's philosophy that she was supposed to stay home and take care of him and the kids. But after I left home she found herself with plenty of spare time on her hands and decided to go back to school. Dad wasn't too crazy with the idea but decided to indulge her, anyway, thinking she'd only last a few months. I'm proud to say that she graduated three years ago with a graduate degree in education."

Jamal set his empty coffee cup aside. "For some reason I have a feeling that you influenced your mother's sudden need to educate herself."

Delaney chuckled. "Of course. I've always known she had a brilliant mind—a mind that was being wasted doing nothing but running a house and taking care of her family. You know what they say. A mind is a terrible thing to waste. And why should men have all the advantages while women get stuck at home, barefoot and pregnant?"

Jamal shook his head. He hoped to Allah that Delaney Westmoreland never had the opportunity to visit his country for an extended period of time. She would probably cause a women's rights revolution with her way of thinking.

He stretched his body, tired of the conversation. It was evident that somewhere along the way Delaney had been given too much freedom. What she needed was some man's firm hand of control.

And what he needed was to have his head examined.

Even now his nostrils were absorbing her feminine scent, and it was nearly driving him insane. As she sat on the steps, her drawn-up knees exposed a lot of bare thigh that the shorts she was wearing didn't hide.

"Do you have female doctors in your country?"

He looked at her when her question pulled him back into the conversation. It was the same conversation he had convinced himself a few moments ago that he no longer wanted to indulge in. "Yes, we have women that deliver babies."

"That's all they do?" she asked annoyed.

He thought for a second. "Basically, yes."

She glared at him as she pursed her lips. "Your country is worse off than I thought."

"Only you would think so. The people in my country are happy."

She shook her head. "That's sad."

He lifted a brow. "What's sad?"

She drew his gaze. "That you would think they are happy."

Jamal frowned, feeling inordinately annoyed. Had she given him the opportunity, he would have told her that thanks to Fatimah, a highly educated woman herself, things had begun to change. The women in his country were now encouraged to pursue higher education, and several universities had been established for that purpose. And if they so desired, women could seek careers outside of the home. Fatimah was a strong supporter of women enjoying political and social rights in their country, but she was not radical in her push for reform. She simply used her influence over his father to accomplish the changes she supported.

He moved from the rail. It was time to practice his kickboxing, but first he needed to take a walk to relieve the anger consuming his mind and the intense ache that was gripping the lower part of his body. "I'm going down to the lake for a while. I'll see you later."

Delaney scooted aside to let him walk down the steps, tempted to tell him to take his time coming back. She watched as he walked off, appreciating how he filled out his jeans from the back. There was nothing like a man with a nice-looking butt.

She pulled in a deep breath and let it out again. Every time he looked at her, directly in her eyes, sparks of desire would go off inside of her. Now she fully understood what Ellen Draper, her college roommate at Tennessee State, meant when she'd tried explaining to her the complexities of sexual chemistry and physical attraction. At the time she hadn't had a clue because she hadn't yet met a man like Jamal Yasir.

Standing, she stretched. Today she planned to explore

the area surrounding the cabin. Then later she intended to get more sleep. For the past three weeks she had studied all hours of the day and night preparing for final exams and had not gotten sufficient rest.

Now that she could, she would take advantage of the opportunity to relax. Besides, the less she was around Jamal, the better.

Jamal kept walking. He had passed the lake a mile back but intended to walk off as much sexual frustration as he could. The anger he'd felt with Delaney's comment about the people in his country not being happy had dissolved. Now he was dealing with the power of lust.

He stopped walking and studied the land surrounding the cabin. From where he stood the view was spectacular. This was the first time since coming to the cabin that he had actually taken the time to walk around and appreciate it.

He remembered the first time Philip had mentioned the cabin in the Carolinas, and how the view of the mountains had been totally breathtaking. Now he saw just what his friend had meant.

His mind then went back to Delaney, and he wondered if she had seen the view from this spot and if she would find it as breathtaking as he did. He doubted she had seen anything, since she rarely left the confines of her bedroom for long periods of time.

Jamal leaned against a tree when he heard his cell phone ring. He unsnapped it from the waist of his jeans and held it to his ear. "Yes, Asalum, what is it?"

"I'm just checking, Your Highness, to make sure all is well and that you don't need anything."

He shook his head. "I'm fine, but I have received an unexpected visitor."

"Who?"

He knew that Asalum was immediately on alert. In addition to serving as his personal secretary, Asalum had been his bodyguard from the time Jamal had been a child to the time he had officially reached manhood at eighteen.

He told him about Delaney's arrival. "If the woman is being a nuisance, Your Highness, perhaps I can persuade her to leave."

Jamal sighed. "That won't be necessary, Asalum. All she does most of the time is sleep, anyway."

There was a pause. Then a question. "Is she pregnant?"

Jamal arched a brow. "Why would you think she is pregnant?"

"Most women have a tendency to sleep a lot when they are pregnant."

Jamal nodded. If anyone knew the behavior of a pregnant woman it would be Asalum. Rebakkah, Asalum's wife, had borne him twelve children. "No, I don't think she's pregnant. She claims she's just tired."

Asalum snorted. "And what has she been doing to be so tired?"

"Studying for finals. She recently completed a medical degree at the university."

"Is that all? She must be a weak woman if studying can make her tired to the point of exhaustion."

For some reason Jamal felt the need to defend Delaney. "She is not a weak woman. If anything she's too strong. Especially in her opinions."

"She sounds like a true Western woman, Your Highness."

Jamal rubbed his hand across his face. "She is. In

every sense of the words. And, Asalum, she is also very beautiful."

For the longest moment Asalum didn't say anything, then he said quietly, "Beware of temptation, my prince."

Jamal thought about all that he had been experiencing since Delaney had arrived. Even now his body throbbed for relief. "Your warning comes too late. It has gone past temptation," Jamal said flatly.

"And what is it now?"

"Obsession."

Chapter 3

After being at the cabin a full week, Delaney finally completed the task of unpacking and put away the last of her things. With arms folded across her chest she walked over to the window and looked out. Her bedroom had a beautiful view of the lake, and she enjoyed waking up to it every morning. A number of thoughts and emotions were invading her mind, and at the top of the list was Jamal Yasir. She had to stop thinking about him. Ever since their talk that morning a few days ago, he had been on her mind although she hadn't wanted him there. So she had done the logical thing and avoided him like the plague.

A bit of anger erupted inside of her. In the past she had been able to school her thoughts and concentrate on one thing. And with that single-minded focus she had given medical school her complete attention. Now it seemed that with school behind her, her mind had gotten a life of its own and decided Jamal deserved her full consideration.

She was always consumed with thoughts of him. Intimate thoughts. Wayward thoughts. Thoughts of the most erotic kind. She wasn't surprised, because Jamal was the type of man who would elicit such thoughts from any woman, but Delaney was annoyed that she didn't have a better handle on her mental focus. Even with medical school behind her, she was still facing two years of residency, which would require another two years of concentration. An intimate relationship with any man should be the last thing on her mind.

But it wasn't.

And that's what had her resentful, moody and just plain hot, to the highest degree. Deciding to take a walk to cool off—like she really thought that would help—she grabbed her sunglasses off the dresser. She stepped outside of her room only to collide with the person who had been dominating her thoughts.

Jamal reached out to grab her shoulders to steady her and keep her from falling. She sucked in a quick breath when she noticed he was shirtless. Dark eyes gazed down into hers making her knees go weak, and the intensity of her lust went bone deep.

The rate of her breathing increased when his hand moved from her shoulder to her neck and the tip of his fingers slowly began caressing her throat. She could barely breathe with the magnitude of the sensations consuming her. The chemistry radiating between them was disturbingly basic and intrinsically sexy, and it was playing havoc with all five of her senses.

The sound of thunder roared somewhere in the distance and jolted them. He slowly released his hold, dropping his hands to his side. "Sorry, I didn't mean to bump into you," he said, the sound a throaty whisper that hummed through every nerve in Delaney's body before flowing through her bloodstream. And from the look in his eyes she could tell he wasn't immune. He was as aware as she was of the strong sexual tension that held both of them in its clutches.

"That's okay since I wasn't looking where I was going," she said softly, also offering an apology and inhaling deeply to calm her racing heart. She watched as his gaze slowly raked over her. She was wearing a pair of shorts and a crepe halter top. Suddenly she felt more naked than covered. More tensed than relaxed. And hotter than ever.

"Delaney?"

With the sound of her name spoken so sensually from his lips, her gaze locked with his, and at the same time he began leaning down closer to her. It was too close. Not close enough. And when she felt the warm brush of his breath against her throat, she responded softly, in an agonized whisper, "Yes?"

"It's going to rain," he said huskily.

She saw flickers of desire darken his gaze. "Sounds that way, doesn't it?" she managed to get out with extreme effort. She licked her lips slowly, cautiously. She was no longer aware of her surroundings, and barely heard the sound of the first drops of rain that suddenly began beating against the rooftop. Nor did she feel the tartness of the cold, damp air that suddenly filled the room.

All of her thoughts, her total concentration, was on the imposing figure looming before her. And she didn't consider resisting when he gently pulled her to him.

Go ahead, let him kiss you, a voice inside her head said. *Indulge yourself. Get it out of your system. Then the two of you can stop acting like two animals in heat. All it will take is this one, single kiss.*

A deep, drugging rush of desire filled Delaney. Shivers of wanting and need coursed down her spine. Yes, that's all it would take to get her head back on straight. A sexual attraction between a man and woman was healthy. Normal. Fulfilling. She'd just never had time to indulge before, but now she was ready. Now, with Jamal, indulging was necessary.

That was her last thought before Jamal's mouth covered hers.

Jamal took Delaney's lips with expertise and desperation. The need to taste her was elemental to him. Relentlessly his tongue explored her mouth, tasting and stroking, slowly moving beyond sampling to devouring. And when that wasn't enough he began sucking, drawing her into him with every breath.

He slipped his hand behind her head to hold her mouth in place while he got his fill, thinking it was impossible to do so, but determined to try anyway. He was at a point where he was willing to die trying.

He had kissed many women in his lifetime but had never felt a need to literally eat one alive. Never had any woman pushed him to such limits. He had been raised in an environment that accepted sex and intimacy for what they were—pleasure of the most tantalizing kind and a normal, healthy part of life.

But something deep within him believed there wasn't anything normal about this. What could be normal about wanting to stick your tongue down a woman's throat to see how far it could go? What was normal about wanting to suck her tongue forever if necessary to get the taste he was beginning to crave?

He pressed his body closer to hers, wanting her to feel him and know how much he desired her. He wanted her to know he wanted more than just a kiss. He wanted everything. He wanted it all.

And he intended to get it.

Jamal's fingers were insistent as they moved down her body to come to rest on her backside, gently pulling her closer. His body hardened at the feel of the tips of her nipples pressing against his bare chest through the material of her top. The contact was stimulating, inflaming, arousing.

And it was driving him insane.

The area between his thighs began to ache and get even harder. Grasping her hips he brought her more firmly against him, wanting her to feel his arousal, every throbbing inch. He knew she had gotten the message when he felt her fingers tangle in his hair, holding him close as he continued to devour her mouth.

Moments later, another loud clap of thunder, one that seemed to shake the entire earth, broke them apart. Delaney gasped so hard she almost choked. She bent over to pull air into her lungs, and seconds later, when she looked up and met Jamal's hot gaze, she felt her body responding all over again.

One kiss had not gotten him out of her system. That thought made her aware that unless she backed away, she would be in too deep. Already she felt herself sinking, drowning, being totally absorbed by him.

She backed up and he moved forward, cornering her against the wall. "I don't think we should have done that," she said softly, unconvincingly. Her voice was shaky, husky.

Jamal was glad they had done it and wanted to do it again. "It's been a week. We would have gotten around to kissing eventually," he said in a low, raspy voice. His body was still radiating an intimate intensity, although they were no longer touching.

"Why?" she asked, her curiosity running deep. When she saw the way his eyes darkened, a part of her wished that she hadn't asked him. He was looking at her in that way that made certain parts of her body get hot. And at the moment she couldn't handle the heat and doubted that she ever would.

"Because we want each other. We want to have sex," he replied, bluntly and directly. Although the words sounded brusque even to his ears, it was the truth and when it came to satisfying his body he believed in complete honesty. In his country such things were understood, expected and accepted.

Delaney's body trembled with Jamal's words. He'd made having sex sound so simple and basic. She thought of all the guys she had dated in her lifetime. She'd never wanted to have sex before. But Jamal was right—she *was* tempted now. But a part of her held back.

"I'm not a woman who makes a habit of getting into a man's bed," she said softly, feeling the need to let him know where she stood, and determined not to let him know that for the first time she was rethinking that policy.

"We don't have to use a bed if you don't want. We can use the table, the sofa or the floor. You pick the place. I'm bursting at the seams ready."

Delaney glanced down and saw his erection pressing against his zipper and knew he was dead serious. She inhaled deeply. He had missed her point entirely.

"What I mean is that I don't sleep with a man just for the fun of it."

He nodded slowly. "Then what about for the pleasure

of it? Would you sleep with a man just for the pleasure it would give you?"

Delaney stared at him blankly. Indulging in sex mainly for pleasure? She knew her brothers did it all the time. They were experts in the field. None of them had a mind to marry, yet they bought enough condoms during the year to make it cost-efficient to form their own company.

"I've never thought about it before," she answered truthfully. "When I think of someone being horny, I immediately think of men, more so than I do women."

"Horny?"

She shook her head, thinking he was probably not familiar with a lot of American slang. "Yes, horny. It means needing sex in a bad way, almost to the point where your body is craving it."

Jamal leaned down close to her mouth. "In that case, I'm feeling *horny*," he murmured thickly against it. "Real horny. And I want to make you feel horny, too."

"That's not possible," she whispered softly, barely able to breathe.

A half smile lifted one corner of his mouth. "Yes, it is."

Before she could say anything, his hand reached down and touched her thigh at the same time his tongue licked her lips, before slowly easing inside her mouth. Once there he began stroking her tongue with his, as if he had all the time in the world and intended to do it all day at his leisure.

Delaney's entire body shivered when she felt his fingers at the zipper of her shorts, and a part of her wanted to push his hand away. But then another part, that foolish part that thrived on curiosity, the one that was slowly getting inflamed again, wanted to feel his touch and wanted to know how far he would take it.

She held her breath when he lowered the zipper slowly

and deliberately, easing her into submission. His breathing was getting just as difficult as hers, and her entire body felt hot all over.

And then he inserted his hand inside her shorts, boldly touching her through the flimsy material of her panties. He touched her in a place no man had ever touched her before, and with that intimate touch, every cell in her body ignited. He began stroking her, slowly, languidly, making her feel horny. Just as he said he would do.

Never had she experienced anything so mind-numbing, so unbelievably sensuous as one of his hands gently pushed her thighs apart even more while his fingertip gave complete erotic attention to that ultrasensitive, highly stimulated spot between her legs, while his tongue continued to suck on hers.

The combination of his fingers and his tongue was too much. She felt faint. She felt scandalized. She was feeling pleasure of the highest magnitude.

Another rumble of thunder with enough force to shake the cabin jolted Delaney out of her sexual haze and back to solid ground. She pushed Jamal away. Taking a deep breath she slumped against the wall, not believing what had just happened between them. What she had let him do. The liberties she had given him.

She had been putty in his arms.

A totally different woman beneath his fingers.

She appreciated the fact that evidently someone up there was looking out for her and had intervened before she could make a total fool of herself. Just as she'd thought, Jamal was a master at seduction. He had known just how to kiss her and just where to touch her to make her weak enough to throw caution to the wind. And she was determined not to let it happen again.

Forcing her gaze to his, she knew she was dealing

with a man who was probably used to getting what he wanted whenever he wanted it. All he had to do was snap his fingers, ring a bell or do whatever a prince did when he needed sexual fulfillment.

Did he think she would fit the same bill while he was in America? The thought that he did angered her. She was not part of his harem and had no intentions of being at his beck and call.

Furious with herself for letting him toy with her so easily, she glared at him. "I plan to take a cold shower. I suggest you do the same."

He didn't say anything for a long moment, and then he smiled at her. It was a smile that extended from his eyes all the way to each corner of his lips.

"A cold shower won't help, Delaney."

"Why won't it?" she all but snapped, refusing to admit he was probably right.

"Because now I know your taste and you know mine. When you get hungry enough you will want to be fed, and when that happens I will feed you until your body is full and content. I will provide it with all the sexual nourishment it needs."

Without giving her an opportunity to say anything, he turned and walked away.

After pacing the confines of her bedroom for what seemed like the longest time, Delaney sat on the edge of the bed. She couldn't ever remember being so irritated, so frustrated...so just plain mad.

"I'll feel better once I get my head back on straight," she said, as she stood and began pacing again. How could one man have the ability to set a body on fire the way Jamal had hers still burning?

All she had to do was close her eyes and she could actually still feel the essence of his tongue inside her mouth or the feel of his hands…more specifically, his fingers, on her flesh. And she could still feel the hardness of him pressed against her stomach.

A silky moan escaped her lips, and she knew she had to leave the cabin for a while and take a walk. But the problem was that it was raining, and not just a little sprinkle but a full-fledged thunderstorm.

She touched a finger to her lips, thinking that it was too bad the thundershowers couldn't wash away the memories of her kiss with Jamal.

A part of her wondered what Jamal was doing right now. Was his body being tormented like hers?

She sighed deeply. She had to stay determined. She had to stay strong. And most important, she had to continue to avoid Jamal Ari Yasir at all costs.

Chapter 4

"Going someplace?"

Delaney stopped in her trek across the room to the door. She wished she had waited until she'd been absolutely sure Jamal was asleep before leaving to go to the store. After their encounter a few days ago, she had avoided him by staying in her room most of the time.

But she had been too keyed-up to hide out in her room any longer. Heated desire flowed like warm wine through all parts of her body, making her feel things she had never felt before. Restless. On edge. Horny.

The rain for the past two days had kept them both inside the cabin. And whenever she got too hungry to stay in her room, she would go into the kitchen to find him sitting at the wobbly table sketching something out on paper. His black gaze would pierce her, nearly taking her breath away, and although he didn't say anything, she knew he watched her the entire time she was in close range. Like a wolf watching his prey.

She sighed as her gaze moved slowly down the length of him. He was dressed in a pair of white silk pajamas. The first thought that entered her mind was that she had seen her brothers in pajamas many times, but none of them had looked like this. And then there was the white kaffiyeh that he wore on his head. Silhouetted in the moonlight that flowed through the window, he looked the epitome of the tall, dark and handsome prince that he was.

Inhaling deeply, she needed all of the strength she could muster to hold her own with him, especially after the kiss they had shared; a kiss that made her breathless just remembering it. And it didn't help matters that she was noticing things she hadn't noticed before; like his hands and how perfect they looked. The fingers of those hands were long, deft and strong. They were fingers that had once swallowed hers in a warm clasp while he had kissed her; fingers whose tips had touched her cheek, traced the outline of her lips, and fingers that had touched her intimately. Then there were his eyebrows. She had been so taken with his eyes that she had failed to notice his brows. Now she did. They were deep, dark, slanted, and together with his eyes were deadly combination.

"Delaney, I asked if you were going somewhere," Jamal said.

She swallowed as she gazed across the room at him and nearly came undone when he nailed her with his dark, penetrating eyes and those slanted brows.

"I'm going to the store," she finally responded. "There are some items I need to pick up."

"At this time of night?"

Even in the dim light Delaney could see the frown

darkening his face. She met his frown with one of her own. "Yes, this time of night. Do you have a problem with it?"

For a long moment they stood there staring at each other—challenging. Delaney refused to back down, and so did he. To her way of thinking he reminded her of her brothers in their attempts to be overprotective. And that was the last thing she wanted or would tolerate.

"No, I don't have a problem with it. I was just being concerned," he finally said. "It's not safe for a woman to be out at night alone."

The quiet tone of his voice affected her more than she wanted it to. And the way he was looking at her didn't help matters. Intentionally or not, he was igniting feelings she had been experiencing lately; feelings she had tried ridding herself of by staying in her room. But now she felt the slow pounding of blood as it rushed to her head and back down to her toes. She also heard the ragged pant of her breathing and wondered if he heard it.

"I'm used to living alone, Jamal," she finally responded. "And I can take care of myself. Because of my study habits, I'm used to going shopping at night instead of in the daytime."

He nodded. "Do you mind some company? There are some things I need to pick up, as well."

Delaney narrowed dark eyes, wondering if he actually needed something or if he was using that as an excuse to tag along. If it was the latter, she wasn't having any of it. "If I wasn't here, how would you have managed to get those things?"

He shrugged. "I would have called Asalum. And although he would be more than happy to do my shopping for me, I prefer doing things for myself. Besides, it's after midnight and he needs his rest."

Delaney was glad to hear that he was considerate of the people who worked for him. Slowly nodding, she said, "Then I guess it will be all right if you come along."

Jamal laughed. It was a deep, husky, rich sound that made heat spread through the lower part of her body. She slanted him a look. "Something funny?"

"Yes. You make it seem such a hardship to spend time with me."

Delaney sighed, looking away. He didn't know the half of it. Moments later she returned her attention to him. "Mainly because I had thought I would be here alone for the next few weeks."

He grinned at her suddenly. It was so unexpected that her anger lost some of its muster. "So had I," he said huskily, slowly crossing the room to stand in front of her. "But since we're not alone and it was your decision to stay, don't you think we should stop avoiding each other and make the most of it and get along?"

Delaney fought her body's reaction to his closeness. It wasn't easy. "I suppose we can try."

"What do we have to lose?"

Oh, I can think of a number of things I have to lose. My virginity for one, Delaney thought to herself. Instead of responding to his question, she turned and headed for the door. "I'll wait in the car while you change clothes."

"Did you get everything you need?" Delaney asked Jamal as they got back into her car to return to the cabin. Once they had gone inside the all-night supermarket he seemed to have disappeared.

"Yes, I got everything I need. What about you?"

"Yes. I even picked up a few things I hadn't intended to get," she said, thinking of the romance novel she had talked herself into buying. She couldn't remember the last time she'd been able to read a book for pleasure.

They drove back to the cabin in silence. Delaney kept her eyes on the road but felt Jamal's eyes on her all the while.

"What kind of doctor are you?" he asked after they had ridden a few miles.

His question got him a smile. She enjoyed talking about her profession and was proud of the fact that she was the only doctor in the Westmoreland family. "I will be a pediatrician, but first I have to complete my residency, which will take another two years."

"You like working with children?"

Delaney's response was immediate. "Not only do I enjoy working with kids, I love kids, period."

"So do I."

Delaney was surprised by his comment. "You do?" Most men, especially a single man, wouldn't admit that fact.

"Yes. I'm looking forward to getting married one day and having a family."

She nodded. "Me, too. I want a houseful."

Jamal chuckled and gave her a curious look. "Define a houseful."

The words leaped from Delaney's mouth without thinking about it. "At least six."

He smiled, finding it amazing that she wanted pretty close to the same number of children that he did. "You are asking for a lot, aren't you?"

She grinned. That was what her brothers always told her. They were convinced it would be hard to find a man who'd want that many kids. "Not a whole lot, just a good even number to make me happy and content."

When the car stopped at a traffic light, Jamal glanced

over at Delaney. He thought she was too beautiful for
words. Even with a face scrubbed clean of makeup and
a fashionable scarf around her head to keep her hair in
place, she was definitely one nice feminine package, a
right sassy one at that.

His thoughts drifted to Najeen. She would remain his
mistress even after he took a wife. That was understood
and it would also be accepted. He knew that Western
women tended to be possessive after marriage. They
would never tolerate a husband having a mistress. But
then, most American women fancied themselves marrying for love. In his country you married for benefits—
usually heirs. His marriage would be no different. Since
he didn't believe in love he didn't plan on marrying for
it. His would be an arranged marriage. Nothing more.
Nothing less.

He could not see Delaney ever settling for that type
of arrangement with any man. She would want it all: a
man's love, his devotion, and his soul if there was a way
she could get it.

Jamal cringed inwardly. The thought of any woman
having that much control over a man was oddly discon-
certing. The possibility that a woman would demand such
a relationship would be unheard of in his country.

"Think you can juggle a career and motherhood?" he
asked moments later. He wondered how she would respond. Western women also tended to be less domesti-
cated. They enjoyed working just as hard as a man. He
smiled. The woman he married would have only one
job—to give him children. She could walk around naked
all day if she chose to do so. She would be naked and
pregnant the majority of the time.

"Sure," Delaney said smiling. "Just like you'll be able
to handle being a prince *and* a father, I'll be able to han-

dle being a doctor and a mom. I'm sure it will be a little hectic at times but you'll be successful at it and so will I."

Jamal frowned. "Don't you think your child would need your absolute attention, especially in the early years?"

Delaney heard the subtle tone of disapproval in his voice. "No more than your child would need *yours* as his father."

"But you are a woman."

She smiled in triumph, pleased with that fact. "Yes, and you are a man. So what's your point? There's nothing written that says a mother's role in a child's life is more important than a father's. I tend to think both parents are needed to give the child love and structure. The man I marry will spend just as much time with our children as I do. We will divide our time equally in the raising of our child."

Jamal thought about the amount of time his father had spent with him while he'd been growing up. Even when his father had been in residence in the palace, Jamal had been cared for by a highly regarded servant—specifically, Asalum's wife, Rebakkah. And although his father had not spent a lot of time with him, he had always understood that he loved him. After all, he was his heir. Now that he was older, he knew their relationship was built on respect. He saw his father as a wise king who loved his people and who would do anything for them. Being his father's successor one day would be a hard job and he hoped he was at least half the man his father was.

Delaney was fully aware that Jamal had become quiet. Evidently she had given him something to think about. The nerve of him thinking that a woman's job was to stay barefoot and pregnant. He and her father, as well as her brother Storm, would get along perfectly.

It was a long-standing joke within the family that her youngest brother wanted a wife who he could keep in the bedroom, 24/7. The only time he would let her out of bed was when she needed to go to the bathroom. He wanted her in the bed when he left for work and in the bed when he came back home. His wife's primary job would be to have his children and to keep him happy in the bedroom, so it wouldn't matter to him if she were a lousy cook in the kitchen. He would hire a housekeeper to take care of any less important stuff.

Delaney shook her head. And all this time she'd thought that Storm was a rare breed. Evidently not. When they had made Storm, the mold hadn't been broken after all.

She glanced quickly at Jamal and wondered how she had gotten herself in this predicament. When she hadn't been able to sleep, going to the store in the middle of the night for some things she needed had seemed like a good idea. But she hadn't counted on Jamal accompanying her.

She sighed as the car traveled farther and farther away from the city and back toward the cabin. She stole another glance at him and saw that he was watching her. She quickly returned her gaze to the road.

When they finally arrived back at the cabin, Delaney felt wired. Too keyed-up to sleep. She decided to start cutting back on the hours of sleep she was putting in during the day. At night, while the cabin was quiet, her mind had started to wander and she didn't like the direction it was taking.

She quickly walked past Jamal when he opened the door, intending to make a path straight for her room. The last thing she could handle was another encounter like the one shared before. The man was definitely an experienced kisser.

What he had predicted was true. She hated admitting it but her body was hungry for him. A slow ache was beginning to form between her legs, and heat was settling there, as well.

"Would you like to share a cup of coffee with me, Delaney?"

The sound of his voice, husky and sexy, like always, did things to her insides. It also made that ache between her legs much more profound. Sharing a cup of coffee with him was the last thing she wanted to do. She would never make it through the first sip before jumping his bones. "No, thanks, I think I'll go on to bed."

"If you ever get tired of sleeping alone, just remember that my room is right across the hall."

Delaney tightened her lips. "Thanks for the offer, but I *won't* keep that in mind."

He reached out and brought his hand to her face and caressed her cheek. The action was so quick she hadn't had time to blink. His touch was soft, tender, gentle, and her breathing began a slow climb. He leaned toward her and whispered. "Won't you?"

Delaney closed her eyes, drinking in the masculine scent of him. Desire for him was about to clog her lungs. Fighting for control, she took a step back as she opened her eyes. "Sorry, *Your Highness,* but no, I won't." She then turned and walked quickly to her room, thinking she had lied to him and that she *would.*

"Oh, my goodness." Delaney shifted her body around in the hammock while keeping her eyes glued to the book, not believing what she was reading.

She hadn't read a romance novel in nearly eight years

and then the ones she'd read had been those sweet romances. But nothing was sweet about the book she had purchased last night. The love scenes didn't leave you guessing about anything.

She had awakened that morning, and while Jamal had been outside doing his kickboxing routine, she'd sat at the wobbly table and had eaten a bagel and had drunk a cup of orange juice. Jamal was still outside by the time she had finished. She had passed him when she had left to find a good spot near the lake to read her book.

She took in a deep breath, then returned to the book once more. A few minutes later the rate of her heart increased, and she wondered if two people could actually perform that many positions in bed.

Stretching her body and giving herself a chance to catch her breath, she admitted that reading the book had turned her on. In her imagination, the tall, dark, handsome hero was Jamal and she was the elusive and sexy heroine.

Rolling onto her back she decided she had read enough. There was no use torturing her body anymore. The next thing Delaney knew, she had drifted off to sleep with thoughts of romancing the sheikh on her mind.

She dreamed she was being kissed in the most tantalizing and provocative way; not on her lips but along her shoulder and neck. Then she felt a gentle tug on her tank top as it was lifted up to expose her bare breasts. It had been too hot for a bra so she'd not worn one, and now, with the feel of her imaginary lover's tongue moving over her breasts, tasting her, nibbling on her, she was glad that she hadn't. A rush of heated desire spread through the lower part of her legs as a hot, wet tongue took hold of a nipple and gently began sucking, feasting on the budding tip.

A name, one she had given to her imaginary lover, came out on a gasp of a sound. Her mind began spinning, her breathing became even more erratic and her body hotter. A part of her didn't want the dream to end, but then another part was afraid for it to continue. It seemed so real that she was almost tortured beyond control, just on the edge of insanity.

Then suddenly her lover lowered her top and ceased all action without warning. Her breathing slowed back to normal as she struggled to gain control of her senses.

Moments later, Delaney lifted her dazed eyes and glanced around her. She was alone, but the dream had seemed so real. The nipples on her breasts were still throbbing and the area between her legs was aching for something it had never had before—relief.

She closed her eyes, wondering if she could dream up her lover again and decided she couldn't handle that much pleasure twice in the same day. Besides, she was still sleepy and tired. As she drifted off to sleep she couldn't help remembering her dream and thought it had been utterly amazing.

Jamal breathed deeply as he leaned back against the tree. What had possessed him to do what he'd just done to Delaney? It didn't take long for him to have his answer. He had been attracted to her from the first, and when he had come upon her sleeping in the hammock wearing a short midriff top and shorts, with a portion of her stomach bare to his gaze, he couldn't resist the thought of tasting her. A taste he had thought about a lot lately.

Her breasts, even while she slept, had been erect with the dark tips of her nipples showing firmly against her blouse. Without very much thought, he had gone to her and had knelt before her to feast upon every inch of her body. But he hadn't gotten as far as he wanted before coming to his senses.

Just thinking about making love to her made him aroused to the point that his erection, pressing against the fly of his jeans, was beginning to ache. And when she had moaned out his name, he'd almost lost it.

A woman had been the last thing on his mind when he had arrived at the cabin. Now a woman, one woman in particular, was the only thing he could think about.

His body felt hot. It felt inflamed. He wondered if he should pack his things and ask Asalum to come for him. Maybe it was time for him to return to Tahran. Never before had he wanted any woman to the point of seducing her while she slept.

But he knew he couldn't leave. She had moaned out his name. He hadn't imagined it. She may deny wanting him while she was awake, but while she slept it was a different matter.

His libido stirred. He wanted to taste her again. In truth, he wanted more than that. He wanted to make love with her. And every muscle in his body strained toward that goal.

Chapter 5

Jamal was sitting at the wobbly table drinking a cup of tea when Delaney came inside for lunch a few hours later. She glanced over at him as she made her way to the refrigerator to take out the items she needed for a sandwich.

"I'm making a sandwich for lunch," she said, opening the refrigerator. "Would you like one, too?"

Jamal shifted in the chair as he looked at her. He didn't want a sandwich. He wanted sex. And as a result, he felt restless and on edge. Earlier in the week he had tasted her mouth, today he had feasted on her nipples. There wasn't much of her left to discover, but what there was sent his hormones into overdrive.

When he didn't answer, she turned away from the refrigerator and looked at him curiously. "Jamal?"

"Yes?"

"I asked if you wanted a sandwich?"

He nodded, deciding to take her up on her offer. He

needed to eat something, since he would need all his strength later for something he would enjoy. At least that was what he was hoping. "Yes, thank you. I would love to have a sandwich." *I would love to have you.*

He continued to watch as she took items out of the refrigerator and assembled them on the counter. The enticing scent of her perfume was filling the kitchen and he found himself getting deeply affected by it. And it didn't help matters that he knew she wasn't wearing a bra under her top and that her breasts were the best kind to lick and suck. The moment his tongue had touched the taut nipple, the tip of it had hardened like a bud, tempting him to draw the whole thing in his mouth and gently suck and tease it with a pulling sensation. And the way she had moaned while squirming around on the hammock had let him know she enjoyed his actions.

He shifted his gaze from her chest to her bottom. Her backside had been what had caught his attention that very first day. It was also the main thing that had him hard now. She liked wearing shorts, the kind that showed just what a nice behind she had. Nice thighs, too. The shorts placed emphasis on the curve of her hips. He wondered what her behind looked like without clothes. He bet her buttocks were as firm and as lush as her breasts.

"Do you want mayonnaise on your bread?"

Her questions made him return his gaze to her face when she tossed him a glance over her shoulder. "No, mustard is fine," he answered, briefly considering pinning her against the counter and taking her from behind. He could just imagine pumping into her while pressed solidly against her backside.

He took another sip of his herbal tea. Usually the sweet brew calmed him. But not today and certainly not now.

"Be prepared to enjoy my sandwich," she was saying. "My brothers think they're the bomb and would give anything for me to make them one. They have my special touch."

He nodded. He could believe that and suddenly felt envious of a slice of bread and wished he could trade places with it. He would love to have her hands on him, spreading whatever she wanted over his body, preferably kisses. She wouldn't even have to toast him since her touch would burn him to a crisp, anyway.

She glanced over his shoulder and smiled again. "You're quiet today. Are you okay?"

He was tempted to tell her that no, he wasn't okay, and if he were to stand up she would immediately see why he wasn't. But instead he said, "Yes, I'm fine."

Satisfied with his response, she turned back around to continue making their sandwiches. He leaned back in his chair. He watched her pat her foot on the hardwood floor while she worked. She was also humming. He wondered what had her in such a good mood. Unlike him, she must be sleeping at night and not experiencing sexual torment.

"Did you finish your book?" he decided to ask. She had been reading it all morning. The only time he noticed her not reading was when she'd fallen asleep on the hammock.

"Oh, yes, and it was wonderful," she said, reaching up in the cabinets to get two plates. "And of course there was a happy ending."

He lifted his brow. *So she had been reading one of those kinds.* "A happy ending?"

She nodded, turning around. "Yes. Marcus realized just how much Jamie meant to him and told her that he loved her before it was too late."

Jamal nodded. "He loved this woman?"

Delaney smiled dreamily. "Yes, he loved her."

Jamal frowned. "Then what you read was pure fantasy. Why waste your time reading such nonsense and foolishness?"

Delaney's smile was replaced with a fierce frown. "Nonsense? Foolishness?"

"Yes, nonsense and foolishness. Men don't love women that way."

Delaney braced herself against the counter and folded her arms across her chest. Her legs, Jamal noted, were spread apart. Seeing her stand that way almost made him forget what they were discussing. Instead his gaze moved to the junction of those legs and wondered how it would feel fitting his hard body there.

"And just how do men love women?"

Jamal's gaze left her midsection and moved up to her face. She was still frowning. Evidently she was no longer in such a good mood. "Usually they don't. At least not in my country."

Delaney lifted a brow. "People do get married in your country, don't they?"

"Of course."

"Then why would a man and a woman marry if not for love?"

Jamal stared at her, suddenly feeling disoriented. She had a way of making him feel like that whenever he locked on her dark brown eyes and lush lips. "They would marry for a number of reasons. Mainly for benefits," he responded, not taking his gaze off her eyes and lips. Especially her lips.

"Benefits?"

He nodded. "Yes. If it's a good union, the man brings to the table some kind of wealth and the woman brings strong family ties, allegiances and the ability to give him an heir. Those things are needed if a sheikhdom is to grow and prosper."

Delaney stared into his eyes, amazed at what he had just said. "So the marriages in your country are like business arrangements?"

He smiled. "Basically, yes. That's why the most successful ones are arranged at least thirty years in advance."

"Thirty years in advance!" she exclaimed, shaking her head in disbelief.

"Yes, at least that long, sometimes even longer. More often than not, the man and woman's family plans their union even before they are born. Such was the case with my father and mother. She was of Berber descent. The Berbers were and still are a proud North African tribe that inhabits the land in northwestern Libya. As a way to maintain peace between the Berbers and the Arabs, a marriage agreement between my mother, an African princess, and my father, an Arab prince, was made. Therefore, I am of Arab-Berber descent, just as the majority of the people of Tahran are. My parents were married a little more than a year when my mother died giving birth to me."

Delaney leaned back against the counter. At the moment what he was telling her was more interesting than making a sandwich. "What if your father, although pledged to your mother, had found someone else who he preferred to spend the rest of his life?"

"That would have been most unfortunate. And it wouldn't have meant a thing. He would still marry the woman he'd been pledged to marry. However, he could take the other woman he fancied as a mistress for the rest of his days."

"A mistress? And what would his wife have to say about something like that?"

He shrugged. "Nothing. It's common practice for a man to have both a wife and mistress. That sort of an arrangement is accepted."

Delaney shook her head. American men knew better. "That's such a waste, Jamal. Why would a man need both a wife *and* a mistress? A smart man would seek out and fall in love with a woman who can play both roles. In our country wives are equipped to fulfill every desire her husband may have."

Jamal lifted a brow. He could see her fulfilling every man's desire since he saw her as a very sensual woman. She would probably make a good *American* wife, if you liked the outspoken, sassy and rebellious type. She would keep a man on his toes and no doubt on his knees. But he had a feeling she would also keep him on his back—which would be well worth the trouble she would cause him.

He sighed, deciding he didn't want to talk about wives and mistresses any longer, especially when he knew how possessive American women were. "Are the sandwiches ready?"

Evidently, she wasn't ready to bring the subject to an end and asked, "The first day we met you indicated you were to marry next year."

He nodded. "Yes, that's true. In my country it's customary for a man to marry before his thirty-fifth birthday. And I'll be that age next summer."

"And the woman you're marrying? Was your marriage to her prearranged?"

Seeing she would not give the sandwich to him until her curiosity had been appeased, he said, "Yes, and no. My family had arranged my marriage to the future princess of Bahan before she was born. I was only six at the time. But she and her family were killed a few years ago while traveling in another country. That was less than a year before we were to marry. She was only eighteen at the time."

Delaney gave a sharp intake of air into her lungs. "Oh, that must have been awful for you."

Jamal shrugged. "I guess it would have been had I known her." *Like I know you now,* he thought, watching her eyes lift in confusion. The thought of anything ever happening to her…

"What do you mean if you had known her? You didn't know the woman you were going to marry?" Her mouth gaped open in pure astonishment.

"No, I had never met her. There was really no need. We were going to marry. Her showing up at the wedding would have been soon enough."

"But…but what if she was someone you didn't want?"

Jamal looked at her, smiling as if she had asked a completely stupid question. "Of course I would have wanted her. She was pledged to be my wife, and I was pledged to be her husband. We would have married regardless."

Delaney inhaled slowly. "And you would have kept your mistress." She said the words quietly, not bothering to ask if he had one. A man like him would, especially a man who thought nothing of marrying a woman he had never met to fulfill a contract his family had made. He would bed his wife for heirs, fulfilling his duty, then bed his mistress for pleasure.

"Yes, I would keep my mistress." He thought of Najeen, then added, "I would never think of giving her up."

Delaney stared at him and his nonchalant attitude about being unfaithful. Her brothers, possibly with the exception of Thorn when he was in one of his prickly moods, were players, enjoying being bachelors to the fullest. But there was no doubt in her mind that when…

and if they each found their soul mate, that woman would make them give up their players' cards. They would not only give her their complete love but their devotion and faithfulness, as well.

She was suddenly swamped by a mixture of feelings. There was no way she could get serious about a man like Jamal and accept the fact that he would be sleeping with another woman. She appreciated differences in cultures, but there were some things she would not tolerate. Infidelity was one of them. Violation of marriage vows was something she would not put up with.

Crossing the room with both plates in her hands, she set his sandwich down in front of him with a thump, glaring down at him. "Enjoy your sandwich. I hope you don't choke on it. I'm eating in my room, since I prefer not to share your company at the moment."

Jamal was out of his chair in a flash. He reached out and grabbed hold of her wrist and brought her closer to him. "Why?"

Her eyes darkened. "Why what?"

He studied her features. "Why did my words, spoken in total honesty, upset you? It's the way we do things in my country, Delaney. Accept it."

She tried pulling her hand free but he held on tight. "Accept it?" Her laugh was low, bitter and angry. She tilted her head back and glared up at him. "Why should I accept it? How you live your life is your business and means nothing to me."

Their faces were close. If they moved another inch their mouths would be touching. She tried to pull back, but he wouldn't let her. "If you truly mean that, then it would make things a lot easier."

Delaney tried not to notice that his eyes were focused on her mouth. "What do you mean by that?" she snapped, hating the fact that even now desire for him was spreading through all parts of her body. How could she still want him, after he admitted he would not marry for love and proudly boasted of having a mistress? A mistress he would never give up.

"If how I live my life means nothing to you, then it won't be an issue when we sleep together."

"What!"

"You heard what I said, Delaney. Western women tend to be possessive, which is one of the reasons I've never gotten too involved with one. You sleep with them once and they want to claim you forever. I've pretty much spelled out to you how my life will be when I will return to Tahran. I want you to fully understand that, before you share my bed. I make you no promises other than I will pleasure you in ways no man has pleasured you before."

Delaney shook her head, not believing the audacity of Jamal. He was as arrogant as they came. In his mind it was a foregone conclusion the two of them would sleep together. Well, she had news for him. It would be a damn cold day in July before she shared his bed.

She snatched her hand from his. "Let me get one thing straight, Prince." Her breath was coming in sharp, as sharp as her anger. "I have no intention of sleeping with you," she all but screamed, thumping him on his solid chest a few times for good measure. "I don't plan on being number three with any man, no matter the degree of pleasure. Your body could be made of solid gold and sprinkled with diamonds, I still wouldn't touch it unless it was mine exclusively. Do you hear me? I get exclusive rights from a man or nothing at all."

His gaze hardened as he stared at her. "I would never give any woman exclusive rights on me. Never."

"Then fine, we know where we stand, don't we?" She turned around to leave the room.

"Delaney…"

She told herself not to turn around, but found herself turning around, anyway. "What?"

He was frowning furiously. "Then I suggest you leave here. Now. Today."

Delaney inhaled deeply. Of all the nerve. "I've told you, Jamal, that I'm not leaving."

He stared at her for a long moment, then said, "Then you had best be on your guard, Delaney Westmoreland. I want you. I want you so badly I practically ache all over. I want you in a way I have never wanted a woman. I like inhaling your scent. I like tasting you and want to do so again…every part of you. I want to get inside your body and ignite us both with pleasure. Ever since you got here all I do is dream about having you, taking you, getting on top of you, inside of you and giving you the best sex you've ever had."

He slowly crossed the room to her. Ignoring the apprehension in her eyes, he lifted his hand to her cheek and continued. "For the two of us it all comes down to one word. *Lust.* So it doesn't matter who or what comes after we leave here. What we're dealing with, Delaney, is lust of the thickest and richest kind. Lust so strong it can bring a man to his knees. There is no love between us and there never will be. There will only be lust."

He stared deeply into her eyes. "Chances are when we leave here we will never see each other again. So what's wrong with enjoying our time together? What's wrong with engaging in something so pleasurable it will give us beautiful memories to feast on for years to come?"

His hand slowly left her cheek and moved to her neck. "I want to have sex with you every day while we're here,

Delaney, in every position known to man. I want to fulfill your fantasies as well as my own."

Delaney swallowed. Everything he said sounded tempting, enticing. And a lesser woman would abandon everything, including her pride, and give in to what he was suggesting. But she couldn't.

For too many years she had watched her brothers go from woman to woman. She would shake her head in utter amazement at how easily the women would agree to a night, a week or whatever time they could get from one of the Westmoreland brothers, with the attitude that something was a lot better than nothing.

Well, she refused to settle for just anything. She wasn't that hard up. Besides, you couldn't miss what you never had, and although she would be the first to admit that Jamal had awakened feelings and desires within her that she hadn't known existed, she could control her urge to sample more.

With a resolve and a stubborn streak that could only match her brother Thorn, she took a step back. "No, Jamal, I meant what I said. Exclusive or nothing."

His eyes darkened and she watched his lips tilt in a seductive smile. "You think that now, Delaney, but you will be singing a different tune in the end."

His voice was husky, and the look in his eyes was challenging. She swallowed the lump in her throat. "What do you mean?"

His smile became biting. "I mean that when it comes to something I want, I don't play fair."

Delaney stared pointedly into his eyes; her heart slammed against her ribs, completely understanding what he meant. He would try to wear down her defenses and didn't care how he did it as long as the end result was what he wanted—her in his bed.

Well, she had news for him. Westmorelands, among other things, were hard as nails when they chose to be. They were also stubborn as sin, and some were more stubborn than others were. They didn't back down from a challenge. A light flickered in her eyes. The prince had met his match.

Delaney smiled, and her eyes were lit with a touch of humor. "You may not play fair, but you can ask any one of my brothers and they will tell you that when it comes to competition, I play to win."

"This is one game you won't win, Delaney."

"And this is one game I can't afford to lose, *Your Highness*."

His eyes darkened as he frowned. "Don't say I didn't warn you."

She met his frown with one of her own. "And don't say I didn't warn *you*." With nothing else to say, Delaney turned, and with her head held high she strutted out of the kitchen and headed to the porch to eat her sandwich alone.

Chapter 6

Jamal looked up when Delaney walked into the living room later that evening. War had been declared and she was using every weapon at her disposal to win. She was determined to flaunt in his face what she thought he would never have. Which he assumed was the reason for the outfit she had changed into. There was only one way to describe it—sinfully sensual.

It was some sort of lounging outfit with a robe. But the robe enticed more than it covered. He couldn't do anything but lean back in his chair and look at her from head to toe. A surge of raw, primitive possessiveness, as well as arousal of the most intense kind, rushed through him. He couldn't pretend indifference even if he wanted to, so there was no sense trying. Instead he tossed the papers he was working on aside and placed his long legs out in front of him and gave her his full attention, since he knew that is what she wanted, anyway.

He knew her game. She wanted to bring him to his knees with no chance of him getting between her legs. But he had news for her. He would let her play out this little scene, then he intended to play out his.

The outfit she wore was peach in color and stood out against the color of her dark skin. The material was like soft silk, beneath a lacy robe that gave the right amount of feminine allure. The sway of the material against her body as she crossed the room clearly indicated she didn't have on a stitch of undergarments. The woman was foreplay on legs.

His groin throbbed as he watched her sit on the sofa across the room from him, real prim and proper and looking incredibly hot. Of its own accord his breathing deepened, making it difficult to pass oxygen through his lungs, yet he continued to torture himself by looking at her.

"So, what's up?" she asked in a deep, sultry voice.

He blinked when it occurred to him that she had spoken, and the sexy tone and the way she was looking at him made him aware of every male part of his body. "I can tell you of one thing in particular that's up, Delaney," he said smoothly. He may as well state the obvious since it had to be evident to her, even from across the room, that he had an erection the size of Egypt.

She didn't answer him. Instead she smiled saucily, as if she had scored a point. And he had to concede that she had. He wondered if she enjoyed seeing him sweat. He would remember just what she was putting him through when it was his turn to make his move. And when that time came he wouldn't let her retreat. She had started this, and he damn well intended to see her finish it. He intended to teach her a thing or two about tempting a desert sheikh.

The CD he had been listening to stopped playing, and a lingering silence filled the room. She watched him and he watched her. Inside he smoldered, his body was heating to a feverish pitch and from the look on her face she was savoring every moment.

"Do you want me to put on some more music?" he asked, slowly standing, not caring that she could see his obvious masculine display.

After taking it all in, seeing how big he was, she just nodded, unable to respond. The look on her face gave him pause, and he couldn't help but smile. Hell, what had she expected? Granted he'd been told by a number of women that he was very well endowed, but he thought surely she had seen a fully aroused male before.

Crossing the room he walked over to the CD player. "Is there anything in particular you would like to hear?" he asked huskily, in a quiet whisper. When she didn't answer he glanced at her over his shoulder.

She shrugged. He saw the deep movement of her throat as she swallowed before responding. "No. Whatever you decide to play is fine."

He picked up on her nervousness. Evidently, she didn't have this game of hers down as pat as she thought she did. With five brothers she should have known that a woman didn't stand a chance against a man with one thing on his mind. You play with fire, you get burned, and he was going to love scorching her in the process. By the time he lit her fire she would be ready to go up in smoke.

He put on Kenny G and it wasn't long before the sound of the saxophone filled the room. He turned around slowly and walked over to the sofa toward her. *Stalked* over to the sofa was probably a better word. He intended to see just how much temptation she could take.

Coming to a stop in front of her he reached out his

hand. "Would you like to dance?" He saw the movement of her throat as she swallowed deeply again. Her gaze held his and he knew she was giving his question some thought.

He had an idea what her response would be. She had started this and she intended to finish it. There was no way she would let him get the upper hand, even if it killed her. He smiled. He definitely didn't want her dead. He wanted a live body underneath him tonight when he made her admit defeat.

She slowly slid off the sofa, bringing her body so close to his that his nostrils flared with her scent. "Yes, I'll dance with you," she said softly, taking the hand he offered.

He nodded and pulled her into his arms. They both let out a deep rush of breath when their bodies connected. He closed his eyes, forcing his body to remain calm. She felt good against him, and when she leaned closer he groaned.

Neither of them said a word, but he could hear her indrawn breath each and every time his erection came into contact with her midsection, which he intentionally made happen a lot.

As Kenny G skillfully played the sax, he masterfully began his seduction to prove to Miss Westmoreland that she couldn't play with the big boys, no matter what her intent. When she rested her head against his chest, he opened his hand wide over her backside, cupping her to him as he slowed their movements even more.

He groaned again as he felt her lush bottom in his hand. He smoothly rubbed his hand over it, loving the way it felt. He decided not to speak. Words would only break the sensuous spell they were in. So he pulled her closer to his swollen erection, wishing they were in bed together instead of dancing, but grateful for what he could get, especially after she had been so adamant about him not getting anything.

When the music stopped playing, he didn't want to release her from his arms. And since she didn't take a step back he got the distinct impression she wasn't ready for the moment to end yet, either.

He knew what he had to do and what he wanted to do. And if tasting her led to other things, then so be it.

He leaned back slightly from her, which forced her head to lift from his chest. She met his gaze and he saw desire, just as potent, just as raw, in her eyes. He had to kiss her.

She must have had the same idea since without any protest her lips parted for him. A ragged moan escaped the moment he captured her mouth in his.

The movement of his tongue in her mouth was methodically slow and she reacted with a groan deep in her throat, which he absorbed in the kiss. He was an expert on kissing and used that expertise on her. He had been schooled in various places but found he had learned more during his stay in the Greek Isles than any other place. It was there he had mastered Ares, an advanced form of French kissing.

Some people preferred not using it because it could get you in such an aroused state, if you weren't careful things would be over for you before you even started. Only men with strong constitutions, those capable of extending the peak of their pleasure could use it. And it wasn't unusual for a woman to climax from the pleasure it gave her. Ares was developed around the belief that certain parts inside of your mouth, when stroked in the right way, gave you immense pleasure. He had never tried it on any other woman other than the person who had taught it to him at the age of twenty-one. It boggled his mind that he had never wanted to try it on Najeen, yet more than anything he wanted to experience it with Delaney. It was something about her taste that made it imperative for his state of mind.

Closing his eyes he took their kiss to another level. He could tell she noted the change but continued kissing him. Moments later he felt her arms reach up and encircle his neck as she became as much a part of their kiss as he did.

Moments later, startled, she pushed back out of his arms, her breasts rising and falling with every uneven breath she took. He wasn't through with her mouth yet. He'd barely started.

"Give me your tongue back, Delaney," he whispered in a low guttural tone. "Just stick it out and I'll take it from there."

She stared at him for a moment. Then, closing her eyes, she opened her mouth and darted her tongue out to him. Angling his head so he wouldn't bump her nose he captured it with his and drew it into his mouth. Slowly, gently, he set out to seduce her with the kiss he now controlled.

Delaney heard a soft moan from deep within her throat as she stroked her hands through Jamal's hair. She was in a state of heated bliss. She had no idea what he was doing to her but whatever it was, she didn't want him to stop. There were certain areas in her mouth that his tongue was touching that were driving her insane to the point that the heat between her legs was becoming unbearable.

She felt him rubbing against her and that combined with what he was doing to her mouth was too much. He sucked her tongue deep when she felt the first inkling of desire so strong it shot through her body like a missile and exploded within her.

She groaned, long and deep in her throat. Her body began to tremble. Every nerve ending seemed electrified. Her knees felt weak, her head began spinning and the last conscious thought that flooded her mind was that she was dying.

Delaney slowly opened her eyes and gazed up at Jamal. She was draped across him, sitting in his lap on the sofa. She blinked, her breathing was heavy, ragged. "What happened?" she asked in a whisper, surprised that she was able to get the words out. She felt so weak.

"You passed out."

She blinked again, not sure she had heard him correctly. "I passed out?"

He nodded slowly. "Yes. While I was kissing you."

Taking a deep breath, she closed her eyes, remembering. She may be a novice but she had the sense to recognize a climax when she experienced one. Her first and she was still a virgin. It seemed that every part of her body had become detached, as pleasure the degree of which she had never felt before had flooded through her. It had been just that intense.

She took another deep breath, closing her eyes, trying to gather her thoughts. She was a doctor, right out of medical school, and fully understood the workings of the human body. All through life she had aced all her biology classes. Under normal circumstances people didn't pass out during a kiss.

She frowned. But what she had shared with Jamal had not been a regular kiss. It had been a kiss that had made her climax all the way to her toes. She opened her eyes and looked up at him. He was studying her intently. "What did you do to me?" she asked breathlessly, as the aftereffects sent shivers through her body. Her mouth felt sensitive, raw, and his taste was embedded so deeply in the floor and roof of her mouth that she savored him every time she spoke.

He smiled and it was a smile that made her stomach clench in heat. "I kissed you in a very special way."

She licked her lips before asking, "And what way was that?"

"Ares. It's a very volatile form of French kissing."

Delaney stared up at him, unable to say a word. When she had entered the room earlier that evening she had thought she had everything under control. In the end he had brought out his secret weapon. But he had warned her from the very beginning that he didn't play fair.

"Is that the way you kiss your mistress?" she whispered, suddenly wanting to know, although she knew how she would feel when he gave her the answer.

His eyes darkened and a surprised look came into his face. "No, I've never kissed Najeen that way. Other than the woman who taught me the technique when I was twenty-one, I've never used it on anyone."

Delaney blinked. Now she was the one surprised. Not only had he given her the name of his mistress, but had admitted to sharing something with her he had not shared with any other woman. For some reason she felt pleased.

"You climaxed while I was kissing you."

Delaney's mouth opened in silent astonishment, not believing he had said that. A part of her started to deny such a thing but knew he was experienced enough to know she would be lying through her teeth. She searched her brain for a response. What could a woman say after a man made a statement such as that?

Before she could gather her wits he added, "You're wet."

She swallowed; the soreness of her mouth almost made

the task difficult. She knew what he meant and wondered how he knew? Had he checked? She was sitting in his lap, draped over him in a position that was downright scandalous. Had he slipped his hand inside her clothes and fingered her the way he had done the last time? Evidently the question showed on her face. He responded.

"No, I didn't touch you there, although I was tempted to. Your scent gave you away. It was more potent and overpowering, which is usually the case after a woman has a climax."

Delaney stared at him, not believing the conversation they were having. At least, he was talking. She was merely listening, being educated and suddenly, thanks to him, was becoming aware of the intensity of her femininity.

He smiled again and as before her stomach clenched. He stood with her in his arms. "I think you've had enough excitement for one night. It's time for you to go to bed."

He began walking down the hall and she was surprised when he carried her into her bedroom instead of the one he was using. He gently placed her in the middle of the bed, then straightened and looked down at her.

"I want you, Delaney, but I refuse to take advantage of you at a weak moment. I will not have accomplished anything if you wake up in my arms in the morning regretting sleeping with me."

He sighed deeply before continuing. "As much as I want to bury myself inside of you, it's important to me that you come to me of your own free will, accepting things the way I have laid them out for you. All I can and will ever offer you is pleasure. What you got tonight was just a fraction of the pleasure I can give you. But it has to be with the understanding that my life is in Tahran, and once I leave here you can't be a part of it. I have obligations that I must fulfill and responsibilities I must take on."

He leaned down and cupped her cheek, his dark gaze intense. "All you can and ever will be to me is a beautiful memory that I will keep locked inside forever. Our two cultures make anything else impossible. Do you understand what I'm saying?" he asked quietly in a husky voice filled with regret.

Slowly Delaney nodded her head as she gazed up at him. "Yes, I understand."

Without saying anything else Jamal dropped his hand from her face, turned and walked out of the room, closing the door behind him.

Delaney buried her head in the bedcovers as she fought back the tears that burned her eyes.

Chapter 7

Delaney slowly opened her eyes to the brilliance of the sun that was shining through her bedroom window. Refusing to move just yet, she looked up at the ceiling as thoughts and memories of the night before scrambled through her brain.

She lifted her fingers to her mouth as she remembered the kiss she and Jamal had shared. Her mouth still felt warm and sensitive. It also felt branded. He had left a mark on her that he had not left on another woman. He had given her his special brand of kissing that had been so passionate it had made her lose consciousness.

Closing her eyes, Delaney gave her mind a moment to take stock of everything that had happened last night, as well as come to terms with the emotions she was feeling upon waking this morning.

Yesterday Jamal had pretty much spelled everything out to her. He had told her in no uncertain terms that he wanted her. But then in the same breath he had let her know that the time they spent at the cabin was all they would have together. He had obligations and responsibilities in his country that he would not turn his back on. He had a life beyond America that did not include her and never would. In other words, she would never have a place in his life.

As a woman who had never engaged in an affair, casual or otherwise, she had felt indignant that he would even suggest such a thing to her. But last night after he had left her alone in her bedroom, she had been able to think things through fully before drifting off to sleep.

Jamal's life was predestined. He was a prince, a sheikh, and his people and his country were his main concerns. He admitted he wanted her, not loved her. And he had stated time and time again that what was between them was lust of the strongest kind, and as two mature adults there was nothing wrong in engaging in pleasure with no strings attached.

What he offered was no different from what her brothers consistently offered the women they dated. And she had always abhorred the very thought of any woman being weak enough to accept so little. But now a part of her understood.

Things had become clear after Jamal had brought her into the room and placed her on the bed. And after listening to what he had said then, she had known: she was falling in love with Jamal. And now, in the bright of day, she didn't bother denying the truth.

Although her brothers were dead set against ever falling in love, a part of her had always known that she would be a quick and easy victim. Everyone knew that her parents had met one weekend at a church function and less than two weeks later had married. They claimed they had fallen in love at first sight and always predicted their children would find love the same way.

Delaney smiled, thinking of her brothers' refusal to believe their parents' prediction. But she had, which was one of the reasons she had remained a virgin. She had been waiting for the man she knew would be her one true love, her soul mate, and had refused to sell herself short by giving herself to someone less deserving.

Over the years she assumed the man would be a fellow physician, someone who shared the same love for medicine that she did. But it appeared things didn't turn out that way. Instead she had fallen for a prince, a man whose life she could never share.

She opened her eyes. What Jamal had said last night was true. When they parted ways, chances were they would never see each other again. Somehow she would have to accept that the man she loved would never fully belong to her. He would never be hers exclusively. But if she accepted what he was offering, at least she could have memories to treasure in the years to come.

She inhaled deeply, no longer bothered that there would not be a happy ending to her situation with Jamal. But until it was time for them to leave, she would take each day as it came and appreciate the time she would spend with him, storing up as many memories as she could.

She wanted him, the same way he wanted her, but in her heart she knew that for her, lust had nothing to do with it. Her mind and her actions were ruled by love.

"Are you sure you are all right, my prince?" Asalum asked Jamal as he gave him a scrutinizing gaze.

"Yes, Asalum, I am fine," Jamal responded drily.

Asalum wasn't too sure of that. His wise old eyes had

assessed much. He had arrived at the cottage to deliver some important papers to His Highness to find him sitting outside on the steps, drinking coffee and looking like a lost camel. There were circles under his eyes, which indicated he had not gotten a good night's sleep, and his voice and features were expressionless.

Asalum glanced over to the car that was parked a few feet from where they stood. "I take it the Western woman is still here."

Jamal nodded. "Yes, she is still here."

"Prince, maybe you should—"

"No, Asalum," Jamal interrupted, knowing what his trusted friend and confidant was about to suggest. "She stays."

Asalum nodded slowly. He hoped Jamal knew what he was doing.

Delaney walked into the kitchen to the smell of rich coffee brewing. She was about to pour a cup when her cell phone rang. "Hello?"

"I just thought I would warn you that the Brothers Five are on the warpath."

Delaney smiled, recognizing Reggie's voice. "And just what are they up to now?"

"Well, for starters they threatened me with missing body parts if I didn't tell them where you were."

Delaney laughed. She needed to do that and it felt good. "But you didn't, did you?"

"No, only because I knew their threats were all bluster. After all, I'm family, although I must admit I had to remind them of that a few times, especially Thorn. The older he gets, the meaner he gets."

Delaney shook her head. "Didn't Mom and Dad assure them I was all right and just needed to get away and rest for a while?"

"Yeah, I'm sure they did, Laney, but you know your brothers better than anyone. They feel it's their God-given right to keep tabs on you at all times, and not knowing where you are is driving them crazy. So I thought I'd warn you about what to expect when you return home."

Delaney nodded. She could handle them. Besides, when she returned home they would provide the diversion that she needed to help get over Jamal. "Thanks for the warning."

"How are things going otherwise? Is the prince still there?" Reggie asked between bites of whatever he was eating.

"Yes, he's still here and things are going fine." Now was not the time to tell Reggie that she had fallen in love with Jamal. A confession like that would prompt Reggie to tell her brothers her whereabouts for sure. His loyalty to her only went so far. She decided a change of topic was due at this point.

"There is something I need to ask you about," she said, fixing her focus on one object in the kitchen.

"What?"

"The table in the kitchen. Did you and Philip know that it wobbles?"

She could hear Reggie laughing on the other end. "The table doesn't wobble. It's the floor. For some reason it's uneven in that particular spot. If you move the table a foot in either direction it will be perfect."

Delaney nodded, deciding to try it. "Thanks, and thanks again for keeping my brothers under control."

Reggie chuckled. "Laney, no one can keep your brothers under control. I merely refused to let them intimidate me. For now your secret is safe. However, if I figure they will really carry out their vicious threats, then I'll have to rethink my position."

Delaney grinned. "They won't. Just avoid them for the next three weeks and you'll be fine. Take care, Reggie."

"And you do the same."

After hanging up the phone, Delaney poured a cup of coffee, then took a sip. She wondered if Jamal, who was an early riser, was outside practicing his kickboxing as he normally did each morning.

Glancing out the window, she arched her brow when she noted another car parked not far from hers, a shiny black Mercedes. And not far from the vehicle stood Jamal and another man. The two were engaged in what appeared to be intense conversation. She immediately knew the man with Jamal was Asalum. However, with his height and weight, the older man resembled more of a bodyguard than the personal secretary Jamal claimed he was.

Her gaze moved back to Jamal. There was such an inherent sensuality to him that it took her breath away. In her mind everything about him was perfect. His bone structure. His nose. His ebony eyes. His dark skin. And especially his seductive mouth that had kissed her so provocatively last night.

He was dressed in his Eastern attire, which reminded her that he was indeed a sheikh, something she tended to forget at times; especially when he dressed so American, the way he had last night. He'd been casually dressed in a pair of khakis and a designer polo shirt. Today he was wearing a long, straight white tunic beneath a loosely flowing top robe of royal blue. He also wore a white kaffiyeh on his head.

Delaney thought about the decision she had made. Feeling somewhat shaky, she took another sip of her coffee. She knew exactly what would happen once she told him that she had decided to take what he offered. There was no way he would ever know that she loved him, since she had no intention of ever admitting that to him. His knowing wouldn't change a thing, anyway.

She sighed deeply. She had to make him believe she no longer had any reservations about their future and she had accepted the way things would be.

No longer satisfied with watching him through the kitchen window, she decided to finish her coffee out on the porch the way she normally did each morning. She wanted him to see her. She wanted to feel the warmth of his eyes when they came in contact with hers. And she needed to look into them and know his desire for her was still there.

At the sound of the door opening, Jamal and Asalum turned. Delaney became the object of both men's intense stares but for entirely different reasons. Asalum was studying her as the woman who had his prince so agitated. Having been with His Highness all of his life, he read the signs. Jamal wanted this woman sexually, and in a very bad way. No other woman would do, so there was no need for him to suggest a substitute. He could only pray to Allah that Jamal didn't take drastic measures. He had never seen his prince crave any woman with such intensity.

Jamal's gaze locked with Delaney's the moment she stepped outside of the door. The first thing he thought was that she was simply beautiful. The next thing he thought was that she looked different today. Gone were the shorts and tops she normally wore, instead she was wearing a sundress that had thin straps at the shoulders.

Her curly hair was no longer flowing freely around her face but was up and contained by a clip.

"I must be going, Your Highness," Asalum said, reclaiming Jamal's attention, or at least trying to. Jamal kept his gaze on Delaney as he nodded to Asalum's statement.

As far as Asalum was concerned that in itself spoke volumes. Shaking his head, he inwardly prayed for Allah's intervention as he got into the car and drove away.

Inhaling deeply, Delaney released the doorknob and walked to the center of the porch. Her gaze never left Jamal's and she read in his what she wanted to read. The dark eyes holding hers were intense, forceful and sharp; and the nerve endings in her body began to tighten and the area between her legs filled with warmth with the look he was giving her.

And when he began walking toward her, he again reminded her of a predatory wolf and gave her the distinct impression that he was stalking her, his prey. There was something about him that was deliciously dangerous, excitingly wild and arrogantly brazen. A part of her knew that no matter how far he went today in this game of theirs, she would be there with him all the way. In the end he would succeed in capturing her, but she would not make it easy. She intended to make him work.

When Jamal came to a stop in front of her, dark eyes held hers in sensual challenge. "Good morning, Delaney," he murmured softly.

"Good morning, Jamal," she responded in kind. She then looked him up and down. "You're dressed differently this morning."

A smile twitched his lips, and amusement lit his eyes

as he looked her up and down, just as she had done him. "Yes, and so are you."

Delaney smiled to herself. She was beginning to like this game of theirs. "I thought today would be a good day to do something I haven't done since I got here."

"Which is?"

"To try out the hot tub on the back deck. It's roomy enough for two, and I was wondering if you would like to join me?"

Jamal raised a brow, evidently surprised by her invitation but having no intention of turning it down. "Yes, I think I will."

A tense silence followed. Delaney knew that he wasn't anyone's fool and saw her ploy as seduction in the making and was determined, as he'd done the night before, to turn things to his advantage. He didn't play fair.

She was hoping he wouldn't. In fact, she was counting on it.

"I'll go on out back," she said, her voice only a notch above a whisper. "My swimming suit is under my dress."

"And it won't take long for me to change clothes and join you," he said huskily.

She turned to leave, then suddenly turned back to him. "And one more thing, Jamal."

"Yes?"

"You have to promise to keep your hands to yourself."

A rakish grin tilted the corner of his lips, and a wicked gleam lit his eyes. "All right, I promise."

Delaney blinked, surprised he had made such a promise. She really hadn't expected him to. Without saying another word, she opened the door and went back into the house, wondering if he really intended to keep his promise.

* * *

Delaney was already settled in the hot tub when Jamal appeared on the back deck. She found it difficult to breathe or to look away. She finally let out a deep whoosh of air when she broke eye contact with him to take a more detailed look at his outfit.

The swimming trunks he wore were scantier than the boxer trunks he usually wore for kickboxing. Everything about him oozed sex appeal, and she felt inwardly pleased that for the next three weeks he belonged only to her.

"The water looks warm," Jamal said, breaking into Delaney's thoughts.

She smiled up at him. "It is."

Tossing a towel aside, he eased onto the edge of the tub. She watched his every move, mesmerized, as he swung into the water and took the seat in the hot tub that faced her. He sank lower, allowing the bubbly, swirling water to cover him from the shoulders down.

"Mmm, this feels good," he said huskily, closing his eyes and resting his head against the back of the tub.

"Yes, it does, doesn't it," Delaney said, raising a brow. Was he actually not going to try anything? He seemed perfectly content to sit there and go to sleep. He hadn't even tried taking a peek at her swimming outfit beneath the water. If he had, he would have known that she was wearing very little. On a dare from one of her college roommates, she had purchased the skimpy, sheer, two-piece flesh-tone bikini, although she had never worn it out in public.

Feeling frustrated and disappointed, she was about to close her own eyes when she felt him. He had stretched out his foot and it had come to rest right smack between her legs. Before she could take a sharp intake of breath, he had tilted his toes to softly caress her most sensitive area. She closed her eyes and sucked in a deep breath as his foot gently massaged and kneaded her center in tantalizing precision, slowly through the thin material of her swimsuit.

But he didn't plan to stop there. He lifted his foot higher to rest between her breasts. Then with his big toe leading the pack, he caressed the right nipple through the thin material of her bikini top, and when he had her panting for breath, he moved on to the other breast.

When all movement ceased, Delaney opened her eyes to find Jamal had covered the distance separating them and was now facing her in the tub.

"I don't need hands to seduce you, Delaney," he whispered softly yet arrogantly, his lips mere inches from hers. "Let me demonstrate."

And he did.

Leaning toward her he used his teeth to catch hold of the material of her bikini top to lift it up. Growling like the wolf she thought him to be, he sought out her naked breasts with a hunger that nearly made her scream in pleasure. Using his knee he shifted her body so that her breasts were above water. His tongue tasted, sucked, devoured each breast, and she became a writhing mass of heated bliss.

Moments later a moan of protest escaped her lips when he leaned back. She slowly opened her eyes to find him staring at her with raw, primitive need reflected in his eyes.

Her breasts, tender from the attention he had given them, rose and fell with every uneven breath she took. As she continued to look at him, he smiled hotly, boldly, and she knew he was not finished with her yet.

Not by a long shot.

She held her breath when he leaned toward her again

and with the tip of his tongue traced the lines of her lips before traveling the complete fullness of her mouth. Automatically her lips parted, just as he'd known they would, and he slipped his tongue inside.

A shudder of desire swept through her, and she wondered what madness had possessed her to forbid him to use his hands. Improvising, Jamal was using his tongue to seduce her as effectively as he would have used his hands. Jamal was an expert kisser and he was using that expertise on her, showing her just how much he enjoyed kissing her. And by her response he knew just how much she enjoyed being kissed.

Moments later he ended the kiss and pulled back. A sexy smile tilted the corners of his lips. "I want to see you naked, Delaney."

His words, murmured softly in the most sensual voice, touched Delaney deeply and sent a surge of emotions through her body. Once again he was able to shake up passion within her that she hadn't known existed—passion she wanted to explore with him.

Moaning, she leaned toward him. She was free to use her hands even if he wasn't. Feeling bold she circled her arms around his neck and kissed him again. Already used to each other, their tongues met, mingled and began stroking intimately.

When she finally lifted her mouth from his, she drew back, looked into his eyes and whispered thickly, "And I want to see you naked, as well."

His eyes darkened even more. "When you are nude will I be able to use my hands?" he asked in a deep, husky tone.

She smiled and instead of answering she asked a question of her own. "When you are nude will I be able to use *my* hands?"

His voice lowered to a growl when he answered. "You can use anything you want."

Her smile widened. "And so can you."

Chapter 8

Jamal was nearly at his wit's end as he watched Delaney towel herself dry. The swimming suit she had on was too indecent, too improper and too obscene for any woman to wear, but he was getting a tremendous thrill seeing her in it. His already ragged pulse had picked up a notch, and his breath was becoming so thick it could barely pass through his lungs.

She would be arrested and jailed if she wore anything so scandalous in his country with the pretense of going swimming in it. The material was so sheer he had to widen his eyes to make sure he wasn't seeing naked skin. And both pieces clung to her curves in the most provocative way, nearly exposing everything. Everything he wanted. Everything he had dreamed about. Everything he craved. And everything he intended to have.

He frowned. She was deliberately driving him mad.

"Like what you see, *Your Highness?*"

And she was deliberately provoking him.

Awareness joined the arousal already flaring in his eyes. He crossed his arms and looked at her assessingly, eager for her to strip. "Yes, I like what I see, but I want to see more." She was inflaming him one minute and frustrating him the next. He knew this was a game to her, a game she intended to play out until the end...and win. She may be amused now but when this was over he would be the one cackling in sensuous delight.

"Anxious, aren't you, Jamal?"

There was no reason for him to lie. "Yes."

She grinned, tossing the towel aside. "I think we should go inside."

He lifted a dark brow. As far as he was concerned here was just as good a place as anywhere. "Why?"

Delaney silently considered his question, sending him a sidelong glance. Did he actually think she would strip naked out in the open? "Because I prefer being inside when I take off my clothes."

Jamal favored her with a long, frustrated sigh. "It doesn't matter where you are as long as you take them off, Delaney. I'm holding you to your word."

"And I'm holding you to yours." She turned to go inside.

Following behind, close on her heels, he crossed the deck and quickly reached out and opened the back door for her.

She looked back over her shoulder and smiled. "Thanks, Jamal. You are such a gentleman," she said in a low, throaty voice.

Jamal smiled. He hoped she thought that same thing a few hours from now. A true gentleman couldn't possibly be thinking of doing some of the things that he planned to do to her. He would try to be a *gentle man* but beyond that he couldn't and wouldn't make any promises. As soon as they were inside with the door closed he said, "Okay, do it."

Delaney shook her head thinking Jamal must have a fetish for a woman's naked body. But she knew the reason he was challenging her and was so anxious to see her naked was because he really didn't believe she would go through with it. He thought she was stringing him along. After all, she had told him she played to win. She glanced around. "Be real, Jamal. I can't strip naked in a kitchen."

He frowned at her. "Why not?"

She shrugged. "It's not decent."

Jamal couldn't help but laugh. "You're worried about decency dressed in an outfit like that?"

"Yes."

Jamal rolled his eyes heavenward. "It's not like you have a whole lot to take off, Delaney. You're stalling."

"I'm not stalling."

"Then prove it."

"All right. I'd feel better taking off my clothes in the bedroom."

Jamal nodded, wondering what excuse she would come up with once he got her into the bedroom. Although he was frustrated as sin, he had to admit he was getting some excitement out of her toying with him, however he much preferred that she toyed with him in quite a different way. This game of hers had gone on long enough.

"Okay, Delaney, let's go to the bedroom."

"I'll need a few minutes to get things ready," she said quickly.

Jamal could only stare at her. Surely she had to be joking. What was there to get ready? She was half-naked already. Before he could open his mouth to voice that very opinion, she said, "Just five minutes, Jamal. That's all I'm asking." She turned and rushed off, not waiting for his response.

"Five minutes, Delaney, is all you will get," he called after her. "Then I'm going to join you, whether you're ready or not."

Delaney glanced around the room. She was ready.

Because her bedroom was on the side facing the mountains, at this time of the day it was the one with the least amount of sunlight, which was perfect for the darkened effect she needed. The curtains in the room were drawn and lit candles were placed in various spots in the room. Already their honeysuckle scent had filled the midday air.

She had removed the top layer of bedcovering and the two pillows from the bed; arranging them on the floor and adorning each side with the two tall artificial ficus trees in the room.

She smiled. Everything was set up to make the room resemble a lovers' haven, and as far as she was concerned it was fit for a prince…or a wolf in prince's clothing. It was time the hunter got captured by his game.

She turned when she heard the gentle knock on the door. Taking a deep breath, she crossed the room. Taking another quick glance around, she took another deep breath and slowly opened the door.

Jamal swallowed with difficulty and somehow remembered to breathe when Delaney opened the door, wearing a short, shimmering, baby-doll-style nightie that was sheerer than her bikini had been. Where the swimming suit had left a little to the imagination, this outfit told the full story.

Completely white, the material was a sharp contrast

to her dark skin, and he could easily make out certain parts of her body, clearly visible through the transparent chiffon material. The first question that came to his mind was, why would a woman who thought she would be spending a month alone in a cabin out in the middle of nowhere bring such intensely feminine apparel? He would have to ask her that question later...but not now. The only thing he wanted to do now, other than get his breathing back on track, was to touch her.

But first he needed to think...and then he conceded that his brain had shut down. He was now thinking with another body part. He forced his gaze to move to her face. She was looking at him, just as entranced with him as he was with her. He had changed into a silk robe and from the way it hung open it was obvious he wasn't wearing anything underneath.

The look of desire in her eyes made a deep, heated shudder pass through him, and when she took a step back into the room, he followed, closing the door behind him. He quickly took in his surroundings: the drawn curtains, the candles and the bedcovers and pillows strewn on the floor.

He then gave Delaney his full attention. Reaching out, he placed a finger under her chin. "Take it off, Delaney," he whispered, holding her gaze. "No more excuses, no more games. You have succeeded in pushing me to my limit."

Delaney stared at him, unable to do anything else. Through the haze of passion she saw him, really saw him, and knew that he might not love her, but she had something he desperately wanted. And from the way he was breathing and the size of the arousal he wasn't trying to hide, she had something he urgently needed.

A ray of hope sprang within her. He may be predestined to marry another woman, and he may have a mistress waiting for him in his native land, but now, today, right at this very moment, *she* was the woman he wanted and desired with an intensity that took her breath away.

"Take it off."

His words, Delaney noted, had been spoken...or a better word would be *growled*...through clenched teeth and heated frustration. She would bet no woman had ever given him such a hassle to see her naked. The one thing he would remember about her was that she hadn't been easy.

Reaching up to ease the spaghetti straps off her shoulders, she gave the top part of her body a sensuous wiggle, which prompted the gown to ease down past her small waist, over her curvaceous thighs and land in a pool at her feet.

She met Jamal's gaze when she heard his sharp intake of breath. She watched as his eyes became darker still, and saw how he was focusing entirely on her naked body, seemingly spellbound by what he saw. His eyes roamed over her like a lover's caress, the deep penetration of his gaze blazing a heated path from the tips of each of her breasts to the area between her legs. Then he reached up and released the clip on her hair, which tumbled around her shoulders.

A thickness settled deep in her throat, and her chest inhaled tightly a faint whisper of air. She thought she would always remember this moment when she had openly displayed herself to him, the man she loved. He was seeing her as no man ever had.

"Now it's your turn," she managed to say in the silence that had settled between them. She watched as he slowly pushed the robe from his shoulders, then stood before her proud, all male, intensely enlarged and naked for her. The glow from the candles reflected off his brown skin.

"I want you, Delaney." His whispered plea penetrated the room. "I want to take you in all the ways a man can take a woman. And I promise to give you pleasure of the richest, purest and most profound kind. Will you let me do that? Will you accept me as I am, accept the things that cannot be and accept that this is all we can have together?"

Delaney stared at him, knowing what her answer would be. This wasn't a cold day in July, and he wasn't coming to her exclusively. Yet she would go to him willingly, without shame and with no regrets. She lifted her head proudly as she fought back the burning in her eyes, inwardly conceding yet again that she loved him. And because she loved him, for whatever time they had left to spend together she would be his, the sheikh's woman, and he would be hers, Delaney's desert sheikh.

She met his gaze, knowing he waited for her response. As much as he wanted her, if she denied him he would accept her decision. But she had no intention of denying him. "Yes, Jamal, I want to experience the pleasure you offer, knowing that is all I can and will ever get from you."

For a moment Delaney could have sworn she saw regret, deep and profound, flash in his eyes just before he reached out and gathered her in his arms, sealing his lips with hers.

An insurmountable degree of passion flared quickly between them the moment his tongue touched hers, and the only thing she could do was revel in the fiery sensations bombarding her. His skin felt hot pressed against hers, and when his hand began caressing her backside, instinctively she got closer, feeling him large and hot, intimately pressing against her.

The kiss seemed to go on and on, neither wanting to break it, both wanting to savor every moment they spent together and not rush toward what they knew awaited them. The more they kissed the more fire ignited between them. They began devouring each other's mouths with a hunger that bordered on obsession. His tongue was familiar with every inch of her mouth, every nook and cranny, and it tasted and stroked her to oblivion.

When breathing became a necessity that neither could any longer deny, Jamal broke off the kiss but immediately leaned her back over his arms and went to her breasts. Delaney didn't think her mind or senses could take anything more, with the way his mouth and tongue felt locked on her breasts.

Displaying an expertise that had her weak in the knees, he paid sensual homage to her breasts, lavishing them with gentle bites and passionate licks. The scalding touch of his tongue on her nipples flooded her insides with heat so intense she thought she would burn to a crisp right there in his arms.

"Jamal…"

He didn't answer. Instead he picked her up in his arms and carried her to the area she had prepared for them on the floor. He quickly glanced around the room and saw what she had tried to do. She had attempted to turn a section of her bedroom into an exotic, romantic haven.

Whispering something in Arabic, then Berber, he eased down on the floor with her in his arms, suddenly feeling a deep tightening in his chest when full understanding hit him. She was giving herself to him on a level that was deeply passionate, erotically exotic and painstakingly touching.

Quickly forcing the foreign emotions he felt to the back of his mind, he took her lips once again. While holding her mouth captive to his, his fingers sought out every area of her body, flicking light touches over her dark skin, trailing from the tip of her breasts, down to her waist and navel and along her inner thigh before claiming the area between her legs.

Delaney broke off their kiss, closed her eyes and shuddered a moan when she felt Jamal's fingers touch her intimately, stroking, probing, caressing. She struggled to breathe, to maintain control and to not drown in the sensations he enveloped her in.

She opened her eyes and looked at him. His gaze was locked on hers, and she could tell from the taut expression covering his dark face that he was one step from sexual madness. The erection she felt against her hip was big and hard, and she didn't think it could possibly get much bigger or harder. Nor did she think she could take much more of what he was doing to her.

"I want you in a way I have never wanted another woman, Delaney," he murmured seductively as his fingers continued to stroke the very essence of her. "I want this," he said hot against her ear, pushing his fingers deeper inside of her so she would know just what "this" was.

Delaney could barely breathe. Her only response was a shuddering moan.

He slowly moved his fingers in and out, relishing the tiny purrs and moans she made, knowing he was giving her pleasure.

A sudden tremble passed through his body, and he knew at that moment he couldn't last any longer. He had to get inside of her. Shifting his body to where she lay under him, he sat back on his haunches and looked down at her, glorying in the beautiful darkness of her skin, the magnificent curves of her hips, the flatness of her stomach and the rich sharp scent that was totally her.

Her gaze was holding his, and he saw desire so profound in her eyes he almost lost it. He had to connect with her and sample the very essence of the gift she was offering him. "Are you protected, Delaney?" he asked in a voice so low he wasn't sure she had heard him.

She shook her head. "No, I..."

Whatever it was she was going to say she decided not to finish it. But that was all right, he would protect her. Standing, he quickly crossed the room to gather his robe off the floor. He had placed packs of condoms in the pockets. After putting one on he returned to her and knelt back in place before her, pausing to admire her lying there, waiting for him. Unable to help himself he leaned down and captured her lips again, in a passion that shook him to the core and made everything inside of him feel the need for her.

He tasted her richness as his tongue stroked hers to a hunger that matched his, tantalizing them into a feverish pitch. Breaking off the kiss he whispered something in Arabic as he slid her body beneath him, his gaze locked to hers. A part of him knew that he would always remember this moment as he fitted his body over her, parting her thighs.

His erection was like a radar and guided him unerringly to his destination, the part of her it desperately wanted, probing her entrance before slowly slipping inside, wanting to savor the feel of entering her body. Her heated muscles that encompassed him were tight, almost unbearably so, and held him as he inched his way forward.

He watched as she drew in a deep breath as her body's

silkiness sheathed him, and he kept moving forward slowly, until he came to an unexpected resistance. He frowned, then stared at her, not believing what he had come up against, but knowing it was the truth.

"You're a virgin," he whispered softly. Amazed. Dazed. Confused.

She suddenly lifted her legs to wrap around his waist, holding him captive. Meeting his astonished gaze, she whispered sassily, "And your point is, *Your Highness?*"

Jamal couldn't help but smile, although this was not one of those rare times he usually did so. He was always a very serious person when having sex with a woman. He frowned when it suddenly occurred to him that he was doing more with Delaney than merely having sex. With his full concentration on her he responded, "My point is that I don't do virgins."

She reached up and placed her arms around his neck, lifted her chin and met his stare. "You'll do this one, Prince."

He held her gaze, feeling angry because he knew she was right. There was no way he could retreat. "Why didn't you tell me, Delaney?"

She shrugged and whispered softly, "I didn't think it was such a big deal."

His face became hard as granite. "It *is* a big deal. In my country I would be honor-bound to marry any woman I deflowered."

"Then it's a good thing we're not in your country, isn't it?" She could see the dark storm gathering in his eyes.

"But what about your family? They would expect me to do the right thing."

Delaney's eyes widened when she immediately thought of her brothers. They wouldn't give him a chance to do the right thing. They would take him apart piece by piece instead. "My family has nothing to do with this. I'm a grown woman and make my own decisions. Women in this country can do that, Jamal."

"But—"

Instead of letting him finish whatever he intended to say, she deliberately shifted her body, bringing him a little deeper inside of her. She smiled when she heard his sharp intake of breath. She had him just where she wanted him.

Almost.

"Stop that!" he said, frowning down at her. "I have to think about this."

"Wrong answer, Prince. There's no time to think," she said, as the feel of him throbbing inside of her sent her senses spinning and heat flaring in all parts of her body. She writhed beneath him and felt him place his hands on her hips to hold her still.

"Delaney, I'm warning you."

She stared at him, at the hardness of his face, the darkness of his eyes and the sweat that beaded his brow. He wanted her but was fighting it.

It was time to end his fight. She wanted her memories and she intended to get them.

She lifted her body to capture his mouth and before he could pull back, her tongue skated over his lips. When he let out a deep moan she slipped inside, stroking his tongue into sweet surrender, the way he had done her mouth several times. She knew that once she had his mouth under her control, the rest would be history. There was no way he would not concede.

He groaned deep in his throat and grabbed her wrists, but he didn't release her. Nor did he break their kiss. Instead he became a willing participant, a prisoner of desire of the hottest kind. She knew he was still fighting her, trying to hold on to his last shred of will, his ingrained inclination to do the right thing. But she was beyond that and wanted him beyond it, too.

She felt his hands release her wrists and move to her hips, lifting her to him, and with one hard thrust, he had completely filled her.

Delaney gasped at the first sensation of pain, but it subsided when he slowly began moving inside of her. He broke off their kiss and held her gaze in the fiery darkness of his. "I brand you mine," he growled, nuzzling his nose against her neck as he rode her the way he had dreamed of since that first day, with an urgency that bordered on mania. His hands that were locked at her hips lifted her, held her in place to meet his every thrust.

Delaney closed her eyes, drowning in the pleasure he was giving her. Her fingers dug deeply into his shoulders, and her legs were wrapped tightly around his waist. She opened her eyes to see him looking at her, almost into her soul, and she whispered in a voice filled with quivering need, mind-stealing pleasure. "If you brand me, then I brand you, too, Jamal."

Her words sent Jamal's mind reeling and he knew she *had* branded him. Closing his eyes, he reared his head back, feeling his body connect to her, becoming a part of her, lured to a place he didn't want to go but found himself going anyway. In the back of his mind he heard her whimpering sounds of pleasure as his body continued to pump repeatedly into hers, taking her on a journey he had never traveled before with any woman. And when he felt the tip of her tongue softly lick the side of his face, tracing a path down his neck, he knew then and there he would always remember this but the memories would never be enough.

"Jamal!"

He felt her draw in a shuddering breath. He felt her body quiver tightly around him, clenching him, milking him and elevating him to the same plane she was on. He inhaled deeply, his nostrils flaring when the scent of her engulfed him, surrounded him. Sensations he had never experienced before took control, flooding him to the point where he couldn't think; he could only feel.

He released a huge, guttural groan when the world exploded around him and forged them tighter in each other's arms, as extreme sexual gratification claimed their bodies, their minds and their senses.

And for the first time in his entire life, Jamal felt mind-boggling pleasure and body-satisfying peace. He knew then and there that he would never get enough of this woman.

Chapter 9

Jamal stirred awake as the flickering candles cast shadows in the room. He glanced down at the woman he still held in his arms. She was getting much-deserved rest.

After making love that first time, they had both succumbed to sexual oblivion, quickly falling asleep, only to wake up an hour or so later just as hungry for each other as they had been before. He had been concerned that it was too soon again for her, but Delaney took matters into her own hands, straddling him and seducing him to the point where he had finally flipped her underneath him and given her what they both wanted.

Once again he had experienced something with her he had never experienced before, and knew when they separated he would never find peace. She would always be a clinging memory for the rest of his days.

In the past after having slept with a woman, he would quickly send her away, then shower to remove the smell of lingering sex. But the only place he wanted Delaney was just where she was, in his arms, and he didn't want to shower. In fact, he wanted to smother in the sexual scent their bodies had created.

He looked down at the way they were still intimately locked together, their limbs tangled and their arms around each other as if each was holding the other captive, refusing to let go. He reached out and stroked a lock of hair back from her face thinking how peaceful she looked asleep. She had the same blissful expression on her face that she had the night she had passed out from him kissing her.

He inhaled deeply. He had made love to other Western women, but nothing had prepared him for the likes of Delaney Westmoreland. She was a woman who could hold her own with him. She called him Your Highness with a haughtiness that was outright disrespectful for a man of his stature and distinction. She didn't hesitate to let him know she couldn't care less for those things, and that in his country he might be an Arabian prince but to her he was just a man. No more, no less. Other women gave in to him too easily and were quick to let him have his way. But that wasn't the case with the passionate, provocative and smart-mouthed Delaney.

And then there was the fact that she had been a virgin. Never in a thousand years would he have considered such a possibility, not with the body she had and especially with her nonconservative views. The woman was definitely full of surprises.

He shifted when he began to harden inside of her. As much as he wanted her again, he needed to take care of her. The best thing for her body right now was a soak in a tub of hot water.

"Delaney?" He whispered her name and gently nudged her awake. She lifted sleep-drugged eyes up at him, and her lips, swollen from his kisses, eased into a smile. That smile pulled at something inside of him. It also made him become larger. He saw her startled expression when she felt her body automatically stretch to take him deeper.

He had to find a way to stop this madness. His body was becoming addicted to her. He moved to pull out, but she tightened the leg she had entangled with his. Frowning, he looked down at her. "You need to soak in a tub of hot water," he rasped softly, trying to reason with her and gain her cooperation.

She shook her head. "No. Not now, maybe later." The sound of her voice came out in a sultry purr.

He tried ignoring it. "No, now. Besides, I need to put on another condom before we do this again. If I don't, we run the risk of an accident happening."

He figured that explanation would work on her good sense.

It didn't.

He felt the muscles of her body holding him inside of her tighten. He closed his eyes to pull out of her, but the more he tried the more her muscles held him.

He glared down at her, despising himself for wanting her so much. She was torturing him, and she damn well knew it. "Do you know what you're asking for?"

She met his gaze. "Yes," she murmured softly, while her body continued to milk him into a state of mindless pleasure. "I'm asking for *you,* Jamal."

"Delaney..." Her words were like a torch, sending his body up in flames. He captured her mouth with his at the same time his body thrust deep inside of her, giving her just what she had asked for.

*   *   *

"Mmm, this feels good," Delaney said, leaning back in the hot tub.

After they had made love, he had gathered her naked body up in his arms and taken her outside and placed her in the hot tub then got in with her. "It will help relieve the soreness," Jamal said slowly, looking at her. He had decided to sit on the other side of the tub, at what he considered a safe distance away. He couldn't trust himself to keep his hands off her.

"I'll survive a little soreness, Jamal. I am not a weak woman."

He chuckled, thinking that was an understatement. "No, Delaney, you are definitely not a weak woman. You're as strong as they come."

Delaney quirked a brow, not knowing whether he meant it as a compliment or an insult. She knew he was used to docile women; women who were meek and mild. She doubted it was in her makeup to ever be that way.

She glanced around. The sun had gone down, and dusk was settling in around them. "Are you sure it's all right for us to be out here naked? What if someone sees us?"

"I don't have a problem being seen naked."

Delaney lifted eyes heavenward. "Well, I do."

Jamal leaned back and closed his eyes. "This is private property, you said so yourself. And besides, they can look at you all they want, but they'd better not touch."

Delaney stared at him. "Getting a little possessive, aren't we?"

Jamal slowly opened his eyes and met her stare. "Yes." His attitude about that was something he couldn't quite understand. He had never been possessive of any woman, not even Najeen. That thought didn't sit too well with him. Deciding to change the subject, he said, "Tell me about this job of yours as a doctor."

Delaney spent the next half hour telling him about how she had to go through a period of residency where she would work at the hospital in a pediatric ward.

"Is this hospital a long way from your home in Atlanta?" he asked as he shifted his body below the water line some more.

"Far enough. It's in Bowling Green, Kentucky, so I'm leasing an apartment for the two years I'll be working there." She didn't add that she needed that distance away from her brothers.

When she had first left home for college she made the mistake of going to a school that was less than a two-hour drive from Atlanta. Her brothers nearly drove her crazy with their frequent impromptu visits. The only people who enjoyed seeing them had been the females living in her dorm who thought her brothers were to die for.

For medical school she had decided on Howard University in D.C. Although her brothers' trips to see her weren't as frequent, they still managed to check on her periodically just the same, claiming their parents' concern was the reason for their visits.

"After your residency do you plan to open up your own medical office?" Jamal asked.

"Yes, it's my dream to open up a medical office somewhere in the Atlanta area."

Jamal nodded. "And I hope your dream comes true, Delaney."

She knew he meant that with all sincerity and was deeply touched by it. "Thanks."

Later that evening they ate a light meal that the two of them prepared together. He noticed she had slid the table closer to the window and that it wasn't wobbling.

She told him of her conversation with Reggie, who had told her that the problem had not been with the table but with the floor.

"So as you can see, Jamal, things aren't always as they seem to be."

He had lifted a brow at her comment but said nothing.

She smiled. He knew she had been trying to make a point about something, but from his expression it was quite obvious he didn't get it. Delaney felt confident that one day he would.

After dinner she sat in the living room watching television while he sat on the opposite end of the sofa sketching on something. It was the same papers that he had occasionally worked on since she had arrived.

"What are you doing?" she asked curiously when he had finally placed the documents aside.

He reached out his arms to her and she covered the distance and went to him. He placed her in his lap while he showed her what he had been working on. "This is something I plan to build in my country. It will be a place my people can go for their necessities."

She studied the sketch, admiring the structural design. "It's sort of like an open market."

He smiled, glad she had recognized it for what it was. "Yes. It will be similar to the places you refer to in your country as a one-stop shop. Here they will be able to buy their food, clothing and any other miscellaneous items they might need. I also want it as a place for them to socialize while doing so, to come together. Although the majority of my people are like me, both Arab and Berber descent, and are in harmony for the most part, there are those who every once in a while try to cause friction between the two ethnic groups."

Delaney lifted her head. "What sort of friction?"

He smiled at her, feeling her genuine interest. "It's a feud that's dated back hundreds of years. The reason my mother and father married to begin with was to unite the Arabs and the Berbers, producing me, an heir of both heritages. The disagreement is about what should be recognized as the official language of our nation. Right now it's Arabic and has been for hundreds of years, but a group of African-born descendants believes it should be Berber."

Delaney nodded. "You mainly speak Arabic, right?"

"Yes, but I am fluent in both. When I become the king, my biggest challenge will be how to get everyone to embrace both languages, since both are a part of my country's heritage."

Delaney studied his features. "What are your views on the matter, Jamal?"

He smiled down at her. "I understand the need for both sides. There is a need to teach the Berber language and preserve and promote the Berber culture. However, since Arabic is the official language, everyone is duty bound to speak it. But I'm not for Arabization being imposed on the Berbers who reside in isolated regions and who want to keep their heritage intact, just as long as they remain loyal to Tahran and its leadership. The needs of all of my people are important to me."

Delaney nodded. A thought then struck her. "Speaking of needs, what about medical care? How do your people get the medical care they need?"

He looked at her as if surprised by her question. "We have hospitals."

She twisted in his arms, the concern in her features evident. "But what about those people living in smaller cities who can't make it to a hospital? Don't you think you may want to consider having a clinic just for them?"

Jamal lifted a brow. "In a market?"

She shook her head, smiling. "Not necessarily in the market but adjacent to it. I believe this entire idea has merit as a way to get people out and about in an open marketplace-type setting. But think of how convenient it would be to them. It might prompt more people who need it to seek medical care."

Jamal nodded, thinking she had a point. He had often approached his father with concerns of the need for more medical facilities. Keeping his people healthy was another way of keeping them safe. He looked down at the plans he had designed. "And where do you suggest this facility be placed?"

Delaney's smile widened. She was pleased that he had asked her opinion. For the next hour or so they discussed his designs. She had been surprised when he told her that although his master's degree from Harvard had been in business administration, he had also received a bachelor degree from Oxford in structural engineering.

That night when they retired to his bedroom, he again told her of his intent to not touch her anymore that day. He just wanted to hold her in his arms.

"Why did you change your mind about us?" he asked her quietly, holding her close, loving the feel of her softness next to him.

Delaney knew she could not tell him the truth. She did not want him to know that she had fallen in love with him. There was nothing to gain by doing so. "I took another look at things, Jamal, and decided that I wasn't getting any younger and it was time I did something about being a virgin."

He was surprised. Women in his country remained virgins until they married. "You had a problem with being a virgin?"

She heard the censure in his voice. "No, I didn't have

a problem with it, but then I didn't want to die a virgin, either."

He took her hand in his, letting his fingers curl around hers and ignoring the sexual rush just touching her invoked. "There were never any plans in your future to marry?"

"Yes, but no time soon. I wanted to establish myself as a doctor before getting serious about anyone."

Jamal nodded. He then thought of another question that he wanted to ask her. "What about your lingerie?"

She lifted a brow. "My lingerie?"

"Yes."

"What about them?"

He cleared his throat. "They are the type a woman normally wears to entice a man. Why would you bring such sleeping attire when you had planned to be at this cabin alone?"

Delaney smiled, understanding his question. She enjoyed going shopping for sexy lingerie and feminine undergarments. Her bras and panties were always purchased in matching sets, and she tended to be attracted to bright colors and for the most part shied away from plain-looking white underthings.

"I like looking and feeling sexy, Jamal, even when there's no one there to notice but me. Whenever I buy lingerie and underthings, I buy what I like for me with no man in mind."

"Oh."

"Now I have a question for you, Jamal," Delaney said softly.

"Yes?"

"Why would you bring all those packs of condoms with you when you had planned to be here alone?"

He grinned sheepishly at her. "I didn't bring them. I purchased them after I got here."

"When?" she asked lifting a curious brow.

"The night you and I went to that all-night supermart," he said, studying her features and wondering how she felt knowing he had planned her seduction even then. He reached out and touched her chin with his finger. "Are you upset?"

"No," she said as a smile curved her lips. "I'm not upset. I'm glad you did have the good sense to buy them."

Long after Delaney had fallen asleep, Jamal was still awake. For some reason the thought of another man sleeping with her, holding her in his arms the way he was doing bothered him. It also disturbed him that one day there would be a man in her life who would see her in all those sexy lingerie and underthings that she liked buying for herself.

When he finally dozed off to sleep, his mind was trying to fight the possessiveness he felt for the beautiful woman asleep in his arms.

"I take it that you enjoyed the movie," Jamal said when he pulled Delaney's car to a stop in front of the cabin.

She smiled, showing perfect white teeth and very sensuous lips. "What woman wouldn't enjoy a movie with Denzel Washington in it?"

He searched her face, amazed at the tinge of jealousy he was feeling. "You really like him, don't you?"

"Of course," she responded, getting out of the car and walking up the steps to the door. "What woman could resist Denzel?"

Jamal frowned. "And you would go out on a date with him if he were to ask you?"

Delaney stopped walking and turned around. She

studied Jamal's expression, seeing his frown and clenched teeth. As she continued to observe him, she had a sudden flash of insight when something clicked in her brain. He's jealous! Of all the outrageous...

She inwardly smiled. If that was true it meant, just possibly, that he cared something for her. But then a voice within her taunted, *Not necessarily. It could also mean that now that he has slept with you he sees you as a possession he wants to keep and add to the other things he owns.*

"Yes, I would go out with him," she finally answered, and saw the frown on his face deepen. "However, I don't plan on losing sleep waiting for such a miracle to happen. Besides, I doubt he would ask any woman out on a date since he's a married man." She quirked a brow. "Why do you want to know?"

He walked past her and said, "Curious."

She fell silent as she followed him to the porch. When she had awakened that morning he had already left the bed and was outside practicing his kickboxing. By the time she had made coffee and placed a few Danish rolls in the oven he had come inside. They had enjoyed a pleasant conversation, then he had suggested that they take in a midday matinee at the movie theater.

She knew his intention had been to get her out of the cabin for most of the day so he wouldn't be tempted to touch her again. He wanted to give her body time to adjust to their making love before they did it again, although she had tried convincing him that her body had adjusted just fine. She sighed deeply. It was time for her to take matters into her own hands.

Jamal's hands tightened like fists at his sides when he stood aside to let Delaney enter the cabin. He didn't understand why an irrational stab of envy had consumed him, making him angry, since he was familiar with Western women's fascination with movie actors and sports figures. But it rubbed him the wrong way to include Delaney in that number.

Closing the door behind them, he watched as she tossed her purse on the sofa. He had admired her outfit the moment she had emerged from the bedroom wearing it. She certainly knew how to dress to show off her attributes to the maximum. The short blue dress stopped way above her knees and showed off her curves and shapely legs. Her high-heeled sandals were sexy enough to drive him to distraction.

Then there was that lush behind of hers that always kept his pulse working overtime. He was just dying to touch it, run his hand all over it. He took a deep, fortifying breath as he let his gaze trace her legs from the tip of her polished toes, past her ankles, beyond her knees and up to her thighs that met the hem of her dress. He couldn't help but think about what was under that dress. He shook his head. How had he thought he could go a whole day without making love to her again?

"How does soup and a sandwich sound, Jamal?"

Jamal swallowed. His low reserve of willpower was pitiful. It took every ounce that he had to move his gaze away from her legs and focus on her face. "That sounds good and I'd like to help."

She smiled. "You're getting pretty handy in the kitchen. You seem to enjoy being there."

Jamal's brows furrowed. Not really, he wanted to say. She was the one who enjoyed being in the kitchen. He merely enjoyed being wherever she was. "Things are not always as they seem to be, Delaney."

She studied him for a long moment, then turned toward the kitchen. He followed, trying his best not to notice how the soft material of the dress hugged her hips as she walked ahead of him.

"Do you want to chop the veggies for the soup?"

His mind clicked when he heard a sound. He thought he heard her speak but wasn't sure. "Did you say something?"

She stopped walking and turned around. Her eyes smiled fondly at him as if he was a dim-witted human being. The way he was lusting after her, he was certainly feeling like one. "I asked if you wanted to chop the veggies for the soup I'm making."

"Oh, sure. Whatever you need me to do. I'm at your disposal."

"Are you always this generous to the women you sleep with?"

Jamal tensed, not liking her question and wondering how she could ask such a thing. While he was with her he didn't want to think about other women. "I'm considered a very generous man to a lot of people, Delaney," he said, holding her gaze, refusing to let her bait him.

She nodded and continued her walk to the kitchen.

Jamal sighed. He knew there was an American saying that...if you can't stand the heat, stay out of the kitchen. He muttered a low curse. He was following the heat right into the kitchen.

Delaney stopped stirring the ingredients she had already put in the pot and glanced over at Jamal. He was standing at the counter slicing vegetables. "How are you doing over there?"

He lifted his head from his task, and his gaze met hers across the room. "I'm just about finished."

"Good. The vegetables will be ready to go into the pot in a few minutes."

He swallowed hard. "It smells good. I bet it will taste good, too."

She gave a casual shrug. "There's nothing like something smelling good and tasting good," she said before turning back around.

Jamal was doing his best not to remember how good she smelled and how good she tasted. He also tried not to remember other things. Like the feel of her beneath his hands as he held her hips firmly, lifting her as he had entered her; how her eyes would darken each time he thrust into her, pulled out and thrust into her again. And the sounds of pleasure she made, and how her body would tighten around him, holding him deep inside of her, milking him bone-dry. At least trying to.

Jamal diced mercilessly into a tomato, furious with his lusty thoughts and knowing his control was slipping. Taking a deep breath he gathered the chopped vegetables in a bowl and on unsteady legs slowly made his way across the room to Delaney.

She turned and smiled at him, taking the bowl he offered. "You did a good job," she said, dumping the chopped vegetables into the steaming pot. "Now all we have to do is wait for another boil and then let things simmer awhile."

Jamal nodded. He knew all about boiling and simmering. He came damn close to telling her that he was already doing both from the feminine heat she generated. For the past thirty minutes he had tried to distract himself from watching her move about in the kitchen. Every move she made had turned him on. When she had reached up into the cabinets looking for garlic salt, her already short dress had risen, showing more leg and thigh and making sweat pop out on his brow. The sight had been pure temptation.

He took a step closer to her. "So what kind of soup are you making?"

She chuckled good-naturedly. "Vegetable soup."

The lower part of his body throbbed from the intensity of his need. He forced a smile. "That was simple enough to figure out, so why couldn't I think of that?"

Delaney placed the lid on the pot, turned the dial to simmer and looked up at him. "Maybe you have your mind on other things." She stepped away from the stove and walked over to the sink.

He followed her. He should have been expecting this, her being one step ahead of him. He wouldn't put it past her to have set him up. "So what do you think I have on my mind?" he asked, looking at her intently.

She shrugged and met his gaze squarely. "I'm not a mind reader, Jamal."

"No," he said, raking his gaze over her body. "Only because you're too busy being a seductress."

"No, I'm not."

"Yes, you are. Do you think I don't know what you've deliberately been doing to me for the past half hour?"

For a long moment neither said anything as their gazes clashed. Then Delaney asked in a deep, sultry voice, "Well, did it work?"

Jamal took a step closer as he muttered under his breath. He reached out and brought her body tightly against him, letting her feel how well her ploy had succeeded. "What do you think?"

She moaned softly and shifted her stance to spread her legs, wanting the feel of the hard length of him between them. Even through the material of their clothing there was simmering heat. Her eyes were half-closed when she said, "I think you should give your body what it wants and stop trying to play hard to get."

He lowered his head and licked her lips, slowly, thoroughly. "I was trying to spare you and give your body a chance to adjust."

Delaney's breath quickened with the feel of his tongue licking her lips as if he was definitely enjoying the taste. "I don't want to be spared, and my body doesn't need to adjust. The only thing it needs is you," she said quietly, shivering inside as his tongue continued to torment her. "I want to be made love to and satisfied. I want you inside of me, Jamal. Now."

The only thing Jamal remembered after that was taking her mouth with an intensity that overwhelmed him as he picked her up in his arms. He wanted her now, too. Quickly crossing the room, he set her on the table and pushed up her dress to her waist and lifted her hips to pull her panties completely off.

Like a desperate man he tore at the zipper of his jeans and set himself free just long enough to push her legs apart. Pulling her to him he then entered her. "Oh, yes," he said, throwing his head back when he felt her heat clutch him, surround him.

"You make me crazy, Delaney," he said, squeezing his eyes shut and placing a tight hold on her thighs, savoring how she felt. He didn't want her to move. He just wanted to stand there, between her legs, locked inside of her.

"Don't move," he ordered when he felt her body shift. "Just let me feel myself inside of you for a minute. Let me feel how wet you are around me and how tight." He wondered how a body so wet could hold him so snugly.

He inhaled her scent. It was like an aphrodisiac, making his sexual hunger all the more intense. "Lie back," he whispered hoarsely, and held on to her hips while she did so. When she was flat on her back on the table he leaned in and pulled her closer to him, going deeper inside of her. He opened his eyes when he felt her thighs quiver and stretch wide to wrap her legs around his waist.

What little control he had left vanished when he leaned down and caught her mouth with his. He closed his eyes and began making love to her with the intensity of a madman, a wolf mating, someone engaging in sex for the last time before facing a firing squad; he was just that greedy, besotted, possessed. He didn't think he could go another single day without getting some of this. All of it. And for a quick crazy moment he thought of taking her back to Tahran with him—against her will if he had to—just to keep her with him forever.

Forever.

He opened his eyes and muttered an Arabic curse then he mumbled an even worse one in Berber, not believing the path his thoughts had taken. Nothing was forever with him—especially a woman. But as he arched his back to go even deeper inside of Delaney, he knew that with her he had a different mindset. His body had a mind of its own. It wanted to devour her, every chance it got. Sexual intensity flared throughout his body, and he thought nothing could and would ever compare to this.

And moments later when she screamed out her climax, he sucked in a deep whiff of her scent at the same time that he exploded deep in her feminine core. It was then that he realized he wasn't wearing a condom. Too late to do anything about it now, since he had no intention of pulling out, and he continued to pour his seed deep within her as his body responded to the pleasure of their lovemaking.

He clenched his teeth as he drove into her hard, wanting to give her everything that was his, everything he had never given another woman. Finally admitting at that moment that what he was sharing with Delaney West-moreland went beyond appeasing sexual appetites.

She had somehow found a way to erode his resolve and raw emotions. All his defenses were melting away, the dam around his heart had crumbled. When he realized what was happening to him, shock reverberated through his body, only intensifying his climax.

Then another emotion, one stronger, more powerful, ripped through him. Up to now it had been a foreign element, but at that moment he felt it, from the depths of his loins to the center of his heart.

Love.

He loved her.

Chapter 10

The next week flew by as Jamal and Delaney enjoyed the time they were spending together. Jamal was awakened before dawn one morning by the insistent ringing of his cell phone. He automatically reached for it off the nightstand next to the bed, knowing who his caller would be. "Yes, Asalum?"

He felt Delaney stir beside him; her arms were tight around him, and her naked limbs were tangled with his. Last night they'd had dinner outside on the patio, preferring to enjoy the beauty of the moon-kissed lake while they ate. Then later in his bed they had made love all through the night.

Something Asalum said grabbed Jamal's attention. "Say that again," he said, immediately sitting up. "When?" he asked, standing, and at the same time he grabbed for his robe.

He turned and met Delaney's curious gaze. "I'll contact my father immediately, Asalum," he was saying into the phone. He let out a heavy sigh. When he disconnected the call he sat down on the edge of the bed and pulled Delaney into his arms. Before she could ask him anything he kissed her.

"Good morning, Delaney," he whispered huskily, close to her ear when he finally released her mouth. He cradled her gently in his arms.

"Good morning, Prince," she said smiling up at him. Then her dark brow puckered in concern. "Is anything wrong?"

Jamal shifted positions to lean back against the headboard, taking Delaney with him. "I won't know until I talk to my father. Before I came to this country I had been involved in important negotiations involving several countries that border mine. The usual issues were under discussion, and after three months everyone left satisfied. But according to Asalum, the sheikh of one of those countries is trying to renege on the agreement that was accepted by everyone."

Delaney nodded. "So in other words, he's causing problems and being a pain in the butt."

Jamal chuckled, appreciating the way Delaney put things. "Yes, he is."

Delaney placed a quick kiss on his lips before slipping out of his arms and getting out of the bed. "Where are you going?" he asked, when she began gathering up her clothes off the floor. Seeing her naked was making his body stir in desire.

She turned and smiled at him. "I'm going to take a shower. I know you have an important call to make and I want to give you complete privacy to do so."

He grinned, looking her over from head to toe. "And without any distractions?"

She chuckled. "Yeah, and without any distractions." She gave him a saucy look. "You're welcome to join me in the shower after you finish your call." She then left his bedroom, closing the door behind her.

Jamal didn't finish the call in time to join Delaney in the shower. After talking to his father he discovered the situation was more serious than he had thought and he was needed in Tahran immediately.

He had placed a call to Asalum with instructions to make the necessary arrangements for his return to the Middle East. All his life he had known what was expected of him when duty called, but this was the first time he had something important in his life that meant everything to him.

He hadn't told Delaney how he felt because the emotions were new to him and he wasn't sure it changed anything. She was who she was, and he was who he was. Love or no love, they could never have a future together. But could he give her up?

He knew that somehow he had to let her go. She could never be his queen, and he loved her too much to ask her to be his mistress, especially knowing how she felt about the subject. And then there was that other problem his father had conveniently dumped in his lap. The old sheikh of Kadahan wanted Jamal to marry his daughter as soon as it could be arranged. The thought of marrying, which a few weeks ago he would have merely accepted as his duty, now bothered him to no end. He felt angered at the prospect of having any woman in his life other than Delaney. And he did not appreciate the pressure his father was putting on him to return home and consider marriage to Raschida Muhammad, princess of Kadahan, at once, just to make her father happy.

Jamal shook his head. And why the sudden rush for a wedding? Why did Sheikh Muhammad feel the urgency to marry his daughter off? Jamal had posed the question to his father, and the only answer he got was that the old sheikh's health was failing and he wanted to make sure his daughter, as well as his people, were in good hands should anything happen.

Jamal refused to believe Sheikh Muhammad had serious health problems. He had spent three months with the man while negotiating that contract, and Sheikh Muhammad had still been actively bedding his French mistress when Jamal had left to come to America.

He tightened his fists at his sides, wondering what the hell was going on. He suddenly felt as if he was headed for the gallows and wished there were some other eligible sheikh the princess could marry. For once he did not want to be the sacrificial lamb.

He inhaled a deep breath. There was nothing left to do but to return to Tahran. It seemed that life had landed him a crushing blow. He felt frustrated and shaken. He was about to leave the only woman he truly loved to return home and marry someone he cared nothing about. A part of him died at the thought, but he knew what he had to do.

He also knew he owed it to Delaney to let her know that he was leaving and the reason why. She deserved his honesty. Chances were that news of his engagement would go out over the wire service, and he didn't want her to find out about it from the newspapers.

It took several moments for him to compose himself, then he left his bedroom to find Delaney.

She was nowhere to be found in the cabin, so he walked toward the lake looking for her. It was a warm, sunny day and birds were flying overhead. A part of him wished he could be that carefree, with no responsibilities and only the commitments that would make him happy. But that wasn't the case. As his father had not hesitated to remind him a few minutes earlier, he was a prince, a sheikh, and he had responsibilities and obligations.

Jamal stopped walking when he saw Delaney. She was sitting on the dock with her legs dangling over the edge, letting her toes play in the water. A light breeze stirred her hair about her face. She tossed it back in place, then leaned back on her hands to stare up at the birds; the same flock he had seen earlier.

Leaning against a tree, he continued to stare at her. He smiled. Seeing her sitting there, peaceful and serene, was the most beautiful sight he had ever seen, and he wanted to keep it in his memory forever. And knew that he would.

A battle was raging within him, love versus responsibility. Deep in his heart he knew which would win. He had been groomed and tutored to take on responsibilities all his life. But this thing called love was new to him. It was something he had never experienced, and for the first time in his life he felt lost, like a fish out of water.

A shiver passed through him. He loved her with a passion he hadn't known was possible, yet he had to let her go because duty called.

He forced himself to walk toward her, and when he got to the edge of the dock, he whispered her name and she turned and met his gaze. The look in her eyes and the expression on her face told it all. She didn't know the why of it, but she knew he was leaving.

And from the way her lips were quivering and from the way she was looking at him, she didn't have to say the words, because he immediately knew how she felt.

The silent message in her eyes told him everything, just as he knew the silent message in his was exposing his very soul to her. For the first time it was unguarded... just for her.

They had both played the game and won...but at the same time they had both lost. He hadn't played fair and she had played to win and in the end they had gotten more than they had bargained for—each other's hearts. But now they were losing even more—the chance to be together.

"Come here," he whispered softly, and she stood and came into his arms willingly. He held her like a dying man taking his last drink, pulling her to him and holding her close, so close he could hear the unevenness of her breathing and the feel of her spine trembling. But at the moment all he wanted to do was hold her tight in his arms, close to his aching heart.

They stood that way, for how long he didn't know. He stepped back and looked at her, wondering how he would survive the days, weeks, months and years, without her. Wondering how a woman he had met only three weeks ago could change his life forever. But she had.

He swallowed the thick lump in his throat and said, "Duty calls."

She nodded slowly as she studied his features. Then she asked, "It's more than the business with the sheikh of that other country, isn't it?"

He met her gaze. Deep regret was in his eyes. "Yes. I've been summoned home to marry."

He watched as she took a deep breath, saying nothing for a few moments. Hurt and pain appeared in her features although he could tell she was trying not to let them show. Then she asked in a very quiet voice, "How soon will you be leaving?"

He thought he could feel the ground under his feet crumble when he said, "As soon as Asalum can make the necessary arrangements."

She tried to smile through the tears he saw wetting her eyes. "Need help packing, Your Highness?"

A surge of heartache and pain jolted through him. This was the first time she had called him Your Highness without the usual haughtiness in her voice. He reached out and clasped her fingers and brought them to his lips. In a voice rough with emotion, tinged with all the love he felt, he whispered, "I would be honored to accept your help, My Princess."

He pulled her into his arms and covered her mouth with his, zapping her strength as well as his own. The inside of her mouth was sweet, and he kissed her the way he had kissed her so many other times before, putting everything he had into it.

Without breaking the kiss he gathered her up into his arms and carried her over to the hammock. He wanted and needed her now. And she had the same wants and needs as he did, and began removing her clothes with the same speed he removed his. He then gathered her naked body in his arms and placed her flat on her back in the hammock. Straddling her, he used his legs to keep the hammock steady as he entered her body, almost losing it before he could push all the way inside. His entire body filled with love as he sank deeper and deeper into her. All his thoughts were concentrated on her.

For a moment, like the hammock, he felt his life was hanging by cords, but when she wrapped her legs around his waist and looped her arms around his neck, he knew she was all he would ever need and was the one thing he could never have.

But he would have these lasting memories of the time

they had spent together. They were memories that would have to last him a lifetime. He began moving, thrusting in and out of her, his hunger for her at its highest peak, knowing this may very well be the last time he had her this way. Over and over again, he withdrew, then pushed forward again, wanting her and needing her with a passion.

Under the clear blue sky, with the sunshine beaming brightly overhead, he made love to his woman with an urgency that overwhelmed both of them. The muscles inside of her squeezed him, as he pumped into her relentlessly.

In the deep recesses of his mind he heard Delaney cry out as completion ripped through her, once, twice and a third time, before he finally let go, letting wave after wave of sensations swamp his body, and he shuddered deep into her, filling her fully.

He dug his heels into the solid ground to hold the hammock in place as he held her hips in a tight grip, experiencing the ultimate in sexual pleasure with the woman he loved.

Jamal and Delaney heard the sound of Asalum's car when it pulled up in the driveway. The older man had phoned earlier to say a private plane had arrived to take the prince back to his homeland and was waiting for them at the airport.

After making love outside they had come inside and showered together, only to make love again. She had sat on the bed and watched him dress in his native garb, trying not to think about the fact that one day soon another woman would be the one to be by his side.

When he had finished dressing, looking every bit a dashing Arab prince, a handsome desert sheikh, she helped him pack without a word being exchanged between them. There was nothing left to say. He had to do what he had to do.

Delaney inhaled deeply. She had known this day would eventually come, but she had counted on another week with him. But that was no longer possible. It was time for him to return to the life he had without her to marry another. She looked up and saw him watching her. She had been determined to make their parting easier but now…

"Will you walk me to the porch, Delaney?"

"Yes." She felt tears gathering in her throat. Crossing the room to him, she stood on tiptoe and kissed him on his lips. "Take care of yourself, Jamal."

He reached out and stroked her hair back from her face—a face he would remember forever. "You do the same." He inhaled deeply and said, "There were times when I wasn't as careful with you as I should have been, Delaney. If you are carrying my child, I want to know about it. I've left Asalum's number on the nightstand next to your bed. He knows how to reach me at any time, day or night. Promise you will call and let me know if you carry my heir."

Delaney looked up at Jamal, questions evident in her eyes. He knew what she was asking. "It doesn't matter," he said softly. "If you are pregnant, the child is mine and I will recognize it as such. Your child will be *our* child, and I will love it…just as much as I will always love you, its mother."

Tears streamed down her face with his admission of love. It had not been his intent to tell her how he felt, but he couldn't leave without letting her know their time together had meant everything to him, and without letting her know that he had fallen in love with her.

"And I love you, too, Jamal," she whispered, holding him tight to her.

He nodded. "Yes, but this is one of those times when love is not enough," he said hoarsely. "Duty comes before love."

Asalum blew the horn, letting them know it was time for him to leave. Delaney walked him to the door, then stood silently on the porch as she watched his trusted servant help him with his luggage. When that had been done Jamal turned and looked at her after taking a small box Asalum had handed to him.

Walking back to her he presented the box to her. "This is something I had Asalum make sure arrived with the plane. It is something I want you to have, Delaney. Please accept it not as a gift for what has passed between us, because I would never cheapen what we shared that way. But accept it as a token of my undying love and deep affection. And whenever you need to remember just how deeply I love you, just how much I care, take a look at it," he said, opening the box for her to see.

Delaney released a sharp intake of breath. Sitting on a surface of white velvet was the largest diamond ring she had ever seen. It was all of eight or nine carats. But what really caught her eye was the inscription on the inside of the wide band. It read—"My Princess." "But... but I can't take this."

"Yes, you can, Delaney. It belonged to my mother and is mine to give to the woman I choose."

"But what about the woman you must marry, and—"

"No, she is the woman being given to me. In my heart you are the woman I love and the woman I would choose if I could. This is mine and I want to give it to you."

Delaney shook her head as tears began clouding again in her eyes. "This is too much, Jamal. It is so special."

"Because you are too much, Delaney, and you are so special. And no matter who walks by my side, remember that things aren't as they seem to be. You are the one who will always have my heart."

He leaned and tenderly kissed her one last time before turning and walking to the car. He looked over his shoulder before getting inside, and waved goodbye.

She waved back, then stood rooted to the spot, watching the car drive away. She once remembered him saying that he didn't like leaving anything behind broken.

Evidently, it didn't include her heart.

She stood until the vehicle was no longer in sight. It was then that she allowed the floodgates to open, and she gave in to the rest of her tears.

The sun was low on the horizon by the time Delaney finished her walk. The cabin held too many memories, and she hadn't been ready to go there after Jamal left, so she'd taken a stroll around the cabin. But she had found no peace in doing that, either.

Every path she took held some memory of Jamal.

Already every cell in her body missed him, longed for him and wanted him. There was so much she'd wanted to say and wished she had said, but none of it would have mattered.

He had chosen duty over love.

Delaney's heart sank, yet a part of her both understood and accepted. She had known all along that things would end this way. There had been no other way for them to end. Jamal had been totally honest with her from the very beginning. He had not given her false hope or empty promises.

He was who he was. A man of honor. A man whose life was not his own, so it could never be hers.

She sighed when she reached the porch, remembering how they had often eaten breakfast while sitting on the steps enjoying the sun. She also remembered a particular time when he had said something to make her laugh just moments before claiming her mouth and kissing her in a way that had melted her insides.

Inhaling deeply, Delaney knew there was no way she could stay at the cabin any longer. She walked up the steps after making the decision to pack up her things and leave.

Delaney had just closed the last of her luggage when she heard a car door slam outside. Thinking, hoping, wishing that Jamal had returned for some reason, she raced out of the bedroom to the front door. When she opened it, she swallowed deeply, recognizing her visitors.

Five men were leaning against a sports utility vehicle, and each man had his arms crossed over his chest and a very serious look on his face. Delaney sighed as she studied them.

Dare stood every bit of six-four and was the most conservative of the five. As a sheriff he demanded respect for the law, and those who knew him knew he meant business and not to call his bluff. Thorn stood an inch or so taller than Dare and was considered the prickliest of the five. He was moody and temperamental when it suited him. And he was the daredevil in the family, the one who took risks by racing the motorcycles he built. Chase was basically easygoing when the others weren't around. He stood six-two and relished the success of his soul-food restaurant that had recently been named one of the best eating places in the Atlanta area. Stone was the most serious of the five, or at least he tried to be. His height fell somewhere between Chase's and Dare's. He enjoyed taking trips to different places, doing research for his books. So far all ten novels had appeared on the *New York Times* bestseller list. Last, but not least, was Storm, Chase's twin. He was as tall as Chase and had dimples to die for. It had always been his dream to become a fireman, and now because of a recent promotion, he was a proud lieutenant in the Atlanta Fire Department.

Even Delaney had to admit they were a handsome group, but at the moment she wasn't in the mood to be intimidated by the likes of the Westmoreland brothers. "You guys are a long way from home, aren't you?" she asked, moving her gaze from one to the other.

Of course it had to be the prickly Thorn who spoke up by saying, "What the hell are you doing out here by yourself in the middle of nowhere, Laney?"

Before she could answer, Dare chimed in. "I see another set of tire tracks, you guys. It looks like Laney wasn't here by herself, or she had a visitor."

Delaney raised her eyes heavenward. "Always the cop, aren't you, Dare?" She sighed. "Why the show of force? Didn't Mom and Dad tell you I was okay and wanted to be left in seclusion for a while?"

"Yes, they told us," Stone said easily, but eyed her suspiciously as if she would be the perfect villain for his next book. "But we had to check things out for ourselves. And who did that other car belong to?"

Delaney refused to answer. In fact, she had a question of her own. "How did you find me?"

Storm laughed. "Dare put your picture out over the FBI wire service as a most-wanted fugitive and we got a tip."

At her frown, Storm held up his hand and said, "I was just kidding, Laney. For goodness sakes, cut the 'I will kill you dead if that's true' look. Chase took a peek at the folks' caller ID and got your new cell number. The telephone company was able to trace where the roaming fees were being charged. Once we had that pinpointed the rest was a piece of cake."

Delaney shook her head. "Yeah, I bet it was, like none of you have anything better to do with your time than to hunt me down. I am twenty-five, you know."

Stone rolled his eyes. "Yeah, and the cost of milk was two-fifty a gallon yesterday, so what's your point?"

Delaney glared at the five of them as she came down off the porch. "My point is this. I can take care of myself, and if you start trying to get into my business, I will do the same for yours."

Four of the men looked uneasy. Of course it was Thorn who took her threat in stride. "You're welcome to mess things up with me and the woman I'm presently seeing. She's the clingy type, and I've been trying to get rid of her for weeks."

Delaney glared at him. "If your mood hasn't run her off then nothing will." She inhaled deeply, knowing her brothers were hopeless. They would never treat her like the adult she was. "Well, since you're all here, you may as well help carry my stuff to the car."

Chase lifted a brow. "You're leaving?"

"Yes."

"You never said whose car those tire tracks belonged to," Dare reminded her.

Delaney turned to go into the house, knowing her brothers would follow. She decided to tell them the truth since she knew they wouldn't believe her, anyway. "The car belonged to a prince, a desert sheikh from the Middle East," she tossed back over her shoulder.

She smiled when she heard Storm say to the others, "And she thinks we're stupid enough to believe that."

Chapter 11

Jamal gazed out of the window of the private plane as it landed at the Tahran airport. Any other time he would have thought it was good to be home, but tonight was an exception. His heart still ached for Delaney.

What was she doing? Was she thinking of him the way he was thinking of her?

"It is time to disembark, My Prince."

He lifted his gaze and met Asalum's concerned frown. Only someone as close to him as Asalum could know the pain he was feeling. He turned his head to look back out of the window, not saying anything for the longest time, then he said quietly, "I'm no longer filled with obsession, Asalum."

Asalum nodded. "And what is it now, Your Highness?"

"Depression."

Asalum shook his head. That much he had already concluded. The loss of the American woman was having a powerful effect on the prince.

Jamal slowly stood. He had noted the long, black limo parked on the runway. As usual his father had sent an entourage to welcome him home. With a grim set of his jaw he walked off the plane.

Within less than an hour's time he arrived at the palace. Sitting high on a hill it looked like a magnificent fortress, commanding its own respect and admiration, and had served as home for the Yasir family for hundreds of years.

After going through the massive wrought-iron gate, the limo had barely come to stop when a beautiful, young dark-haired woman raced from the front of the house into the courtyard.

"Jamal Ari!"

Jamal smiled for the first time since leaving America and watched his sister come to a stop next to the car, anxious for him to get out. A few moments later he found himself standing next to the car and embracing his sister, Johari.

"It's so good to have you home, Jamal Ari. I have so much to tell you," she said excitedly, pulling him through the huge wooden door she had come out of.

Jamal shook his head. If anyone could pull him out of his despairing mood, it would be Johari.

Later that night Jamal heard a soft knock on his door. He had claimed complete exhaustion, and his father had agreed to put off their talks until the next morning. Jamal had escaped to his private apartment in the palace, the entire west wing that was his. Rebakkah, Asalum's wife and the woman who had been his personal servant since birth, had brought him a tray of food a while ago that sat untouched on the table. He had no appetite to eat.

He opened the door to find his stepmother, Fatimah,

standing there. A beautiful woman with golden-brown skin and long, black wavy hair that flowed to her waist, she had retained her petite figure even after giving birth to two children. It seemed she never aged and was just as radiant at forty-four as she had been when she had come into his and his father's lives twenty-two years ago. He was not surprised to see her. Like Asalum, Fatimah knew him well and she knew when something was bothering him.

She stepped into his apartment and turned to face him. Concern was etched in her dark eyes. They were beautiful eyes that were all seeing, all knowing. "What is it, Jamal Ari?" she asked softly, studying him intently. "You are not yourself. Something is bothering you, and I want you to tell me what it is so I can make it better."

Jamal leaned against the door. He couldn't help but smile. When he was younger it seemed Fatimah had always been able to do that—make things better. Even if it pitted her against his father. She had never been outright disobedient, but she had definitely let the king know how she felt about certain things.

"I don't think you can make this one better, Fatimah," he said quietly. "This is something I have to work out for myself."

Fatimah looked at him for a long moment, then nodded, accepting his right to request that she not interfere. *For now.* "Well, whatever has you in such a sour mood will soon be forgotten. I sent word to Najeen that you had returned."

A frown covered Jamal's face. "Najeen?"

Fatimah's feminine chuckle bathed the air. "Yes, Najeen. Have you forgotten who she is?"

Jamal walked away from the door. He didn't want to see Najeen or any woman for that matter. The woman he wanted to see was millions of miles away. "Najeen will no longer be my mistress," he said softly.

Fatimah raised a dark brow. "Why? Do you have another?"

"No." He sighed deeply, not in the mood to explain. But seeing the surprised look on Fatimah's face he knew that he should. "I will be sending Najeen away, back to her homeland where she will be taken care of in the comfort she has become accustomed to until she takes another benefactor," he quietly decreed.

Fatimah nodded as she studied him. Her distress level rose. He was acting in a most peculiar way. "Is there a reason for your decision?"

His lashes lifted and his dark eyes met her even darker ones. Fatimah saw anxiety in their depths. She also saw something else that alarmed her. "Jamal Ari? What is it?"

He crossed the room to the window. The view outside was magnificent, but for the first time he didn't appreciate it. "While in America I met someone, Fatimah. A woman who stirred me in a way no other woman has. A Western woman who initially fought me at every turn, a woman who is just as proud and stubborn as I am, someone who was my complete opposite on some things but then my total equal on others. And…"

Silence. Across the room Fatimah watched his profile. She saw the way his hands balled into fists at his sides; the way his jaw hardened and the sharp gaze that was looking out the window without really seeing anything. "And what?" she prompted, hoping he would continue.

Slowly, he turned to face her and she saw the torment in his features. "And someone I fell helplessly and hopelessly in love with."

Fatimah's heart took a lurching leap of surprise in her throat. "A Western woman?"

He met her gaze thinking, *my* Western woman. From the moment Delaney had gotten out of the car that day she had arrived at the cabin, a part of him had known she would be his. He just hadn't known that he, in turn, would become hers. "Yes," he finally responded.

Fatimah studied him. "But you've never liked Western women, Jamal Ari. You always thought they were too modern, headstrong and disobedient."

A smile forced its way to his lips when he thought of Delaney. In her own way she was all those things. "Yes, but I fell in love with her, anyway."

Fatimah nodded. "So what are you going to do? You love one but are planning to wed another?"

Jamal inhaled a deep breath. "I must do what I must do, Fatimah. I am duty bound to do what is needed for my country."

"And what about what is needed for your heart, Jamal Ari?" she asked, crossing the room to him. She had taken him into her heart as her son the moment she had seen him many years ago. "Your heart is breaking. I can sense it."

"Yes," he said, not bothering to deny it. "A good leader's decisions should not be ruled by love, Fatimah. They should be ruled by what is in the best interest of his people. My feelings matter not."

Fatimah looked at him, aware of the coldness settling in him. The bitterness, as well. She smiled sadly. For as long as she had known him, Jamal Ari had always had a mind and a will of his own. Yes, he was as dedicated to the people as his father, but still, he did exactly what pleased him, which usually had been fast cars and beautiful women. But now for what he considered to be the good of his people, he was willing to bend his mind and his will. And in doing so he was slowly destroying himself.

"Your father once thought that way, Jamal Ari, but now he thinks differently," she finally said, hoping to make him see reason before it was too late. "And I hope you will open your mind to do the same. Love is a powerful beast. It can bring the strongest of beings to their knees."

Without saying anything else, she turned and walked out of the room. The door closed stiffly behind her, bathing the room in dead silence.

That night Jamal dreamed.

Delaney was with him, in his bed while he made love to her. Not caring that he wasn't using protection of any kind, his body repeatedly thrust into hers, glorying in the feel of her beneath him, of him being inside of her. In the darkness he could hear her moans of pleasure that combined with his own. He could actually feel the imprint of her nails on his back and shoulders as she gripped him, her fingers relentlessly pressing deeply into his skin. He felt his body moving closer to the edge and knew what he wanted more than anything. He wanted to impregnate her with his heir, just in case she wasn't pregnant already. He could envision a son with dark, copper-colored skin and a head of jet-black curls and eyes the color of dark chocolate.

His hand reached up and cupped her cheek, bringing her lips to his; lips he now hungered for all the time; lips he would tease into submission. They were also lips whose touch could arouse him to no end, drive him literally insane; lips belonging to a mouth he had branded.

He then gave his attention to her breasts as they thrust firmly and proudly from her body, taunting him to taste, which he did. He loved the feel of them against his tongue, wished he could love her this way forever and never have to stop. Around her he always felt primal, needy, lusty.

So he continued to make love to her, holding her tightly in his arms and whispering his words of love.

Thousands of miles away Delaney was in bed having that same dream.

Her body felt stretched, filled and hot. Her breasts felt soul-stirringly tender from Jamal's caress, and she could feel him loving her in a way she had become used to: determined, forceful. And very thorough.

His touch felt so right, and she felt a simmering sense that relief was near. She moaned a low, needy sound when a shiver passed through her body, and she gloried in the feel of being made love to this way. Then she exploded into tiny pieces.

Sometime later she opened her eyes, letting them adjust to the darkness. Rejoining reality she found that she was in bed alone. She curled her body into a ball as the waves of passion subsided, sending tremors through her.

She lay there, too shaken to move. Her dream had seemed so real. It had been as if Jamal had actually been with her, inside of her, making love to her. Taking a deep breath she swung her legs down to the floor and eased out of bed.

Going into the bathroom she washed her face in cool water, still feeling the heat of her dream. She inhaled deeply, glad she had returned to her apartment and not done as her brothers had suggested and gone to her parents' home.

She needed time alone—time to deal with everything. Her brothers had relented and had given in to her request for privacy. But she knew their placidness wouldn't last long. For the moment they were humoring her.

Glancing up at the mirror, she studied her red, swollen eyes. After her brothers had left, indicating they would be back to check on her within a few weeks, she had lain across the bed and cried.

She knew she couldn't continue on this way. Jamal was gone and wasn't coming back. She had to get on with her life, and the best way to do that was to go to work. She was not supposed to report to the hospital for another two weeks, but she wanted to go to work now. She would call the chief of staff to see if she could start earlier than planned.

The best thing to do was to keep her mind occupied. She had to stop thinking about Jamal.

Jamal got out of bed drenched in sweat as chills from the night air touched his body, making him tremble. His dream had seemed so real. He inhaled deeply. There wasn't the lingering aroma of sex, that special scent that he and Delaney's mated bodies generated.

He momentarily closed his eyes, memorizing her scent and visualizing in his mind the nights he had been pleasured by her body in reality and not in a dream. He could never forget the sight of her lying on her back…waiting for him. Her legs were shapely, long and sleek, and her breasts, there for him to touch and taste, and he had thoroughly enjoyed doing both. But what took his breath away to just think about it was her rear, perfectly rounded and curvy, making him hard each time he saw it.

The memories were making his body hard, and his breath was ragged. A part of him cursed the fate that had taken him away from Delaney. He acknowledged he would have left eventually, anyway. But knowing that had made every moment with her precious as time had clicked away. The time they had spent together had not been nearly long enough.

He reached for his robe from a nearby chair and put it on, then walked across the room to the door leading to the balcony. Stars dotted the midnight sky and softly lit the courtyard below. With its numerous lush plants, beautiful flowers and exotic shrubs, the courtyard had always been his favorite place to hide out as a child. But no matter how well he thought he could hide, Asalum would always find him. He smiled at the memory, breathing in the scent of gardenias and jasmine.

He then smiled at the thought of what Delaney would think if she ever saw the palace. A part of him could see her feeling right at home here. There was no doubt in his mind that with her Western views she would be a breath of fresh air. Her liberal way of thinking would no doubt scandalize some, but her caring would capture the hearts of others. The same way she had captured his.

Just thinking about her was torment. He straightened slowly and sighed. After he met with his father in the morning he would leave for Kuwait to meet with the other members of the coalition to reach another agreement with the Sheikh of Caron.

Then he would travel to Ranyaa, his estates in northern Africa. And there he would stay until the marriage arrangements had been worked out. He didn't want to be around anyone any more than necessary. He wanted to be left alone…to drown in his misery.

Chapter 12

Delaney returned the squiggling baby to its mother. "She seems to be doing a whole lot better, Mrs. Ford. Her fever has broken, and her ears no longer look infected."

The woman shook her head, smiling. "Thanks, Dr. Westmoreland. You have been so nice to my Victoria. She likes you."

Delaney grinned. "I like her, too. And to be on the safe side, I'd like to see her again in a few weeks to re-check her ears."

"All right."

Delaney watched as the woman placed the baby in the stroller and left, waving goodbye before getting on the elevator. She sighed deeply. During the three weeks since she had started working she was getting used to being called Dr. Westmoreland. Her heart caught in her chest each time she heard it. All of her hard work and dedication to her studies had paid off. She was doing something she loved and that was providing medical care to children.

Someone behind her chuckled, and she half turned and saw it was Tara Matthews. Tara was a fellow resident pediatrician whom she had met when she began working at the hospital. They had quickly become good friends.

"Okay, what's so funny?" she asked Tara, smiling.

"You are," Tara said, shaking her head, grinning. "You really like babies, don't you?"

Managing a chuckle, Delaney said, "Of course I do. I'm a pediatrician, for heaven's sake. So are you, and I have to assume you like babies, too."

Tara took the stethoscope from around her neck and placed it in the pocket of her doctor's scrubs. "But not as much as you do. I wished I had a camera for the look of awe on your face when you were holding Victoria Ford. You were in hog heaven. And that's with every baby you care for."

Delaney chuckled, knowing that was true. "I already told you that I'm the only girl with five brothers and I was also the youngest. By the time I came along there weren't any babies in my family. And my brothers have declared themselves bachelors for life, which means I won't be getting any nieces or nephews anytime soon."

Tara folded her arms under her breasts and nodded. "And for me it was the complete opposite. I'm the oldest of four and I had to take care of my younger sister and brothers, so I can hold off having any children of my own for years to come."

Delaney laughed. She really liked Tara and appreciated their friendship. Like her, Tara had moved to Bowling Green without knowing a soul, and the two of them had hit it off. They lived in the same apartment building and carpooled to work occasionally, and on the weekends they would go shopping and to the video store, then stay up late for hours talking and watching old movies. Being the same age, they shared similar interests, and like her, Tara was unattached at the moment, although Delaney couldn't understand why. With her dark mahogany complexion, light brown eyes and dark brown hair, not to mention her hourglass figure, Tara was simply gorgeous. Delaney knew that a number of doctors had asked her out and she had turned them down without blinking an eye.

But then so had she.

It wasn't uncommon for the single doctors to check out the new unattached female residence physicians. Although Delaney had been asked out several times, like Tara, she had declined the offers. Usually in the afternoons when she left work, unless she and Tara had made plans to do something together that night, she went home, took a shower and went to bed.

And each night she dreamed of Jamal.

"Tara to Delaney. Tara to Delaney. Come in, please."

Delaney laughed when she realized Tara had been trying to get her attention. "I'm sorry, what were you saying?"

"I asked if you have any plans for tonight."

Delaney shook her head. "No, what about you?"

"No, none. Do you want to check out Denzel's new movie?"

Wincing, Delaney sucked in a deep breath. Tara's question reminded her that she had already seen the movie…with Jamal. She closed her eyes as she tried to blot out the memory.

"Delaney, are you all right?"

Delaney snapped her eyes back open and met Tara's concerned stare. "Yes, I'm fine." She took in another deep breath of air. "I've already seen the movie, but if you really want to go I can see it again."

Tara looked at her for a moment before saying, "You went with him, didn't you?"

Delaney took a deep breath. "Him who?"

"The guy you won't talk about."

Delaney didn't say anything for the longest time and then she nodded. "Yes, and you're right, I don't want to talk about him."

Tara nodded and reached out a hand to touch Delaney's arm. "I'm sorry. I didn't mean to pry. I have no right."

Delaney shook her head. "No, you don't." A smile softened her features when she added, "Especially since you're harboring secrets of your own."

A gentle smile tilted the corners of Tara's lips. "Touché, my friend. One day, after I've taken one sip of chardonnay too many, I'll spill my guts."

Delaney's expression became serious. "And one day when my pain gets too unbearable and I can use a shoulder to cry on, I'll tell you about him."

Tara nodded, understanding completely. "Good enough."

"I can't marry Princess Raschida," Jamal said, meeting his father's deep stare. He had arrived back at the palace after having been gone three weeks. It had taken all that time for him to make decisions he knew would change his life forever. But there was nothing he could do about that. Delaney was the woman he wanted, and she was the woman he would have...if she still wanted him.

King Yasir held his son's gaze. "Do you know what you're saying?" he asked, pushing himself up from the wing chair he had been sitting in.

Jamal stared into the face of the man who had produced him, a man loved, respected and admired by many—a man Jamal knew would do anything for his people and a man who, in addition to everything else, believed in honor.

"Yes, Father," he answered quietly. "I know what I'm saying and I also know what this means. I truly thought I could go through with it, but now I know that I can't. I'm in love with someone else, and there is no way I can marry another."

King Yasir looked deep into his son's face. He had known when Jamal arrived home three weeks ago that something had been troubling him. Subsequently, Fatimah had shared with him what that something was. But he had turned a deaf ear to the thought that his son was in love with a Western woman. But now, seeing was believing. Jamal looked tormented and his features were those of a man who was hurting and whose very soul had been stripped away. With all the arrogance and lordliness Jamal was known to have, King Yasir was shocked that a woman had brought his son to this.

"This woman you love is a Western woman, is she not?" he asked gruffly.

Jamal continued to meet his father's gaze. "Yes," he said calmly.

"And you're willing to walk away from a woman of your people and marry someone not like you, of your faith and nationality?"

Chin up, head lifted and body straight, Jamal answered stiffly, "Yes, because, although not like me, she is of me. She is a part of me just as I am a part of her, Father. Love has united us as one."

The king's eyes darkened. "Love? And what do you know of love?" he declared. "Are you sure it's not your libido talking? Lust can be just as strong an emotion as love," he persisted.

Jamal walked closer into the room to face his father. "Yes, I'm aware of that, and I do admit I was attracted to her from the moment I first saw her. I even thought it to be lust for a while, but it is not. At thirty-four I know the difference. I have had an ongoing affair with Najeen for a number of years, yet I've never thought about falling in love with her."

"You wouldn't have. You knew her position in your life. She was your mistress. If a man of your status were to fall in love it should be with his wife."

"But things don't always happen that way, Father, as you well know. Look at the number of other dignitaries who are besotted with their mistresses. And to answer your question as to what I know about love, I can honestly say that I know more now than I did some weeks ago," he concluded heavily. "I know love is what has me willing to stand before you now and plead for your understanding that I marry the woman who has my heart. Love is what has me in total misery, torment and depression. Love is also what has kept me functioning regardless of those things."

He took a deep breath and continued, "Love is what I see whenever you and Fatimah are together, and love is what has me willing to abdicate my right to succession if I have to."

Shock was reflected in his father's face. "You will give up the right to be my heir—the crown prince, the future king—for this woman?"

Jamal knew his words had caused his father pain, but they had to be said to make him understand just what Delaney meant to him. "Yes, Father, I would. Fatimah was right. Love is powerful enough to bring even the

strongest man to his knees. I love Delaney Westmoreland, and I want her for my princess."

"But does this woman want you? What if she refuses to
accept our ways? What if she refuses to change, and—"

"I don't want her to change," Jamal said vehemently.
"I love her just the way she is. I believe she would be
willing to meet me halfway on certain things, and in my
heart I also believe she will love our people as much as I
do. But Delaney is not a woman who will bend because
a man says she has to."

"This woman is disobedient?" the king asked, trou-
bled, astounded.

"No more so than Fatimah was when she first came
here. If I remember correctly there was some rumbling
among the people when you married an Egyptian princess instead of one of your own. But over the years they
have come to love and respect her."

King Yasir didn't say anything for a long moment,
because what Jamal had just said was true. Fatimah was
loved and admired by all. Finally he released a long, deep
sigh. "Sheikh Muhammad isn't going to be happy with
the news that you refused to marry his daughter. He may
declare that our sheikhdom lacks honor. Are you willing
to abide with that, Jamal?"

Jamal shook his head. That was the hardest thing he
had to contend with. "I will talk to the sheikh and if I
have to I will agree to scour the entire countryside and
find a replacement that pleases him. But I will not marry
his daughter."

The king nodded solemnly. He then picked up documents off his desk. "Finding a replacement might not be
necessary. Fatimah brought something to my attention
a few weeks ago, gossip that was circulating among the

servants. It seems that the servants in the Muhammads' household had been whispering, and even with the distance separating our sheikhdoms, the wind carried some of those whispers here. Rebakkah felt it was her duty to make her queen aware of what was being said."

"And what was being said?" Jamal asked, watching lines of anger form in his father's face.

"Word that Princess Raschida is with child, which is the reason Sheikh Muhammad is in such a hurry to marry her off."

Jamal was taken aback. "I would have married her, not knowing this, and the child would not have been my true heir?"

"Yes," the king answered in a disgruntled voice. "Evidently they were hoping no one would be the wiser since she is in her very early stages."

Jamal became furious. "I can't believe Sheikh Muhammad would do such a thing."

"He was trying to save both himself and his daughter from embarrassment, Jamal. But I agree that what he had planned was dishonorable." He gazed down at the papers he held in his hand. "This report tells everything. When Fatimah brought me word, I had my men look into it, discreetly. It seemed that the princess has been involved in a secret affair—right under her father's nose—with a man who is a high-ranking official in his army."

"Well, the man can have her!" Jamal was appalled at how close he had come to being taken in. And here Delaney could be—and for some reason he believed that she was—pregnant with his legitimate heir.

"I think you should know, Father," he said, drawing his father's attention, "there is a possibility that Delaney carries my child."

His father's eyes widened. "Do you know that for certain?"

Jamal shook his head. "No. I haven't had any contact with her since I left America. I can only cite my beliefs on male intuition or possibly a revelation from Allah. But I plan to go to her and find out. I also plan to ask her to marry me and return with me as my bride."

"And if she doesn't want to do that?"

"Then I will convince her otherwise. Whatever it takes."

King Yasir nodded, knowing just how persuasive Jamal Ari could be when it suited him. "I much prefer that you marry someone from our country, Jamal, however, you are right, I do understand love doesn't recognize color, national origin or religion."

"Do I have your blessings, Father?"

The king slowly nodded his head. "Yes, although I am certain you would still marry her without my blessings. However, before I can fully accept her as the woman who will one day stand by your side to rule our people, I must meet her and get to know her. That is the best I can do," he quietly conceded.

Jamal nodded. "And that is all I ask, Father. You are more than fair."

King Yasir hugged his son in a strong display of affection, which Jamal returned. After the king released him from his embrace, Jamal turned and walked out of his father's study.

"Delaney, are you sure you're feeling all right?" Tara asked for the third time that day. "I hate to be a nuisance but you don't look well."

Delaney nodded. She didn't feel well, either, but then she wouldn't be feeling well for a number of days to come. She had missed her period and an over-the-counter pregnancy test she had taken that morning confirmed she was carrying Jamal's child. She planned to keep her word and let him know, but decided to wait until after her first appointment with the doctor in a few weeks.

A baby.

The thought that she was carrying Jamal's baby made her extremely happy, and if it wasn't for the bouts of morning sickness she had started having a few days ago, she would be fine. At least as fine as a woman could be who was still pining over the man she loved. Each day she had checked the international news section of the paper for word of his engagement or marriage. So far she hadn't seen anything.

Lovingly she caressed her stomach. Jamal had planted a baby inside of her. His baby, a part of him that she would love as much as she loved him.

"Delaney?"

Delaney looked up and met Tara's concerned stare. She was not ready to share her news with anyone yet. "I'm fine, Tara. I've just been busy lately, preparing for my brothers' visit. I have to get ready, both mentally and physically, for them. They can be rather tiring and taxing to one's peace of mind."

Tara chuckled. "When do you expect them?"

"Sometime later today. They had to wait for Storm to get off work before driving up. And I really appreciate you letting a couple of them stay at your place. There is no way all five of them will fit in my tiny apartment."

"Hey, don't mention it, and I'm looking forward to meeting them."

And there was no doubt in Delaney's mind that her brothers would definitely want to meet Tara. She couldn't wait to see their reaction to her, as well as her reaction to them. Tara was a woman who didn't tolerate arrogance in any man, and the Westmoreland brothers were as arrogant as they came.

On a private plane bound for America, Jamal sat back in the seat, relaxed. Asalum, using his connection with certain international security firms, had been able to obtain a residence address for Delaney in Bowling Green, Kentucky. Jamal planned to go straight to her home from the airport as soon as the plane landed.

He smiled at the thought of seeing her again. Inside of him the yearning to hold her in his arms was so intense it pulled at his inner strength. He laid his head back against the seat. They had been in the air eight hours already, and according to the pilot they had another four hours to go before they arrived in Kentucky.

Asalum appeared with a pillow. "For you, Prince."

Jamal took the pillow and placed it behind his head. "Thank you, Asalum." He looked up into the older man's world-weary and rugged face. "I'm no longer feeling depression."

Asalum couldn't hide his smile. "And what are you feeling now, My Prince?"

Jamal grinned heartily. "Jubilation."

Chapter 13

Tara leaned against the closed bathroom door. Concern was etched on her face as she heard the sound of Delaney throwing up on the other side. "Delaney? Are you sure you're going to be okay? That's the second time you've thrown up today."

Delaney held her head over the toilet thinking it was actually the third time. And all this time she thought morning sickness was just for the morning. "Yes, Tara, I'll be fine, just give me a second."

At that moment she could hear the sound of the doorbell. *Oh, my gosh! My brothers are here!* "Tara, please get the door. More than likely it's my brothers, and no matter what, please don't tell them I'm in the bathroom sick."

Tara smiled. "Okay, I'll do my best to stall them, but only if you promise to see Dr. Goldman tomorrow. Sounds like you might be coming down with a virus."

She turned and crossed the room when the doorbell sounded a second time.

Opening the door, Tara's breath caught and held at the sight of the four men standing there. Then just as quickly she regained her composure. It took some doing. Delaney's brothers were definitely good-looking and oozing in raw sexuality. Dressed in jeans and T-shirts that advertised the Thorn-Byrd motorcycle, they all had massive shoulders, solid chests and firm thighs.

She cleared her throat. For the longest moment no one spoke. They just stood there staring at her in a way that made her glance down to make sure her T-shirt wasn't transparent or something. She decided it was time to say something. "You're Delaney's brothers?"

A crooked smiled tipped up the side of one of their mouths. He seemed to be a little older than the rest. "Yes, I'm Dare. And who are you?" he prompted curiously, not taking his eyes off her.

"I'm Tara Matthews, Delaney's friend, neighbor and fellow physician," she said, reaching her hand out to him. He took it and held it, a bit longer than she thought necessary, before shaking it. The others did the same when Dare introduced them. She took a step back. "Please come in. Delaney is in the bathroom."

Tara closed the door behind them thinking they appeared bigger than life. All of them were well over six feet tall. "I thought there were five of you," she said when they still gazed at her curiously.

The one whose name was Stone and whose smile was just as sexy as the one called Dare spoke up. "Our brother Thorn had a last-minute appointment and is flying in. He'll get here in the morning."

Tara nodded as she leaned back against the door while the four men continued to look at her. She started to ask them if anyone had ever told them it wasn't polite to stare when Delaney entered the room.

"I see you guys made it okay." Delaney shook her head when they didn't take their eyes off Tara to acknowledge her entrance into the room. They were behaving like any typical male animals that had an irresistible female within their scope.

"Yeah, we made it," Chase said smiling, but not at her, since his gaze was still on Tara.

Delaney bit her lip to keep from laughing. Most women fawned over Chase's killer smile, but Tara didn't appear the least flattered. In fact, it appeared she was beginning to get annoyed at her brothers' attention, if her frown was any indication. "Hey you guys, let up and give Tara a break. She's my friend."

Storm finally released his gaze from Tara and met Delaney's glare. "What are we doing?" he asked innocently.

"The four of you are checking her out like she's a piece of fried chicken just waiting to be eaten." She then glanced around the room. "Where's Thorn?"

"Not in our side," Chase said, finally breaking eye contact with Tara and turning to Delaney and smiling. His response was the usual one the brothers had given over the years whenever someone asked them about Thorn.

"So where is he?" Delaney asked again, hating it when they gave her their smart responses.

"He had a last-minute appointment, some very important customer he had to take care of, so he'll be flying in tomorrow morning," Dare said, finally turning to look at her and leaving his brothers to finish their appraisal of Tara.

"And how long are you guys staying?" Delaney asked. She didn't want to run the risk of being sick around them.

Dare smiled. "Trying to get rid of us already, Laney?"

Delaney frowned. If she'd had her choice they would never have come. She loved her brothers to death but they could get on her last nerve at times. She didn't want to think about how they were going to handle the news of her pregnancy. "No, I'm not trying to get rid of you, as if it would do me any good even if I were. I just wanted to know for sleeping-arrangement purposes. As you can see this place is rather small, and Tara has graciously offered to put two of you up at her place during your visit."

As she had known it would, that statement got her brothers' attention. All eyes returned to Tara, who merely shrugged and said, "It's the least I can do for a friend, but it seems that I need to put some ground rules in place."

Dare gave her a sexy smile. "Such as?"

"I expect you to be good."

Storm smiled and Tara and Delaney didn't miss the byplay gaze that passed between the brothers. "We're always *good,*" he said slowly.

Tara lifted a brow and crossed her arms over her chest. "What I mean is *good* as in good behavior. You're to behave like gentlemen and treat me just like a member of the family."

Chase chuckled. "That's going to be a real challenge since you aren't a member of the family."

Tara laughed. "But I get the distinct feeling that the four of you like challenges."

Storm shook his head, grinning. "Thorn is the one who likes challenges. We prefer things to be made easy for us."

Tara laughed again as she came to stand before them in the center of the room. "Sorry, I don't do easy. Nor do I do hard, just to set the record straight in case you might be curious. I'm not looking for a serious relationship nor am I looking for a nonserious one. In other words, I'm not into casual affairs. I'm single and although I'm a die-hard heterosexual, I'm not interested in a man at the present time. Do we understand each other, guys?"

Dare nodded and smiled. "Yeah, you're definitely a challenge, so we'll leave you for Thorn."

Before Tara could open her mouth and give him the retort Delaney knew was coming, the doorbell sounded. Giving Tara a quick glance, she grinned and said, "Hold that thought," then crossed the room to answer the door.

She opened the door and drew in a breath so sharp her heart missed a beat and a wave of dizziness swept over her. "Jamal!"

Jamal took a step inside and closed the door behind him. Without saying a word and without noticing the other people in the room he pulled Delaney into his arms and kissed her. Automatically Delaney molded her body to his and placed her arms around his neck and kissed him back.

The intimate scene shocked the other five people in the room; four in particular.

"What the hell is going on!" Dare's voice bellowed, almost shaking the windows and causing Jamal and Delaney to abruptly end their kiss.

"No!" Delaney shouted when she saw the murderous expressions of anger on the faces of her brothers when they began walking toward her and Jamal. She leaned back against Jamal, blocking him, and felt him stiffen behind her before he gently eased her to his side.

Her four brothers stopped then, looking Jamal up and down as if he was someone from another planet instead of someone dressed in his native Arab garb.

Likewise, Jamal sized them up. He immediately knew who they were. The gaze he gave each one of them was dispassionate, but his features were fierce, sharp, lethal. He was letting them know he would protect Delaney, even from them if he had to.

"I can explain," Delaney said quickly, trying to defuse her brothers' anger before the situation got too far out of hand.

"You can explain things after he's taken care of," Stone said furiously. "Who the hell is this guy? And what is he doing kissing you like that?" And then, noticing Jamal's arms firmly around Delaney's waist, he met the man's dark stare. "And take your damn hands off of her."

"Stone, stop it!" Delaney all but screamed. "The four of you are acting like barbarians, and you're an officer of the law, Dare, for heaven's sake. If you give me a chance I can explain things."

Delaney stopped talking when suddenly a wave of dizziness and queasiness swept over her and she leaned against Jamal. His sharp gaze left her brothers and concentrated on her, turning her quickly into his arms. "Are you all right?" he whispered in concern.

She muttered a barely audible response, saying softly, "Take me to the bathroom, Jamal. Now!"

Reacting with unerring speed, Jamal picked her up in his arms and followed Tara out of the room, leaving the Westmoreland brothers too shocked by the whole scene to speak.

As soon as Jamal placed Delaney on her feet in the bathroom and locked the door behind them, she sank weakly to her knees in front of the commode and threw up for the fourth time that day. When she had emptied her stomach completely for what she hoped would be the last time, she flushed the toilet and tried standing, only to find herself engulfed in powerful arms.

Jamal picked her up and walked over to the counter and sat her on it. He then took a washcloth and wet it and wiped it over her face. Moments later he placed her back on her feet and while he held her around the waist, giving her support, she stood in front of the sink and brushed her teeth and rinsed out her mouth.

After that, he picked her up and sat her back on the counter and stood in front of her. "The prince is already causing problems, I see," he said softly, as he tenderly wiped her face again with the damp cloth.

Delaney gazed up at him, still amazed that he was actually there with her. Breath slowly slipped through her teeth as she gazed at him. If it was possible, he was more handsome than before. The dark eyes that were looking at her were gentle yet intent, and his chin was no longer clean shaven but was covered with a neatly trimmed beard that made him look as sexy as sin.

She inhaled deeply. She had so many questions to ask, but what he had just said suddenly came back to her. "What did you say?" She needed him to repeat it to make sure she had heard him correctly.

He looked amused but answered her, anyway. "I said the prince is already causing you problems." And this time he placed a gentle hand over her stomach.

She met his gaze. "How did you know I'm pregnant?"

His smile widened. "I had a feeling that you were. I've been dreaming about you every single night since we've been apart, and the dreams were so real that I would wake up in a sweat and sexually spent. And each time we made love in my dreams, I flooded your womb with my seed, which reminded me of the times I had actually done so at the cabin. I believe the dreams were Allah's way of letting me know of your condition."

Delaney nodded and looked down at his hand on her

stomach. "Is that the reason you're here, Jamal? For confirmation that I'm having your baby?"

He lifted her chin. "No. I'm here because I was missing you too much to stay away and couldn't think about marrying another woman. So I told my father I loved you and wanted you as the woman in my life."

Delaney's eyes widened. "But what about the princess from that sheikhdom who you were to marry?"

Jamal stiffened. "It seems the princess needed to marry quickly since she was secretly with child from someone else. It was her dishonorable intent to try and pass the child off as mine."

"And what about Najeen? Was she well?"

Jamal lifted a brow, knowing what Delaney was trying to ask him in a roundabout way. He decided to rest her concerns in that area. "I didn't see Najeen. The first night I returned I told my stepmother to make sure she returned to her homeland. She is no longer my mistress."

Delaney reached out and touched his cheek, remembering how he had once said he would never give his mistress up. "Do you regret sending her away?"

He met her gaze and smiled. "The only thing I regret is leaving you, Delaney. I was so miserable without you. The only thing I had to survive on were my dreams," he said, his voice soft and husky.

She smiled. "And I had mine, too. And when I discovered I was pregnant I was so happy."

"How long have you known?"

"I had an idea when I missed my period last week, and then when I started experiencing bouts of sickness throughout the day I thought I'd better check things out. I took a pregnancy test this morning which pretty much confirmed things. I've made an appointment to see the doctor in two weeks." She traced her fingertips softly around his features, especially his lower lip. "How do you feel about me being pregnant, Jamal?"

He grinned. "The thought that you carry my child inside of you makes me extremely happy, Delaney. I didn't intentionally get you pregnant, but I was more lax with you than I have been with any other woman, so I think subconsciously I wanted you, and only you, to have my heir."

Happiness flooded Delaney. "Oh, Jamal."

"And you are the woman that I want for my princess, Delaney. Please say that you will marry me and come live with me in Tahran. There are a number of Americans in your military and private businesses living close by in Kuwait, and if you get homesick we can always come back here to visit at any time. We can even live in your country half the year and in mine the other half if that pleases you. I see my father being king for a long time, which means I won't I have to live permanently in Tahran for a number of years to come."

He leaned over and kissed her lips. "Say yes you will marry me so I can be yours exclusively."

Delaney knew there was no way she could refuse him. Her love for him was too great, and she knew she wanted to be with him for the rest of her life.

"Yes, Jamal. I will marry you."

Filled with joy of the richest kind, Jamal leaned in closer, and captured her lips with his, feeling a jolt of desire shoot down his spine at the contact. His hand moved to the back of her neck, and he ran his fingers through the thick, glossy curls before holding her neck firmly in place to let his mouth make love to hers, wanting to consume her.

He wanted to be reunited with her taste, and he focused his attention on the bone-melting kiss he was giving her. His tongue explored inside her mouth as he licked everywhere before taking her tongue in his and sucking on it in a way he knew would make her scream.

But he didn't want her to scream, or else he would have to hurt her brothers when they broke the door down to see what was going on. So he gentled the kiss, not quite ready to end it. He wanted to taste her some more. He needed to make sure this was the real thing and not a dream.

Jamal continued to let his tongue mate with hers, reacquainting himself with the pleasures he could find only with her.

"What the hell is going on in that bathroom?" Dare asked in a loud, sharp voice as he paced the floor. "I can't believe we're out here and not knocking the damn door down to find out for ourselves what's happening."

Tara glared at him, the same way she had been glaring at the other three since that man had taken Delaney into the bathroom and locked them in. "You're acting just like Delaney wants you to act, calm and civilized, and not like barbarians. She has a right to privacy."

"Privacy hell, she was sick," Stone implored. "And why is he in there taking care of her instead of one of us? We're her brothers."

Yes, but he is the father of her child, Tara wanted to tell them, now that she had figured things out. She sighed deeply. The least she could do for her friend was to keep her brothers under control. "While the four of you are waiting, can I get you to help me with something? I need help with this piece of exercise equipment I'm trying to put together."

They looked at her as if she was crazy. "Nice try, Tara, but we're not moving until we know for sure that Laney is okay," Dare said, smiling at her.

Tara shrugged. "All right. I'm sure it won't be too much longer before they—"

Everyone stopped talking when the bathroom door opened. Everyone who had been sitting down shot up out of their seats. "Laney, are you all right?" Storm asked with a worried look. He glared at Jamal when he saw the man's hand was back around his sister's waist. "I thought you were told about your hands," Storm said, filled with hostility.

Delaney actually chuckled. "Storm, that is no way to talk to your future brother-in-law." Before anyone could recover from what she had just implied, she said, "I never got around to making introductions. Everyone, this is Sheikh Jamal Ari Yasir of Tahran. We met last month at the cabin and fell in love. Before we could make plans for our future he had to leave unexpectedly to return home. Now he's back and has asked me to marry him and I've accepted."

Mixed emotions went around the room. Tara screamed out her excitement, and the Westmoreland brothers stood frozen in shock.

"Marry?" Chase finally found his voice enough to ask, almost in a shout. "Are you nuts! He's not even from this country. Where in the hell will the two of you live?"

Delaney smiled sweetly. "Although we plan to spend a lot of time in America, we will mainly live in Tahran, which is located not far from Kuwait. All of you are welcome to visit anytime."

"You can't marry him!" Stone stormed.

"She can and she will." The room suddenly became quiet when Jamal spoke to everyone for the first time. The tone of his voice reflected authority, certainty and invincibility. "I appreciate all the care and concern you have shown to Delaney for the past twenty-five years and I find your actions nothing but admirable. But as my intended bride, the future princess of Tahran, she now becomes my responsibility. At the exact moment that she consented to marry me, she fell under the protection of my country. My father, King Yasir, has given his blessings and—"

"Your father is King Yasir?" Dare asked in total amazement.

Jamal lifted a brow. "Yes, do you know him?"

Dare shook his head, still semishocked at everything. "No, of course I don't know him, at least not personally, anyway. But a few years ago while I was in the Marines stationed near Saudi Arabia, I got the honor of meeting him when I was in charge of security for a political function he attended. That meeting left me very impressed with the way he carried himself and the care, concern and love he bestowed on his people."

Jamal nodded. "Thank you. I will pass on to him your compliment." He then studied Dare a moment before asking, "So you have resided in the Middle East?"

"Yes. I was stationed there for two years and I must admit the entire area is beautiful and the Persian Gulf is simply magnificent."

Jamal smiled, pleased at the compliment given to his homeland. "You must visit there again. Delaney and I will have private quarters in the palace and as she has indicated, all of you are welcome to visit."

"Damn," Storm said. "An actual palace?" He grinned. "That day when you told us those tire tracks belonged to a prince, we thought you were fooling." He laughed. "Nobody on the squad is going to believe my sister actually nabbed herself a real-live prince. John Carter walked around with his chest poked out when his sister flew to

Tampa and married a professional football player. Just wait until I tell them that Laney is going to be a princess."

Chase frowned at his brother, then turned his full attention to Delaney. Uncertainty and concern were etched in his features. "Are you sure this is what *you* want, Laney? I have to know that this is what *you* want, no matter what *he* wants," Chase said, looking at Jamal. "Is marrying this guy going to make you happy? What about your career in medicine?"

Delaney glanced around the room at her brothers. The deep love and concern she saw in their eyes touched her. Although she had whined and complained about their overprotectiveness through the years, deep down in her heart she knew they had behaved in such a manner because they loved her and had cared for her well-being.

"Yes," she whispered softly, yet loud enough for all to hear. She glanced up at Jamal before turning back to everyone. "I love Jamal, and becoming his wife will be my greatest joy." *As well as being the mother of his child,* she decided not to add. Her brothers had to adjust to the idea of her getting married. She didn't want to complicate matters with the news that she was pregnant, as well. "And as for my career in medicine, I'm sure it will come in handy in some capacity in Tahran."

"I'm so happy for you, girlfriend," Tara said, smiling brightly and going over to Delaney and giving her a fierce hug.

Storm laughed. "Well, I guess that's that."

Dare shook his head solemnly. "No, that's not that. Thorn doesn't know yet. And, personally, I don't want to be around when he gets in tomorrow and finds out."

Chapter 14

That evening Delaney left her brothers in Tara's care while she and Jamal went out to dinner. Although he had invited everyone to join them, she was grateful they had declined, so she could spend an evening alone with him.

However, they had indicated to Jamal, engaged or not engaged, they expected her to sleep in her bed and *alone* tonight. They had made it clear that until there was a wedding they intended to protect their sister's honor. It had been hard for Delaney to keep a straight face at that one. And eye contact across the room with Tara indicated that her friend had figured out her condition and would keep her secret and would do everything she could to help keep the Westmoreland brothers busy until she returned—which Delaney intended to be rather late.

She nervously bit her bottom lip when she thought about Thorn. He could be rather irrational at times and was more overprotective than the others. She would have to talk to him privately just as soon as he arrived in the morning.

"Are you ready to leave, Delaney?"

Jamal's question broke into her thoughts, and she lovingly gazed across the table at him. Earlier that day, after getting nearly everything straightened out with her brothers, he had left to change clothes and had returned two hours later to take her to dinner.

Tonight he was dressed like a Westerner and looked absolutely stunning in a dark gray suit, white shirt and navy-blue tie. She smiled, thinking he was certainly a very handsome man. His dark eyes held her seductively in their gaze and had been doing so all night. "Yes," she said softly. "But it's early yet. You aren't planning to take me straight home, are you?"

He stood and walked around the table to pull her chair back for her. "No. I thought you might be interested in seeing the town house I've purchased to live in while I'm here."

Delaney raised a brow. "You've purchased a town house? But you just arrived today."

He nodded. "Asalum is most efficient when it comes to handling business matters. He took care of all the details and made the necessary arrangements from the jet while we were flying over here."

Delaney shook her head. She doubted she would ever get used to such extravagance. "Must be nice."

He chuckled. "It is nice, as you will soon see." He took her hand in his as they walked out of the restaurant. "And there is another reason I want to take you to my town house."

Delaney had a good idea just what that other reason was but wanted him to tell her, anyway. "And what reason is that, *Your Highness?*"

Jamal leaned down and whispered in her ear. Even with the darkness of her skin, she actually blushed, then smiled up at him. "Um, I think something like that can be arranged, Prince."

Back at Delaney's apartment the Westmoreland brothers and Tara were involved in a game of bid whist. Tara excused herself from the next game and went into the kitchen to check on the cookies that she had baking in the oven.

They had ordered pizza earlier, and with Stone's complaint of not having anything sweet to eat, she had taken a tube of frozen cookie dough from Delaney's freezer and had baked a batch of chocolate chip cookies.

Tara smiled, inwardly admitting that now that she was getting to know them better, she liked Delaney's brothers. Although she thought their overprotectiveness was a bit much, it was definitely a show of the love they had for their sister.

She was taking the tray of baked cookies from the oven when Delaney's doorbell sounded. She hoped it wasn't one of the neighbors complaining that too much noise was coming from the apartment. Storm had a tendency to groan rather loudly whenever he lost, which was frequently. She smiled, thinking he was definitely a sore loser.

Back in the living room, Chase got up from the table to open the door. He snatched it open, wondering who would have the nerve to interrupt their card game.

He winced when he saw the person standing there. *Damn, all hell is about to break loose,* he thought, frowning. "Thorn! What are you doing here? We weren't expecting you until the morning."

Thorn Westmoreland shook his head and looked questioningly beyond Chase to the table where his other brothers sat playing cards. At least they *had* been playing cards. Stone had stopped and sat unmoving, like a "stone" right in the middle of dealing out the cards, and both Dare and Storm looked at him as if he was a Martian.

He frowned, wondering what the hell had everyone spooked. Entering the apartment, he walked into the center of the room. "What the hell is everyone staring at? Do I have mud on my face or something?"

Dare, regaining his wits, returned to shuffling the cards. "We're just surprised to see you tonight."

"Yeah," Stone chimed in. "We weren't expecting you until the morning."

Thorn threw his overnight bag on the sofa. "Yes, that's what I heard, twice already. First from Chase and now you guys. So you're all surprised I showed up tonight. What's going on?"

Chase closed the door and walked across the room to reclaim his seat at the table. "What makes you think something is going on?"

"Because the four of you are looking guilty as sin about something."

Dare chuckled. "That's just your imagination, bro." As usual everyone was trying to decipher Thorn's mood and until they did, they weren't making any waves. And they definitely weren't going to say anything about Delaney's engagement. "I take it you got that customer satisfied."

"Yeah, and got a free flight here on his private jet." Thorn glanced around the apartment. "Where's Laney?"

Storm threw out a card. "She went out."

Thorn frowned and checked his watch. It was almost midnight. "She went out where?"

"She didn't say," Stone said, studying his hand.

Thorn's frown deepened. "When is she coming back?"

"We don't know exactly," Chase said, watching his brother, knowing that at any minute they would start seeing smoke come from his ears. It didn't take much to set Thorn off when he was in one of his foul moods. Usually this kind of mood meant he was overdue for getting laid, but it was Thorn's own fault for being so damn nitpicky when it came to women.

Thorn slowly walked over to the table. "And just what do you know, *exactly?*"

Dare chuckled. "Trust us, Thorn, you don't want to hear it. At least not from us. Just have a seat and sit tight until Laney comes home. Or better yet, pull up a chair and join the game. My truck needs a new engine so I need to win some money off you."

Thorn slammed his fist hard on the table, sending cards flying. When he was sure he had everyone's attention he proceeded to say, "I don't know what's going on but I have a feeling it involves Laney. And you guys know how much I hate secrets. So which one of you is going to spill your guts?"

Dare stood. So did Stone, Chase and Storm. Usually it took a combined effort to make Thorn see reason and cut the moody crap. "We aren't telling you anything so sit down and shut up," Dare said through clenched teeth.

At that moment Tara came charging out of the kitchen. She had heard enough. Thorn Westmoreland had some nerve, barging in here at this late hour and causing problems. Just who did he think he was?

Thorn caught her in his peripheral vision the moment she flew out of the kitchen. She stopped walking when he turned and stared at her.

Tara swallowed, wondering why the air had suddenly left the room, making it almost impossible for her to breathe. Her gaze held the muscular, well-built man who stood so tall she had to stretch her neck to look up at him. Dressed in a pair of jeans—and wearing them in a way she'd never known a man to wear them before—he utterly oozed sexuality and sensuality, all rolled into one. He was without a doubt the most gorgeous hunk of man she had ever laid eyes on.

He was staring at her, and his stare was burning intimate spots all over her body, branding her. She blinked, not appreciating the fact that any man, especially this man with his foul mood, could have this effect on her. She didn't have time for such foolishness. Sexual chemistry was too much bother, too time-consuming. Her job and her career came first. Physical attraction, love, sex, babies…and all the other stuff that went with it…was definitely a low priority on her totem pole.

She inhaled deeply, thinking that the best thing to do would be to say her peace and get the hell of out there, on the fastest legs she had. Once she was safe in her apartment, she would try and figure out what was happening to her and why.

With a deep frown she resumed walking until she stood directly in front of Thorn. She placed her hands on her hips and glared at him. "How dare you come here causing problems? Just who do you think you are? The Mighty Thorn? All we need is to give the neighbors a reason to complain. So why don't you do like you've been told and sit down and shut up!"

Taking a deep breath, she then turned her attention to the other four brothers. "I put the cookies on a plate in the kitchen. Help yourselves." After glaring one last time at Thorn, she quickly crossed the room and walked out the door, slamming it behind her.

Thorn forced his gaze away from the whirlwind who had told him off. He slowly turned and looked at his brothers, who for some reason were staring steadfastly at him…with smirks on their faces. "Who the hell is that?"

Dare chuckled as he crossed his arms over his chest. "*That,* Thorn, is *your* challenge."

The same sexual tension that had totally consumed Jamal and Delaney from the moment he had picked her up for dinner increased by umpteen degrees once he had her settled in the warm intimacy of the Mercedes sports car he was driving. Every look they exchanged was hot.

Delaney knew that each time he stopped for a traffic light he took his eyes off the road and turned his gaze to her. Then there was the hand that he simply refused to keep on the steering wheel—the one he preferred to use to caress her legs and thighs instead. And the short dress she had on made her body all that more accessible. It barely covered her thighs.

Her brothers' jaws had almost dropped when she'd walked out of the bedroom wearing it, but thank goodness they hadn't said anything. The look Jamal had given her had been totally different from her brothers' and she had hurriedly ushered him out of her apartment before anyone noticed what seeing her in it had done to a certain part of his body.

"Open."

Jamal's husky command filled the quiet stillness of the car's interior. Delaney couldn't help but notice his hand had worked its way up her inner thigh. Knowing just what he meant for her to do, she slowly opened her legs while studying his profile intently. His eyes were still on the road but she detected his breathing had shifted from steady to unsteady.

Her eyes fluttered shut when she felt the tenderness of his fingers touch the center of her panty hose between her legs. Boy, she had missed his fingers. Her dream was nothing compared to the real thing. The man was filling her with a purely sexual rush.

Her breathing became heavy when the tip of his finger worked insistently until it poked a hole in her panty hose, to get to just what it wanted. Tonight her panty hose was serving as both panty and hosiery, so once he found his way past the silky nylon all that was left was bare flesh, and his finger found her hot and wet.

"I can't wait to get you home, Delaney," he whispered softly, as his busy fingers continued to touch her, tease her and explore her fully. Her body shivered at the intimate contact, and she felt herself getting hotter and wetter. He felt it, too.

Her mind and thoughts concentrated on what he was doing to her when his fingers began a rhythm that made her arch her back against the seat. She opened her legs wider, which made her dress rise higher on her thighs, thankful that the people riding in the car next to them could not see what was happening inside theirs. Her mouth opened, then closed, along with her eyes, unable to get any words out, just moans…excruciating moans.

"When we get to my place, Delaney, I won't be using my finger. Do you know what I'll be using?"

She slowly opened her eyes and looked at him and saw they had come to a traffic light. He leaned over and whispered hotly in her ear, and the only thing she could think to say was, "My goodness."

Her breath suddenly became shaky and her body began shivering when he began rubbing inside of her harder, increasing the rhythm. The palms of her hands pressed hard against the car's dashboard when everything inside of her exploded, reeling her into a climax. Her body continued to shudder violently.

"Jamal!"

Her head went back and she moaned one final time as pleasure consumed her, slowly leaving her sated, breathless and feeling weak. Once she could get her breathing under control she found the strength to glance over at Jamal. She was too overwhelmed to even feel embarrassed at the fact that he had made her climax in a car while he had been driving with one hand.

"Are you okay, My Princess?"

"Yes," she replied weakly. At some point they had arrived at their destination when she noted he had brought the car to a complete stop in front of a massive group of elegant buildings. As she met his gaze, his lips tilted into an intense sexual smile. He slowly leaned over and placed a light, yet passionate kiss on her lips. "No matter how real my dreams seemed at night, whenever I woke up I could never conjure this."

"What?" she asked softly, barely able to speak.

"The scent of you having a climax. It's a scent that is purely you, private, individual and totally sensual. I wish like hell I could bottle it." He leaned over and kissed her again. "Stay put. I'm coming around the car to get you," he said when he finally released her lips.

She watched as he got out of the car and came around to her side and opened the door. Undoing her seat belt he scooped her up into his arms and, as if she was a precious bundle, he held her gently to him and carried her inside his home.

Jamal took Delaney straight to the bedroom and placed her on his bed. "I'll be right back. I need to lock the door."

Delaney nodded, closing her eyes, feeling blissful yet totally drained. Moments later she slowly reopened her eyes and glanced around. The bedroom was huge, probably big enough to fit two of her bedrooms in. She had noticed the same thing about the other parts of the house when he carried her through to the bedroom. She sat up, and when she noted her dress had risen up past her hips, tried tugging it back down.

"There's no need to pull it down since I'll be taking it completely off you in a second."

Heat filled Delaney's cheeks when she met Jamal's gaze across the room. He was standing in the doorway removing his jacket, which was followed by his tie. Her gaze stayed glued to him, while she watched him undress. She continued to look at him, thinking he was such a fine specimen of a man and that he was hers.

"Jamal?"

"Yes?"

"How soon do you want to get married?"

He smiled as he pulled the belt out of his pants. "Is tonight soon enough?"

She returned his smile. "Yes, but I'd like you to meet my parents first."

He nodded. "Only if you won't let them talk you out of marrying me."

Delaney didn't blink, not once when she said, "No one could do that. I love you too much."

Jamal had taken off all his clothes except for his pants. She remembered the first time she had seen him without a shirt and how her body had responded to the sheer masculinity of him. And her body was responding to him now.

He walked over to where she sat in the middle of the bed. "And I love you, too. I hadn't realized just how much until I had to leave you. Being without you was hard on me. You totally consumed my every thought. There were days when I wondered if I would make it without you."

Delaney looked at Jamal. She knew an admission like that had probably been hard for him to make. "I will make you a good princess, Jamal."

He sat on the edge of the bed and reached out and pulled her into his lap. "Mmm, will you, Delaney?" he asked, smiling. "Are you willing to salaam me each and every time you see me?"

She lifted a dark brow at him. "No."

"Well, then, are you willing to always walk two paces behind me?"

"No. Nor will I hide my face behind some veil," she decided to add.

Jamal couldn't keep the amusement out of his gaze. "You won't?"

"No, I won't."

"Mmm. Then will you be obedient and do *everything* that I say?"

She didn't give that question much thought, either, before quickly shaking her head. "No."

He chuckled as he looked at her. "All right, Delaney, then what *will* you do to make me a good princess?"

She shifted positions in his lap so that she was sitting facing him, straddling his hips. She placed her arms around his neck and met his gaze intently. "On the day I become your desert princess, you will become my desert sheikh. And I will love you more than any woman has ever loved you before. I will honor you and be by your side to do what I can for your people who will become *my* people. I will obey you to a point, but I will retain my right to disagree and make my own decisions about things, always respecting your customs when I do so."

Her gaze became intense when she added, "And I will give you sons and daughters who will honor you and respect you and who will grow up strong in our love and the love of their people. They will share two cultures and two countries, and I believe they will always love and appreciate both."

She inhaled deeply when she added, "And last but not least, I will be your wife *and* your mistress. I will take care of *all* your needs and make sure that you stay extremely happy and never regret making me your princess."

For the longest moment Jamal didn't say anything. Then he kissed her. First softly, then tenderly and finally hotly as his mouth slanted over hers, tasting her fully. He broke off the kiss and slowly stood with her in his arms, her legs still wrapped around his waist.

Placing her on her feet, he pulled her dress over her head, leaving her bare, except for her panty hose and chemise, which he quickly removed. When she stood before him completely naked, he removed his pants and boxer shorts, desperately wanting to be inside of her, with his body stroking hers.

Gathering her into his arms, he placed her back in the middle of the bed and joined her there. "How soon can I meet your parents?" he asked her, pulling her into his arms.

"I'm scheduled to be off this weekend so we can go to Atlanta then. I plan on calling them in the morning and telling them our good news."

"Even the news about the baby?"

"No, I want them to get used to the idea of me getting married and moving away before I tell them they will also become grandparents."

Jamal nodded. "I told my father there was a possibility you were carrying my heir."

Delaney raised a brow. "And what did he say?"

Jamal smiled. "Not much at the time but I could tell

that the thought pleased him. He will enjoy being a grandfather as much as I'm going to enjoy being a father."

He then placed his body on top of hers, supporting
himself on his elbows. "But right now I want to hurry up
and become a husband. Your husband, Delaney."

He leaned down and kissed her, wanting to take their
kiss to another level like he had that night in the cabin.
After tasting her mouth for a few moments, he pulled
back. "Stick out your tongue to me."

She blinked, then did what he instructed, knowing
what was coming.

"Don't worry," he said huskily. "I won't let you pass
out on me again."

When he captured her tongue in his mouth, she gasped
for breath at the intensity of his tongue mating so sensually with hers. She moaned with pleasure when he
touched those certain places in her mouth that gave her
the greatest sexual gratification. The pleasure was so intense, she began to writhe beneath him and he placed his
hands on her hips to keep her still.

He finally let go of her mouth and went to her breasts
and paid the same homage there, nibbling, sucking and
laving her with his tongue.

"Oh, Jamal."

The sound of his name from her lips was like an aphrodisiac, making him want to taste her everywhere. So
he did. The scent of her spiraled him on to new heights,
new territory and for both of them, a new adventure.

"I can't get enough of you, Delaney," he whispered
against her hot flesh before easing his body upward to
enter her. The tightness of her surrounded him, stroking
the already-blazing fire within him.

"My Princess," he whispered softly as his body began

pumping into her as he held her gaze, forcing her to look at him with each and every stroke into her body.

She wrapped her arms around him and targeted his mouth. "My Sheikh," she whispered before thrusting her tongue inside, intent on taking ownership and making love to his mouth the same way and with the same rhythm that he was using on her body.

Delaney released his mouth to look at him. Each time he thrust into her, his neck strained and the tension etched in his face showed the degree of strength he had. Each time he pulled out her thighs trembled as flesh met flesh. Then suddenly he pushed deeper, nearly touching her womb, holding himself still inside of her, refusing to pull out.

He lowered his face to hers and came close to her lips and kissed her in such a way that made both their bodies simultaneously explode in ecstasy, as he filled her completely with the essence of his release making the three weeks they had spent apart well worth the reunion.

He strained forward, lifting her hips to receive him as their bodies exploded yet again, making them groan out when yet another climax struck.

And moments later, completely sated and totally pleasured, they collapsed in each other's arms.

A few hours later Jamal leaned forward over Delaney, breathed in deeply to inhale her scent, before kissing her awake.

He leaned back and watched as she opened her eyes slowly and smiled at him. "You can wake me up anytime, Your Highness."

Jamal chuckled and ran a finger along her cheek. "It's time for me to take you home. I did promise your brothers that I would have you back at a reasonable hour."

Delaney reached down and caressed him, and her smile widened. "And of course you will want to make love again before you take me home, right?"

"That had been my plan." He grinned, placing his body over hers. "I will love you forever, Delaney."

"And I will love you forever, too. Who would have thought that what was supposed to be a secluded vacation would bring us together? And to think we didn't even like each other at first."

Jamal leaned down and kissed her lips tenderly. "You know what they say, don't you?" he asked, tracing a path with his tongue down her throat.

"No," Delaney whispered, just barely. "What do they say?"

He smiled down at her. "Things are not always as they seem to be." He kissed her again, then said, "But the love that we share is everything we will ever want it to be and more."

Epilogue

Six Weeks Later

"Another marriage ceremony?" Delaney asked Jamal as they captured some stolen moments in the palace courtyard. All around them, the atmosphere of the desert was hot and humid, yet the fragrance of jasmine and gardenias permeated the air, creating a seductive, erotic overtone. "This makes the fourth."

Their first wedding had been a beautiful garden wedding on her parents' lawn three weeks ago in Atlanta. The second ceremony had taken place last week when they arrived at the palace, with the king, queen and other dignitaries and their wives present. The third had been in the town square, arranged by the people of Tahran as a way to welcome the prince and his chosen princess.

A smile tilted the corners of Jamal's lips. "But think

of how much fun we have with the wedding nights that follow each one."

Delaney reached out and placed her arms around her husband's neck, leaned up and kissed his lips. "Mmm, that is true."

She then turned in his arms so her back pressed against his front while his hand splayed across her stomach where their child rested. She didn't think she could ever be as happy as she was now.

Upon her arrival at the palace last week, she was immediately summoned to hold a private meeting alone with Jamal's father, King Yasir. At first the king had presented himself as the fierce, dictatorial ruler, and had relentlessly interrogated her about her views and beliefs.

She had answered all of his questions, honestly, truthfully and respectfully. In the end he had told her that her sharp tongue and tough stance reminded him of Queen Fatimah, and that he knew she would have no problem being understood, respected and loved. He had hugged her and accepted her into the family.

Jamal's sisters, Johari and Arielle, had also made her feel welcome and said they did not consider her as their brother's wife but as their sister. But it was Queen Fatimah who had endeared herself to Delaney's heart forever by meeting with her and sharing some of the things she had come up against as a foreigner in her husband's land and how she had set about changing things, in a subtle way.

She had even suggested that Delaney give some thought to using her medical knowledge to educate the women of Tahran about childhood diseases and what they could do to prevent them. As well, she suggested Delaney could practice medicine in the hospital the two of them would convince the king he needed to build.

"Ready to go back inside, Princess?" Jamal asked, leaning down and placing a kiss on her forehead.

"Is there another dinner party we must attend tonight?" she asked, twisting around to face him, suddenly captured by his dark gaze. Her body began feeling achy, hot and hungry. She wondered if there would ever be a time she would not be sexually attracted to her husband.

"No. In fact I thought that we could spend a quiet evening in our apartment," he said reaching down and tracing a finger along her cheek.

"That sounds wonderful, Jamal," she said smiling. They hadn't found a lot of time to spend alone except at night when they finally went to bed. She enjoyed the nights he made love to her, reminding her over and over again just how much she meant to him and just how much she was loved. She would fall asleep in his arms at night and be kissed awake by him each morning.

"Everyone should fall in love, shouldn't they, Jamal?" she asked smiling.

He grinned. "Yes, but I bet you would never convince your brothers of that."

She nodded, knowing that was true. "But they were happy for us, even Thorn, once he got used to the idea that I was indeed getting married."

Jamal shook his head, grinning. Thorn Westmoreland had taken great pleasure in being a thorn in his side. "Yes, but look how long it took him to come around. I almost had to call him out a few times. I've never known anyone so stubborn, man or woman, and that even includes you. I don't envy the woman who tries to capture his heart. I doubt such a thing is possible."

I wouldn't be too sure of that, Delaney thought. She couldn't help but recall how Thorn kept looking at Tara at her wedding when he thought no one was watching. Tara had been her maid of honor, and all her brothers had been openly friendly to her, treating her like a member of the family. But for some reason Thorn had kept his distance. She found that rather interesting.

"What are you thinking, sweetheart?"

"Oh, just that it wouldn't surprise me if there is a woman out there who can capture Thorn's heart. In fact, I have an idea who she is."

Jamal raised a curious brow. "Really? Who?"

Her mouth curved into that smile that he adored. "Um, you'll find out soon enough."

Later that night, after making love to his wife, Jamal slipped from the bed, leaving Delaney sleeping. Putting on his robe, he left the confines of their apartment and walked down the stairs to the courtyard to find a private place to give thanks.

A half hour later on his way back to his apartment he met Asalum lurking in the shadows, always on guard to protect his prince.

Asalum studied Jamal's features. "Is all well with you, Your Highness?"

Jamal nodded. "Yes, my trusted friend and companion, all is well."

Silence filled the space between them, then a few moments later Jamal asked, "Do you know what I'm feeling now, Asalum?"

A smile curved the older man's lips. He had a good idea but asked anyway. "And what are you feeling, My Prince?"

Suddenly Jamal began to laugh. It was laughter of happiness, joy and contentment, and the rapturous sound punctured the silence of the night and echoed deep into the courtyard.

Moments later Jamal spoke when his laughter subsided. "Exultation."

* * * * *

If you loved DELANEY'S DESERT SHEIKH,
pick up all the Westmoreland books by
USA TODAY *and* New York Times
bestselling author Brenda Jackson!

A LITTLE DARE
THORN'S CHALLENGE
STONE COLD SURRENDER
RIDING THE STORM
JARED'S COUNTERFEIT FIANCÉE
THE CHASE IS ON
THE DURANGO AFFAIR
IAN'S ULTIMATE GAMBLE
SEDUCTION, WESTMORELAND STYLE
SPENCER'S FORBIDDEN PASSION
TAMING CLINT WESTMORELAND
COLE'S RED-HOT PURSUIT
QUADE'S BABIES
TALL, DARK...WESTMORELAND!

A LITTLE DARE

Ponder the path of thy feet,
and let all thy ways be established.
—*Proverbs* 4:26

To my husband, the love of my life
and my best friend, Gerald Jackson, Sr.

And to everyone who asked for Dare's and
Thorn's stories, this book is for you!

Chapter 1

Two weeks later—early September

Sheriff Dare Westmoreland leaned forward in the chair behind his desk. From the defiant look on the face of the boy standing in front of him he could tell it would be one of those days. "Look, kid, I'm only going to ask you one more time. What is your name?"

The boy crossed his arms over his chest and had the nerve to glare at him and say, "And I've told you that I don't like cops and have no intention of giving you my name or anything else. And if you don't like it, arrest me."

Dare stood to his full height of six-feet-four, feeling every bit of his thirty-six years as he came from behind his desk to stare at the boy. He estimated the kid, who he'd caught throwing rocks at passing cars on the highway, to be around twelve or thirteen. It had been a long time since any kid living in his jurisdiction had outright sassed him. None of them would have dared, so it stood to reason that the kid was probably new in town.

"You will get your wish. Since you won't cooperate and tell me who you are, I'm officially holding you in police custody until someone comes to claim you. And while you're waiting you may as well make yourself useful. You'll start by mopping out the bathroom on the first floor, so follow me."

Dare shook his head, thinking he didn't envy this kid's parents one bit.

Shelly had barely brought her car to a complete stop in front of the sheriff's office before she was out of it. It had taken her a good two hours in Atlanta's heavy traffic to make it home after receiving word that AJ had not shown up at school, only to discover he wasn't at home. When it had started getting late she had gotten worried and called the police. After giving the dispatcher a description of AJ, the woman assured her that he was safe in their custody and that the reason she had not been contacted was because AJ had refused to give anyone his name. Without asking for any further details Shelly had jumped into her car and headed for the police station.

She let out a deep sigh. If AJ hadn't given anyone his name that meant the sheriff was not aware she was AJ's mother and for the moment that was a comforting thought. As she pushed open the door, she knew all her excuses for not yet meeting with Dare and telling him the truth had run out, and fate had decided to force her hand.

She was about to come face-to-face with Sheriff Dare Westmoreland.

"Sheriff, the parent of John Doe has arrived."

Dare looked up from the papers he was reading and

met his secretary's gaze. "Only one parent showed up, Holly?"

"Yes, just the mother. She's not wearing a wedding ring so I can only assume there isn't a father. At least not one that's around."

Dare nodded. "What's the kid doing now?" he asked, pushing the papers he'd been reading aside.

"He's out back watching Deputy McKade clean up his police motorcycle"

Dare nodded. "Send the woman in, Holly. I need to have a long talk with her. Her son needs a lot more discipline than he's evidently getting at home."

Dare moved away from his desk to stand at the window where he could observe the boy as he watched McKade polish his motorcycle. He inhaled deeply. There was something about the boy that he found oddly familiar. Maybe he reminded him of himself and his four brothers when they'd been younger. Although they had been quite a handful for their parents, headstrong and in some ways stubborn, they had known just how far to take it and just how much they could get away with. And they'd been smart enough to know when to keep their mouths closed. This kid had a lot to learn.

"Sheriff Westmoreland, this is Ms. Rochelle Brockman."

Dare swung his head around and his gaze collided with the woman he'd once loved to distraction. Suddenly his breath caught, his mouth went dry and every muscle in his body froze as memories rushed through his spiraling mind.

He could vividly recall the first time they'd met, their first kiss and the first time they had made love. The last time stood out in his mind now. He dragged his gaze from her face to do a total sweep of her body before returning to her face again. A shiver of desire tore through him, and he was glad that his position, standing behind his desk, blocked a view of his body from the waist down. Otherwise both women would have seen the arousal pressing against the zipper of his pants.

His gaze moved to her dark brown hair, and he noted that it was shorter and cut in one of those trendy styles that accented the creamy chocolate coloring of her face as well as the warm brandy shade of her eyes.

The casual outfit she wore, a printed skirt and a matching blouse, made her look stylish, comfortable and ultrafeminine. Then there were the legs he still considered the most gorgeous pair he'd ever seen. Legs he knew could wrap around his waist while their bodies meshed in pleasure.

A deep sigh escaped his closed lips as he concluded that at thirty-three she was even more beautiful than he remembered and still epitomized everything feminine. They'd first met when she was sixteen and a sophomore in high school. He'd been nineteen, a few weeks shy of twenty and a sophomore in college, and had come home for a visit to find her working on a school project with his brother Stone. He had walked into the house at the exact moment she'd been leaning over Stone, explaining some scientific formula and wearing the sexiest pair of shorts he had ever seen on a female. He had thought she had a pair of legs that were simply a complete turn-on. When she had glanced up, noticed him staring and smiled, he'd been a goner. Never before had he been so aware of a woman. An immediate attraction had flared between them, holding him hostage to desires he'd never felt before.

After making sure Stone didn't have designs on her himself, he had made his move. And it was a move he'd never regretted making. They began seriously dating a few months later and had continued to do so for six long years, until he had made the mistake of ending things between them. Now it seemed the day of reckoning had arrived.

"Shelly."

"Dare."

It was as if the years had not passed between them, Dare suddenly thought. That same electrical charge the two of them always generated ignited full force, sending a high voltage searing through the room.

He cleared his throat. "Holly, you can leave me and Ms. Brockman alone now," he thought it best to say.

His secretary looked at Shelly then back at him. "Sure, Sheriff," she murmured, and walked out of the office, pulling the door shut behind her.

Once the door closed, Dare turned his full attention back to Shelly. His gaze went immediately to her lips; lips he used to enjoy tasting time and time again; lips that were hot, sweet and ultraresponsive. One night he had thrust her into an orgasm just from gnawing on her lips and caressing them with the tip of his tongue.

He swallowed to get his bearings when he felt his body begin responding to just being in the same room with her. He then admitted what he'd known for years. Shelly Brockman would always be the beginning and the end of his most blatant desires and a part of him could not believe she was back in College Park after being gone for so long.

Shelly felt the intensity of Dare's gaze and struggled to keep her emotions in check, but he was so disturbingly gorgeous that she found it hard to do so. Wearing his blue uniform, he still had that look that left a woman's mind whirling and her body overheated.

He had changed a lot from the young man she had fallen in love with years ago. He was taller, bigger and more muscular. The few lines he had developed in the corners of his eyes, and the firmness of his jaw made his face more angular, his coffee-colored features stark and disturbingly handsome and still a pleasure to look at.

She noted there were certain things about him that had remained the same. The shape of his mouth was still a total turn-on, and he still had those sexy dimples he used to flash at her so often. Then there were those dark eyes—deep, penetrating—that at one time had had the ability to read her mind by just looking at her. How else had he known when she'd wanted him to make love to her without her having to utter a single word?

Suddenly Shelly felt nervous, panicky when she remembered the reason she had moved back to town. But there was no way she could tell Dare that he was AJ's father—at least not today. She needed time to pull herself together. Seeing him again had derailed her senses, making it impossible for her to think straight. The only thing she wanted was to get AJ and leave.

"I came for my son, Dare," she finally found her voice to say, and even to her own ears it sounded wispy.

Dare let out a deep breath. It seemed she wanted to get right down to business and not dwell on the past. He had no intention of letting her do that, mainly because of what they had once meant to each other. "It's been a long time, Shelly. How have you been?" he asked raspily, failing to keep his own voice casual. He found the scent of her perfume just as sexy and enticing as the rest of her.

"I've been fine, Dare. How about you?"

"Same here."

She nodded. "Now may I see my son?"

Her insistence on keeping things nonpersonal was

beginning to annoy the hell out of him. His eyes narrowed and his gaze zeroed in on her mouth; bad timing on his part. She nervously swiped her bottom lip with her tongue, causing his body to react immediately. He remembered that tongue and some of the things he had taught her to do with it. He dragged air into his lungs when he felt his muscles tense. "Aren't you going to ask why he's here?" he asked, his voice sounding tight, just as tight as his entire body felt.

She shrugged. "I assumed that since the school called and said he didn't show up today, one of your officers had picked him up for playing hooky."

"No, that's not it," he said, thinking that was a reasonable assumption to make. "I'm the one who picked him up, but he was doing something a bit more serious than playing hooky."

Shelly's eyes widened in alarm. "What?"

"I caught him throwing rocks at passing motorists on Old National Highway. Do you know what could have happened had a driver swerved to avoid getting hit?"

Shelly swallowed as she nodded. "Yes." The first thought that came to her mind was that AJ was in need of serious punishment, but she'd tried punishing him in the past and it hadn't seemed to work.

"I'm sorry about this, Dare," she apologized, not knowing what else to say. "We moved to town a few weeks ago and it hasn't been easy for him. He needs time to adjust."

Dare snorted. "From the way he acted in my office earlier today, I think what he needs is an attitude adjustment as well as a lesson in respect and manners. Whose kid is he anyway?"

Shelly straightened her spine. The mother in her took offense at his words. She admitted she had spoiled AJ somewhat, but still, considering the fact that she was a single parent doing the best she could, she didn't need Dare of all people being so critical. "He's my child."

Dare stared at her wondering if she really expected him to believe that. There was no way the kid could be hers, since in his estimation of the kid's age, she was a student in college and his steady girl about the same time the boy was born. "I mean who does he really belong to since I know you didn't have a baby twelve or thirteen years ago, Shelly."

Her gaze turned glacial. "He *is* mine, Dare. I gave birth to him *ten* years ago. He just looks older than he really is because of his height." Shelly watched Dare's gaze sharpen and darken, then his brows pulled together in a deep, furious frown.

"What the hell do you mean *you* gave birth to him?" he asked, a shocked look on his face and a tone of voice that bordered on anger and total disbelief.

She met his glare with one of her own. "I meant just what I said. Now may I see him?" She made a move to leave Dare's office but he caught her arm.

"Are you saying that he was born after you left here?"

"Yes."

Dare released her. His features had suddenly turned to stone, and the gaze that focused on hers was filled with hurt and pain. "It didn't take you long to find someone in California to take my place after we broke up, did it?"

His words were like a sharp, painful slap to Shelly's face. He thought that she had given birth to someone else's child! How could he think that when she had loved him so much? She was suddenly filled with extreme anger. "Why does it matter to you what I did after I left here, Dare, when you decided after six long years that you wanted a career with the FBI more than you wanted me?"

Dare closed his eyes, remembering that night and what he had said to her, words he had later come to regret. He slowly reopened his eyes and looked at her. She appeared just as stricken now as she had then. He doubted he would ever forget the deep look of hurt on her face that night he had told her that he wanted to break up with her to pursue a career with the FBI.

"Shelly, I…"

"No, Dare. I think we've said enough, too much in fact. Just let me get my son and go home."

Dare inhaled deeply. It was too late for whatever he wanted to say to her. Whatever had once been between them was over and done with. Turning, he slowly walked back over to his desk. "There's some paperwork that needs to be completed before you can take him with you. Since he refused to provide us with any information, we couldn't do it earlier."

He read the question that suddenly flashed in her gaze and said, "And no, this will not be a part of any permanent record, although I think it won't be such a bad idea for him to come back every day this week after school for an hour to do additional chores, especially since he mentioned he's not into any after-school activity. The light tasks I'll be assigning to him will work off some of that rebellious energy he has."

He met her gaze. "However, if this happens again, Shelly, he'll be faced with having to perform hours of community service as well as getting slapped with a juvenile delinquent record. Is that understood?"

She nodded, feeling much appreciative. Had he wanted to, Dare could have handled things a lot more severely. What AJ had done was a serious offense. "Yes, I understand, and I want to thank you."

She sighed deeply. It seemed fate would not be forcing her hand today after all. She had a little more time before having to tell Dare the truth.

Dare sat down at his desk with a form in front of him and a pen in his hand. "Now then, what's his name?"

Shelly swallowed deeply. "AJ Brockman."

"I need his real name."

She couldn't open her mouth to get the words out. It seemed fate wouldn't be as gracious as she'd thought after all.

Dare was looking down at the papers in front of him, however, the pause went on so long he glanced up and looked at her. He had known Shelly long enough to know when she was nervous about something. His eyes narrowed as he wondered what her problem was.

"What's his real name, Shelly?" he repeated.

He watched as she looked away briefly. Returning her gaze, she stared straight into his eyes and without blinking said, "Alisdare Julian Brockman."

Chapter 2

Air suddenly washed from Dare's lungs as if someone had cut off the oxygen supply in the room and he couldn't breathe. Everything started spinning around him and he held on to his desk with a tight grip. However, that didn't work since his hands were shaking worse than a volcano about to explode. In fact his entire body shook with the force of the one question that immediately torpedoed through his brain. Why would she name her son after him? Unless...

He met her gaze and saw the look of guilt in her eyes and knew. Yet he had to have it confirmed. He stood on non-steady legs and crossed the room to stand in front of Shelly. He grasped her elbow and brought her closer to him, so close he could see the dark irises of her eyes.

"When is his birth date?" he growled, quickly finding his equilibrium.

Shelly swallowed so deeply she knew for certain Dare

could see her throat tighten, but she refused to let his re-action unsettle her any more than it had. She lifted her chin. "November twenty-fifth."

He flinched, startled. "Two months?" he asked in a pained whisper yet with intense force. "You were two months pregnant when we broke up?"

She snatched her arm from his hold. "Yes."

Anger darkened the depths of his eyes then flared through his entire body at the thought of what she had kept from him. "I have a son?"

Though clearly upset, he had asked the question so quietly that Shelly could only look at him. For a long moment she didn't answer, but then she knew that in spite of everything between them, there was never a time she had not been proud that AJ was Dare's son. That was the reason she had returned to College Park, because she felt it was time he was included in AJ's life. "Yes, you have a son."

"But—but I didn't know about him!"

His words were filled with trembling fury and she knew she had to make him understand. "I found out I was pregnant the day before my graduation party and had planned to tell you that night. But before I got the chance you told me about the phone call you'd received that day, offering you a job with the Bureau and how much you wanted to take it. I loved you too much to stand in your way, Dare. I knew that telling you I was pregnant would have changed everything, and I couldn't do that to you."

Dare's face etched into tight lines as he stared at her. "And you made that decision on your own?"

She nodded. "Yes."

"How dare you! Who in the hell gave you the right to do that, Shelly?"

She felt her own anger rise. "It's not who but what. My love for you gave me the right, Dare," she said and without giving him a chance to say another word, she angrily walked out of his office.

Fury consumed Dare at a degree he had never known before and all he could do was stand there, rooted in place, shell-shocked at what he had just discovered.

He had a son.

He crossed the room and slammed his fist hard on the desk. Ten years! For ten years she had kept it from him. Ten solid years.

Ignoring the pain he felt in his hand, he breathed in deeply when it hit him that he was the father of John Doe. No, she'd called him AJ but she had named him Alisdare Julian. He took a deep, calming breath. For some reason she had at least done that. His son did have his name—at least part of it anyway. Had he known, his son would also be wearing the name Westmoreland, which was rightfully his.

Dare slowly walked over to the window and looked out, suddenly seeing the kid through different eyes—a father's eyes, and his heart and soul yearned for a place in his son's life; a place he rightly deserved. And from the way the kid had behaved earlier it was a place Dare felt he needed to be. It seemed that Alisdare Julian Brockman was a typical Westmoreland male—headstrong and stubborn as hell. As Dare studied him through the windowpane, he could see Westmoreland written all over him and was surprised he hadn't seen it earlier.

He turned when the buzzer sounded on his desk. He took the few steps to answer it. "Yes, Holly?"

"Ms. Brockman is ready to leave, sir. Have you completed the paperwork?"

Dare frowned as he glanced down at the half-completed form on his desk. "No, I haven't."

"What do you want me to tell her, Sheriff?"

Dare sighed. If Shelly for one minute thought she could just walk out of here and take their son, she had another thought coming. There was definitely unfinished business between them. "Tell Ms. Brockman there're a few things I need to take care of. After which, I'll speak with her again in my office. In the meantime, she's not to see her son."

There was a slight pause before Holly replied. "Yes, sir."

After hanging up the phone Dare picked up the form that contained all the standard questions, however, he didn't know any answers about his son. He wondered if he could ever forgive Shelly for doing that to him. No matter what she said, she had no right to have kept him in the dark about his son for ten years.

After the elder Brockmans had retired and moved away, there had been no way to stay in touch except for Ms. Kate, the owner of Kate's Diner who'd been close friends with Shelly's mother. But no matter how many times he had asked Kate about the Brockmans, specifically Shelly, she had kept a stiff lip and a closed mouth.

A number of the older residents in town who had kept an eye on his and Shelly's budding romance during those six years had been pretty damn disappointed with the way he had ended things between them. Even his family, who'd thought the world of Shelly, had decided he'd had a few screws loose for breaking up with her.

He sighed deeply. As sheriff, he of all people should have known she had returned to College Park; he made it his business to keep up with all the happenings around town. She must have come back during the time he had been busy apprehending those two fugitives who'd been hiding out in the area.

With the form in one hand he picked up the phone with the other. His cousin, Jared Westmoreland, was the attorney in the family and Dare felt the need for legal advice.

"The sheriff needs to take care of a few things and would like to see you again in his office when he's finished."

Shelly nodded but none too happily. "Is there anyway I can see my son?"

The older woman shook her head. "I'm sorry but you can't see or talk to him until the sheriff completes the paperwork."

When the woman walked off Shelly shook her head. What had taken place in Dare's office had certainly not been the way she'd envisioned telling him about AJ. She walked over to a chair and sat down, wondering how long would it be before she could get AJ and leave. Dare was calling the shots and there wasn't anything she could do about it but wait. She knew him well enough to know that anger was driving him to strike back at her for what she'd done, what she'd kept from him. A part of her wondered if he would ever forgive her for doing what she'd done, although at the time she'd thought it was for the best.

"Ms. Brockman?"

Shelly shifted her gaze to look into the face of a uniformed man who appeared to be in his late twenties. "Yes?"

"I'm Deputy Rick McKade, and the sheriff wants to see you now."

Shelly stood. She wasn't ready for another encounter

with Dare, but evidently he was ready for another one with her.

"All right."

This time when she entered Dare's office he was sitting behind his desk with his head lowered while writing something. She hoped it was the paperwork she needed to get AJ and go home, but a part of her knew the moment Dare lifted his head and looked up at her, that he would not make things easy on her. He was still angry and very much upset.

"Shelly?"

She blinked when she realized Dare had been talking. She also realized Deputy McKade had left and closed the door behind him. "I'm sorry, what did you say?"

He gazed at her for a long moment. "I said you could have a seat."

She shook her head. "I don't want to sit down, Dare. All I want is to get AJ and take him home."

"Not until we talk."

She took a deep breath and felt a tightness in her throat. She also felt tired and emotionally drained. "Can we make arrangements to talk some other time, Dare?"

Shelly regretted making the request as soon as the words had left her mouth. They had pushed him, not over the edge but just about. He stood and covered the distance separating them. The degree of anger on his face actually had her taking a step back. She didn't ever recall seeing him so furious.

"Talk some other time? You have some nerve even to suggest something like that. I just found out that I have a son, a ten-year-old son, and you think you can just waltz back into town with my child and expect me to turn my head and look away and not claim what's mine?"

Shelly released the breath she'd been holding, hearing the sound of hurt and pain in Dare's voice. "No, I never thought any of those things, Dare," she said softly. "In fact, I thought just the opposite, which is why I moved back. I knew once I told you about AJ that you would claim him as yours. And I also knew you would help me save him."

Eyes narrowed and jaw tight, Dare stared at her. She watched as immediate concern—a father's concern—appeared in his gaze. "Save him from what?"

"Himself."

She paused, then answered the question she saw flaring in his eyes. "You've met him, and I'm sure you saw how angry he is. I can only imagine what sort of an impression he made on you today, but deep down he's really a good kid, Dare. I began putting in extra hours at the hospital, which resulted in him spending more time with sitters and finding ways to get into trouble, especially at school when he got mixed up with the wrong crowd. That's the reason I moved back here, to give him a fresh start—with your help."

Anger, blatant and intense, flashed in Dare's eyes. "Are you saying that the only reason you decided to tell me about him and seek my help was because he'd started giving you trouble? What about those years when he was a *good* kid? Did you not think I had a right to know about his existence then?"

Shelly held his gaze. "I thought I was doing the right thing by not telling you about him, Dare."

A muscle worked in his jaw. "Well, you were wrong. You didn't do the right thing. Nothing would have been more important to me than being a father to my son, Shelly."

A twinge of regret, a fleeting moment of sadness for

the ten years of fatherhood she had taken away from him touched Shelly. She had to make him understand why she had made the decision she had that night. "That night you stood before me and said that becoming an FBI agent was all you had ever wanted, Dare, all you had ever dreamed about, and that the reason we couldn't be together any longer was because of the nature of the work. You felt it was best that as an agent, you shouldn't have a wife or family." She blinked back tears when she added, "You even said you were glad I hadn't gotten pregnant any of those times we had made love."

She wiped at her eyes. "How do you think I felt hearing you say that, two months pregnant and knowing that our baby and I stood in the way of you having what you desired most?"

When AJ's laughter floated in from the outside, Shelly slowly walked over to the window and looked into the yard below. The boy was watching a uniformed officer give a police dog a bath. This was the first time she had heard AJ laugh in months, and the sheer look of enjoyment on his face at that moment was priceless. She turned back around to face Dare, knowing she had to let him know how she felt.

"When I found out I was pregnant there was no question in my mind that I wouldn't tell you, Dare. In fact, I had been anxiously waiting all that night for the perfect time to do so. And then as soon as we were alone, you dropped the bomb on me."

She inhaled deeply before continuing. "For six long years I assumed that I had a definite place in your heart. I had actually thought that I was the most important thing to you, but in less than five minutes you proved I was wrong. Five minutes was all it took for you to wash six years down the drain when you told me you wanted your freedom."

She stared down at the hardwood floor for a moment before meeting his gaze again. "Although you didn't love me anymore, I still wanted our child. I knew that telling you about my pregnancy would cause you to forfeit your dream and do what you felt was the honorable thing— spend the rest of your life in a marriage you didn't want."

She quickly averted her face so he wouldn't see her tears. She didn't want him to know how much he had hurt her ten years ago. She didn't want him to see that the scars hadn't healed; she doubted they ever would.

"Shelly?"

The tone that called her name was soft, gentle and tender. So tender that she glanced up at him, finding it difficult to meet his dark, piercing gaze, though she met it anyway. She fought the tremble in her voice when she said, "What?"

"That night, I never said I didn't love you," he said, his voice low, a near-whisper. "How could you have possibly thought that?"

She shook her head sadly and turned more fully toward him, not believing he had asked the question. "How could I not think it, Dare?"

Her response made him raise a thick eyebrow. Yes, how could she not think it? He had broken off with her that night, never thinking she would assume that he had never loved her or that she hadn't meant everything to him. Now he could see how she could have felt that way.

He inhaled deeply and rubbed a hand over his face, wondering how he could explain things to her when he really didn't understand himself. He knew he had to try anyway. "It seems I handled things very poorly that night," he said.

Shelly chuckled softly and shrugged her shoulders. "It depends on what you mean by poorly. I think that you accomplished what you set out to do, Dare. You got rid of a girlfriend who stood between you and your career plans."

"That wasn't it, Shelly."

"Then tell me what was *it*," she said, trying to hold on to the anger she was beginning to feel all over again.

For a few moments he didn't say anything, then he spoke. "I loved you, Shelly, and the magnitude of what I felt for you began to frighten me because I knew what you and everyone else expected of me. But a part of me knew that although I loved you, I wasn't ready to take the big step and settle down with the responsibility of a wife. I also knew there was no way I could ask you to wait for me any longer. We had already dated six years and everyone—my family, your family and this whole damn town—expected us to get married. It was time. We had both finished college and I had served a sufficient amount of time in the marines, and you were about to embark on a career in nursing. There was no way I could ask you to wait around and twiddle your thumbs while I worked as an agent. It wouldn't have been fair. You deserved more. You deserved better. So I thought the best thing to do was to give you your freedom."

Shelly dipped her chin, no longer able to look into his eyes. Moments later she lifted her gaze to meet his. "So, I'm not the only one who made a decision about us that night."

Dare inhaled deeply, realizing she was right. Just as she'd done, he had made a decision about them. A few moments later he said, "I wish I had handled things differently, Shelly. Although I loved you, I wasn't ready to become the husband I knew you wanted."

"Yet you want me to believe you would have been

ready to become a father?" she asked softly, trying to make him see reason. "All I knew after that night was that the man I loved no longer wanted me, and that his dream wasn't a future with me but one in law enforcement. And I loved him enough to step aside to let him fulfill that dream. That's the reason I left without telling you about the baby, Dare. That's the only reason."

He nodded. "Had I known you were pregnant, my dreams would not have mattered at that point."

"Yes, I knew that better than anyone."

Dare finally understood the point she'd been trying to make and sighed at how things had turned out for them. Ten years ago he'd thought that becoming an FBI agent was the ultimate. It had taken seven years of moving from place to place, getting burnt-out from undercover operations, waking each morning cloaked in danger and not knowing if his next assignment would be his last, to finally make him realize the career that had once been his dream had turned into a living nightmare. Resigning from the Bureau, he had returned home to open up a security firm about the same time Sheriff Dean Whitlow, who'd been in office since Dare was in his early teens, had decided to retire. It was Sheriff Whitlow who had talked him into running for the position he was about to vacate, saying that with Dare's experience, he was the best man for the job. Now, after three years at it, Dare had forged a special bond with the town he'd always loved and the people he'd known all of his life. And compared to what he had done as an FBI agent, being sheriff was a gravy train.

He glanced out of the window and didn't say anything for the longest time as he watched AJ. Then he spoke. "I take it that he doesn't know anything about me."

Shelly shook her head. "No. Years ago I told him that

his father was a guy I had loved and thought I would marry, but that things didn't work out and we broke up. I told him I moved away before I had a chance to tell him I was pregnant."

Dare stared at her. "That's it?"

"Yes, that's it. He was fairly young at the time, but occasionally as he got older, he would ask if I knew how to reach you if I ever wanted to, and I told him yes and that if he ever wanted me to contact you I would. All he had to do was ask, but he never has."

Dare nodded. "I want him to know I'm his father, Shelly."

"I want him to know you're his father, too, Dare, but we need to approach this lightly with him," she whispered softly. "He's going through enough changes right now, and I don't want to get him any more upset than he already is. I have an idea as to how and when we can tell him, and I hope after hearing me out that you'll agree."

Dare went back to his desk. "All right, so what do you suggest?"

Shelly nodded and took a seat across from his desk. She held her breath, suddenly feeling uncomfortable telling him what she thought was the best way to handle AJ. She knew her son's emotional state better than anyone. Right now he was mad at the world in general and her in particular, because she had taken him out of an environment he'd grown comfortable with, although that environment, as far as she was concerned, had not been a healthy one for a ten-year-old. His failing grades and the trouble he'd gotten into had proven that.

"What do you suggest, Shelly?" Dare asked again, sitting down and breaking into her thoughts.

Shelly cleared her throat. "I know how anxious you are to have AJ meet you, but I think it would be best, considering everything, if he were to get to know you as a friend before knowing you as his father."

Dare frowned, not liking the way her suggestion sounded. "But I am his father, Shelly, not his friend."

"Yes, and that's the point. More than anything, AJ needs a friend right now, Dare, someone he can trust and connect with. He has a hard time making friends, which is why he began hanging out with the wrong type of kids at the school he attended in California. They readily accepted him for all the wrong reasons. I've talked to a few of his teachers since moving here and he's having the same problems. He's just not outgoing."

Dare nodded. Of the five Westmoreland brothers, he was the least outgoing, if you didn't count Thorn who was known to be a pain in the butt at times. Growing up, Dare had felt that his brothers were all the playmates he had needed, and because of that, he never worried about making friends or being accepted. His brothers were his friends—his best friends—and as far as he'd been concerned they were enough. It was only after he got older and his brothers began seeking other interests that he began getting out more, playing sports, meeting people and making new friends.

So if AJ wasn't as outgoing as most ten-year-old kids, he had definitely inherited that characteristic from him. "So how do you think I should handle it?"

"I suggest that we don't tell him the truth about you just yet, and that you take the initiative to form a bond with him, share his life and get to know him."

Dare raised a dark brow. "And just how am I supposed to do that? Our first meeting didn't exactly get off to a great start, Shelly. Technically, I arrested him, for heaven's sake. My own son! A kid who didn't bat an eye when he informed me he hated cops—which is what I definitely am. Then there's this little attitude problem of his that I feel needs adjusting. So come on, let's be real here. How am I supposed to develop a relationship with *my kid* when he dislikes everything I stand for?"

Shelly shook her head. "He doesn't really hate cops, Dare, he just thinks he does because of what happened as we were driving from California to here."

Dare lifted a brow. "What happened?"

"I got pulled over in some small Texas town and the officer was extremely rude. Needless to say he didn't make a good impression on AJ."

She sighed deeply. "But you can change that, Dare. That's why I think the two of you getting together and developing a relationship as friends first would be the ideal thing. Ms. Kate told me that you work with the youth in the community and about the Little League baseball team that you coach. I want to do whatever it takes to get AJ involved in something like that."

"And he can become involved as my son."

"I think we should go the friendship route first, Dare."

Dare shook his head. "Shelly, you haven't thought this through. I understand what you're saying because I know how it was for me as a kid growing up. At least I had my brothers who were my constant companions. But I think you've forgotten one very important thing here."

Shelly raised her brow. "What?"

"Most of the people in College Park know you, and most of them have long memories. Once they hear that you have a ten-year-old son, they'll start counting months, and once they see him they'll definitely know the truth. They will see just how much of a Westmoreland he is. He favors my brothers and me. The reason I didn't see it before was because I wasn't looking for it. But you better believe the good people of this town will be. Once you're seen with AJ they'll be looking for anything to link me to him, and it will be easy for them to put two and two together. And don't let them find out that he was named after me. That will be the icing on the cake."

Dare gave her time to think about what he'd said before continuing. "What's going to happen if AJ learns that I'm his father from someone other than us? He'll resent us for keeping the truth from him."

Shelly sighed deeply, knowing Dare was right. It would be hard to keep the truth hidden in a close-knit town like College Park.

"But there is another solution that will accomplish the same purpose, Shelly," he said softly.

She met his gaze. "What?"

Dare didn't say anything at first, then he said. "I'm asking that you hear me out before jumping to conclusions and totally ditching the idea."

She stared at him before nodding her head. "All right."

Dare continued. "You said you told AJ that you and his father had planned to marry but that we broke up and you moved away before telling him you were pregnant, right?"

Shelly nodded. "Yes."

"And he knows this is the town you grew up in, right?"

"Yes, although I doubt he's made the connection."

"What if you take him into your confidence and let him know that his father lives here in College Park, then go a step further and tell him who I am, but convince him that you haven't told me yet and get his opinion on what you should do?"

Since Dare and AJ had already butted heads, Shelly had a pretty good idea of what he would want her to do—keep the news about him from Dare. He would be dead set against developing any sort of personal relationship with Dare, and she told Dare so.

"Yes, but what if he's placed in a position where he has to accept me, or has to come in constant contact with me?" Dare asked.

"How?"

"If you and I were to rekindle our relationship, at least pretend to do so."

Shelly frowned, clearly not following Dare. "And just how will that help the situation? Word will still get out that you're his father."

"Yes, but he'll already know the truth and he'll think I'm the one in the dark. He'll either want me to find out the truth or he'll hope that I don't. In the meantime I'll do my damnedest to win him over."

"And what if you can't?"

"I will. AJ needs to feel that he belongs, Shelly, and he does belong. Not only does he belong to you and to me, but he also belongs to my brothers, my parents and the rest of the Westmorelands. Once we start seeing each other again, he'll be exposed to my family, and I believe when that happens and I start developing a bond with him, he'll eventually want to acknowledge me as his father."

Dare shifted in his chair. "Besides," he added smiling. "If he really doesn't want us to get together, he'll be so busy thinking of ways to keep us apart that he won't have time to get into trouble."

Shelly lifted a brow, knowing Dare did have a point. However, she wasn't crazy about his plan, especially not the part she would play. The last thing she needed was to pretend they were falling in love all over again. Already, being around him was beginning to feel too comfortably familiar.

She sighed deeply. In order for Dare's plan to work, they would have to start spending time together. She couldn't help wondering how her emotions would be able to handle that. And she didn't even want to consider what his nearness might do to her hormones, since it had been a long time since she had spent any time with a man. A very long time.

She cleared her throat when she noticed Dare watching her intently and wondered if he knew what his gaze was doing to her. Biting her lower lip and shifting in her seat, she asked, "How do you think he's going to feel when he finds out that we aren't really serious about each other, and it was just a game we played to bring him around?"

"I think he'll accept the fact that although we aren't married, we're friends who like and respect each other. Most boys from broken relationships I come in contact with have parents who dislike each other. I think it's important that a child sees that although they aren't married, his parents are still friends who make his well-being their top priority."

Shelly shook her head. "I don't know, Dare. A lot can go wrong with what you're proposing."

"True, but on the other hand, a lot can go right. This way we're letting AJ call the shots, or at least we're letting him think that he is. This will give him what he'll feel is a certain degree of leverage, power and control over the situation. From working closely with kids, I've discovered that if you try forcing them to do something they will rebel. But if you sit tight and be patient, they'll eventually come around on their own. That's what I'm hoping will happen in this case. Chances are he'll resent me at first, but that's the chance I have to take. Winning him over will be my mission, Shelly, one I plan to accomplish. And trust me, it will be the most important mission of my life."

He studied her features, and when she didn't say anything for the longest time he said, "I have a lot more to lose than you, but I'm willing to risk it. I don't want to spend too much longer with my son not knowing who I am. At least this way he'll know that I'm his father, and it will be up to me to do everything possible to make sure that he wants to accept me in his life."

He inhaled deeply. "So will you at least think about what I've proposed?"

Shelly met his gaze. "Yes, Dare, I'll need time," she said quietly.

"Overnight. That's all the time I can give you, Shelly."

"But, I need more time."

Dare stood. "I can't give you any more time than that. I've lost ten years already and can't afford to lose any more. And just so you'll know, I've made plans to meet with Jared for lunch tomorrow. I'll ask him to act as my attorney so that I'll know my rights as AJ's father."

Shelly shook her head sadly. "There's no need for you to do that, Dare. I don't intend to keep you and AJ apart. As I said, you're the reason I returned."

Dare nodded. "Will you meet me for breakfast at Kate's Diner in the morning so we can decide what we're going to do?"

Shelly felt she needed more time but knew there was no way Dare would give it to her. "All right. I'll meet you in the morning."

Chapter 3

Dare reached across his desk and hit the buzzer.

"Yes, Sheriff?"

"McKade, please bring in John Doe."

Shelly frowned when she glanced over at Dare. "John Doe?"

Dare shrugged. "That's the usual name for any unidentified person we get in here, and since he refused to give us his name, we had no choice."

She nodded. "Oh."

Before Dare could say anything else, McKade walked in with AJ. The boy frowned when he saw his mother. "I wondered if you were ever going to come, Mom."

Shelly smiled wryly. "Of course I was going to come. Had you given them your name they would have called me sooner. You have a lot of explaining to do as to why you weren't in school today. It's a good thing Sheriff

Westmoreland stopped you before you could cause harm to anyone."

AJ turned and glared at Dare. "Yeah, but I still don't like cops."

Dare crossed his arms on his chest. "And I don't like boys with bad attitudes. To be frank, it doesn't matter whether or not you like cops, but you'd sure better learn to respect them and what they stand for." This might be his son, Dare thought, but he intended to teach him a lesson in respect, starting now.

AJ turned to his mother. "I'm ready to go."

Shelly nodded. "All right."

"Not yet," Dare said, not liking the tone AJ had used with Shelly, or how easily she had given in to him. "What you did today was a serious matter, and as part of your punishment, I expect you to come back every day this week after school to do certain chores I'll have lined up for you."

"And if I don't show up?"

"AJ!"

Dare held up his hand, cutting off anything Shelly was about to say. This was between him and his son. "And if you don't show up, I'll know where to find you and when I do it will only make things a lot worse for you. Trust me."

Dare's gaze shifted to Shelly. This was not the way he wanted to start things off with his son, but he'd been left with little choice. AJ had to respect him as the sheriff as well as accept him as his father. From the look on Shelly's face he knew she understood that as well.

"Sheriff Westmoreland is right," she said firmly, giving Dare her support. "And you *will* show up after school to do whatever he has for you to do. Is that understood?"

"Yeah, yeah, I understand," the boy all but snapped. "Can we go now?"

Dare nodded and handed her the completed form. "I'll walk the two of you out to the car since I was about to leave anyway."

Once Shelly and AJ were in the car and had buckled up their seat belts, Dare glanced into the car and said to the boy, "I'll see you tomorrow when you get out of school."

Ignoring AJ's glare, he then turned and the look he gave Shelly said that he expected to see her tomorrow as well, at Kate's Diner in the morning. "Good night and drive safely."

He then walked away.

An hour later, Dare walked into a room where four men sat at a table engaged in a card game. The four looked up and his brother Stone spoke. "You're late."

"I had important business to take care of," Dare said grabbing a bottle of beer and leaning against the refrigerator in Stone's kitchen. "I'll wait this round out and just watch."

His brothers nodded as they continued with the game. Moments later, Chase Westmoreland let out a curse. Evidently he was losing as usual, Dare thought, smiling. He then thought about how the four men at the table were more than just brothers to him; they were also his very best friends, although Thorn, the one known for his moodiness, could test that friendship and brotherly love to the limit at times. At thirty-five, Thorn was only eleven months younger than him, and built and raced motorcycles for a living. Last year he'd been the only African-American on the circuit.

His brother Stone, known for his wild imagination,

had recently celebrated his thirty-third birthday and wrote action-thriller novels under the pen name, Rock Mason. Then there were the fraternal thirty-two-year-old twins, Chase and Storm. Chase was the oldest by seven minutes and owned a soul-food restaurant in downtown Atlanta, and Storm was the fireman in the family. According to their mother, she had gone into delivery unexpectedly while riding in the car with their dad. When a bad storm had come up, he chased time and outran the storm to get her to the hospital. Thus she had named her last two sons Chase and Storm.

"You're quiet, Dare."

Dare looked up from studying his beer bottle and brought his thoughts back to the present. He met Stone's curious stare. "Is that a crime?"

Stone grinned. "No, but if it was a crime I'm sure you'd arrest yourself since you're such a dedicated lawman."

Chase chuckled. "Leave Dare alone. Nothing's wrong with him other than he's keeping Thorn company with this celibacy thing," he said jokingly.

"Shut up, Chase, before I hurt you," Thorn Westmoreland said, without cracking a smile.

Everyone knew Thorn refrained from having sex while preparing for a race, which accounted for his prickly mood most of the time. But since Thorn had been in the same mood for over ten months now they couldn't help but wonder what his problem was. Dare had a clue but decided not to say. He sighed and crossed the room and sat down at the table. "Guess who's back in town."

Storm looked up from studying his hand and grinned. "Okay, I'll play your silly guessing game. Who's back in town, Dare?"

"Shelly."

Everyone at the table got quiet as they looked up at him. Then Stone spoke. *"Our* Shelly?"

Dare looked at his brother and frowned. "No, not *our* Shelly, *my* Shelly."

Stone glared at him. *"Your* Shelly? You could have fooled us, the way you dumped her."

Dare leaned back in his chair. He'd known it was coming. His brothers had actually stopped speaking to him for weeks after he'd broken off with Shelly. "I did not dump her. I merely made the decision that I wasn't ready for marriage and wanted a career with the Bureau instead."

"That sounds pretty much like you dumped her to me," Stone said angrily. "You knew she was the marrying kind. And you led her to believe, like you did the rest of us, that the two of you would eventually marry when she finished college. In my book you played her for a fool, and I've always felt bad about it because I'm the one who introduced the two of you," he added, glaring at his brother.

Dare stood. "I did not play her for a fool. Why is it so hard to believe that I really loved her all those years?" he asked, clearly frustrated. He'd had this same conversation with Shelly earlier.

"Because," Thorn said slowly and in a menacing tone as he threw out a card, "I would think most men don't walk away from the woman they claim to love for no damn reason, especially not some lame excuse about not being ready to settle down. The way I see it, Dare, you wanted to have your cake and eat it too." He took a swig of his beer. "Let's change the subject before I get mad all over again and knock the hell out of you for hurting her the way you did."

Chase narrowed his eyes at Dare. "Yeah, and I hope

she's happily married with a bunch of kids. It would serve you right for letting the best thing that ever happened to you get away."

Dare raised his eyes to the ceiling, wondering if there was such a thing as family loyalty when it came to Shelly Brockman. He decided to sit back down when a new card game began. "She isn't happily married with a bunch of kids, Chase, but she does have a son. He's ten."

Stone smiled happily. "Good for her. I bet it ate up your guts to know she got involved with someone else and had his baby after she left here."

Dare leaned back in his chair. "Yeah, I went through some pretty hard stomach pains until I found out the truth."

Storm raised a brow. "The truth about what?"

Dare smirked at each one of his brothers before answering. "Shelly's son is mine."

Early the next morning Dare walked into Kate's Diner. "Good morning, Sheriff."

"Good morning, Boris. How's that sore arm doing?"

"Fine. I'll be ready to play you in another game of basketball real soon."

"I'm counting on it."

"Good morning, Sheriff."

"Good morning, Ms. Mamie. How's your arthritis?"

"A pain as usual," was the old woman's reply.

"Good morning, Sheriff Westmoreland."

"Good morning, Lizzie," Dare greeted the young waitress as he slid into the stool at the counter. She was old man Barton's granddaughter and was working at the diner part-time while taking classes at the college in town.

He smiled when Lizzie automatically poured his coffee. She knew just how he liked it. Black. "Where's Ms. Kate this morning?" he asked after taking a sip.

"She hasn't come in yet."

He raised a dark brow. For as long as he'd known Ms. Kate—and that had been all of his thirty-six years—he'd never known her to be late to work at the diner. "Is everything all right?"

"Yes, I guess so," Lizzie said, not looking the least bit worried. "She called and said Mr. Granger was stopping by her house this morning to take a look at her hotwater heater. She thinks it's broken and wanted to be there when he arrived."

Dare nodded. It had been rumored around town for years that old man Granger and Ms. Kate were sweet on each other.

"Would you like for me to go ahead and order your usual, Sheriff?"

He rolled his shoulders as if to ease sore muscles as he smiled up at her and said. "No, not yet. I'm waiting on someone." He glanced at his watch. "She should be here any minute."

Lizzie nodded. "All right then. I'll be back when your guest arrives."

Dare was just about to check his watch again when he heard the diner's door open behind him, followed by Boris's loud exclamation. "Well, my word, if it isn't Shelly Brockman! What on earth are you doing back here in College Park?"

Dare turned around on his stool as other patrons who'd known Shelly when she lived in town hollered out similar greetings. He had forgotten just how popular she'd been with everyone, both young and old. That was one of the reasons the entire town had all but skinned him alive when he'd broken off with her.

A muscle in his jaw twitched when he noticed that a few of the guys she'd gone to school with—Boris Jones, David Wright and Wayland Miller—who'd known years ago that she was off-limits because of him, were checking her out now. And he could understand why. She looked pretty damn good, and she still had that natural ability to turn men on without even trying. Blue was a color she wore well and nothing about that had changed, he thought, as his gaze roamed over the blue sundress she was wearing. With thin straps tied at the shoulders, it was a decent length that stopped right above her knees and showed off long beautiful bare legs and feet encased in a pair of black sandals. When he felt his erection straining against the crotch of his pants, he knew he was in big trouble. He was beginning to feel a powerful and compelling need that he hadn't felt in a long time; at least ten years.

"Is that her, Sheriff? The woman you've been waiting on?"

Lizzie's question interrupted Dare's musings. "Yes, that's her."

"Will the two of you be sitting at the counter or will you be using a table or a booth?"

Now that's a loaded question, Dare thought. He wished—doubly so—that he could take Shelly and use a table or a booth. He could just imagine her spread out on either. He shook his head. Although he'd always been sexually attracted to Shelly, he'd never thought of her with so much lust before, and he couldn't help wondering why. Maybe it was because in the past she'd always been his. Now things were different, she was no longer his and he was lusting hard—and he meant hard!—for something he had lost.

"Sheriff?"

Knowing Lizzie was waiting for his decision, he glanced toward the back of the diner and made a quick decision. "We'll be sitting at a booth in the back." Once he was confident he had his body back under control, he stood and walked over to where Shelly was surrounded by a number of people, mostly men.

Breaking into their conversation he said, "Good morning, Shelly. Are you ready for breakfast?"

It seemed the entire diner got quiet and all eyes turned to him. The majority of those present remembered that he had been the one to break Shelly's heart, which ultimately had resulted in her leaving town, and from the way everyone was looking at him, the last thing they wanted was for her to become involved with him again.

In fact, old Mr. Sylvester turned to him and said, "I'm surprised Shelly is willing to give you the time of day, Sheriff, after what you did to her ten years ago."

"You got that right," eighty-year-old Mamie Potter agreed.

Dare rolled his eyes. That was all he needed, the entire town bringing up the past and ganging up on him. "Shelly and I have business to discuss, if none of you mind."

Allen Davis, who had worked with Dare's grandfather years ago, crossed his arms over his chest. "Considering what you did to her, yes, we do mind. So you better behave yourself where she is concerned, Dare Westmoreland. Don't forget there's an election next year."

Dare had just about had it, and was about to tell Mr. Davis a thing or two when Shelly piped in, laughing, "I can't believe all of you still remember what happened ten years ago. I'd almost forgotten about that," she lied. "And to this day I still consider Dare my good friend," she lied again, and tried tactfully to change the subject. "Ms. Mamie, how is Mr. Fred?"

"He still can't hear worth a dime, but other than that he's fine. Thanks for asking. Now to get back to the subject of Dare here, from the way he used to sniff behind you and kept all the other boys away from you, we all thought he was going to be your husband," Mamie mumbled, glaring at Dare.

Shelly shook her head, seeing that the older woman was determined to have her say. She placed a hand on Ms. Mamie's arm in a warm display of affection. "Yes, I know you all did and that was sweet. But things didn't work out that way and we can't worry about spilled milk now, can we?"

Ms. Mamie smiled up at Shelly and patted her hand. "I guess not, dear, but watch yourself around him. I know how crazy you were about him before. There's no need for a woman to let the same man break her heart twice."

Dare frowned, not appreciating Mamie Potter talking about him as if he wasn't there. Nor did it help matters that Shelly was looking at him as though she'd just been given good sound advice. He cleared his throat, thinking that it was time he broke up the little gathering. He placed his hand on Shelly's arm and said, "This way, Shelly. We need to discuss our business so I can get to the office. We can talk now or you can join Jared and I for lunch."

From the look on her face he could tell his words had reminded her of why he was meeting Jared for lunch. After telling everyone goodbye and giving out a few more hugs, she turned and followed Dare to a booth, the farthest one in the back.

He stood aside while she slipped into a soft padded seat and then he slid into the one across from her. Nervously she traced the floral designs on the place mat. Dare's nearness was getting to her. She had experienced the same thing in his office last night, and it aggravated the heck out of her that all that anger she'd felt for him had not been able to defuse her desire for him; especially after ten years.

Desire.

That had to be what it was since she knew she was no longer in love with him. He had effectively put an end to those feelings years ago. Yet, for some reason she was feeling the same turbulent yearnings she'd always felt for him. And last night in her bed, the memories had been at their worse…or their best, depending on how you looked at it.

She had awakened in the middle of the night with her breath coming in deep, ragged gasps, and her sheets damp with perspiration after a hot, steamy dream about him.

Getting up and drinking a glass of ice water, she had made a decision not to beat herself up over her dreams of Dare. She'd decided that the reason for them was understandable. Her body knew Dare as it knew no other man, and it had reminded her of that fact in a not-too-subtle way. It didn't help that for the past ten years she hadn't dated much; raising AJ and working at the hospital kept her busy, and the few occasions she had dated had been a complete waste of her time since she'd never experienced the sparks with any of them that she'd grown accustomed to with Dare.

"Would you like some more coffee, Sheriff?"

Shelly snatched her head up when she heard the sultry, feminine voice and was just in time to see the slow smile that spread across the young woman's lips, as well as the look of wanton hunger in her eyes as she looked at Dare. Either he didn't notice or he was doing a pretty good job of pretending not to.

"Yes, Lizzie, I'd like another cup."

"And what would you like?" Lizzie asked her, and Shelly couldn't help but notice the cold, unfriendly eyes that were staring at her.

Evidently the same thing you would like, Shelly thought, trying to downplay the envy she suddenly felt, although she knew there was no legitimate reason to feel that way. What was once between her and Dare had ended years ago and she didn't intend to go back there, no matter how much he could still arouse her. Sighing, she was about to give the woman her order when Dare spoke. "She would like a cup of coffee with cream and one sugar."

The waitress lifted her brow as if wondering how Dare knew what Shelly wanted. "Okay, Sheriff." Lizzie placed menus in front of them, saying, "I'll bring your coffee while you take a look at these."

When Lizzie had left, Shelly leaned in closer to the center of the booth and whispered, "I don't appreciate the daggered looks coming from one of your girlfriends." She decided not to tell him that she'd felt like throwing a few daggered looks of her own.

Lifting his head from the menu, Dare frowned. "What are you talking about? I've never dated Lizzie. She's just a kid."

Shelly shrugged as she straightened in her seat and glanced over to where Lizzie was now taking another order. Her short uniform showed off quite nicely the curves of her body and her long legs. Dare was wrong. Lizzie was no kid. Her body attested to that.

"Well, kid or no kid, she definitely has the hots for you, Dare Westmoreland."

He shrugged. "You're imagining things."

"No, trust me. I know."

He rubbed his chin as his mouth tipped up crookedly

into a smile. Settling back in his seat, he asked, "And how would you know?"

She met his gaze. "Because I'm a woman." *And I know all about having the hots for you,* she decided not to add.

Dare nodded. He definitely couldn't deny that she was a woman. He glanced over at Lizzie and caught her at the exact moment she was looking at him with a flirty smile. He remembered the other times she'd given him that smile, and now it all made sense. He quickly averted his eyes. Clearing his throat, he met Shelly's gaze. "I've never noticed before."

Typical man, Shelly thought, but before she could say anything else, Lizzie had returned with their coffee. After taking their order she left, and Shelly smiled and said, "I can't believe you remembered how I like my coffee after all this time."

Dare looked at her. His gaze remained steady when he said, "There are some things a man can't forget about a woman he considered as his, Shelly."

"Oh." Her voice was slightly shaky, and she decided not to touch that one; mainly because what he said was true. He had considered her as his; she had been his in every way a woman could belong to a man.

She took a deep breath before taking a sip of coffee. Emotions she didn't want to feel were churning inside her. Dare had hurt her once and she refused to let him do so again. She would definitely take Ms. Mamie's advice and watch herself around him. She glanced up and noticed Dare watching her. The heat from his gaze made her feel a connection to him, one she didn't want to feel, but she realized they did have a connection.

Their son.

She cleared her throat, deciding they needed to engage in conversation, something she considered a safe topic. "How is your family doing?"

A warm smile appeared on Dare's face. "Mom and Dad and all the rest of the Westmoreland clan are fine."

Shelly took another sip of her coffee. "Is it true what I've heard about Delaney? Did she actually finish medical school and marry a sheikh?" she asked. She wondered how that had happened when everyone knew how overprotective the Westmoreland brothers had been of their baby sister.

Dare smiled and the heat in his gaze eased somewhat. "Yeah, it's true. The one and only time we took our eyes off Laney, she slipped away and hid out in a cabin in the mountains for a little rest and relaxation. While there she met this sheikh from the Middle East. Their marriage took some getting used to, since she up and moved to his country. They have a five-month-old son named Ari."

"Have you seen him yet?"

Dare's smile widened. "Yes, the entire family was there for his birth and it was some sort of experience." A frown appeared on his face when he suddenly thought about what he'd missed out on by not being there when AJ had come into the world. "Tell me about AJ, Shelly. Tell me how things were when he was born."

Shelly swallowed thickly. So much for thinking she had moved to a safe topic of conversation. She sighed, knowing Dare had a right to what he was asking for. "He was born in the hospital where I worked. My parents were there with me. I didn't gain much weight while pregnant and that helped make the delivery easier. He wasn't a big baby, only a little over six pounds, but he was extremely long which accounts for his height. As soon as I saw him I immediately thought he looked like you. And I knew at that moment no matter how we had separated, that my baby was a part of you."

Shelly hesitated for a few moments and added. "That's why I gave him your name, Dare. In my mind he didn't look like a Marcus, which was the name I had intended to give him. To me he looked like an Alisdare Julian. A little Dare."

Dare didn't say anything for the longest time, then he said, "Thank you for doing that."

"You're welcome."

Moments later, Dare cleared his throat and asked, "Does he know he was named after his father?"

"Yes. You don't know how worried I was before arriving at the police station yesterday. I was afraid that you had found out his name, or that he had found out yours. Luckily for me, most people at the station call you Sheriff, and everyone in town still calls you Dare."

Dare nodded. "Except for my family, few people probably remember my real name is Alisdare since it's seldom used. I've always gone by Dare. If AJ had given me his full name I would have figured things out."

After a few brief quiet moments, Dare said, "I told my parents and my brothers about him last night, Shelly."

She nervously bit into her bottom lip. "And what were their reactions?"

Dare leaned back against his seat and met her gaze. "They were as shocked as I was, and of course they're anxious to meet him."

Shelly nodded slowly. She'd figured they would be. The Westmorelands were a big family and a rather close-knit group. "Dare, about your suggestion on how we should handle things."

"Yes?"

She didn't say anything for the longest time, then she

said, "I'll go along with your plan as long as you and I understand something."

"What?"

"That it will be strictly for show. There's no way the two of us could ever get back together for any reason. The only thing between us is AJ."

Dare raised a brow and gave her a deliberate look. He wondered why she was so damn sure of that, but decided to let it go for now. He wanted to start building a relationship with his son immediately, and he refused to let Shelly put stumbling blocks in his way. "That's fine with me."

He leaned back in his chair. "So how soon will you tell AJ about me?"

"I plan to tell him tonight."

Dare nodded, satisfied with her answer. That meant they could put their plans into action as early as tomorrow. "I think we're doing the right thing, Shelly."

She felt the intensity of his gaze, and the force of it touched her in a way she didn't want. "I hope so, Dare. I truly hope so," she said quietly.

Chapter 4

Dare glanced at the clock again and sighed deeply. Where was AJ? School had let out over an hour ago and he still hadn't arrived. According to what Shelly had told him that morning at breakfast, AJ had ridden his bike to school and been told to report to the sheriff's office as soon as school was out. Dare wondered if AJ had blatantly disobeyed his mother.

Although Shelly had given him her cell-phone number—as a home healthcare nurse she would be making various house calls today—he didn't want to call and get her worried or upset. If he had to, he would go looking for their son himself and when he found him, he intended to—

The sound of the buzzer interrupted his thoughts. "Yes, McKade, what is it?"

"That Brockman kid is here."

Dare nodded and sighed with relief. Then he recalled

what McKade had said—*that Brockman kid.* He frowned. The first thing he planned to do when everything settled was to give his son his last name. *That Westmoreland kid* sounded more to his liking. "Okay, I'll be right out."

Leaving his office, Dare walked down the hall toward the front of the building and stopped dead in his tracks when he saw AJ. His frown deepened. The kid looked as though he'd had a day with a tiger. "What happened to you?" he asked him, his gaze roaming over AJ's torn shirt and soiled jeans, not to mention his bruised lip and bloodied nose.

"Nothing happened. I fell off my bike," AJ snapped.

Dare glanced over at McKade. They both recognized a lie when they heard one. Dare crossed his arms over his chest. "You never came across to me as the outright clumsy type."

That got the response Dare was hoping for. The anger flaring in AJ's eyes deepened. "I am not the clumsy type. Anyone can fall off a bike," he said, again snapping out his answer.

"Yes, but in this case that's not what happened and you know it," Dare said, wanting to snap back but didn't. It was apparent that AJ had been in a fight, and Dare decided to cut the crap. "Tell me what really happened."

"I'm not telling you anything."

Wrong answer, Dare thought taking a step forward to stand in front of AJ. "Look, kid, we can stand here all day until you decide to talk, but you *will* tell me what happened."

AJ stuck his hands in the pockets of his jeans and glanced down as if to study the expensive pair of Air Jordans on his feet. When seconds ticked into minutes and he saw that Dare would not move an inch, he finally raised his head, met Dare's gaze, squared his shoulders and said, "Caleb Martin doesn't like me and today after school he decided to take his dislike to another level."

Dare leaned against the counter and raised a brow. "And?"

AJ paused, squared his shoulders again and said, "And I decided to oblige him. He pushed me down and when I got up I made sure he found out the hard way that I'm not someone to mess with."

Dare inwardly smiled. He hated admitting it but what his son had said had been spoken like a true Westmoreland. He didn't want to remember the number of times one of the Westmoreland boys came home with something bloodied or broken. Word had soon gotten around school that those Westmorelands weren't anyone to tangle with. They never went looking for trouble, but they knew how to handle it when it came their way.

"Fighting doesn't accomplish anything."

His son shrugged. "Maybe not, but I bet Caleb Martin won't be calling me bad names and pushing me around again. I had put up with it long enough."

Dare placed his hand on his hips. "If this has been going on for a while, why didn't you say something about it to your mother or to some adult at school?"

AJ's glare deepened even more. "I'm not a baby. I don't need my mother or some teacher fighting my battles for me."

Dare met his son's glare with one of his own. "Maybe not, but in the future I expect you not to take matters into your own hands. If I hear about it, I will haul both you and that Martin kid in here and the two of you will be sorry. Not only will I assign after-school duties but I'll give weekend work duties as well. I won't tolerate that kind of foolishness." Especially when it involved his son,

Dare decided not to add. "Now go into that bathroom and get cleaned up then meet me out back."

AJ shifted his book bag to his other shoulder. "What am I supposed to do today?"

"My police car needs washing and I can use the help."

AJ nodded and rushed off toward the bathroom. Dare couldn't hide the smile that lit his face. Although AJ had grumbled last night about having to show up at the police station after school, Dare could tell from his expression that he enjoyed having something to do.

"Sheriff?"

Dare glanced up and met McKade's gaze. "Yes?"

"There's something about that kid that's oddly familiar."

Dare knew what McKade was getting at. His deputy had seen the paperwork he'd completed last night and had probably put two and two together; especially since Rick McKade knew his first and middle names. The two of them were good friends and had been since joining the FBI at the same time years back. When Dare had decided to leave the Bureau, so had McKade. Rick had followed Dare to Atlanta, where he'd met and fallen in love with a schoolteacher who lived in the area.

"The reason he seems oddly familiar, McKade, is because you just saw him yesterday," Dare said, hoping that was the end of it.

He found out it wasn't when McKade chuckled and said, "That's not what I mean and you know it, Dare. There's something else."

"What?"

McKade paused a moment before answering. "He looks a lot like you and your brothers, but *especially* like you." He again paused a few moments then asked, "Is there anything you want to tell me?"

Dare's lips curved into a smile. He didn't have to tell McKade anything since it was obvious he had figured things out for himself. "No, there's nothing I want to tell you."

McKade chuckled again. "Then maybe I better tell you, or rather I should remind you that the people in this town don't know how to keep a secret if that's what you plan to do. It won't be long before everyone figures things out, and when they do, someone will tell the kid."

Dare's smile widened when he thought of that happening. "Yes, and that's what his mother and I are counting on." Knowing what he'd said had probably confused the hell out of McKade, Dare turned and walked through the door that led out back.

The kid was a hard worker and a darn good one at that, Dare decided as he watched AJ dry off the police cruiser. He had only intended the job to last an hour, but he could tell that AJ was actually enjoying having something to do. He made a mental note to ask Shelly if AJ did any chores at home, and if not, maybe it wouldn't be a bad idea for her to assign him a few. That would be another way to keep him out of trouble.

"Is this it for the day?"

AJ's statement jerked Dare from his thoughts. AJ had placed the cloth he'd used to dry off the car back in the bucket. "Yes, that's it, but make sure you come back tomorrow—and I expect you to be on time."

A scowl appeared on AJ's face but he didn't say anything as he picked up his book bag and placed it on his shoulder. "I don't like coming here after school."

Dare shook his head and inwardly smiled, wondering who the kid was trying to convince. "Well, you should have thought of that before you got into trouble."

Their gazes locked for a brief moment and Dare detected a storm of defiance brewing within his son. "How much longer do I have to come here?" AJ asked in an agitated voice.

"Until I think you've learned your lesson."

AJ's glare deepened. "Well, I don't like it."

Dare raised his gaze upward to the sky then looked back to AJ. "You've said that already, kid, but in this case what you like doesn't really matter. When you break the law you have to be punished. That's something I suggest you remember. I also suggest that you get home before your mother starts worrying about you," he said, following AJ inside the building.

"She's going to do that anyway."

Dare smiled. "Yeah, I wouldn't put it past her, since mothers are that way. I'm sure my four brothers and I worried my mother a lot when we were growing up."

AJ raised a brow. "You have four brothers?"

Dare's smile widened. "Yes, I have four brothers and one sister. I'm the oldest of the group."

AJ nodded. "It's just me and my mom."

Dare nodded as well. He then stood in front of the door with AJ. "To answer your question of how long you'll have to come here after school, I think a full week of this should make you think twice about throwing rocks at passing cars the next time." Dare rubbed his chin thoughtfully then added, "Unless I hear about you getting involved in a fight again. Like I said, that's something I won't tolerate."

AJ glared at him. "Then I'll make sure you don't hear about it."

Not giving Dare a chance to respond, AJ raced out of the door, got his bike and took off.

* * *

"Ouch, that hurts!"

"Well, this should teach you a lesson," Shelly said angrily, leaning over AJ as she applied antiseptic to his bruised lip. "And if I hear of you fighting again, I will put you on a punishment like you wouldn't believe."

"He started it!"

Shelly straightened and met her son's dark scowl. "Then next time walk away," she said firmly.

"People are going to think I'm a coward if I do that. I told you I was going to hate it here. Nobody likes me. At least I had friends in L.A."

"I don't consider those guys you hung around with back in L.A. your friends. A true friend wouldn't talk you into doing bad things, AJ, and as far as anyone thinking you're a coward, then let them. I know for a fact that you're one of the bravest persons I know. Look how long you've had to be the man of the house for me."

AJ shrugged and glanced up at his mother. "But it's different with you, Mom. I don't want any of the guys at school thinking I'm a pushover."

"Trust me, you're not a pushover. You're too much like your father." She then turned to walk toward the kitchen.

Shelly knew she had thrown out the hook and it wouldn't take long for AJ to take the bait. She heard him draw in a long breath behind her and knew he was right on her heels.

"Why did you mention him?"

She looked back over her shoulder at AJ when she reached the kitchen. "Why did I mention who?"

"My father."

She leaned against the kitchen cabinet and raised a curious brow. "I'm not supposed to mention him?"

"You haven't in a long time."

Shelly nodded. "Only because you haven't asked about him in a long time. Tonight when you said something about being a pushover, I immediately thought of him because you're so much like him and he's one of the bravest men I know."

AJ smiled. He was glad to know his father was brave. "What does he do, fly planes or something?"

Shelly smiled knowing of her son's fixation with airplanes and spaceships. "No." She inhaled deeply. "I think it's time we had a talk about your father. I've been doing a lot of thinking since moving back and I need you to help me make a decision about something."

AJ lifted a brow. "A decision about what?"

"About whether to tell your father about you."

Surprise widened AJ's eyes. "You know where he is?"

Shelly shook her head. "AJ, I've always known where he is. I've always told you that. And I've always told you if you ever wanted me to contact him to just say the word."

Uncertainty narrowed his eyes, then he glanced down as if to study his sneakers. "Yeah, but I wasn't sure if you really meant it or not," he said quietly.

Shelly smiled weakly and reached out and gently gripped his chin to bring his gaze back to hers. "Is that why you stopped asking me about him? You thought I was lying to you about him?"

He shrugged. "I just figured you were saying what you wanted me to believe. Nick Banner's mom did that to him. She told him that his dad had died in a car accident when he was a baby, then one day he heard his grandpa tell somebody that his dad was alive and had another family someplace and that he didn't want Nick."

Shelly's breath caught in her throat. She felt an urgent need to take her son into her arms and assure him that unlike Nick's father, his father did want him. But she knew he was now at an age where mothers' hugs were no longer *cool*. Her heart felt heavy knowing that AJ had denied himself knowledge of his father in an attempt to save her from what he thought was embarrassment.

"Come on, let's sit at the table. I think it's time for us to have a long talk."

AJ hung his head thoughtfully then glanced back at her. His eyes were wary. "About him?"

"Yes, about him. There are things I think you need to know, so come on."

He followed her over to the table and they sat down. Her gaze was steady as she met his. "Now then, just to set the record straight, everything I've ever told you about your father was true. He was someone I dated through high school and college while I lived here in College Park. Everyone in town thought we would marry, and I guess that had been my thought, too, but your father had a dream."

"A dream?"

"Yes, a dream of one day becoming an FBI agent. You have your dream to grow up and become an astronaut one day, don't you?"

"Yes."

"Well, your father had a similar dream, but his was one day to become an FBI agent, and I knew if I had told him that I was pregnant with you, he would have turned his back on his dream for us. I didn't want him to do that. I loved him too much. So, without telling him I was pregnant with you, I left town. So he never knew about you, AJ."

Shelly sighed. Everything she'd just told AJ was basically true. However, this next part would be a lie; a lie Dare was convinced AJ needed to believe. "Your father still doesn't know about you, and this is where I need your help."

AJ looked confused. "My help about what?"

"About what I should do." When his confusion didn't clear she said, "Since we moved back, I found out your father is still living here in College Park."

She could tell AJ was momentarily taken aback by what she'd said. He stared at her with wide, expressive eyes. "He's here? In this town?" he asked in a somewhat shaky yet excited voice.

"Yes. It seems that he moved back a few years ago after he stopped working for the FBI in Washington, D.C." Shelly leaned back in her chair. "I want to be fair to the both of you. You're getting older and so is he. I think it's time that I finally tell him about you, just like I'm telling you about him."

AJ nodded and looked at her and she saw uncertainty in his eyes. "But what if he doesn't want me?"

Shelly smiled and then chuckled. "Trust me, when he finds out about you he will definitely want you. In fact I'm a little concerned about what his reaction will be when he realizes that I've kept your existence from him. He is a man who strongly believes in family and he won't be a happy camper."

"Had he known about me, he would have married you?"

Shelly's smiled widened, knowing that was true. "Yes, in a heartbeat, which is the reason I didn't tell him. And although it's too late for either of us to think of ever having a life together again, because we've lived separate lives for so long, there's no doubt in my mind that once I tell him about you he'll want to become a part of your life. But I need to know how you feel about that."

AJ shrugged. "I'm okay with it, but how do you feel about it, Mom?"

"I'm okay with it, too."

AJ nodded. He then lowered his head as his finger made designs across the tablecloth. Moments later he lifted his eyes and met her gaze. "So when can I get to meet him?"

Shelly took a deep breath and hoped that her next words sounded normal. "You've already met your father, AJ. You met him yesterday."

She inhaled deeply then broke it down further by saying, "Sheriff Dare Westmoreland is your father."

Chapter 5

"Sheriff Westmoreland!" AJ shouted as he jumped out of his seat. He stood in front of his mother and lifted his chin angrily, defiantly. "It can't be him. No way."

Shelly smiled slightly. "Trust me, it *is* him. I of all people should know."

"But—but, I don't want *him* to be my father," he huffed loudly.

Shelly looked directly at AJ, at how badly he was taking the news, which really wasn't unexpected, considering the way he and Dare had clashed. "I'm sorry you feel that way because he is and there's nothing you can do about it. Alisdare Julian Westmoreland *is* your father."

When she saw the look that crossed his face, she added. "And I didn't make up that part, either. You really were named after him, AJ. He merely shortens the Alisdare to Dare."

She felt AJ's need to deny what she'd just told him, but

there was no way she could let him do that. "The question is, now that you know he's your father, what are we going to do about it?"

She watched his forehead scrunch into a frown, then he said, "We don't have to do anything about it since he doesn't have to know. We can continue with things the way they are."

She lifted a brow. "Don't you think he has every right to know about you?"

"Not if I don't want him to know."

Shelly shook her head. "Dare will be very hurt if he ever learns the truth." She studied her son. "Can you give me a good reason why he shouldn't be told?"

"Yes, because he doesn't like me and I don't like him."

Shelly met his gaze. "With your disrespectful attitude, you probably didn't make a good impression on him yesterday, AJ. However, Dare loves kids. And as far as you not liking him, you really don't know him, and I think you should get to know him. He's really a nice guy, otherwise I would not have fallen in love with him all those years ago." A small voice whispered that that part was true. Dare had always been a caring and loving person. "How did things go between the two of you today?"

AJ shrugged. "We still don't like each other, and I don't want to get to know him. So please don't tell him, Mom. You can't."

She paused for a moment knowing what she would say, knowing she would not press him anymore. "All right, AJ, since you feel so strongly about it, I won't tell him. But I'm hoping that one day *you* will be the one to tell him. I'm hoping that one day you'll see the importance of him knowing the truth."

She stood and walked over to AJ and placed her hand

on his shoulder. "There's something else you need to think about."

"What?"

"Dare is a very smart man. Chances are he'll figure things out without either one of us telling him anything."

He frowned and his eyes grew round. "How?"

Shelly smiled. "You favor him and his four brothers. Although he hasn't noticed it yet, there's a good chance that he will. And then there's the question of your age. He knows I left town ten years ago, the same year you were born."

AJ nodded. "Did he ask you anything when you saw him yesterday?"

"No. I think he assumes your father is someone I met after leaving here, but as I said, there's a chance he might start putting two and two together."

AJ's features drew in a deeper frown at the thought of that happening. "But we can't let him figure it out."

She shook her head. Shelly hated lying to AJ although she knew it was for a good reason. She had to remember that. "Whoa. Don't include me in this, AJ. It's strictly your decision not to let Dare know about you, it isn't mine. I'm already in hot water for not having told him that you exist at all. But I'll keep my word and not tell him anything if that's the way you want it."

"Yes, that's the way I want it," AJ said, not hiding the relief on his face.

His lips were quivering, and Shelly knew he was fighting hard to keep his tears at bay. Right now he was feeling torn. A part of him wanted to be elated that his father did exist, but another part refused to accept the man who he'd discovered his father was, all because of that Westmoreland pride and stubbornness.

Shelly shook her head when she felt tears in the back of her own eyes. Dare's mission to win his son's love would not be easy.

Later that night, after AJ had gone to bed Shelly received a phone call from Dare.

"Did you tell him?"

She leaned against her kitchen sink. "Yes, I told him."

There was a pause. "And how did he take it?"

Shelly released a deep sigh. "Just as we expected. He doesn't want you to know that he's your son." When Dare didn't respond, she said, "Don't take it personally, Dare. I think he's more confused than anything right now. Tonight I discovered why he had stopped asking me about you."

"Why?"

"Because he didn't really believe you existed, at least not the way I'd told him. It seems that a friend of his had shared with him the fact that his mother had told him his father had died in a car accident when he was a baby, and then he'd discovered that his father was alive and well and living somewhere with another family. So AJ assumed what I had told him about you wasn't true and that I really didn't know how to contact you if he ever asked me to. And since he never wanted to place me in a position that showed me up as a liar, he just never bothered."

Again she released a sigh as she fought back the tears that threaten to fall. "And to think that he probably did want to know you all this time but refrained from asking to save me embarrassment in being caught in a lie."

A sob caught in her throat as she blinked back a tear. "Oh, Dare, I feel so bad for him, and what he's going through is all my fault. I thought I was making all the right decisions for all the right reasons and now it seems I caused more harm than good."

Dare lay in bed, his entire body tense. He could no longer hold back the anger he felt for Shelly, even knowing he had made a couple of mistakes himself in handling things ten years ago. Had he not chosen a career over her then, things would have worked out a whole lot differently. So, in reality, he was just as much to blame as Shelly, but together they had a chance to make things work to save their son.

"Things are going to work out in the end, Shell, you'll see. You've done your part tonight, now let me handle things from here. It might take months, but in the end I believe that AJ will accept me as his father. In my heart I believe that one day he'll want me to know the truth."

Shelly nodded, hearing the confidence in Dare's voice and hoping he was right. "So now we move to the second phase of your plan?"

"Now we move to the second phase of *our* plan."

The next morning, after AJ had left for school, a gentle knock on the door alerted Shelly that she had a visitor. Today was her day off and she had spent the last half hour or so on the computer paying her bills online, and was just about to walk into the kitchen for a cup of coffee.

Crossing the living room she glanced out of the peephole. Her breath caught. Dare was standing on her porch, and his tall, muscular frame was silhouetted by the mid-morning sunlight that was shining brightly behind him. He looked gorgeous; his uniform, which showcased his solid chest, firm stomach and strong flanks, made him look even more so.

She shivered as everything about her that was woman jolted upward from the soles of her feet, to settle in an area between her legs. She inhaled and commanded her body not to go there. Whatever had been between her and Dare had ended ten years ago, and now was not the time for her body to go horny on her. She'd done without sex for this long, and she could continue to go without it for a while longer. But damn if Dare Westmoreland didn't rattle and stir up those urges she'd kept dormant for ten years. She couldn't for the life of her forget how it had felt to run her hands over his chest, indulging in the crisp feel of his hair and the masculine texture of his skin.

She closed her eyes and took a deep breath at the memory of his firm stomach rubbing against her own and the feel of his calloused palm touching her intimately on the sensitive areas of her body. She remembered him awakening within her a passion that had almost startled her.

His second knock made her regain her mental balance, and warning signals against opening the door suddenly went off in her head as she opened her eyes. A silent voice reminded her that although she might want to, there was no way to put as much distance between herself and Dare as she'd like. No matter how much being around him got to her, their main concern was their son.

Inhaling deeply, she slowly opened the door and met his gaze. Once again she felt every sexual instinct she possessed spring to life. "Dare, what are you doing here?" she asked, pausing afterwards to take a deep, steadying breath.

He smiled, that enticingly sexy smile that always made her want to go to the nearest bed and get it on with him. There was no way she could see him and not think of crawling into bed next to him amidst rumpled sheets while he reached out and took her into his arms and…

"I tried calling you at the agency where you worked and they told me you were off today," he said as he leaned in her doorway, breaking into her wayward thoughts and sending her already sex-crazed mind into turmoil. Why did he still look so good after ten years? And why on earth was her body responding to the sheer essence of him this way? But then she and Dare always had had an abundant amount of overzealous hormones and it seemed that ten years hadn't done a thing to change that.

"Why were you trying to reach me?" she somehow found her voice to ask him. "Is something wrong?"

He shook his head, immediately putting her fears to rest. "No, but I thought it would be a good idea if we talked."

Shelly's eyebrows raised. "Talk? But we talked yesterday morning at Kate's Diner and again last night. What do we have to talk about now?" she asked, trying not to sound as frustrated as she felt.

"I thought you'd like to know how my meeting went with Jared yesterday."

"Oh." She had completely forgotten about his plans to meet with his attorney cousin for lunch. She'd always liked his cousin Jared Westmoreland, who, over the years, had become something of a hotshot attorney. "I would." She took a step back as she fought to remain composed. "Come in."

He stepped inside and closed the door behind him and then glanced around. "It's been years since I've been inside this house. It brings back memories," Dare said meeting her gaze once again.

She nodded, remembering how he used to stand in that same spot countless times as he waited for her to come down the stairs for their dates. And even then, when she breezed down the stairs her mind was filled with thoughts of their evening, especially how it would finish. "Yes, it does."

A long, seemingly endless moment of silence stretched between them before she finally cleared her throat. "I was about to have a cup of coffee and a Danish if you'd like to join me," she offered.

"That's a pretty tempting offer, one that I think I'll take you up on."

Shelly nodded. If he thought *that* was tempting he really didn't know what tempting was about. *Tempting* was Dare Westmoreland standing in the middle of her living room looking absolutely gorgeous. And it didn't help matters one iota when she glanced his way and saw a definite bulge behind his fly. Apparently he was just as hot and bothered as she was.

She quickly turned around. "Follow me," she said over her shoulder, wondering how she was going to handle being alone in the house with him.

Following Shelly was the last thing Dare thought he needed to do. He tried not to focus on the sway of the backside encased in denim shorts in front of him. He was suddenly besieged with memories of just how that backside had felt in his hands when he'd lifted it to thrust inside her. Those thoughts made his arousal harden even more. He suppressed a groan deep in his throat.

He tried to think of other things and glanced around. He liked the way she had decorated the place, totally different from the way her parents used to have it. Her mother's taste had been soft and quaint. Shelly's taste made a bold statement. She liked colors—bright, cheery colors—evident in the vivid print of the sofa, loveseat and wingback chair. Then there were her walls, painted in a variety of colorful shades, so different from his plain off-white ones. He was amazed how she was able to tie everything together without anything clashing. She had managed to create a cozy and homey atmosphere for herself and AJ.

As they entered the kitchen, Dare quickly sat down at the table before she could note the fix his body was in, if she hadn't done so already. But he soon discovered that sitting at the table watching her move around the kitchen only intensified his problem. He was getting even more turned on by the fluid movements of her body as she reached into a cabinet to get their coffee cups. The shorts were snug, a perfect fit, and his entire body began throbbing in deep male appreciation.

"You still like your coffee black and your Danish with a lot of butter, Dare?"

"Yes," he managed to respond. He began to realize that he had made a mistake in dropping by. Over the past couple of days when they'd been together there had been other people around. Now it was just the two of them, alone in this house, in this room. He had to fight hard to dismiss the thought of taking her right there on the table.

He inhaled deeply. If Shelly knew what thoughts were running through his mind she would probably hightail it up the stairs, which wouldn't do her any good since he would only race up those same stairs after her and end up making love to her in one of the bedrooms.

That was something they had done once before when her parents had been out of town and he had dropped by unexpectedly. A slow, lazy smile touched the side of his mouth as he remembered the intensity of their lovemaking that day. That was the one time they hadn't used protection. Perhaps that was the time she had gotten pregnant with AJ?

"What are you smiling about?"

Her question invaded his thoughts and he shifted in the chair to alleviate some of the tension pressing at the zipper of his pants. He met her gaze and decided to be completely honest with her, something he had always done. "I was thinking about that time that we made love upstairs in your bedroom without protection, and wondered if that was the time you got pregnant."

"It was."

He regarded her for a second. "How do you know?"

She stared at the floor for a moment before meeting his gaze again. "Because after that was the first time I'd ever been late."

He nodded. The reason they had made love so recklessly and intensely that day was because he had received orders a few hours earlier to leave immediately for an area near Kuwait. It was a temporary assignment and he would only be gone for two months. But at the time, two months could have been two years for all she cared. Because of the danger of his assignment, the news had immediately sent her in a spin and she had raced up the stairs to her bedroom so he wouldn't see her cry. He had gone after her, only to end up placing her on the bed and making frantic, uncontrolled love to her.

"What did Jared have to say yesterday?" Shelly asked him rather than think about that particular day when they had unknowingly created their son. Straightening, she walked over to the table and placed the coffee and rolls in front of him, then sat down at the table.

He took a sip of coffee and responded, "Jared thinks that whatever we decide is the best way to handle letting AJ know I'm his father is fine as long as we're in agreement. But he strongly thinks I should do whatever needs to be done to compensate you from the time he was born. And I agree. As his father I had certain responsibilities to him."

"But you didn't know about him, Dare."

"But I know about him now, Shelly, and that makes a world of difference."

Shelly nodded. She knew that to argue with Dare would be a complete waste of her time. "All right, I have a college fund set up and if you'd like to contribute, I have no problem with that. That is definitely one way you can help."

Dare leaned back in his chair and met her gaze. "Are you sure there's no other way I can help?"

For a moment she wondered if he was asking for AJ or for her. Could he detect the deep longing within her, the sexual cravings, and knew he could help her there? She sighed, knowing she was letting her mind become cluttered. AJ was the only thing between them, and she had to remember that.

"Yes, I'm sure," she said softly. "My job pays well and I've always budgeted to live within my means. The cost of living isn't as high here as it is in L.A., and my parents aren't charging me any rent, so AJ and I are fine, Dare, but thanks for asking."

At that moment the telephone rang; she hoped he didn't see the relief on her face. "Excuse me," she said, standing quickly. "That's probably the agency calling to let me know my hours and clients for next week."

As Shelly listened to the agency's secretary tell her what her schedule would be for the following week, she tried to get her thoughts back together. Dare had stirred up emotions and needs that she'd thought were dead and buried until she'd seen him two days ago. His presence had blood racing through her body at an alarming speed.

"All right, thanks for calling," she said before hanging up the phone. She quickly turned and bumped into a massive solid chest. "Oh."

Dare reached out and quickly stopped Shelly from

falling. "Sorry, I didn't mean to scare you," he said, his words soft and gentle.

She took a step back when he released her. Each time he touched her she was reminded of the sensual feelings he could easily invoke. "I thought you were still sitting down."

"I thought it was time for me to leave. I don't want to take you from your work any longer."

She rubbed her hands across her arms, knowing it was best if he left. "Is that all Jared said?"

He nodded. That was all she needed to know. There was no need to tell her that Jared had suggested the possibility of him having legal visitation rights and petitioning for joint custody of AJ. Both suggestions he had squashed, since he and Shelly had devised what they considered a workable plan.

His gaze moved to her hands and he watched her fingers sliding back and forth across her arms. He remembered her doing that very thing on a certain part of his anatomy several times. The memory of the warmth of her fingers touching him so intimately slammed another arousal through his body that strengthened the one already there.

At that moment, he lost whatever control he had. Being around her stirred up memories and emotions he could no longer fight, nor did he want to. The only thing he wanted, he needed, was to kiss her, taste her and reacquaint the insides of his mouth, his tongue, with hers.

Shelly was having issues of her own and took a steadying breath, trying to get the heated desire racing through her body under control. She swallowed deeply when she saw that Dare's gaze was dead-centered on her mouth, and fought off the panic that seized her when he took a step forward.

A Little Dare

"I wonder…" he said huskily, his gaze not leaving her lips.

She blinked, refocused on him. "You wonder about what?" she asked softly, feeling the last shreds of her composure slipping.

"I wonder if your mouth still knows me."

His words cut through any control she had left. Those were the words he had always whispered whenever they were together after being apart for any length of time, just moments before he took her into his arms and kissed her senseless.

He leaned in closer, then lowered his mouth to hers. Immediately, his tongue went after hers in an attempt to lure her into the same rush of desire consuming him. But she was already there, a step ahead of him, so he tried forcing his body to calm down and settle into the taste he'd always been accustomed to. He had expected heat, but he hadn't expected the hot, fiery explosion that went off in his midsection. It made a groan erupt from deep in his throat.

His hands linked around her waist to hold her closer, thigh-to-thigh, breasts to chest. Sensation after sensation speared through him, making it hard to resist eating her alive, or at least trying to, and wanting to touch her everywhere, especially between her legs. Now that he had rediscovered this—the taste of her mouth—he wanted also to relive the feel of his fingers sliding over her heated flesh to find the hot core of her, swollen and wet.

That thought drove a primitive need through him and the erection pressing against her got longer and harder. The thought of using it to penetrate the very core of her made his mind reel and drugged his brain even more with her sensuality.

A shiver raced over Shelly and a semblance of control returned as she realized just how easily she had succumbed to his touch. She knew she had to put a halt to what they were doing. She had returned to College Park not for herself but for AJ.

She broke off their kiss and untangled herself from his arms. When he leaned toward her, to kiss her again, she pushed him back. "No, Dare," she said firmly. "We shouldn't have done that. This isn't about you or me or our inability to control overzealous hormones. It's about our son and doing what is best for him."

And why can't we simultaneously discover what is best for us, he wanted to ask but refrained from doing so. He understood her need to put AJ first and foremost, but what she would soon realize was that there was unfinished business between them as well. "I agree that AJ is our main concern, Shelly, but there's something you need to realize and accept."

"What?"

"Things aren't over between us, and we shouldn't deceive ourselves into thinking there won't be a next time, so be prepared for it."

He saw the frown that appeared in her eyes and the defiance that tilted her lips reminded him of AJ yesterday and the day before. "No, Dare, there won't be a next time because I won't let there be. You're AJ's father, but what was between us is over and has been for years. To me you're just another man."

He lifted a brow. He wondered if she had kissed many men the way she'd kissed him, and for some reason he doubted it. She had kissed him as though she hadn't kissed anyone in years. He had felt the hunger that had raged through her. He had felt it, explored it and, for the moment, satisfied it. "You're sure about that?"

"Yes, I'm positive, so I suggest you place all your concentration on winning your son over and forget about your son's mother."

As he turned to cross the room to leave, he knew that he would never be able to forget about his son's mother, not in a million years. Before walking out the door he looked back at her. "Oh, yeah, I almost forgot something."

She lifted a brow. "What?"

"The brothers four. They're dying to see you. I told them of our plans for AJ and they agreed to be patient about seeing him, but they refuse to be patient about seeing you, Shelly. They want to know if you'll meet them for lunch one day this week at Chase's restaurant in downtown Atlanta?"

She smiled. She wanted to see them as well. Dare's brothers had always been special to her. "Tell them I'd love to have lunch with them tomorrow since I'll be working in that area."

Dare nodded, then turned and walked out the door.

AJ saw the two boys standing next to his bike the moment he walked out the school door. Since his bike was locked, he wasn't worried about the pair taking it, but after his fight with Caleb Martin yesterday the last thing he wanted was trouble. Especially after the talks the sheriff and his mother had given him.

The sheriff.

He shook his head, not wanting to think about the fact that the sheriff was his father. But he had thought about it most of the day, and still, as he'd told his mother last night, he didn't want the sheriff to know he was his son.

"What are you two looking at?" he asked in a tough voice, ignoring the fact that one of the boys was a lot bigger than he was.

"Your bike," the smaller of the two said, turning to him. "We think it's cool. Where did you get it?"

AJ relaxed. He thought his bike was cool, too. "Not from any place around here. My mom bought it for me in California."

"Is that where you're from?" the largest boy asked.

"Yeah, L.A. That's where I was born, and I hope we move back there." He sized up the two and decided they were harmless. He had seen them before around school, but neither had made an attempt to be friendly to him until now. "My name is AJ Brockman. What's yours?"

"My name is Morris Sears," the smaller of the two said, "and this is my friend Cornelius Thomas."

AJ nodded. "Do you live around here?"

"Yeah, just a few blocks, not far from Kate's Diner."

"I live just a few blocks from Kate's Diner, too, on Sycamore Street," AJ said, glad to know there were other kids living not far away.

"We saw what happened with you and Caleb Martin yesterday," Morris said, his eyes widening. "Boy! Did you teach him a lesson! No one has ever done that before and we're glad, since he's been messing with people for a long time for no reason. He's nothing but a bully."

AJ nodded, agreeing with them.

"Would you like to ride home with us today?" Cornelius asked, getting on his own bike. "We know a shortcut that goes through the Millers' land. We saw a couple of deer on their property yesterday."

AJ's eyes lit up. He'd never seen a deer before, at least not a real live one. He then remembered where he had to go after school. "I'm sorry but today I can't. I have to report directly to the sheriff's office now."

"For fighting yesterday?" Morris asked.

AJ shook his head. "No, for cutting school two days

ago. I was throwing rocks at cars and the sheriff caught me and took me in."

Cornelius eyes widened. "You got to ride in the back of Sheriff Westmoreland's car?" he asked excitedly.

AJ raised a brow. "Yes."

"Boy, that's cool. Sheriff Westmoreland is a hero."

AJ gave a snort of laughter. "A hero? And what makes him a hero? He's nothing but a sheriff who probably does nothing but sit in his office all day."

Morris and Cornelius shook their head simultaneously.

"Not Sheriff Westmoreland," Morris said as if he knew that for a fact. "He was in all the newspapers last week for catching those two bad guys the FBI has been looking for. My dad says Sheriff Westmoreland got shot at bringing them in and that a bullet barely missed his head."

"Yeah, and my dad said," Cornelius piped in, "that those bad guys didn't know who they were messing with, since everyone knows the sheriff doesn't play. Why, he used to even be an FBI agent. My dad went to school with him and graduated the same year Thorn Westmoreland did."

AJ looked curiously at Cornelius. "What does Thorn Westmoreland have to do with anything?"

Cornelius lifted a shocked brow. "Don't you know who Thorn Westmoreland is?"

Of course AJ knew who Thorn Westmoreland was. What kid didn't? "Sure. He's the motorcycle racer who builds the baddest bikes on earth."

Cornelius and Morris nodded. "He's also the sheriff's brother," Morris said grinning, happy to be sharing such news with their new friend. "And have you ever heard of Rock Mason?"

"The man who writes those adventure-thriller books?"

AJ asked, his mind still reeling from what he'd just been told—Thorn Westmoreland was the sheriff's brother!

"Yes, but Rock Mason's real name is Stone Westmoreland and he's the sheriff's brother, too. Then there are two more of them, Chase and Storm Westmoreland. Mr. Chase owns a big restaurant downtown and Mr. Storm is a fireman."

AJ nodded. He wondered how Morris and Cornelius knew so much about a family that he was supposed to be a part of, yet he didn't know a thing about.

"And I forgot to mention that their sister married a prince from one of those faraway countries," Morris added, interrupting AJ's thoughts.

"How do you two know so much about the Westmorelands?" AJ asked, wrinkling his forehead.

"Because the sheriff coaches our Little League team and his brothers often help out."

"The sheriff coaches a baseball team?" AJ asked, thinking now he'd heard just about everything. The only time the people in L.A. saw the sheriff was when something bad happened and he was needed to make a statement on TV.

"Yes, and we're on the team and bring home the trophies every year. If you're good he might let you join."

AJ shrugged, not wanting to be around the sheriff any more than he had to. "No thanks, I don't want to join," he said. "Well, I've got to go, since I can't be late."

"How long do you have to go there?" Morris asked, standing aside to let AJ get to his bike.

"The rest of the week, so I'll be free to ride home with you guys starting Monday if you still want me to," AJ said, getting on his bike.

"Yes," Cornelius answered. "We'll still want you to. What about this weekend? Will your parents let you go look at the deer with us this weekend? Usually Mr. Miller gives his permission for us to come on his property as long as we don't get into any trouble."

AJ was doubtful. "I'll let you know tomorrow if I can go. My mom is kind of protective. She doesn't like me going too far from home."

Morris and Cornelius nodded in understanding. "Our moms are that way, too," Morris said. "But everyone around here knows the Millers. Your mom can ask the sheriff about them if she wants. They're nice people."

"Do you want to ride to school with us tomorrow?" Cornelius asked anxiously. "We meet at Kate's Diner every morning at seven-thirty, and she gives us a carton of chocolate milk free as long as we're good in school."

"Free chocolate milk? Hey, I'd like that. I'll see you guys in the morning." AJ put his bike into gear and headed for the sheriff's office, determined not to be late for a second time.

Chapter 6

Her mouth still knew him.

A multitude of emotions tightened Dare's chest as he sat at his desk and thought about the kiss he and Shelly had shared. Very slowly and very deliberately, he took his finger and rubbed it across his lips, lips that a few hours ago had tasted sweetness of the most gut-wrenching kind. It was the kind of sweetness that made you crave something so delightful and pleasurable that it could become habit forming.

But what got to him more than anything was the fact that even after ten years, her mouth still knew him. That much was evident in the way her lips had molded to his, the familiarity of the way she had parted her mouth and the ease in which his tongue had slid inside, staking a claim he hadn't known he had a right to make until he had felt her response.

He leaned back in the chair. When it came to responding to him, that was something Shelly could never hold back from doing. He'd always gotten the greatest pleasure and enjoyment from hearing the sound of her purring in bed. He used to know just what areas on her body to touch, to caress and to taste. Often, all it took was a look, him simply meeting her gaze with deep desire and longing in his eyes, and she would release an indrawn sigh that let him know she knew just what he wanted and what he considered necessary. Those had been the times he hadn't been able to keep his hands off her, and now it seemed, ten years later, he still couldn't. And it didn't help matters any that she had kissed him as though there hadn't been another man inside her mouth in the ten years they'd been apart. Her mouth had ached for his, demanded everything his tongue could deliver, and he'd given it all, holding nothing back. He could have kept on kissing her for days.

Dare ran his hand over his face trying to see if doing so would help him retain his senses. Kissing Shelly had affected him greatly. His body had been aching and throbbing since then, and the painful thing was that he didn't see any relief in sight.

Over the past ten years he had dated a number of women. His sister Delaney had even painted him and his brothers as womanizers. But he felt that was as far from the truth as it could be. After he and Shelly had broken up, he'd been very selective about what women he wanted in his bed. For years he had looked for Shelly's replacement, only to discover such a woman didn't exist. He hadn't met a woman who would hold a light to her, and he'd accepted that and moved on. The women he'd slept with had been there for the thrill, the adventure, but all he'd gotten was the agony of defeat upon realizing that none could make him feel in bed the way he'd always felt with Shelly. Oh, he had experienced pleasure, but not the kind that made you pound your chest with your fists and holler out for more. Not the kind that compelled you to go ahead and remain inside her body since another orgasm was there on the horizon. And not the kind you could still shudder from days later, just thinking about it.

He could only get those feelings with Shelly.

Closing his eyes, Dare remembered how she had broken off their kiss and the words she'd said before he'd left her house. *"You're AJ's father, but what was between us is over and has been for years. To me you're just another man."*

He sighed deeply and reopened his eyes. If Shelly believed that then she was wrong. Granted, AJ was their main concern, but what she didn't know and what he wouldn't tell her just yet was that his mission also included her. He hadn't realized until she had walked into his office two days ago that his life had been without direction for ten years. Seeing her, finding out about AJ and knowing that he and Shelly were still attracted to each other made him want something he thought he would never have again.

Peace and happiness.

The buzzer interrupted his thoughts. Leaning forward he pushed the button for the speakerphone. "Yeah, Holly, what is it?"

"That Brockman kid is here, Sheriff. Do you want me to send him in?"

Dare again sighed deeply. "Yes, send him in."

Dare felt AJ watching him. The kid had been doing so off and on since he'd finished the chores he'd been assigned and had come into his office to sit at a table in the corner and finish his homework.

Dare had sat behind his desk, reading over various reports. The only sound in the room was AJ turning the pages of his science book and Dare shuffling the pages of the report. More than once Dare had glanced up and caught the kid looking at him, as if he were a puzzle he was trying to figure out. As soon as he'd been caught staring, the kid had quickly lowered his eyes.

Dare wondered what was going through AJ's mind now that he knew he was his father? The only reason Dare could come up with as to why he'd been studying him so intently was that he was trying to find similarities in their features. They were there. Even Holly had noticed them, although she hadn't said anything, merely moving her gaze between Dare and AJ several times before comprehension appeared on her face.

Dare glanced up and caught AJ staring again and decided to address the issue. "Is something wrong?" he asked.

AJ glanced up from his science book and glared at him. "What makes you think something is wrong?"

Dare shrugged. "Because I've caught you staring several times today like I've suddenly grown two heads or something."

He saw the corners of AJ lips being forced not to smile. "I hate being here. Why couldn't I just go home after I finished everything I had to do instead of hanging around here?"

"Because your punishment was to come here for an hour after school and I intend to get my hour. Besides, if I let you leave earlier, you might think I'm turning soft."

"That will be the day," AJ mumbled.

Dare chuckled and went back to reading his reports.

"Is Thorn Westmoreland really your brother?"

Dare lifted his head and gazed back across the room at

AJ. My brother and your uncle, he wanted to say. Instead he responded by asking, "Who told you that?"

AJ shrugged. "Morris and Cornelius."

Dare nodded. He knew Morris and Cornelius. The two youngsters usually hung together and were the same age and went to the same school as AJ. "So you know Morris and Cornelius?"

AJ turned the page on his book before answering, pretending the response was being forced from him. "Yeah, I know them. We met today after school."

Dare nodded again. Morris and Cornelius were good kids. He knew their parents well and was glad the pair were developing a friendship with AJ, since he considered them a good influence. Both got good grades in school, sung in the youth choir at church and were active in a number of sports he and his brothers coached.

"Well, is he?"

Dare heard the anxiousness in AJ's voice, although the kid was trying to downplay it. "Yes, Thorn's my brother."

"And Rock Mason is, too?"

"Yes. I told you the other day I had four brothers and all of them live in this area."

AJ nodded. "And they help you coach your baseball team?"

Dare leaned back in his chair. "Yes, pretty much, although Thorn contributes to the youth of the community by teaching a special class at the high school on motorcycle safety and Stone is involved with the Teach People to Read program for both the young and old."

AJ nodded again. "What about the other two?"

Dare wondered at what point AJ would discover they were holding a conversation and revert back to his I-don't-like-cops syndrome. Well, until he did, Dare planned to milk the situation for all it was worth. "Chase owns a restaurant and coaches a youth basketball team during basketball season. His team won the state championship two years in a row."

Dare smiled when he thought of his younger brother Storm. "My youngest brother Storm hasn't found his niche yet." *Other than with women,* Dare decided not to add. "So he helps me coach my baseball team and he also helps Chase with his basketball team."

"And your sister married a prince?"

Dare's smile widened when he thought of the baby sister he and his brothers simply adored. "Yes, although at the time we weren't ready to give her up."

AJ's eyes grew wider. "Why? Girls don't marry princes every day."

Dare chuckled. "Yes, that may be true, but the Westmorelands have this unspoken code when it comes to family. We stick together and claim what's ours. Since Delaney was the only girl, we claimed her when she was born and weren't ready to give her up to anyone, including a prince."

AJ turned a few pages again, pretending further disinterest. A few moments later he asked, "What about your parents?"

Dare met AJ's stare. "What about them?"

"Do they live around here?"

"Yes, they live within walking distance. Their only complaint is that none of us, other than Delaney, have gotten married. They're anxious for grandkids and since they don't see Delaney's baby that often, they would like one of us to settle down and have a family."

Dare knew that what he'd just shared with AJ would get the kid to thinking. He was about to say something else when the buzzer on his desk sounded.

"Yes, McKade, what is it?"

"Ms. Brockman is here to see you."

Dare was surprised. He hadn't expected Shelly to drop by, since AJ had ridden his bike over from school. A quick glance across the room and he could tell by AJ's features that he was surprised by his mother's unexpected visit as well. "Send her in, McKade."

Dare stood as Shelly breezed into his office, dressed in a skirt and a printed blouse. "I hate to drop in like this, but I received an emergency call from one of my patients living in Stone Mountain and need to go out on a call. Ms. Kate has agreed to take care of AJ, and I have to drop him off at her place on my way out. I thought coming to pick him up would be okay since his hour is over."

Dare glanced at the clock on the wall which indicated AJ's hour had been over ten minutes ago. At some point the kid had stopped watching the clock and so had he.

"Since you're in a rush, I can save you the time by dropping him off at Ms. Kate's myself. I was getting ready to leave anyway."

Dare then remembered that since tonight was Wednesday night, his parents' usual routine was to have dinner with their five sons at Chase's restaurant before going to prayer meeting at church. He knew his family would love meeting AJ, and since they'd been told of his and Shelly's strategy about AJ knowing Dare was his father, there was no risk of someone giving anything away.

"And I have another idea," he said, meeting Shelly's gaze, trying not to notice how beautiful her eyes were, how beautiful she was, period. Just being in the same room with her had his mouth watering. She stood in the middle of his office silhouetted by the light coming in through his window and he thought he hadn't seen anything that looked this good in a long time.

"What?" she asked, interrupting his thoughts.

"AJ is probably hungry and I was on my way to Chase's restaurant where my family is dining tonight. He's welcome to join us, and I can drop him off at Ms. Kate's later."

Shelly nodded. Evidently Dare felt he'd made some headway with AJ for him to suggest such a thing. She glanced across the room at AJ who had his eyes glued to his book, pretending not have heard Dare's comment, although she knew that he had.

"AJ, Dare has invited you to dine with his family before dropping you off at Ms. Kate's. All right?"

It seemed AJ stared at her for an endless moment, as if weighing her words. He then shifted his gaze to Dare, and Shelly felt the sudden clash of two very strong personalities, two strong-willed individuals, two people who were outright stubborn. But then she saw something else, something that made her breath catch and her heart do a flip—two individuals who, for whatever reason, were silently agreeing to a give a little, at least for this one particular time.

AJ then shifted his gaze back to her. He shrugged. "Whatever."

Shelly let out a deep sigh. "Okay, then, I'll see you later." She walked across the room to place a kiss on AJ's forehead; ignoring the frown he gave her. "Behave yourself tonight," she admonished.

She turned and smiled at Dare before walking out of his office.

"The only reason I decided to come with you is because I want to meet Thorn Westmoreland. I think he is so cool," AJ said, and then turned his attention back to the scenery outside the vehicle's window.

Instead of using the police cruiser, Dare had decided

to drive his truck instead, the Chevy Avalanche he'd purchased a month ago. He glanced over at AJ when he brought the vehicle to a stop at a traffic light. He couldn't help but chuckle. "I figured as much, but you won't be the first kid who tried getting on my good side just to meet Thorn."

AJ scowled. "I'm not trying to get on your good side," he mumbled.

Dare chuckled again. "Oh, sorry. My mistake."

For the next couple of miles the inside of the vehicle was quiet as Dare navigated through evening traffic with complete ease.

"So, how was your day at school?" Dare decided to ask when the vehicle finally came to a complete standstill as he attempted to get on the interstate.

AJ glanced over at him. "It had its moments."

Dare smiled. "What kind of moments?"

AJ glared. "Why are you asking me all these questions?"

Dare met his gaze. "Because I'm interested."

AJ's glare deepened. "Are you interested in me or in my mother? I saw the way you were looking at her."

Dare decided the kid was too observant, although he was falling in nicely with their plans. "And what way was I looking at her?"

"One of those man-like-woman looks."

Dare chuckled, never having heard it phrased quite that way before. "What do you know about a man-like-woman look?"

"I wasn't born yesterday."

"Not for one minute did I think you had been." After a few moments he glanced back at AJ. "Did you know your mom used to be my girlfriend some years back?"

"So?"

"So, I thought you should know."

"Why?"

"Because she was very special to me then."

When Dare exited off the interstate, AJ spoke. "That was back then. My mother doesn't need a boyfriend, if that's what you're thinking."

Dare gave his son a smile when he brought the vehicle to a stop at a traffic light. "What I think, AJ, is that you should let your mom make her own decisions about those kinds of things."

AJ glared at him. "I don't like you."

Dare shrugged and gave his son a smile. "Then I guess that means nothing has changed." But he knew something *had* changed. As far as he was concerned, AJ consenting to go to dinner with him to meet his family was a major breakthrough. And although the kid claimed that Thorn was the only reason he was going, Dare had no problem using his brother to his advantage if that's what it took. Besides, AJ would soon discover that of all the Westmorelands, Thorn was the one who was biggest on family ties and devotion, and if you accepted one Westmoreland, you basically accepted them all, since they were just that thick.

At that moment Dare's cell phone rang and he answered it. After a few remarks and nods of his head, he said, "You're welcome to join us for dinner if you'd like. I know for a fact that everyone would love to see you." He nodded again and said, "All right. I'll see you later.

Moments later he glanced over at AJ when they came to a stop in front of Chase's restaurant. "That was your mother. The emergency wasn't as bad as she'd thought, and she is on her way back home. I'm to take you there after dinner instead of to Ms. Kate's house."

AJ narrowed his eyes at Dare. "Why did you do that?"

"Do what?" Dare asked, lifting a brow.

"Invite her to dinner?"

"Because I figured that like you, she has to eat sometime, and I know that my family would have loved seeing her again." He hesitated for a few moments, then added, "And I would have liked seeing her again myself. Like I said, your mom used to mean a lot to me a long time ago."

Their gazes locked for a brief moment, then AJ glared at him and said angrily, "Get over it."

Dare smiled slightly. "I don't know if I can." Before AJ had time to make a comeback, Dare unsnapped his seat belt. "Come on, it's time to go inside."

Shelly pulled onto the interstate, hoping and praying that AJ was on his best behavior. No matter what, she had to believe that all the lessons in obedience, honor and respect that he'd been taught at an early age were somewhere buried beneath all that hostility he exhibited at times. But right now she had to cope with the fact that he was still a child, a child who was getting older each day and enduring growing pains of the worst kind. But one thing was for certain, Dare was capable of dealing with it, and for that she was grateful.

When she thought of Dare, she had no choice but to think of her traitorous body and the way it had responded to him earlier that day at her house. As she'd told AJ, Dare was smart. He was also very receptive, and she knew he had picked up on the fact that she had wanted him. All it had taken was one mindblowing kiss and she'd been ready to get naked if he'd asked.

When she came to a traffic light she momentarily closed her eyes, asking for strength where Dare was concerned. If she allowed him to become a part of her life, she could be asking for potential heartbreak all over again, although she had to admit the new Dare seemed more settled, less likely to go chasing after some other dream. But whatever the two of them had once shared was in the past, and she refused to bring it to the present. She had enough to deal with in handling AJ without trying to take on his father, too.

She had to continue to make it clear to Dare that it was his son he needed to work on and win over and not her. Their first and foremost concern was AJ, and no matter how hot and bothered she got around Dare, she would not give in again. She had to watch her steps and not put any ideas into Dare's head. More than anything, she had to stop looking at him and thinking about sex.

Her body was doing a good job reminding her that ten years was a long time to go without. She'd been too busy for the abstinence to cross her mind, but today Dare had awakened desires she'd thought were long buried. Now she felt that her body was under attack—against her. It was demanding things she had no intention of delivering.

Her breath caught and she felt her nipples tingle as she again thought about the kiss they had shared. Once more she prayed for the strength and fortitude to deal with Alisdare Julian Westmoreland.

Chapter 7

"Dad, Mom, I'd like you to meet AJ. He's Shelly's boy." Dare knew his father wouldn't give anything away, but he wasn't so convinced about his mother as he saw the play of emotions that crossed her features. She was looking into the face of a grandson she hadn't known she'd had; a grandson she was very eager to claim.

Luckily for Dare, his father understood the strategy that he and Shelly were using with AJ and spoke up before his wife had a chance to react to the emotions she was trying to hold inside. "You're a fine-looking young man, but I would expect no less coming from Shelly." He reached out and touched AJ's shoulder and smiled. "I'm glad you're joining us for dinner. How's your mother?"

"She's fine," AJ said quietly, bowing his head and studying his shoes.

Dare wondered what kind of docile act the kid was performing, but then another part of him wondered if when taken out of his comfort zone, AJ had a tendency to feel uneasy around people he didn't know. Dare recalled a conversation he'd had with Shelly about AJ not being all that outgoing.

When Dare saw Thorn enter the restaurant he beckoned him over saying, "Thorn, I'd like you to meet someone. From what I gather, he's a big fan of yours."

AJ's mouth literally fell open and the size of his eyes increased. He tilted his head back to gaze up at the man towering over him. "Wow! You're Thorn Westmoreland!"

Thorn gave a slow grin. "Yes, I'm Thorn Westmoreland. Now who might you be?"

To Dare's surprise, AJ grinned right back. It was the first look of happiness he'd seen on his son's face, and a part of him regretted he hadn't been the one to put it there.

"I'm AJ Brockman."

Thorn tapped his chin with his finger a couple of times as if thinking about something. "Brockman. Brockman. I used to know a Shelly Brockman some years ago. In fact she used to be Dare's girlfriend. Are you related to that Brockman?"

"Yes, I'm her son."

Thorn chuckled. "Well, I'll be," he said, pretending he didn't already know that fact. "And how's your mother?"

"She's fine."

At that moment Dare looked up and saw his other brothers enter. More introductions were made, and, just like Thorn, they pretended they were surprised to see AJ, and no one gave anything away about knowing he was Dare's son.

When they all sat down to eat, with AJ sitting between Thorn and Dare, it was obvious to anyone who cared to notice that the boy was definitely a Westmoreland.

* * *

Shelly put aside the novel she'd been reading when she heard the doorbell ring. A glance out the peephole confirmed it was AJ, but he wasn't alone. Dare had walked him to the door, and with good reason. AJ was half asleep and barely standing on his feet.

She quickly opened the door to AJ's mumblings. "I told you I could walk to the door myself without your help," he was saying none too happily.

"Yeah, and I would have watched you fall on your face, too," was Dare's response.

Shelly stepped aside and let them both enter. "How was dinner?" she asked, closing the door behind them.

AJ didn't answer, instead he continued walking and headed for the stairs. She gave a quick glance to Dare, who was watching AJ as he tried maneuvering the stairs. "That kid is so sleepy he can't think straight," he said. "You might want to help him before he falls and breaks his neck. I would do it, but I think he's had enough of me for one evening."

Shelly nodded, then quickly provided AJ a shoulder to lean on while he climbed the stairs.

Dare moved to stand at the foot of the stairs and watched Shelly and AJ until they were no longer in sight. He sighed deeply, thinking how his adrenaline had pumped up when Shelly had opened the door. She'd been wearing the same outfit she'd worn to his office that evening, and his gaze had been glued to her backside all the while she'd moved up the stairs, totally appreciating the sway of her hips and the way the skirt intermittently slid up her thighs with each upward step she took.

He thought that he would do just about anything to be able to follow right behind her and tumble her straight into bed, but he knew that wasn't possible, especially with

AJ in the house. Not to mention the fact that she was still acting rather cautiously around him.

He knew it would probably take her a while to get AJ ready for bed, and since he didn't intend leaving until they had talked, he decided to sit on the sofa and wait for her. He picked up the book she'd been reading, Stone's most recent bestseller, and smiled, thinking it was a co-incidence that he was reading the same book.

Making sure he kept the spot where she'd stopped reading marked, he flipped a couple of chapters ahead and picked up where he'd left off last night before sleep had overtaken him.

Shelly paused on the middle stair when she noticed Dare sitting on her sofa reading the book she had begun reading earlier that day. She couldn't help noticing that her living room appeared quiet and seductive, and the light from a floor lamp next to where he sat illuminated his features and created an alluring scene that was too enticing to ignore.

She silently studied him for a long time, wondering just how many peaceful moments he was used to getting as sheriff. He looked comfortable, relaxed and just plain sexy as sin. His features were calm, yet she could tell by the way his eyes were glued to the page that he was deeply absorbed in the action-thriller novel his brother had written.

He shifted in his seat while turning the page and crossed one leg over the other. She knew they were strong legs, sturdy legs, legs that had held her body in place while his had pumped relentlessly into her, legs that had nudged hers apart again when he wanted a second round and a third.

Swallowing at the memory, she felt her heart rate increase, and decided the best way to handle Dare was to send him home—real quicklike. She didn't think she could handle another episode like the one they had shared earlier that day.

He must have heard the sound of her heavy breathing, or maybe she had let out a deep moan without realizing she'd uttered a single word. Something definitely gave her away, and she felt heat pool between her legs when he lifted his gaze from the book and looked at her. It wasn't just an ordinary look either. It was a hot look, a definite scorcher and a blatant, I-want-to-take-you-to-bed look.

She blinked, thinking she had misread the look, but then she knew she hadn't. He wouldn't say the words out loud, but he definitely wanted her to know what he was thinking. She breathed in deeply. Dare was trouble and she was determined to send him packing.

He stood when she took the last few steps down the stairs. "He's out like a light," she said quietly when he came to stand in front of her. "I could barely get him in the shower and in bed without him falling asleep again. Thanks for taking him to dinner and for making sure he got back home."

Shelly paused, knowing she had just said a mouthful, but she wasn't through yet. "I know you've had a busy day today and need your rest as much as I do, so I'll see you out now. In fact you didn't have to wait around for me to finish upstairs."

"Yes, I did."

She stared at him. "Why?"

"I thought you'd want to know how tonight went."

Shelly inwardly groaned. Of course she wanted to know how tonight went, but she'd been so intent on getting Dare out the door she had forgotten to ask. "Yes, of course. Did he behave himself? How did he take to your family?"

Dare glanced up at the top of the stairs then returned his gaze to her. "Is there somewhere we can talk privately?"

The first place Shelly thought about was the kitchen, and then she remembered what had happened between them earlier that day. She decided the best place to talk would be outside on the porch. That way he would definitely be out of the house. "We can talk outside on the porch," she said, moving in that direction.

Without waiting for his response, she took the few steps to the door and stepped outside.

The night air was crisp and clear. The first thing Shelly noticed was the full moon in the sky, and the next was the zillions of stars that sparkled like diamonds surrounding it. She went to stand next to a porch post, since it was the best spot for the glow of light from the moon. The last thing she needed was to stand in some dark area of the porch with Dare.

She heard him behind her when he joined her, however, instead of standing with her in the light, he went and sat in the porch swing that was located in a darkened corner. She sucked in a breath. If he thought for one minute that she would join him in that swing, he had another thought coming. As far as she was concerned, they could converse just fine right where they were.

"So how did AJ behave tonight?" she asked, deciding to plunge right in, since there was no reason to prolong the moment.

She heard the swing's slow rocking when he replied, "To my surprise, very well. In fact, his manners were impeccable, but then it was obvious that he was trying to impress Thorn." Dare chuckled. "He pretty much tried ignoring me, but my brothers picked up on what he was doing and wrecked those plans. Whenever he tried excluding me from the conversation, they counteracted and included me. Pretty soon he gave up, after finding out the hard way an important lesson about the Westmorelands."

"Which is?"

"We stick together, no matter what."

Shelly nodded. She'd known that from previous years.

"But I must admit there was this one time when they were ready to disclaim me as their brother," Dare said, chuckling.

Shelly rested her back against the post and crossed her legs. "And what time was that?"

"The night I ended things with you. They thought I was crazy to give you up for any reason. And that included a career."

She nervously rubbed her hands up and down her arms, not wanting to talk about what used to be between them. "Well, all that's in the past, Dare. Is there anything else about tonight I should know?" she asked, trying to keep their conversation moving along.

"Yes, there is something else."

She sought out his features, but could barely make them out in the darkened corner of the porch. "What?"

"I gave AJ reason to believe that I'm interested in you again."

Shelly nodded. "And how did he handle that?"

Dare smiled. "He had something to say about it, if that's what you're asking. Just how far he'll go to make sure nothing develops between us I can't rightly say."

Shelly nodded again. Neither could she. Personally, she thought AJ's dislike of Dare was a phase he was going through, but a very important phase in his life, and she didn't want to do anything to make things worse with him. "In that case, more than likely he'll have a talk with me about it."

Dare leaned back against the swing. "And what do you plan to say when he does?"

Shelly sighed. "Basically, everything we agreed I should say. I'm to let him know he's the one who has a beef with you, not me, and therefore I don't have a problem with reestablishing our relationship."

Dare heard her words. Although they were fabricated for AJ's benefit, they sounded pretty damn good to him, and he wished they were true, because he certainly didn't have a problem reestablishing anything with her.

He looked over at Shelly and saw how she leaned against the post while silhouetted by the glow from the moon. His gaze zeroed in on the fact that she stood with her legs crossed. Tight. She had once told him that she had a tendency to stand with her legs crossed really tight whenever she felt a deep throbbing ache between them. Evidently she had forgotten sharing that piece of information with him some years ago.

"Well, if that about covers everything, then we'd best call it a night."

Her words interrupted his thought, and he figured they could do better than just call it a night. Calling it a "night of seduction" sounded more to his liking. Some inner part of him wanted to know if she wanted him as much as he wanted her, and there was only one way to find out.

"Come sit with me for a while, Shelly," he said, his voice husky.

Shelly swallowed and met his gaze. "I don't think that's a good idea, Dare."

"I do. It's a beautiful night and I think we should enjoy it before saying good-night."

Enjoy it or enjoy each other? Shelly was tempted to

ask, but decided she wouldn't go there with Dare. Once he got her in that swing that would be the end of it. Or the beginning of it, depending on the way you looked at it. Her body was responding to him in the most unsettled and provocative way tonight. All he had to do was to touch her one time and...

"Let me give you what you need, Shelly."

He saw her chin lift defiantly, and he saw the way she frowned at him. "And what makes you think that you know what I need?"

"Your legs."

She raised a confused brow. "What about my legs?"

"They're crossed, and pretty damn tight."

Shelly's heart missed a beat and the throbbing between her legs increased. He had remembered. A long, seemingly endless moment of silence stretched out between them. She could see his features. They were as tight as her legs were crossed. And the gaze that held hers was like a magnet, drawing her in, second by tantalizing second.

She shook her head, trying to deny her body what it wanted, what it evidently needed, but it had a mind of its own and wasn't adhering to any protest she was making. The man sitting on the swing watching her, waiting for her, had a history of being able to pleasure her in every possible way. He knew it and she knew it as well.

Breathing deeply, she found herself slowly crossing the porch toward him, out of the light and into the darkness, out from temptation and into a straight path that led to seduction. She came to a stop between his spread knees and when their legs touched, she sucked in a deep breath at the same time she heard him suck in one, too. And when she felt his hand reach under her skirt skimming her inner thigh, her knees almost turned to mush.

His voice was husky and ultrasexy when he spoke. "This morning I had to know if your mouth still knew me. Now I want to find out if this," he said, gliding his warm hand upward, boldly touching the crotch of her panties, "knows me as well."

Her eyes fluttered closed and she automatically reached out and placed both hands on his shoulders for support. A part of her wanted to scream Yes! Her body knew him as the last man...the only man...to stake a claim in this territory, but she was incapable of speech. All she could do was stand there and wait to see what would happen next and hope she could handle it.

She didn't have to wait long; the tips of Dare's fingers slowly began massaging the essence of her as he relentlessly stroked his hand over the center of her panties.

"You're hot, Shelly," he said, his voice huskier than before. "Sit down in my lap facing me."

Dare had to move his body forward then sideways for her to accommodate his request. The arrangement brought her face just inches from his. His hand was still between her legs.

He leaned forward and captured her mouth, giving her a kiss that made the one they'd shared that morning seem complacent. Her senses became frenzied and aroused, and the feel of his hand stroking her only added to her turmoil. And when she felt his fingers inch past the edge of her bikini panties, she released a deep moan.

"Yeah, baby, that's the sound I want to hear," he said after releasing her lips. "Open your legs a little wider and tell me how you like this."

Before she could completely comply with his request, he slid three fingers inside her, and when he found that too tight a fit, backed out and went with two. "You're pretty snug in there, baby," he whispered as his fingers began moving in and out of her in a rhythm meant to drive her insane. "How do you like this?"

"I love it," she whispered, clenching his shoulders with her hands. "Oh, Dare, it's been so long."

He leaned closer and traced the tips of her lips with his tongue before moving to nibble at her ear. She was about to go up in smoke, and he couldn't help but wonder how long it had been for her, since this was making her come apart so quickly and easily. He asked, "How long has it been, Shelly?"

She met his gaze and drew in a trembling breath. "Not since you, Dare."

His fingers went still; his jaw tightened and his gaze locked with hers. "You mean that you haven't done this since we…"

She didn't let him finish as she closed her mouth over his, snatching his words and his next breath in the process. But the thought that no other man had touched her since him sent his mind escalating, his entire body trembling. No wonder her legs had been crossed so tightly and he intended to make it good for her.

His fingers began moving inside her again and her muscles automatically clenched around them. She was tight and wet and the scent of her arousal was driving him insane. He broke off the kiss, desperately needing to taste her.

"Unbutton your top, Shelly."

She released her hands from his shoulders and slowly unbuttoned her blouse, then unsnapped the front opening of her bra. As soon as her breasts poured forth, looming before him, he began sucking, nibbling and licking his way to heaven. He moved his fingers within her using the same rhythm his tongue was using on her breasts.

He felt the moment her body shook and placed his

mouth over hers to absorb her moans of pleasure when spasms tore into her. Her fingernails dug into his shoulders as he continued using his fingers to pleasure her. And when it started all over again, and more spasms rammed through her, signaling a second orgasm, she pulled her mouth from his, closed her eyes and leaned forward to his chest, crying out into the cotton of his shirt.

"That's it, baby, let go and enjoy."

And as another turbulent wave of pleasure ripped through her and she fought to catch her breath, Shelly let go and enjoyed every single moment of what Dare was doing to her.

And she doubted that after tonight her life would ever be the same.

Chapter 8

"Mom? Mom? Are you okay?"

Shelly heard the sound of AJ's voice as he tried gently to shake her awake.

"Mom, wake up. Please say something."

She quickly opened her eyes when her mind registered the panic in his tone. She blinked, feeling dazed and disoriented, and tried to focus on him, but at the moment she felt completely wrung out. "AJ? What are you doing out of bed?"

Confusion appeared in his face. "Mom, I'm supposed to be out of bed. It's morning and I have to go to school today. You forgot to wake me up. And why did you sleep on the sofa all night in the same clothes you had on yesterday?"

Somehow, Shelly found the strength to sit up. She yawned, feeling bone-tired. "It's morning already?" The last thing she remembered was having her fourth or-

gasm in Dare's arms and slumping against him without
any strength left even to hold up her head. He must have
brought her into the house and placed her on the sofa,
thinking she would eventually come around and go up
the stairs. Instead, exhausted, depleted and totally satisfied, she had slept through the night.

"Mom, are you all right?"

She met AJ's concerned gaze. He had no idea just
how all right she was. Dare had given her just what her
body had needed. She had forgotten just what an ace he
was with his fingers on a certain part of her. "Yes, AJ,
I'm fine." She glanced at the coffee table and noticed the
book both she and Dare had been reading and considered
it the perfect alibi. "I must have fallen asleep reading.
What time is it? You aren't late are you?" She leaned back
against the sofa's cushions. After a night like last night,
she could curl up and sleep for the entire day.

"No, I'm not late, but you might be if you have to go
to work today."

Shelly shook her head. "I only have a couple of patients I need to see, and I hadn't planned on going anywhere until around ten." She decided not to mention that
she was also having lunch with Dare's brothers today.
She yawned again. "What would you like for breakfast?"

He shrugged. "I'll just have a bowl of cereal. I met
these two guys at school yesterday and we're meeting up
to ride our bikes together."

Shelly nodded. She hoped AJ hadn't associated himself with the wrong group again. "Who are these boys?"

"Morris Sears and Cornelius Thomas. And we're
going to meet at Kate's Diner every morning for chocolate milk." As an afterthought he added. "And it's free if
we let her know we've been good in school."

Shelly made a mental note to ask Dare about Morris

and Cornelius when she saw him again. Being sheriff he probably knew if the two were troublemakers.

"They're real cool guys and they like my bike," AJ went on to say. "Yesterday they told me all about the sheriff and his brothers." His eyes grew wide. "Why didn't you tell me that Thorn Westmoreland is my uncle?"

"Because he's not."

At AJ's confused frown, Shelly decided to explain. "Until you accept Dare as your father you can't claim any of the Westmorelands as your uncles."

AJ glared. "That doesn't seem fair."

"And why doesn't it? You're the one who doesn't want Dare knowing he's your father, so how can you tell anyone that Thorn and the others are your uncles without explaining the connection? Until you decide differently, to the Westmorelands you're just another kid."

She stood. "Now, I'm going upstairs to shower while you eat breakfast."

AJ nodded as he slowly walked out of the room and headed for the kitchen. Shelly knew she had given him something to think about.

"Is it true?" Morris asked excitedly the moment AJ got off his bike at Ms. Kate's Diner.

AJ raised a brow. "Is what true?"

It was Cornelius who answered, his wide, blue eyes expressive. "That you had dinner with the sheriff and his family last night?"

AJ shrugged, wondering how they knew that. "Yeah, so what about it?"

"We think it's cool, that's what about it. The sheriff is the bomb. He makes sure everyone in this town is safe at night. My mom and dad say so," Cornelius responded without wasting any time.

AJ and the two boys opened the door and walked into the diner. "How did you know I had dinner with the sheriff?" he asked as they walked up to the counter where cartons of chocolate milk had been placed for them.

"Mr. and Mrs. Turner saw all of you and called my grandmother who then called my mom and dad. Everyone was wondering who you were and I told my mom that you were a kid who got in trouble and had to report to the sheriff's office after school every day. They thought you were a family member or something, but I told them you weren't."

AJ nodded. "My mom had to go to work unexpectedly last night and the sheriff offered to take me to dinner with him since I hadn't eaten."

"Wow! That was real nice of him, wasn't it?"

AJ hadn't really thought about it being an act of kindness and said, "Yeah, I guess so."

"Do you think he'll mind if we go with you to his office after school?" Morris asked excitedly.

AJ scrunched his face, thinking. "I guess not, but he might put you to work."

Morris shrugged. "That's all right if he does. I just want him to tell us about the time he was an FBI agent and did that undercover stuff to catch the bad guys."

AJ nodded. He didn't want to admit it, but he wouldn't mind hearing about that himself. He smiled when the nice lady behind the counter handed them each a donut to go along with their milk.

Shelly's hands tightened on the steering wheel after she brought her car to a stop next to the police cruiser marked Sheriff. She'd had no idea Dare would be joining his brothers for lunch. How would she manage a straight face around him and not let anyone know they had spent close to an hour in a darkened area of her porch last night doing something deliriously naughty?

She opened the car door and took a deep breath, thinking that the things Dare had done to her had turned her inside out and whetted her appetite. To put it more bluntly, sixteen hours later she was still aroused. After having gone without sex for so long she now felt downright hungry. In fact *starving* was a better word to use. Would Dare look at her and detect her sexually excited state? If anyone could, it would be Dare, a man who'd once known her better than she'd known herself.

And to think she'd even admitted to him that she hadn't slept with another soul since their breakup ten years ago. Now that he knew, she had to keep her head on straight and keep Dare's focus on AJ and not her.

With a deep sigh she opened the door and went inside.

She paused and watched all five men stand the moment she entered the restaurant. They must have seen her drive up and were ready to greet her. Tears burned the back of her eyes. It had been too long. When she'd been Dare's girlfriend, the brothers had claimed her as an honorary sister, and since she'd been an only child, she'd held that attachment very dear. One of the hardest things about leaving College Park had been knowing that in addition to leaving Dare she'd also left behind a family she had grown very close to.

As she looked at them now, she began to smile. They stood in a line as if awaiting royalty and she walked up to them, one by one. "Thorn," she said to the one closest to Dare in age. She gladly accepted the kiss he boldly placed on her lips and the hug he fondly gave her.

"Ten years is a long time to be gone, Shelly," he said with a serious expression on his face. "Don't try it again."

She couldn't help but smile upon seeing that he was bossy as ever. "I won't, Thorn."

She then moved to Stone, the first Westmoreland she had come to know; the one who had introduced her to Dare. Without saying a word she reached for him, hugging him tightly. After they released each other, he placed a kiss on her lips as well.

"I'm so proud of your accomplishments, Stone," she said, smiling through her tears. "And I buy every book you write."

He chuckled. "Thanks, Shell." His face then grew serious. "And I ditto what Thorn said. Don't leave again." His gaze momentarily left hers and shifted to where Dare was standing. He glared at his brother before returning his gaze to hers and added, "No matter what the reason."

She nodded. "All right."

Then came the twins, who were a year younger than she. She remembered them getting into all sorts of mischief, and from the gleams in their eyes, it was evident they were still up to no good. After they both placed chaste pecks on her lips, Storm said, smiling. "We told Dare that he blew his chance with you, which means you're now available for us."

Shelly grinned. "Oh, am I?"

"Yeah, if you want to be," Chase said, teasingly, giving her another hug.

When Chase released her she drew a deep breath. Next came Dare.

"Dare," she acknowledged softly, nervously.

She figured since she'd already been in his company a few times, not to mention what they had done together last night, that he would not make a big production of seeing her. She soon discovered just how wrong that assumption was when he gently pulled her into his arms and captured her lips, nearly taking her breath in the process. There was nothing chaste about the kiss he gave her and she knew it had intentionally lasted long enough to cause his brothers to speculate and to give anyone who saw them kiss something to talk about.

When he released her mouth, it was Stone who decided to make light of what Dare had done by saying, "What was that about, Dare? Were you trying to prove to Shelly that you could still kiss?"

Dare answered as his gaze held hers. He smiled at Stone's comment and said, "Yeah, something like that."

Shelly never had problems getting through a meal before. But then she'd never had the likes of Dare Westmoreland on a mission to seduce her. And it didn't matter that she was sitting at a table in a restaurant next to him, surrounded by his brothers, or that the place was filled to lunch-crowd capacity.

She took several deep breaths to calm her racing heart, but it did nothing to soothe the ache throbbing through her. It all started when she caught herself staring at his hand as he lifted a water goblet to his lips. Seeing his fingers had reminded her how she had whimpered her way into ecstasy as those same fingers had stroked away ten years of sexual frustration.

She had caught his eyes dark with desire, over the water glass, and had realized he had read her thoughts. And, as smooth as silk, when he placed the glass down he took that same hand and without calling attention to what he was doing, placed it under the table on her thigh.

At first she'd almost jerked at the cool feel of his hand, then she'd relaxed when his hand just rested on her thigh without moving. But then, moments later, she had almost gasped when his hand moved to settle firmly between her legs. And amidst all conversations going on around them, as the brothers tried to bring her up to date on what had been going on in their lives over the past ten years, no one seemed to have noticed that one of Dare's hands was missing from the table while he gently stroked her slowly back and forth through the material of her shorts. He'd tried getting her zipper down, a zipper that, thanks to the way she was sitting, wouldn't budge.

Thinking that she had to do something, anything to stop this madness, she leaned forward and placed her elbows on the table and cupped her face in her hands as she tried to ignore the multitude of sensations flowing through her. She glanced around wondering if any of the brothers had any idea what Dare was up to, but from the way they were talking and eating, it seemed they had more on their minds than Dare not keeping his hands to himself.

"We want you to know that we'll do everything we can to help you with AJ, Shelly."

Shelly nodded at Stone's offer and then felt her cheeks grow warmer when another one of Dare's fingers wiggled its way inside her shorts. "I appreciate that, Stone."

"He's my responsibility," Dare spoke up and glanced at his brothers, keeping a straight face, not giving away just what sidebar activities he was engaged in.

"Yeah, but he belongs to us, too," Thorn said. "He's a Westmoreland, and I think that you did a wonderful job with him, Shelly, considering the fact that you've been a single parent for the past ten years. He's going through growing pains now, but once he sees that he has a family who cares deeply for him, he'll be just fine."

She nodded. She had to believe that as well. "Thanks, Thorn."

"Well, although I truly enjoyed all your company, it's time for me to get back to the station," Dare said, finally removing his hand from between her legs. When he stood she glanced up at him knowing that regardless of whether it was a dark, cozy corner on her porch at night or in a restaurant filled with people in broad daylight, Dare Westmoreland did just what he pleased, and it seemed that nothing pleased him more than touching her.

"So, what did you do next, Sheriff?"

Dare shook his head. When AJ had shown up after school, he had brought Morris and Cornelius with him and explained that the two had wanted to tag along. Dare had made it clear that if they had come to keep AJ company then they might as well help him with the work, and he had just the project for the three of them.

He had taken them to the basement where the police youth athletic league's equipment was stored, with instructions that they bring order to the place. That past year a number of balls, gloves and bats had been donated by one of the local sports stores.

Deciding to stay and help as well as to supervise, he had not been prepared for the multitude of questions that Morris and Cornelius were asking him. AJ didn't ask him anything, but Dare knew he was listening to everything that was being said.

"That's why it pays to be observant," Dare said, unloading another box. "It's always a clue when one guy goes inside and the other stays out in the car with the motor running. They had no idea I was with law enforcement. I pretended to finish filling my tank up with gas, and out of the corner of my eye I could see the man inside acting strangely and I knew without a doubt that a robbery was about to take place."

"Wow! Then what did you do?" Morris asked, with big, bright eyes.

"Although I worked for the Bureau, we had an unspoken agreement with the local authorities to make them aware of certain things and that's what I did. Pretending to be checking out a map, I used my cell phone to alert the local police of what was happening. The only reason I became involved was because I saw that one of the robbers intended to take a hostage, a woman who'd been inside paying for gas. At that point I knew I had to make a move."

"Weren't you afraid you might get hurt?" AJ asked.

Dare wondered if AJ was aware that he was now as engrossed in the story as Morris and Cornelius were. "No, AJ, at the time the only thing I could think about was that an innocent victim was at risk. Her safety became my main concern at that point, and whatever I did, I had to make sure that she wasn't hurt or injured."

"So what did you do?"

"In the pretense of paying for my gas, I entered the store at the same time the guy was forcing the woman out. I decided to use a few martial arts moves I had learned in the marines, and—"

"You used to be in the marines?" AJ asked.

Dare smiled. The look of total surprise and awe on his son's face was priceless. "Yes, I served in the marines for four years, right after college."

AJ smiled. "Wow!"

"My daddy says the marines only picks the most bravest and the best men," Morris said, also impressed.

Dare smiled. "I think all the branches of the military selects good men, but I do admit that marines are a very special breed." He glanced at his watch. "It's a little over an hour, guys. Do I need to call any of your parents to let them know that you're on your way home?"

All three boys shook their heads, indicating that Dare didn't have to. "All right."

"Sheriff, do you think you can teach us some simple martial arts moves?" Cornelius asked.

"Yeah, Sheriff, with bad people kidnapping kids we need to know how to protect ourselves, don't we?" Morris chimed in.

Dare grinned when he saw AJ vigorously nodding his head, agreeing with Morris. "Yes, I guess that's something all of you should know, some real simple moves. Just as long as you don't use it on your classmates for fun or to try to show off."

"We wouldn't do that," Morris said eagerly.

Dare nodded. "All right then. I'll try to map out some time this Saturday morning. How about checking with your parents, and if they say it's all right, then the three of you can meet me here."

He glanced at his watch again. Shelly didn't know it yet, but he intended to see her again tonight, no matter what excuse he had to make to do so. He smiled, pleased with the progress he felt he'd made with AJ today. "Okay, guys, let's get things moving so we can call it a day. The three of you did an outstanding job and I appreciate it."

"Mom, did you know that the sheriff used to be in the marines?"

Shelly glanced up from her book and met AJ's excited gaze. He was stretched out on the floor by the sofa doing his homework. "Yes, I knew that. We dated during that time."

"Wow!"

She lifted a brow. "What's so fantastic about him being a marine?"

AJ rolled his eyes to the ceiling. "Mom, everyone knows that marines are tough. They adapt, improvise and overcome!"

Shelly smiled at her son's Clint Eastwood imitation from one of his favorite movies. "Oh." She went back to reading her book.

"And, Mom, he told us about the time he caught two men trying to rob a convenience store and taking a hostage with them. It was real cool how he captured the bad guys."

"Yeah, I'm sure it was."

"And he offered to teach us martial arts moves on Saturday morning at the police station so we'll know how to protect ourselves," he added excitedly in a forward rush.

Shelly lifted her head from her book again. "Who?"

"The sheriff."

She nodded. "Oh, your father?"

Their gazes locked and Shelly waited for AJ's comeback, expecting a denial that he did not consider Dare his father. After a few minutes he shrugged his shoulders and said softly, "Yes." He then quickly looked away and went back to doing his homework.

Shelly inhaled deeply. AJ admitting Dare was his father was a start. It seemed the ice surrounding his heart was slowly beginning to melt, and he was beginning to see Dare in a whole new light.

Chapter 9

Dare walked into Coleman's Florist knowing that within ten minutes of the time he walked out, everyone in College Park would know he had sent flowers to Shelly. Luanne Coleman was one of the town's biggest gossips, but then he couldn't worry about that, especially since for once her penchant to gab would work in his favor. Before nightfall he wanted everyone to know that he was in hot pursuit of Shelly Brockman.

Due to the escape of a convict in another county, he had spent the last day and a half helping the sheriff of Stone Mountain track down the man. Now, thirty-six hours after the man had been recaptured, Dare was bone tired and regretted he had missed the opportunity to see Shelly two nights ago as he'd planned. The best he could do was go home and get some sleep to be ready for the martial arts training he had promised the boys in the morning.

He also regretted that he had not been there when AJ had arrived after school yesterday. It had officially been the last time he was to report to him. According to McKade, AJ had come alone and had been on time. He had also done the assignment Dare had left for him to do without having much to say. However, McKade had said AJ questioned him a couple of times as to why he wasn't there.

Dare walked around the shop, wondering just what kind of flowers Shelly would like, then decided on roses. According to Storm, roses, especially red ones, said everything. And everyone knew that Storm was an ace when it came to wooing women.

"Have you decided on what you want, Sheriff?"

He turned toward Mrs. Coleman. A woman in her early sixties, she attended the same church as his parents and he'd known her all of his life. "Yes, I'd like a dozen roses."

"All right. What color?"

"Red."

She smiled and nodded as if his selection was a good one, so evidently Storm was right. "Any particular type vase you have in mind?"

He shrugged. "I haven't thought about that."

"Well, you might want to. The flowers say one thing and the vase says another. You want to make sure you select something worthy of holding your flowers."

Dare frowned. He hadn't thought ordering flowers would be so much trouble. "Do you have a selection I can take a look at?"

"Certainly. There's an entire group over on that back wall. If you see something that catches your fancy, bring it to me."

Dare nodded again. Knowing she was watching him

with those keen eyes of hers, he crossed the room to stand in front of a shelf containing different vases. As far as he was concerned one vase was just as good as any, but he decided to try and look at them from a woman's point of view.

A woman like Shelly would like something that looked special, soft yet colorful. His gaze immediately went to a white ceramic vase that had flowers of different colors painted at the top. For some reason he immediately liked it and could see the dozen roses arranged really prettily in it. Without dallying any further, he picked up his choice and walked back over to the counter.

"This is the one I want."

Luanne Coleman nodded. "This is beautiful, and I'm sure she'll love it. Now, to whom will this be delivered?"

Dare inwardly smiled, knowing she was just itching to bits to know that piece of information. "Shelly Brockman."

Her brows lifted. "Shelly? Yes, I heard she was back in town, and it doesn't surprise me any that you would be hot on her heels, Dare Westmoreland. I hope you know that I was really upset with you when you broke things off with her all those years ago."

You and everybody else in this town, Dare thought, leaning against the counter.

"And she was such a nice girl," Luanne continued. "And everyone knew she was so much in love with you. Poor thing had to leave town after that and her parents left not long after she did."

As Luanne accepted his charge card she glanced at him and said, "I understand she has a son."

Dare pretended not to find her subject of conversation much to his interest. He began fidgeting with several key rings she had on display. "Yes, she does."

"Someone said he's about eight or nine."

Dare knew nobody had said any such thing. The woman was fishing, and he knew it. He might as well set himself up to get caught. "He's ten."

"Ten?"

"Yes." Like you didn't already know.

"That would mean he was born soon after she left here, wouldn't it?"

Dare smiled. He liked how this woman's mind worked. "Yes, it would seem that way."

"Any ideas about his father?"

"No."

"No?"

Dare wanted to chuckle. "None."

She frowned at him. "Aren't you curious?"

"No. What Shelly did with her life after she left here is none of my business."

Dare couldn't help but notice that Luanne's frown deepened. She handed his charge card back to him and said, "I have Shelly's address, Sheriff, since she's staying at her parents' old place."

Dare nodded, not surprised that she knew that. "When will the flowers be delivered?"

"Within a few hours. Will that be soon enough?"

"Yes."

"Sheriff, can I offer you a few words of advice?"

He wondered what she would do if he said no. She would probably give him the advice anyway. He could tell she was just that upset with him right now. "Why sure, Ms. Luanne. What words of advice would you like to offer me?"

She met his gaze without blinking. "Get your head out of the sand and stop overlooking the obvious."

"Meaning?"

She frowned. "That's for you to figure out."

Shelly looked at Mr. Coleman in surprise. She then looked at the beautiful arrangement of flowers he held in his hand. "Are you sure these are for me?"

The older man beamed. "Yes, I'm positive. Luanne said for me to get them to you right away," he said handing them to her.

"Thanks, and if you just wait a few minutes I'd like to give you a tip."

Mr. Coleman waved his hand as he went down the steps. "No need. I've already been tipped real nice for delivering them," he said with a grin that said he had a secret that he wouldn't be sharing with her.

"All right. Thanks, Mr. Coleman." She watched as he climbed into his van and drove off. Closing the door she went into the living room and placed the flowers on the first table she came to. Someone had sent her a dozen of the most beautiful red roses that she had ever seen. And the vase they were in was simply gorgeous; she could tell the vase alone had cost a pretty penny.

She quickly pulled off the card and read it aloud. "You're in my thoughts. Dare."

Her heart skipped a beat as she lightly ran her fingers over the card. Even the card and envelope weren't the standard kind that you received with a floral arrangement. They had a rich, glossy finish that caused Dare's bold signature to stand out even more.

For a moment, Shelly could only stare at the roses, the vase they were in and the card and envelope. It was obvious that a lot of time and attention had gone into their selection, and a part of her quivered inside that Dare would do something that special for her.

You're in my thoughts.

She suddenly felt tears sting her eyes. She didn't know what was wrong with her. It seemed that lately her emotions were wired and would go off at the least little thing. Ever since that day of Dare's visit and what he'd done to her on the porch, not to mention that little episode he'd orchestrated at the restaurant, she'd been battling the worst kind of drama inside her body. He had done more than open Pandora's box. He had opened a cookie jar that had been kept closed for ten years, and now she wanted Dare in the worst possible way.

"Who sent the flowers, Mom?"

Shelly lifted her head and met her son's gaze. "Your father."

He shrugged. "The sheriff?"

"One and the same." She glanced back over at the flowers. "Aren't they beautiful?"

AJ came to stand next to her. It was obvious they couldn't see the arrangement through the same eyes when he said, "Looks like a bunch of flowers to me."

She couldn't help but laugh. "Well, I think they're special, and it was thoughtful for him to send them to let me know I was in his thoughts."

AJ shrugged again. "He's looking for a girlfriend, but I told him you weren't interested in a boyfriend."

Shelly arched a brow. "AJ, you had no right to say that."

His chin jutted out. "Why not? You've never had a boyfriend before, so why would you care about one now? It's just been me and you, Mom. Isn't that enough?"

Shelly shook her head. Her son had years to learn about human sexuality and how it worked. She was just finding out herself what ten years of abstinence could do to a person. "AJ, don't you think I can get lonely some-times?" she asked him softly.

He didn't say anything for a little while. Then he said, "But you never got lonely before."

"Yes, and I worked a lot before. That's how you got into all that trouble. I was putting in extra hours at the hospital when the cost of living got high. I needed addi-tional money so the two of us could afford to live in the better part of town. I didn't have time to get lonely. Now with my new job, I can basically make my own hours so I can spend more time with you. But you're away in school a lot during the days, and pretty soon you'll have friends you'll want to spend time with, won't you?"

AJ thought of Morris and Cornelius and the fun they'd had on the playground that day at school. "Yes."

"Well, don't you think I need friends, too?"

"Yes, but what's wrong with having girlfriends?"

"There's nothing wrong with it, but most of the girls I went to school with have moved away, and although I'm sure I'll meet others, right now I feel comfortable associating with people I already know, like Dare and his brothers."

"But it's the sheriff who wants you as his girlfriend. He likes you."

She smiled. Dare must have laid it on rather thick. "You think so?"

"Yes. He said you used to be his special girl. His broth-ers and parents said so, too. And I've got a feeling he wants you to be his special girl again. But if you let him, he'll find out about me."

"And you still see that as a bad thing, AJ?"

He remained silent for a long time, then he hunched his shoulders. "I'm still not sure he would want me."

Shelly felt a knot forming in her stomach. She wondered if he was using his supposed dislike of Dare as an excuse to shield himself from getting hurt. "And why wouldn't he want you?"

"I told you that he didn't like me."

And you also said you didn't like him, she wanted to remind him, but decided to keep quiet about that. "Well, I know Dare, and I know that he likes you. He wouldn't have invited you to dinner with him and his family if he didn't. He would have taken you straight to Ms. Kate's house knowing she would have fed you."

She watched AJ's shoulders relax. "You think so?"

If you only knew, she thought. "Yes, I think so. I believe you remind Dare of himself when he was your age. I heard he was a handful for his parents. All the brothers were."

AJ nodded. "Yes, he said that once. He has a nice family."

She smiled. "Yes, he has."

AJ stuck his hands inside his pockets. "So, he's back now?"

"Who?"

"The sheriff. He left town to help another sheriff catch a guy who escaped from jail. Deputy McKade said so."

"Oh." Shelly had wondered why she hadn't heard from him since the luncheon on Thursday. Not that she had been looking for him, mind you. "Well, in that case, yes, I would say that he's back, since he ordered these flowers."

"Then our lessons for tomorrow morning are still on."

"Your lessons?"

"Yeah, remember, I told you he had said he would teach me, Morris and Cornelius how to protect ourselves at the police station in the morning."

"Oh, I'd almost forgotten about that." She wanted to

meet her son's new playmates and ask Dare about them. "Will they need a ride or will their parents bring them?"

"Their parents will be bringing them. They have to go to the barbershop in the morning."

Shelly nodded, looking at the long hair on her son's head. She'd allowed him to wear it in twists, as long as they were neat-looking. Maybe in time she would suggest that he pay a visit to the barbershop as well.

"And after our class they have to go to church for choir practice."

AJ's words recaptured Shelly's attention. Morris and Cornelius were active in church? The two were sounding better and better every minute. "All right then. Go get cleaned up for dinner."

He nodded. "Do you think the sheriff will call tonight or come by?" AJ asked as he trotted up the stairs.

I wish. "I'm not sure. If he just got back into town he's probably tired, so I doubt it."

"Oh."

Although she was sure he hadn't wanted her to, she had heard the disappointment in his voice anyway. He sounded just how she felt.

Dare couldn't sleep. He felt restless. Agitated. Horny.

He threw back the covers and got out of bed, yanked a T-shirt over his head and pulled on his jeans. His body was a nagging ache, it was throbbing relentlessly and his arousal strained painfully against his jeans. He knew what his problem was, and he knew just how he could fix it.

He sighed deeply, thinking he definitely had a problem, and wondered if at two in the morning, Shelly was willing to help him solve it.

* * *

Shelly couldn't sleep and heard the sound of a pebble the moment it hit her window. At first she'd thought she was hearing things, but when a second pebble hit the window she knew she wasn't. She also knew who was sending her the signal to come to the backyard.

That had always been Dare's secret sign to let her know he was back in town. She would then sneak past her parents' bedroom and slip down the stairs and through the back door to race outside to his arms.

She immediately got out of bed, tugged on her robe and slipped her feet into her slippers. Not even thinking about why he would be outside her window this time of night, she quickly tiptoed down the stairs. Without turning on a light, she entered the kitchen and opened the back door, and, although it was too dark for her to see, she knew he was there. Her nostrils immediately picked up his scent.

"Dare?" she whispered, squinting her eyes to see him.

"I'm here."

And he was, suddenly looming over her, gazing down at her with a look in his eyes that couldn't be disguised. It was desperate, hot, intense, and it made her own eyes sizzle at the same time the area between her legs began to throb. "I heard the pebbles," she said, swallowing deeply.

He nodded as he continued to hold her gaze. "I was hoping you would remember what it meant."

Oh, she remembered all right. Her body remembered, too. "Why are you here?" she asked softly, feeling her insides heat up and an incredible sensation flow between her legs. Desire was surging through every part of her body and she was barely able to stand it. "What do you want, Dare?"

He reached out and placed both hands at her waist, intentionally pulling her closer so she could feel his large, hard erection straining against his jeans. "I think that's a big indication of what I want, Shelly," he murmured huskily, leaning down as his mouth drew closer to hers.

Chapter 10

Shelly felt a moment of panic. One part of her mind tried telling her that she didn't want this, but another part, the one ruled by her body, quickly convinced her that she did. Her mind was swamped with the belief that it didn't matter that it hadn't been a full week since she laid eyes on Dare again after ten years. Nor did it matter that there were issues yet unresolved between them. The only thing that mattered was that this was the man she had once loved to distraction, the man she had given her virginity to at seventeen; the man who had taught her all the pleasures a man and woman could share, and the man who had given her a son. And, she inwardly told herself, this has nothing to do with love but with gratifying our needs.

Realizing that and accepting it, her body trembled as she lifted her face to meet his, and at that moment everything, including the ten years that had separated them, evaporated and was replaced by hunger, intense, sexual hunger that was waiting to explode within her. He felt it, too, and his body reacted, drawing her closer and making a groan escape from her lips.

He covered her mouth with his, zapping her senses in a way that only he could do. Fueled by the greed they both felt, his kiss wasn't gentle. It displayed all the insatiability he was feeling.

And then some.

Dare didn't think he could get enough. He wanted to get inside her, reacquaint her body with his and give her the satisfaction she had denied herself for ten years. He wanted to give her *him*. He felt his blood boil as he pulled his mouth from hers with a labored breath. She was shaking almost violently. So was he.

"Come with me. I've got a place set up for us."

Nodding, she let him lead her off the back porch and through a thicket of trees to a spot hidden by low overhanging branches, a place they had once considered theirs. It was dark, but she was able to make out the blanket that had been spread on the ground. As always, he had thought ahead. He had planned her seduction well this night.

"Where did you park your car?" she asked wondering how he had managed things.

"At the station. I walked from there, using the back way. And nobody saw me."

She nodded. Evidently he had read her mind. From the information she had gotten from Ms. Kate earlier today, the town was buzzing about AJ, wondering if Dare was actually too dim-witted to figure out her son was his.

She met his gaze, which was illuminated by the moonlight. "Thanks for the flowers. They're beautiful. You didn't have to send them."

"I wanted to send them, Shelly."

He drew in a deep breath, and she saw that his gaze was glued to her mouth just as hers was glued to his. She couldn't help but think of the way he tasted, the hunger and intense desire that was still blatant in his loins, making his erection even bigger. Their need for each other had never been this sharp, all-consuming.

"I want you, Shelly," he whispered gently, pulling her down to the blanket with him.

She went willingly, without any resistance, letting him know that she wanted the intimacy of this night as much as he did. She wanted to lose herself in him in the same way he wanted to lose himself in her. Totally. Completely.

She didn't say a word as he gently pushed her robe from her shoulders, and then pulled her nightgown over her head. Nor did she utter a sound when his fingers caressed her breasts then tweaked her nipples before moving lower, past her rib cage and her stomach until he reached the area between her legs.

When he touched her there, dipped into her warmth, her breathing quickened and strained and she almost cried out.

"You're so wet," his voice rumbled against her lips. "All I could think about over the last couple of days is devouring you, wanting the taste of you on my tongue."

Heat built within her body as he pushed her even more over the edge, making her whimper in pleasure. And when pleasure erupted inside her with the force of a tidal wave, he was there to intensify it.

He kissed the scream of his name from her lips, again taking control of her mouth. The kiss was sensual, the taste erotic and it fueled her fire even more. She had ten years to make up for, and somehow, she knew, he was well aware of that.

When her body ceased its trembling, he pulled back, ending their kiss, and stood to remove his clothes. She looked up at him as he tossed his T-shirt aside. He appeared cool and in control as he undressed in front of her, but she knew he was not. His gaze was on her, and she again connected with it. It felt like a hot caress.

She watched as he eased down his jeans, and she gasped. Her mouth became moist, her body got hungrier. He wasn't wearing any underwear and his erection sprang forth—full of life, eager to please and ready to go. The tip seemed to point straight at her, and the only thing she could think about was the gigantic orgasm she knew Dare would give her.

Anticipation surged within her when he kicked his jeans aside and stood before her completely naked. And her senses began overflowing with the scent of an aroused man.

An aroused man who was ready to mate with an aroused woman.

She then noticed the condom packet he held in his hand. It seemed he had planned her seduction down to the last detail. She watched as he readied himself to keep her safe. Inhaling deeply when the task was done, he lifted his head and met her gaze.

"This is where you tell me to stop, Shelly, and I will."

She knew him, trusted him and realized that what he'd said was true. No matter how much he wanted her, he would never force himself on her. But then, he need not worry about her turning him down. Her body was on fire for him, the area between her legs throbbed. He had given her relief earlier, but that hadn't been enough. She wanted the same thing he wanted.

Deep penetration.

They had discovered a long time ago that they were

two intensely sexual human beings. Anytime he had wanted her, all he had to do was touch her and he would have her hot, wet and pulsing within minutes. And anytime they mated, neither had control other than to make sure she was protected from pregnancy, except for that one time when they hadn't even had control for that.

When he dropped down to rejoin her on the blanket, she drew in a deep breath and automatically wrapped her arms around him as he poised his body over hers. He leaned down and placed a kiss on her lips.

"Thank you for my son."

A groan gently left her throat when she felt the head of him pressed against her entrance. Hot and swollen. He nudged her legs apart a little wider with his knees as his gaze continued to hold hers. "Ten years of missing you and not sharing this, Shelly."

And then he entered her, slowly, methodically, trembling as his body continued to push into hers as he lifted her hips. He let out a deep guttural moan. In no time at all he was planted within her to the hilt. The muscles of her body were clenching him. Milking him. Reclaiming him.

She held his gaze and when he smiled, so did she.

And then he began an easy rhythm. Slowly, painstakingly, he increased the pace. And with each deep thrust, he reminded her of just how things used to be between them, and how things still were now.

Hungry. Intense. Overpowering.

His gaze became keen, concentrated and potently dark each time he thrust forward, drove deeper into her, and she felt her body dissolve, dissipate then fuse into his. She felt the muscles of his shoulders bunch beneath her hands, heard the masculine sound of his growl and knew he was fighting reaching sexual fulfillment, waiting for her, refusing to leave her behind. But he couldn't hold back any longer, and, with one last, hard, deep thrust his body began shaking as he reached the pinnacle of satisfaction.

His orgasm triggered hers, and when her mouth formed a chilling scream, he quickly covered it with his, denying her the chance to wake the entire neighborhood. But he couldn't stop her body from quivering uncontrollably. Nor could he stop her legs from wrapping around him, locking their bodies together, determined that they continue to share this. She closed her eyes as a feeling of unspeakable joy and gratification claimed her in the most provocative way, restitution, compensation for ten years of not having access to any of this.

And when the last of the shudders subsided and they both continued to shiver in the aftermath, he sank down, lowered his head to the curve of her neck, released a deep satisfied sigh, and wondered what words he could say to let her know just how overwhelmed he felt.

He forced himself to lift up, to meet her gaze, and she opened her eyes and looked at him. And at that moment, in that instant, he knew words weren't needed. There was no way she couldn't know how he felt.

And as he leaned down and kissed her, he knew that the rest of the night belonged to them.

"Mom? Mom? Are you all right?"

Shelly opened her eyes as she felt AJ nudge her awake. Once again he had found her sleeping on the sofa. After several more bouts of intense lovemaking, they had redressed, then Dare had gathered her into his arms and carried her inside the house. Not wanting to risk taking her upstairs to her own bed and running into AJ, just in case he had awakened during the night to use the bathroom or something, she had asked Dare to place her on the sofa.

Now she turned over to meet AJ's gaze and felt the soreness between her legs as she did so. She had used muscles last night that she hadn't used in over ten years. "Yes, sweetheart, I'm fine."

He lifted a brow. "You slept on the sofa again."

She glanced at the book that was still where it had been the last time she had used it for an alibi. "I guess I fell asleep reading again." She glanced at the clock on the wall. It was Saturday which meant it wasn't a school day so why was he up so early? "Isn't this your day to sleep late?"

He smiled sheepishly, and that smile reminded her so much of Dare that her breath almost caught. "Yeah, but the sheriff is giving us martial arts lessons today, remember?"

Yes, she remembered, then she wondered if after last night Dare would be in any physical shape to give the boys anything today. But then he was a man, and men recovered from intense sessions of lovemaking a lot quicker than most women. Besides, she doubted if he'd gone without sex for ten years as she had. She forced the thought from her mind, not wanting to think about Dare making love to other women.

She shifted her attention back to AJ. "You're excited about taking lessons from Dare, aren't you?"

He shrugged. "Yes, I guess. I've always wanted to learn some type of martial arts, but you never would let me take any classes. Morris said his father told him that the sheriff is an ace when it comes to that sort of stuff, and I'm hoping he'll be willing to give us more than one lesson."

Shelly wondered if AJ would ever stop referring to

Dare as "the sheriff." But then, to call him Dare was even less respectful. "All right, do you want pancakes this morning?"

"Yes! With lots and lots of butter!"

She smiled as she stood, wincing in the process. Her sore muscles definitely reminded her of last night. "Not with lots and lots of butter, AJ, but I'll make sure you get enough."

Shelly saw Dare the moment she pulled her car into the parking lot at the sheriff's office. He walked over to the car and met them. She wasn't surprised to discover that he'd been waiting for them.

"Are we late?" AJ asked quickly, meeting Dare's gaze.

Dare smiled at him. "No, Cornelius isn't here yet, but I understand he's on his way. Morris's mother just dropped him off a few minutes ago. He's waiting inside."

He then looked at Shelly, and his smile widened. "And how are you doing this morning, Shelly?"

She returned his smile, thinking about all the things the two of them had done last night while most of College Park slept. "I'm fine, Dare, what about you?"

"This is the best I've felt in years." He wanted to say ten years to be exact, but didn't want AJ to catch on to anything.

Shelly glanced at her watch. "How long will the lessons last today?"

"At least an hour or so. Why? Is there something you need to do?"

Shelly placed an arm around AJ's shoulders. "Well, I was hoping I'd have enough time to get my nails done in addition to getting my hair taken care of."

"Then do it. I'm going over to Thorn's shop when I leave here to check out the new bike that he's building.

AJ is welcome to go with me if he likes and I can bring him home later."

He shifted his glance from Shelly to AJ. "Would you like to go to Thorn's shop to see how he puts a motorcycle together?"

The expression in AJ's eyes told Dare that he would. "Yes, I'd love to go!" He turned to Shelly. "Can I, Mom?"

Shelly met Dare's gaze. "Are you sure, Dare? I wouldn't want to put you out with having to—"

"No, I'd like his company."

AJ's eyes widened in surprise. "You would?"

Dare grinned. "Sure, I would. You did a great job with all the chores that I assigned to you this week, and I doubt that you'll be playing hooky from school anytime soon, right?"

AJ lowered his head to study his sneakers. "Right."

"Then that does it. My brothers will be there and I know for a fact they'd like to see you again."

AJ smiled. "They would?"

"Yes, they would. They said they enjoyed having you at dinner the other night. Usually on Saturday we all pitch in to give Thorn a hand to make sure any bike he's building is ready to be delivered on time. The one he's working on now is for Sylvester Stallone."

"Wow!"

Dare laughed at the astonishment he heard in AJ's voice and the look of awe on his face. What he'd said about his brothers wanting to see AJ again was true. They were biting at the bit for a chance to spend more time with their nephew.

"Well, I guess that's settled," Shelly said, smiling at Dare and the son he had given her. "I'd better get going if I want to make my hair appointment on time." She turned to leave.

"Shelly?"

She turned back around. "Yes?"

"I almost forgot to mention that Mom called this morning. She heard from Laney last night. She, Jamal and the baby are coming for a visit in a couple of weeks and will stay for about two months. Then they will be moving to stay at their place in Bowling Green, Kentucky, while Laney completes her residency at the hospital there."

Shelly smiled. When she'd last seen Dare's baby sister, Delaney was just about to turn sixteen and the brothers were having a time keeping the young men away. Now she had graduated from medical school and had landed herself a prince from the Middle East. She was a princess and the mother to a son who would one day grow up to be a king. "That's wonderful! I can't wait to see her again."

Dare grinned. "And she can't wait to see you, either. Mom told her that you had moved back and she was excited about it."

Without having to worry about AJ, Shelly decided to throw in a pedicure after getting her hair and nails done. Upon returning home, she collapsed on the bed and took a nap. The lack of sleep the night before still had her tired. After waking up, she was about to go outside on the porch and sit in the swing when she heard a knock at the door. She glanced through the peephole and saw it was Dare and AJ. Both of them had their hands and faces smeared with what looked like motor oil. She frowned. If they thought they were coming inside her house looking like that, they had another thought coming.

"Go around back," she instructed, opening the door just a little ways. "I'll bring you washcloths and a scrub brush to clean up. You can also use the hose." She then quickly closed the door.

She met them in the backyard where they were using the hose to wash oil from their hair. It was then that she noticed several oil spots on AJ's outfit as well. "What on earth happened?"

"Storm happened," Dare grumbled, taking the shampoo and towel she handed him. His frown indicated he wasn't all that happy about it, either. "You know how he likes to play around? Well, for some reason he decided to fill a water gun with motor oil, and AJ and I became his victims."

She shifted her gaze from Dare to AJ. Whereas Dare was not a happy camper because of Storm's childish antics, it seemed AJ was just the opposite. "Storm is so much fun!" he said, laughing. "He told me all about how he had to save this little old lady from a burning house once."

Shelly smiled. "Well, I'm glad you enjoyed yourself, but those clothes can stay out here. In fact, we may as well trash them."

AJ nodded. "Storm said to tell you that he's going to buy me another outfit and he'll call to find out when he can take me shopping."

Shelly crossed her arms over her chest and lifted a brow. "Oh, he did, did he?"

"Yes."

She shifted her gaze back to Dare. "What are we going to do about that brother of yours?"

Dare shrugged, smiling. "What can I do? I guess we could try marrying him off, except so far there's not a woman around who suits his fancy except for Tara, but she's Thorn's challenge."

A bemused look covered Shelly's face. "What?"

"Tara Matthews. She's Laney's friend—a doctor who works at the same hospital in Kentucky where Delaney plans to complete her residency. I'll explain about her being Thorn's challenge at another time."

Shelly nodded, planning to hold him to that. She glanced down at her watch. "I was about to cook burgers and fries, if anyone is interested."

Dare looked pleased. "Only if you let me grill the burgers."

"And I'll help," AJ chimed in, volunteering his services.

Shelly shook her head. "All right, and I'll cook the fries and make some potato salad and baked beans to go along with it. How does that sound?"

"That sounds great, Mom."

Shelly nodded, liking the excitement she heard in her son's voice. "Dare?"

He chuckled. "I agree with AJ. That sounds great."

Dare remained through dinner. He got a call that he had to take care of, but returned later with Chase and Storm close on his heels. They brought a checkers game, intent on showing AJ how to play. It was almost eleven before AJ finally admitted he was too tired to play another game. Chase and Storm left after AJ went to bed, leaving Dare to follow later after they mentioned they were headed over to Thorn's place to wake him up to play a game of poker.

An hour or so later, Shelly walked Dare to the door. He had spent some time telling her how Tara Matthews was a feisty woman that only Thorn could tame and that was why the brothers referred to her as Thorn's challenge. "So you think this Tara Matthews has captured the eye of Thorn Westmoreland?"

Dare chuckled. "Yes, although he doesn't know it yet, and I feel sorry for Tara when he does."

Shelly nodded. Moments later she said, "I hope you know your leaving late is giving the neighbors a lot to say."

He smiled. "Yeah, I heard from McKade that a lot of people around town are questioning my intelligence. They think I haven't figured out that AJ's my son."

Shelly nodded. "Yes, that's what I'm hearing, too, from Ms. Kate."

"How do you think AJ is handling things?"

"I don't think anyone has said anything to him directly, but I know a couple of people have asked him about his father in a roundabout way."

Dare lifted a brow. "When?"

"A couple of days ago at Kate's Diner. He goes there every morning on his way to school."

Dare nodded. "Damn, Shelly, I'm ready to end this farce and let this whole damn town know AJ's mine."

"I know, Dare, but remember we decided to let him be the one to determine when that would be. Personally, I think it'll be sooner than you think, because he's slowly coming around."

Dare raised a questioning brow. "You think so?"

"Yes. The two of you are interacting together a lot better. That's obvious. I can tell, and I know your brothers picked up on it tonight as well."

"Yes, but for some reason he still holds himself back from me," Dare said in a frustrated tone. "I sense it, Shelly, and it bothers the heck out of me. I don't know why he's doing it."

Shelly smiled slightly. "I think I do."

Dare met her gaze. "Then tell me—why?"

She sighed. "I think AJ is beginning to wonder if he's good enough to be your son."

Dare frowned. "Why would he wonder about a thing like that?"

"Because basically he's beginning to see you through a new set of eyes, the same eyes Morris and Cornelius see you with, and AJ's concerned about the way the two of you met. He knows it wasn't a good start and that you were disappointed with him. Now he's afraid that he won't be able to wipe the slate clean with you."

Dare rubbed a hand down his face. "There'll never be a time that I wouldn't want my son, Shelly."

She wrapped her arms around his waist upon hearing the frustration in his voice. She heard the love there as well. "I know that and you know that, but he has to know that, too. Now that you've broken the ice with him, it's time for you to get to know him and for him to get to know you. Then he'll see that no matter what, you'll always be there for him."

Dare let out a deep sigh. "And I thought winning him over would be easy."

She smiled. "In a way, it has been. To be honest with you, I really didn't expect him to come around this soon. Like you, he has somewhat of a stubborn streak about certain things. Him coming around the way he has just goes to show that you evidently have a way with people."

Dare smiled and brought her closer to him. "And do I have a way with you, Shelly?" The only reason he wasn't making love to her again tonight was that he was well aware of the fact that her body was sore. He couldn't help noticing how stiff her movements were when she'd dropped AJ off that morning and again this evening at dinner.

"After last night how can you even ask that, Dare? You know I was putty in your hands," she said, recapturing his attention.

"Then that makes us even, because I was definitely putty in yours as well." He leaned down and kissed her, thinking of just how right she felt in his arms.

Just like always.

Chapter 11

Shelly stretched out in her bed with a sensuous sigh. Almost two weeks had passed since she and Dare had spent the night together on a blanket in her backyard. Since then, nightly meetings in the backyard on a blanket had become almost a ritual. He had become almost a fixture in her home, dropping by for dinner, and inviting her and AJ to a movie or some other function in town.

AJ was beginning to let his guard down around Dare, but as yet he had not acknowledged him as his father. Shelly knew Dare's patience was wearing thin; he was eager to claim his son, but as she had explained to Dare weeks ago, AJ had to believe in his heart that his father wanted him for a son before he could give Dare his complete love and trust.

She then thought about her own feelings for Dare. She had to fight hard to keep from falling in love with Dare all over again. She had to remember they were playacting for AJ's sake. To anyone observing them, it seemed that he was wooing her. He was giving the townspeople something to talk about with the different flower arrangements that he sent her each week.

A couple of people had taken her aside and warned her not to be setting herself up for heartbreak all over again, since everyone knew Dare Westmoreland was a staunch bachelor. But there were others who truly felt he was worthy of another chance, and they tried convincing her that if anyone could change Dare's bachelor status, she could.

What she couldn't tell them was that she was not interested in changing Dare's bachelor status. Although she had detected some changes in him, she could not forget that at one time he had been a man driven to reach out for dreams that had not included her. And she could never let herself become vulnerable to that type of pain again. For six years she had believed she was the most important thing in Dare's life, and to find out that she hadn't been had nearly destroyed her. She had enough common sense to know that what she and Dare were sharing in the backyard at night was not based on emotional but on physical needs, and as long as she was able to continue to know the difference, she would be all right.

She pulled herself up in bed when she heard the knock on her bedroom door. "Come in, AJ."

It was early still, an hour before daybreak, but she knew he was excited. Today was the day that Dare's sister Delaney and her family were arriving from the Middle East. The Westmoreland brothers were ecstatic and had talked about their one and only sister so much over the past two weeks that AJ had gotten caught up in their excitement; after all, the woman was his aunt, although he assumed Delaney didn't know it.

He opened the door and stood just within the shadows

of the light coming in from the hallway. Again, Shelly couldn't help but notice just how much he looked like Dare. No wonder the town was buzzing. "What is it, AJ?"

He shrugged. "I wanted to talk to you about something, Mom."

She nodded and scooted over in bed, but he went and sat in the chair. Evidently, he thought he was past the age to get into his mother's bed. Shelly's heart caught. Her son was becoming a young man and with his budding maturity came a lot of issues that Dare would be there to help her with. Not only Dare but the entire Westmoreland family.

He remained silent for a few minutes, then he spoke. "I've decided to tell the sheriff I'm his son."

Shelly's heart did a flip, and she swallowed slowly. "When did you decide that?"

"Yesterday."

"And what made you change your mind?"

"I've been watching him, Mom. I was in Kate's Diner one morning last week when he came in, but he didn't see me at first. When he walked in, all the people there acted like they were glad to see him, and he knew all their names and asked them how they were doing. Then it hit me that he really wasn't a bad cop or a mean cop at all. No one would like him if he was, and everybody likes him, Mom."

Shelly blinked away the tears from her eyes. AJ was right. Everyone liked Dare and thought well of him. AJ had had to discover that on his own, and it seemed that he had. "Yes, everyone likes Dare. He's a good sheriff and he's fair, AJ."

"Most of the kids at school think he's the bomb and feel that I'm lucky because you're his girlfriend."

Shelly made a surprised face. "The kids at your school think I'm his girlfriend?"

AJ nodded. "Well, aren't you?"

Shelly smiled slightly. She didn't want to give him hope that things would work out between her and Dare, and that once he admitted to being Dare's son they would miraculously become a loving family. "No, AJ, although we're close, Dare and I are nothing more than good friends. We always have been and always will be."

"But he wants you for his girlfriend, I can tell. Everyone can tell and they're all talking about it, as well as the fact they think I'm his son, although they don't want me to hear that part, but I do. The sheriff spends a lot of time with us and takes us places with him. The kids at school say their parents think it's time for him to settle down and marry, and I can tell that he really likes you, Mom. He always treats you special and I like that."

Shelly inhaled deeply. She liked it, too, but she knew a lot more about why Dare was spending time with her than AJ did. It was all part of his plan to gain his son's love and trust. She refused to put too much stock into anything else, not even the many times they had slept together. She knew it had to do with their raging hormones and nothing more. "So, when are you going to tell him?" she asked quietly.

AJ shrugged. "I still don't know that yet. But I wanted to let you know that I would be telling him."

She nodded. "Don't take too long. Like I said, Dare won't be a happy camper knowing we kept it from him, but I believe he'll be so happy about you that he'll quickly come around."

AJ's eyes lit up. "You think so?"

"Yes, sweetheart, I do."

He nodded. "Then I might tell him today. He asked if

I'd like to go with him to meet his sister and her family at the airport. I might tell him then."

Shelly nodded again, knowing that if he did, it would certainly make Dare's day.

AJ thought Dare's truck was really cool. He had ridden in it a couple of times before, and just like the other times, he thought it was a nice vehicle for a sheriff to have when you wanted to stop being sheriff for a little while. But as he looked at Dare out of the corner of his eyes, he knew that the sheriff was always the sheriff. There was probably never a time when he wasn't on the job, and that included times like now when he wasn't wearing his uniform.

"So are you looking forward to that day out of school next Friday for teachers' planning day?" Dare asked the moment he'd made sure AJ had snapped his seat belt in place. Once that was done, he started the engine.

"Yes, although Mom will probably find a lot of work for me to do that day." He didn't say anything else for a little while, then he asked quickly, "Do you like kids?"

Dare glanced over at him and smiled. "Yes, I like kids."

"Do you ever plan to have any?"

Dare lifted his brow. "Yeah, one day. Why do you ask?"

AJ shrugged. "No reason."

Dare checked the rearview mirror as he began backing out of Shelly's driveway. He was headed for the airport like the rest of his family to welcome his sister home. He couldn't help wondering if AJ had started quizzing him for some reason and inwardly smiled, ready for any questions that his son felt he needed to ask.

* * *

Princess Delaney Westmoreland Yasir clutched her son to her breast and inhaled sharply. She leaned against her husband's side for support. Her mother had said Shelly's son favored Dare, but what she was seeing was uncanny. There was no way anyone could take a look at the boy standing next to Dare and not immediately know they were father and son. They had the same coffee coloring, the same dark intense eyes and the same shape mouth and nose. AJ Brockman was a little Dare; a small replica of his father, there was no doubt of that.

"And who do we have here?" she asked after regaining her composure and giving her parents and brothers hugs.

"This is AJ," Dare said, meeting his sister's astonished gaze. "Shelly Brockman's son. I think Mom mentioned to you that she had returned to town."

Delaney nodded. "Yes, that's what I heard." She smiled down at AJ and immediately fell in love. He was a Westmoreland, and she was happy to claim him. "And how are you, AJ?" she asked her nephew, offering him her hand.

"I'm fine, thank you," he said somewhat shyly.

"And how is your mother?"

"She's doing fine. She said she couldn't wait to see you later today."

Delaney smiled. "And I can't wait to see her. She was like a big sister to me."

With love shining in her eyes, Delaney then glanced at the imposing figure at her side and smiled. "AJ, this is my husband, Jamal Ari Yasir."

AJ switched his gaze from Delaney to the tall man standing next to her. He wasn't sure what he should do. Was he supposed to bow or something? He let out a deep sigh of relief when the man stooped down to his level and met his gaze. "And how are you, AJ?" he asked in a deep voice, smiling.

AJ couldn't help but return the man's smile, suddenly feeling at ease. "I'm fine, sir."

When the man straightened back up, AJ switched his gaze to the baby Delaney held in her arms. "May I see him?"

Delaney beamed. "Sure. His name is Ari Terek Yasir." She leaned down and uncovered her son for AJ to see. The baby glanced at AJ and smiled. AJ smiled back, and so did everyone else standing around them at the airport. Delaney looked over at her mother, in whose eyes tears of happiness shone at seeing her two grandsons together, getting acquainted.

Suddenly Prince Jamal Ari Yasir cleared his throat. Everyone had become misty-eyed and silent, and he decided to put the spark and excitement back into the welcome gathering. This was the family he had come to love, thanks to his wife who he truly cherished. His dark eyes shone with amusement as he addressed the one brother who he hadn't completely won over yet. "So, Thorn, are you still being a thorn in everyone's side these days?" he asked, smiling.

Chapter 12

Shelly smiled as she looked at the young woman sitting in the chair across from her on the patio at Dare's parents' home. The last time she had seen Delaney Westmoreland she'd been a teenager, a few months shy of her sixteenth birthday, a rebellious, feisty opponent who'd been trying to stand up to her five overprotective and oftentimes overbearing brothers.

Now she was a self-assured, confident young woman, a medical doctor, mother to a beautiful baby boy and wife to a gorgeous sheikh from a country in the Middle East called Tahran. And from the looks the prince was constantly giving his wife, there was no doubt in her mind that Delaney was also a woman well loved and desired.

And, Shelly thought further, Delaney was breathtakingly stunning. Even all those years back there had never been any doubt in Shelly's mind that Delaney would grow up to become a beauty. She was sure there hadn't been any doubt in the brothers' minds of that as well, which was probably the reason they had tried keeping such a tight rein on her. But clearly they had not been a match for Prince Jamal Ari Yasir.

Delaney and Shelly were alone on the patio. Mrs. Westmoreland was inside, singing Ari to sleep, and AJ had gone with his father and grandfather to the store to buy more charcoal. The brothers and Jamal had taken a quick run to Thorn's shop for Jamal to take a look at Thorn's latest beauty of a bike.

"I'm glad you returned, Shelly, to bring AJ home to Dare and to us. I don't think you know how happy you've made my parents. They thought Ari was their only grandchild and were fretting over the fact they wouldn't be able to see him as often as they wanted to. I felt awful about that, but knew my place was with Jamal, which meant living in his country the majority of the time. One good thing is that as long as his father is king, we have the luxury of traveling as much as we want. But things will change once Jamal becomes king."

When Shelly nodded, she continued, "We hope that won't happen for a while. His father is in excellent health and has no plans to turn things over to Jamal just yet."

After a long moment of silence, Shelly said, "I want to apologize for leaving the way I did ten years ago, Delaney, and for not staying in touch."

Delaney's eyes shone in understanding. "Trust me, we all understood your need to put distance between you and Dare. Everyone got on his case after you left, and for a while there was friction between him and my brothers."

Shelly nodded. Dare had told her as much.

"Mom explained the situation to me about AJ," Delaney added, breaking into Shelly's thoughts. "She told me how you and Dare have decided to let him be the one to tell Dare the truth. What's the latest on that? Is he softening any toward Dare? As someone just arriving on the scene, I'd say they seem to be getting along just fine."

Shelly nodded, remembering AJ's intense dislike of Dare in the beginning. "I think he's discovered Dare isn't the mean cop that he thought he was, and yes, he is definitely softening. He even told me this morning that he plans to tell Dare that he's his father."

A huge smile touched Delaney's features. "When?"

"Now, that I don't know. From what I gather he'll tell Dare when they get a private moment and when he feels the time is right. He's battling his fear that Dare may not want him because of the way he behaved in the beginning."

Delaney shook her head. "There's no way Dare would not want his son."

"Yes, I know, but AJ has to realize that for himself."

Delaney nodded, knowing Shelly was right.

AJ stood next to Dare in the supermarket line. He watched as the sheriff pulled money from his wallet to pay for his purchases. When they walked outside to wait for Mr. Westmoreland, who was still inside buying a few additional items he'd discovered he needed, AJ decided to use that time to ask Dare a couple more questions.

"Can I ask you something?"

Dare looked at him. "Sure. Ask me anything you want to know, AJ."

"Earlier today you said you liked kids. If you ever marry, do you think you'd want more than one child?"

Dare wondered about the reason for that question. Was AJ contented being an only child? Would he feel threatened if Dare told him that he relished the thought of having other children—if Shelly would be their mother? He sighed, deciding to be completely honest with his son.

"Yes, I'd want more than one child. I'd like as many as my wife would agree to give me."

AJ's face remained expressionless, and Dare didn't have a clue if the answer he'd given would help him or hang him. "Any more questions?"

For a long moment, AJ didn't say anything. Then he met Dare's gaze and asked, "Is Dare your real name?"

Dare shook his head. "No, my real name is Alisdare Julian Westmoreland." He continued to hold his son's gaze. "Why do you ask?"

AJ placed his hands into his pockets. "Because my name is Alisdare Julian, too. That's what the AJ stands for."

Dare wasn't sure exactly what he was supposed to say, but knew he should act surprised, so he did. He raised his dark brows as if somewhat astonished. "Your mother named you after me?"

AJ nodded. "Yes."

Dare stared at AJ for a moment before asking. "Why did she do that?"

He watched as his son drew a deep breath. "Because—"

"Sorry I took so long. I bet your mom thinks the three of us have been kidnapped."

Both Dare and AJ turned to see Mr. Westmoreland walking toward them. But Dare was determined his son would finish what he'd been about to say. He returned his gaze to AJ. "Because—?"

AJ looked at the older man walking toward them, and then at Dare and, after losing his nerve, quickly said, "Because she liked your name."

* * *

"Because she liked your name."

Later that night Dare shook his head, remembering the reason AJ had given him for Shelly's choice of his name. He knew without a shadow of a doubt that AJ had come within a second of finally telling him he was his son before his father had unintentionally interrupted them, destroying that chance. But Dare was determined he would get it again.

Once they'd returned to his parents' home, there had been no private time, and on more than one occasion he'd been tempted to suggest that the two of them go back to the store and pick up some item his mother just had to have, but since his brothers and Jamal hadn't yet returned, his mother put him to work helping his father grill the ribs and steaks.

Now it was past eleven and Shelly was gathering her things to take a tired and sleepy AJ home. He had gotten worn out playing table tennis with his uncles for the past couple of hours.

Dare studied Shelly, as he'd been doing most of the night. She was wearing a pair of jeans that molded to her curvaceous hips and a blue pullover top that, to him, emphasized her lush breasts. Breasts he'd been kissing and tasting quite a lot over the past few weeks. Her body had always been a complete turn-on to him, and nothing had changed. He'd been fighting an arousal all night. The last thing he needed was for his brothers to detect what a bad way he was in, although from the smirks they had sent him most of the evening, he was well aware that they knew.

"AJ and I are going to have to say good-night to everyone," Shelly said smiling. "Thanks again for inviting us." She met Dare's gaze and blinked at his unspoken message. He was letting her know that he would be seeing her later tonight.

He slowly crossed the room to her. "I'll walk the two of you out."

She nodded before turning to give Delaney and Jamal, the elder Westmorelands and finally the brothers hugs.

Dare frowned at Storm when he deliberately kissed Shelly on the lips, trying to get a rise out of him and knowing it had worked. As far as Dare was concerned Shelly was his, and he didn't appreciate anyone mauling her. He had put up with it the first time they'd seen her at Chase's restaurant, but now he figured that it was time Storm learned to keep his hands and his lips to himself.

When Shelly and AJ walked ahead of him going out the door, he hung back and growled to Storm. "If you ever do that again, I'll break your arm."

He ignored Storm's burst of laughter and followed Shelly and AJ outside.

It was a beautiful night. The air felt crisp, pleasantly cool as Shelly closed the back door behind her and raced across the backyard to the place where she knew Dare was waiting for her. She hadn't bothered to put on a robe, since he would be taking it off her anyway, and she hadn't bothered to put on a gown, preferring to slip into an oversized T-shirt instead.

It had taken her some time to get AJ settled and into bed after arriving home from the Westmorelands. They had talked; he had told her that he'd come close to telling Dare the truth tonight, but that he'd been interrupted. She knew the longer he put it off, the harder it was going to be for him.

"Shelly?"

She sucked in a deep breath when Dare emerged from

the shadows, dazzling her senses beneath the glow of a full moon. She immediately walked into his arms. Dark, penetrating eyes met hers and then, in a deep, ragged breath, he tipped her head back as his lips captured hers.

The whimpered sounds erupting from deep within her throat propelled him forward, making the urge for them to mate that much more intense, urgent, imperative. He gently lifted her T-shirt and touched her, discovering she was completely bare underneath. With unerring speed he lifted her off her feet, wrapped her legs around his waist and walked a few steps to a nearby tree.

She saw it was another seduction, planned down to every detail. Evidently he'd kept himself busy while waiting for her, she thought, noticing he had securely tied a huge pillow around the tree trunk. It served as a cushion for her backside when he pressed her against it. And then he was breathing hard and heavy while unzipping his pants and reaching inside to free himself. "I knew I couldn't wait, so I've already taken care of protection," he whispered as he thrust forward, entering her.

At her quick intake of breath, he covered her mouth with his, sipping the nectar of surprise from her lips, playing around in her mouth with his tongue as if relishing the taste of her. How long ago had they last kissed? Hadn't it been just last night? You couldn't tell by the way he was eating away at her mouth and the way she eagerly responded, wanting, needing and desiring him with a vengeance.

She opened her legs wider, wrapped them around his waist tighter when he went deeper, sending shock waves of pleasure racing through her. She felt close, so very close to the edge, and she knew she wanted him to be with her when she fell.

She broke off their kiss. "Now, Dare!"

Dare began moving. Throwing his head back he inhaled a deep whiff of her scent—hot, enticing, sensually hers—and totally lost it. His jaw clenched as he thrust deeper, moved faster, when she arched her back. Desperately, he mated with her with quick, precise strokes, giving her all he had and taking all she had to give.

He was past the point of no return and she was right there with him. And when he felt her body tighten and the spasm rip through her, bringing with it an orgasm so powerful that he felt the earth shake beneath his feet, he held her gaze and thrust into her one final time as he joined her in a climax that just wouldn't stop. The sensations started at the top of his head and moved downward at lightning speed, building intense pressure in that part of his body nestled deep inside her, and making him clench his teeth to keep from screaming out her name and stomping his feet.

The sensations kept coming and coming and he leaned forward to kiss her again, capturing the essence of what they were sharing. As his body continued to tremble while buried deep inside of her, he knew that even after ten long years, he was still seductively, passionately and irrevocably hers. She was the only woman he would ever want. The only woman he would ever need. The only woman who could make him understand and appreciate the difference between having mindblowing sex and making earth-shattering, soul-stirring, deep-down-in-your-gut love.

She was the only woman.

And he also knew that she was the only woman he would ever love and that he still loved her.

Moments later, Dare pulled his body from Shelly's and, gathering her gently into his arms, walked over to place her on the blanket. He stretched out on his side facing her as he waited for the air to return back to his lungs and the blood to stop rushing fast and furious through his veins.

"I was beginning to think you weren't coming," he finally said some time later, the tone of his voice still quivering from the afterglow of what they'd just shared.

He couldn't help touching her again, so he slid his hand across her stomach, gently stroking her. He remembered the question AJ had asked him about wanting other children, and he remembered thinking that he'd want more children only if Shelly were their mother. He wouldn't hesitate putting another child of his inside her, in the womb he knew he had touched tonight. Not only had he touched it, he had branded it his.

Shelly slowly opened her eyes as her world settled, and the explosion she'd felt moments ago subsided. She gazed up at him and wondered how was it possible that each time they did this it was better than the time before. She always felt cherished in his arms.

Treasured.

Loved.

She silently shook that last thought away, refusing to let her mind go there; refusing to live on false hope. And she refused to give in to the want, need and desire to give him her heart again, no matter how strong the pull was to do so. She broke eye contact with him and looked away.

"Shelly?"

She returned her gaze to him, to respond to what he'd said. "It took a little longer than expected to get AJ settled tonight. He wanted us to have a long talk."

Dare asked, "Is he all right?"

"Yes. But I think he's somewhat disappointed that he

didn't get the chance to tell you the truth today. He had planned to do so."

Dare sighed deeply. His gut instincts had been right. "Do you think I should talk to him tomorrow?"

Shelly shook her head. "No, I think the best thing to do is to wait until he gets up his courage again. But I suggest you make things a bit easier on him by making sure the two of you have absolute privacy without any interruptions. However, you're also going to have to make sure he doesn't think things are being orchestrated for that purpose. He still has to feel as though he's in control for a while longer, Dare, especially with this. Right now, telling you that he's your son is very important to him."

Dare nodded. It was important to him as well. He slumped down on his back beside her and looked up at the stars. "I think I have an idea."

"What?"

"The brothers and I, along with Jamal, had planned on going to the cabin in the North Carolina mountains to go fishing. AJ knows about it since he heard us planning the trip, so he won't think anything about it. What if I invite him to come along?"

Shelly raised a brow. "Why would you want to take AJ with you guys? I'd think the six of you had planned it as a sort of guys' weekend, right?"

"Right. But I remember AJ mentioning to Thorn that he'd never gone fishing before, and I know that Thorn came close to inviting him. The only reason he didn't was because he knew we would be playing poker in addition to fishing and Storm's mouth can get rather filthy when he starts losing."

Shelly nodded. "But how will this help your situation with AJ? The two of you still won't have any privacy."

"Yes, we will if the others don't come. After AJ and I

arrive, the others can come up with an excuse as to why they couldn't make it."

Shelly raised a doubtful brow. "All five of them?"

"Yes. It has to be a believable reason for all of them though, otherwise AJ will suspect something."

Shelly had to agree. "And while you and AJ are there alone for those three days, you think he'll open up to you?"

Dare sighed deeply. "I'm hoping that he will. At least I'm giving him the opportunity to do so." He met Shelly's stare. "What do you think?"

Shelly shrugged. "I don't know, Dare. It might be just the thing, but I don't want you to get your hopes up and be disappointed. I know for a fact that AJ wants you to know the truth, but I also know that for him the timing has to be perfect."

Dare nodded as he pulled her into his arms. "Then I'm going to do everything in my power to make sure that it is."

Chapter 13

Dare hung up the phone and met AJ's expectant gaze.

"That was Chase. One of his waitresses called in sick. He'll have to pitch in for the weekend and won't be able to make it."

He saw the disappointment cloud AJ's eyes. So far since arriving at the cabin they had received no-show calls from everyone except Thorn, and he expected Thorn to call any minute.

"Does that mean we have to cancel this weekend?" AJ asked in such a disappointed voice that a part of Dare felt like a heel.

"Not unless you want to. There's still a possibility that Thorn might show."

Although he'd said the words, Dare knew they weren't true. His brothers and Jamal had understood his need to be alone with AJ this weekend and had agreed to bow out of the picture and plan something else to do.

When AJ didn't say anything, Dare said. "You know what I think we should do?"

AJ lifted a brow. "What?"

"Enjoy the three days anyway. I've been looking forward to a few days of rest and relaxation, and I'm sure you're glad to have an extra day off school, as well, right?"

AJ nodded. "Right."

"Then I say that we make the most of it. I can teach you how to fish in the morning and tomorrow night we can camp outside. Have you ever gone camping?"

"No."

Dare sadly shook his head at the thought. When they were kids his father had occasionally taken him and his brothers camping for the weekend just to get them out of their mother's hair for a while. "We can still do all the things that we'd planned to do anyway. How's that?"

AJ was clearly surprised. "You'll want to stay here with just me?"

A lump formed in Dare's throat at the hope he heard in his son's voice. He swallowed deeply. *If only you knew how much I want to stay here with just you,* he thought. "Yes," he answered. "I guess I should be asking you if you're sure that you want to stay here with just me."

AJ smiled. "Yes, I want to stay."

Dare returned that smile. "Good. Then come on. Let's get the rest of the things out of the truck."

The next morning Dare got up bright and early and stood on the porch enjoying a cup of coffee. AJ was still asleep, which was fine, since the two of them had stayed up late the night before. Thorn had finally called to say he couldn't make it due to a deadline he had to meet for a bike he had to deliver. So it was final that it would only be the two of them.

After loading up the supplies in the kitchen after Thorn's call, they'd gathered wood for a fire. Nights in the mountains meant wood for the fireplace and they had gathered enough to last all three days. Then, while he left AJ with the task of stacking the wood, Dare had gone into the kitchen to prepare chili and sandwiches for their dinner.

They hadn't said much over their meal, but AJ'd really started talking while they washed dishes. He'd told him about the friends he had left behind in California, and how he had written to them. They hadn't written back. He'd also talked about his grandparents, the Brockmans, and how he had planned to spend Christmas with them.

Now, Dare glanced around, deciding he really liked this place. It had once been jointly owned by one of their cousins and a friend of his, but Jamal had talked the two men into selling it to him and had then presented it to Delaney as one of her wedding gifts. It was at this cabin that Delaney and Jamal had met. While she was out of the country, Delaney had graciously given her brothers unlimited use of it, and all five had enjoyed getting away and spending time together here every once in a while.

Dare turned when he heard a noise behind him and smiled. "Good morning, AJ."

AJ wiped sleep from his eyes. "Good morning. You're up early."

Dare laughed. "This is the best time to catch fish."

AJ's eyes widened. "Then I'll be ready to go in a second." He rushed back into the house.

Dare chuckled and hoped his son remembered not

only to get dressed but to wash his face and brush his teeth. He inhaled deeply, definitely taking a liking to this father business.

Dare smiled as he looked at the sink filled with fish. AJ had been an ace with the fishing pole and had caught just as many fish as he had. He began rolling up his sleeves to start cleaning them. They would enjoy some for dinner today and tomorrow and what was left they would take home with them and split between his mother and Shelly. Maybe he could talk Shelly into having a fish fry and inviting the family over.

His gaze softened as he thought how easy it was to want to include Shelly in his daily activities. He suppressed a groan thinking of all their nighttime activities and smiled as it occurred to him they had yet to make love in a bed. He had to think of a way to get her over to his place for the entire night. Sneaking off to make love in her backyard under the stars had started off being romantic, but now he wanted more than romance, he wanted permanence…forever. He wanted them to talk and plan their future, and he wanted her to know just how greatly she had enriched his life since she had returned.

He shifted his thoughts to AJ. So far they'd been together over twenty-four hours and he hadn't brought up the topic of their relationship. They had spent a quiet, leisurely day at the lake talking mostly about school and the Williams sisters. It seemed his son had a crush on the two tennis players in a big way, especially Serena Williams. Dare was glad he'd let Chase talk him into taking tennis lessons with him last summer; at least he knew a little something about the game and had been able to contribute to AJ's conversation.

Dare sighed, anxious to get things out in the open

with AJ, but as Shelly had said, AJ would have to be the one to bring it up. He glanced over his shoulder when he heard his son enter the kitchen. He had been outside putting away their fishing gear.

"You did a good job today with that fishing rod, AJ," Dare said, smiling over his shoulder. "I can't wait to tell Stone. The rod and reel you used belongs to him. He swears only a Westmoreland can have that kind of luck with it," he added absently.

"Then that explains things."

Dare turned around. "That explains what?"

"That explains why I did so good today—I *am* a Westmoreland."

Dare's breath caught and he swallowed deeply. He leaned back against the sink and stared at AJ long and hard, waiting for him to stop studying his sneakers and look at him. Moments later, AJ finally lifted his head and met his gaze.

"And how are you a Westmoreland, AJ?" Dare asked quietly, already knowing the answer but desperately wanting to hear his son say it anyway.

AJ cleared his throat. "I—I really don't know how to tell you this, but I have to tell you. And I have to first say that my mom wanted to tell you sooner, but I asked her not to, so it's not her fault so please don't be mad at her about it. You have to promise that you won't be mad at my mom."

Dare nodded. At that moment he would promise almost anything. "All right. I won't be mad at your mom. Now tell me what you meant about being a Westmoreland."

AJ put his hands into his pockets. "You may want to sit down for this."

Dare watched AJ's face and noticed how nervous he'd

become. He didn't want to make him any more nervous than he already was, so he sat at the kitchen table. "Now tell me," he coaxed gently.

AJ hesitated, then met Dare's gaze, and said, "Although my last name is Brockman, I'm really a Westmoreland...because I'm your son."

Dare's breath got lodged in his throat. He blinked. Of course, the news AJ was delivering to him didn't surprise him, but the uncertainty and the caution he saw in his son's gaze did. Shelly had been right. AJ wasn't sure if he would accept him as his son, and Dare knew he had to tread lightly here.

"You're my son?" he asked quietly, as if for clarification.

"Yes. That's why I'm ten and that's why we have the same name." He looked down at his sneakers again as he added, "And that's why I look like you a little, although you haven't seemed to notice but I'll understand if you don't want me."

Dare stood. He slowly crossed the room to AJ and placed what he hoped was a comforting hand, a reassuring hand, a loving hand on his shoulder. AJ looked up and met his gaze, and Dare knew he had to do everything within his power to make his son believe that he wanted him and that he loved him.

Choosing his words carefully and speaking straight from his heart and his soul, he said, "Whether you know it or not, you have just said words that have made me the happiest man in the entire world. The very thought that Shelly gave me a son fills me with such joy that it's overwhelming."

AJ searched his father's gaze. "Does that mean you want me?"

Dare chuckled, beside himself in happiness. "That

means that not only do I want you, but I intend to keep you, and now that you're in my life I don't ever intend to let you out of it."

A huge smile crept over AJ's features. "Really?"

"Yes, really."

"And will my name get changed to Westmoreland?"

Dare smiled. "Do you want your name changed to Westmoreland?"

AJ nodded his head excitedly. "Yes, I'd like that."

"And I'd like that, too. We'll discuss it with your mother and see what her feelings are on the matter, all right?"

"All right."

They stared at each other as the reality of what had taken place revolved around them. Then AJ asked quietly, "And may I call you Dad?"

Dare's chest tightened, his throat thickened and he became filled with emotions to overpowering capacity. He knew he would remember this moment for as long as he lived. What AJ was asking, and so soon, was more than he could ever have hoped for. He had prayed for this. A smile dusted across his face as parental pride and all the love he felt for the child standing in front of him poured forth.

"Yes, you can call me Dad," he said, as he reached out and pulled his son to him, needing the contact of father to son, parent to offspring, Westmoreland to Westmoreland. They shared a hug of acceptance, affirmation and acknowledgement as Dare fought back the tears in his eyes. "I'd be honored for you to call me that," he said in a strained voice.

Moments later, Dare sighed, thinking his mission should have been completed, but it wasn't. Now that he had his son, he realized more than ever just how much he wanted, loved and needed his son's mother. His mission wouldn't be accomplished until he had her permanently in his life as well.

Later that night Dare placed calls to his parents and siblings and told them the good news. They took turns talking with AJ, each welcoming him to the family. After dinner Dare and AJ had talked while they cleaned up the kitchen. Already plans were made for them to return to the cabin in a few months, and Dare suggested that they invite Shelly to come with them.

"She won't come," AJ said, drying the dish his father had handed him.

Dare raised a brow. "Why wouldn't she?"

"Because she's not going to be your girlfriend," he said softly. "Although now I wish that she would."

Dare turned and folded his arms across his chest and looked at his son. "And what makes you think your mother won't be my girlfriend, AJ?" he asked, although the title of wife was more in line with what he was aiming for.

"She told me," he said wryly. "That same night we had a cookout at Grandma and Grandpa Westmoreland's house. After we got home we talked for a long time, and I told her that I had come close to telling you that night that I was your son. I asked if the three of us would be a family after I told you and she said no."

Dare remembered that night well. Shelly had been late coming to the backyard and had mentioned she and AJ had had a long talk. He sighed deeply as he tilted his head to the side to think about what AJ had said, then asked, "Did she happen to say why?"

AJ shook his head. "Yes. She said that although the two of you had been in love when you made me, that now you weren't in love anymore and were just friends. She also said that chances were that one day you would marry someone nice and I'd have a second mother who would treat me like her son."

Dare frowned. He and Shelly not being in love was a crock. How could she fix her lips to say such a thing, let alone think it? And what gave her the right to try and marry him off to some other woman? Didn't she know how he felt about her? That he loved her?

Then it suddenly hit him, right in the gut that, no, Shelly had no idea how he felt, because at no time had he told her. For the past month they had spent most of their time alone together, at night in her backyard under the stars making love. Did she think all they'd been doing was having sex? But then why would she think otherwise? He sucked in a breath, thinking that he sure had missed the mark.

"Is that true, Dad? Will you marry someone else and give me a second mother?"

Dare shook his head. "No, son. Your mother is the only mother you'll have, and she's the only woman I ever plan to marry."

Mimicking his father, AJ placed his arms across his chest and leaned against the sink. "Well, I don't think she knows that."

Dare smiled. "Then I guess I'm just the person to convince her." He leaned closer to his son and with a conspiratorial tone, he said. "Listen up. I have a plan."

Chapter 14

The first thing Shelly noticed as she entered the subdivision where Dare's home was located was that all the houses were stately and huge and sat on beautiful acreages. This was a newly developed section of town that had several shopping outlets and grocery stores. She could vividly remember it being a thickly wooded area when she had left town ten years ago.

She glanced at her watch. Dare had called and said that he and AJ had decided to return a day early and asked that she come over to his place and pick up AJ because Dare needed to stay at home and wait for the arrival of some important package. All of it sounded rather secretive, and the only thing she could come up with was that it pertained to some police business.

After reading the number posted on the front of the mailbox, she knew the regal-looking house that sat on a hill with a long, circular driveway belonged to Dare. She and Delaney had spent the day shopping yesterday and one of the things Delaney had mentioned was that Dare had banked most of his salary while working as a federal agent, and when he moved back home he had built a beautiful home.

Moments later, after parking her car, Shelly strolled up the walkway and rang the doorbell. It didn't take long for Dare to answer.

"Hi, Shelly."

"Hi, Dare." Her heart began beating rapidly, thinking she would never tire of seeing him dressed casually in a pair of jeans and a chambray shirt. As she met his gaze, she thought that she had definitely missed him during the two days he and AJ had gone to North Carolina.

"Come on in," he invited, stepping aside.

"Thanks." She glanced around Dare's home when he closed the door behind her. Nice, she thought. The layout was open and she couldn't help noticing how chic and expensive everything looked. "Your home is beautiful, Dare."

"Thanks, and I'm glad you like it."

Shelly saw that he was leaning against the closed door staring at her. She cleared her throat. "You mentioned AJ finally got around to admitting that you're his father."

Dare shook his head. "Yes."

Shelly nodded. "I'm happy about that, Dare. I know how much you wanted that to happen."

"Yes, I did."

A long silence followed, and, with nothing else to say, Shelly cleared her throat again, suddenly feeling nervous in Dare's presence, mainly because he was still leaning against the door staring at her with those dark penetrating eyes of his. Breaking eye contact, she glanced at her watch and decided to end the silence. "Speaking of AJ, where is he?"

Dare didn't say anything for a moment, then he spoke. "He isn't here."

Shelly raised a brow. "Oh? Where is he?"

"Over at my parents'. They dropped by and asked if he could visit with them for a while. I didn't think you would mind, so I told them he could."

Shelly nodded. "Of course I don't mind." After a few minutes she cleared her throat for the third time and said, "Well, I'm sure you have things to do so I'll—"

"No, I don't have anything to do, since the important package I was waiting for arrived already."

"Oh."

"In fact, I was hoping that you and I could take in a movie and have dinner later."

Her dark gaze sank into his. "Dinner? A movie?"

"Yes, and you don't have to worry about AJ. He'll be in good hands."

With a slight shrug, she said, "I know that, Dare. Your parents are the greatest."

Dare smiled. "Well, right now they think their oldest grandson is the greatest. Now that the secret is out, you should have seen my mom. She can't wait to go around bragging to everyone about him since it's safe to do so."

Shelly's stomach tightened. Now that the secret was out, things would be changing…especially her relationship with Dare. He wouldn't have to pretend interest in her any longer. Even now, she knew that probably the only reason he was inviting her to the movies and to dinner was out of kindness.

"Well, what about the movies and dinner?" Dare asked, reclaiming her attention.

She met his gaze. This would probably be the last time

they would be together, at least out in public. There was
no doubt in her mind that until they got their sexual needs
under control they would still find the time to see each
other at night in private.

"Yes, Dare. I'll go out to the movies and to dinner
with you."

"Thanks for going out with me tonight, Shelly."

"Thanks for inviting me, Dare. I really enjoyed myself." And she had. They had seen a comedy featuring
Eddie Murphy at the Magic Johnson Movie Theater near
the Greenbriar Mall. Afterward, they had gone to a restaurant that had served the best-tasting seafood she'd ever
eaten. Now they were walking around the huge shopping
mall that brought back memories of when they had dated
all those years ago and had spent a lot of their time there
on the weekends.

Dare claimed the reason he was in no hurry to end
their evening was because he wanted to give his parents
and siblings a chance to bond with AJ, and he thought
the stroll through Greenbriar Mall would kill some time.

"How do you like the type of work you're doing now,
working outside the hospital versus working inside?"

This was the first time he had ever asked her anything
about her job since she'd moved back. "It took some getting used to, but I'm enjoying it. I get to meet a lot of
nice people and because of the hours I work, I'm home
with AJ more."

Dare nodded. "I never did tell you why I stopped being
an agent for the Bureau, did I?"

Shelly shook her head. "No, you didn't."

Dare nodded again. He then told her all the things he
had liked about working for the FBI and those things he

had begun to dislike. Finally he told her the reason he had returned home.

"And do you like what you're doing now, Dare?" she couldn't help but ask him, since she of all people knew what a career with the FBI had meant to him.

"Yes, I like what I'm doing now. I feel I'm making more of a difference here than I was making with the Bureau. It's like I'm giving back to a community that gave so much to my brothers and me while we were growing up. It's a good feeling to live in a place where you have history."

Shelly had to agree. She enjoyed being back home and couldn't bear the thought of ever leaving again. Although she had lived in L.A. for ten years, deep down she had never considered it as her home.

She sighed and glanced down at her watch. "It's getting late. Don't you think it's time for us to pick up AJ? I don't want him to wear out his welcome with your folks."

Dare laughed, and the sound sent sensations up Shelly's body, making her shiver slightly. He thought she had shivered for a totally different reason and placed his arm around her shoulders, pulling her closer to him for warmth. "He'll never be able to wear out his welcome with my family, Shelly. Come on, let's go collect our son."

Three weeks later, Shelly sat outside alone on her porch swing as it slowly rocked back and forth. It was the third week in October and the night air was cool. She had put on a sweater, but the stars and the full moon were so beautiful she couldn't resist sitting and appreciating them both. Besides, she needed to think.

Ever since that night Dare had taken her to a movie and to dinner, he had come by every evening to spend time with AJ. But AJ wasn't the only person he made sure he spent time with. Over the past few weeks he had often asked her out, either to a movie, dinner or both. Then there was the time he had asked her to go with him to the wedding of one of his deputies.

She sighed deeply. Each time she had tried putting distance between them, he would succeed in erasing the distance. Then there were the flowers he continued to send each week. When she had asked him why he was still sending them, he had merely smiled and said because he enjoyed doing so. And she had to admit that she enjoyed receiving them. But still, she didn't want to put too much stock in Dare's actions and continued to see what he was doing as merely an act of kindness on his part. It was evident that he wanted them to get along and establish some sort of friendly relationship for AJ's sake.

The other thing that confused her was the fact that he no longer sought her out at night. Their late-night rendezvous in her backyard had abruptly come to an end the night Dare had taken her on their first date. He had offered her no explanation as to why he no longer came by late at night, and she had too much pride to ask him.

He came by each afternoon around dinnertime and she would invite him to stay, so she still saw him constantly. And at night, after AJ went to bed, he would sit outside on the porch swing with her and talk about how her day had gone, and she would ask him about his. Their talks had become a nightly routine, and she had to admit that she rather enjoyed them.

She shifted her thoughts to AJ. He was simply basking in the love that his father and the entire Westmoreland family were giving him. Dare had been right when he'd said all AJ had needed was to feel that he belonged. Each time she saw her son in one of his happy moods, she knew that he was glad as well as proud to be a part of the Westmoreland clan, and that she had made the right decision to return to College Park.

She stood, deciding to go inside and get ready for bed. Dare had left immediately after dinner saying he had to go to the station and finish up a report he was working on. As usual, before he left he had kissed her deeply, but otherwise he had kept his hands to himself. However, whenever he pulled her into his arms, she knew he wanted her. His erection was always a sure indicator of that fact. But she knew he was fighting his desire for her, which made things confusing, because she didn't understand why.

As she got ready for bed she continued to wonder what was going on with Dare. Why had he ended all sexual ties between them? Had he assumed she thought things were more serious between them than they really were because of their nightly meetings in her backyard?

As she closed her eyes she knew that if reality could not find her in his arms making love, that she would be there with him in the dreams she knew she would have that night.

Shelly smiled at Ms. Mamie. The older woman had broken her ankle two weeks before and Shelly had been assigned as her home healthcare nurse. "I thought we had talked about you staying off your foot for a while, Ms. Mamie."

Ms. Mamie smiled. "I tried, but it isn't easy when I have so much to do."

Shelly shook her head. "Well, your ankle will heal a lot quicker if you follow my instructions," she said, re-wrapping the woman's leg. She made it a point to check on Ms. Mamie at least twice a week, and she enjoyed her visits. Even with only one good leg, the older woman still managed to get around in her kitchen and always had fresh cookies baked when Shelly arrived.

"So, how are things going with you and the sheriff?"

Shelly looked up. "Excuse me?"

"You and the sheriff. How are the two of you doing? Everyone is talking about it."

Shelly frowned, not understanding. "They are talking about Dare and AJ or about me and Dare?"

"They are talking about you and Dare. Dare and AJ is old news. Everyone knew that boy was Dare's son even if Dare was a little slow in coming around and realizing that fact." Shelly's mind immediately took in what Ms. Mamie had said. She'd had no idea that she and Dare were now the focus of the townspeople's attention. "Why are people talking about me and Dare?"

"Because everyone knows how hard he's trying to woo you."

Shelly stilled in her task and looked at Ms. Mamie. She couldn't help but grin at something so ridiculous. "Why would people think Dare is trying to woo me?"

"Because he is, dear."

The grin was immediately wiped from Shelly's face. Woo her? Dare? She shook her head. "I think you're mistaken."

"No, I'm not," Ms. Mamie answered matter-of-factly. "In fact, me and the ladies in my sewing club are taking bets."

Shelly raised a brow. "Bets?"

"Yes, bets as to whether or not you're going to give him a second chance. All of us know how much he hurt you before."

Shelly's head started spinning. "But I still don't understand why you all would think he was wooing me."

Ms. Mamie smiled. "Because it's obvious, Shelly. Luanne tells us each time he sends you flowers, which I understand is once, sometimes twice a week. Then, according to Clara, who lives across the street from you, he comes to dinner every evening and he takes you out on a date occasionally." The woman's smile widened. "Clara also mentioned that he's protecting your reputation by leaving your house at a reasonable time every night so he won't give the neighbors something to talk about."

Shelly shook her head. "But none of that means anything."

Ms. Mamie gently patted her hand. "That's where you're wrong, Shelly. It means everything, especially for a man like Dare. The ladies and I have watched him over the years ignore one woman after another, women who threw themselves at him. He never got serious about any of them. When you came back things were different. Anyone with eyes can see that he is smitten with you. That boy has always loved you, and I'll be the first to say he made a mistake ten years ago, but I feel good knowing he's trying real hard to win you back." She then grinned conspiratorially. "It even makes me feel good knowing that you're making it hard for him."

Making it hard for him? She hadn't even picked up on the fact that he was trying to win her back. Shelly opened her mouth to say something, then closed it, deciding that she needed to think about what Ms. Mamie had said. Was it true? Was Dare actually wooing her?

That question was still on her mind half an hour later when she pulled out of Ms. Mamie's driveway. She sighed deeply. The only person who could answer that question was Dare, and she decided it was time that he did.

Thunder rumbled in the distance as Dare placed a lid on the pot of chili he'd just made. He had tried keeping himself busy that afternoon since thoughts of Shelly weighed so heavily on his mind.

He knew one of the main reasons for this was that AJ would be spending the weekend with Morris and Cornelius, which meant Shelly would be home all alone, and Shelly all alone was too much of a temptation to think about. He sighed deeply, wondering just how much longer he could hold out in his plan to prove to her that what was between them was more than sex and that he cared deeply for her. For the past three weeks he had been the ardent suitor as he tried easing his way back into her heart. The only thing about it was that he wasn't sure whether his plan was working and exactly where he stood with her.

He paused in what he was doing when he heard his doorbell ring and wondered which of his brothers had decided to pay him a visit. It would be just like them to show up in time for dinner. Leaving the kitchen, he made his way through the living room to open the front door. His chest tightened with emotion when he looked through his peephole and saw that it wasn't one of his brothers standing outside on his porch, but Shelly.

He quickly opened the door and recognized her nervousness. A man in his profession was trained to detect when someone was fidgety or uneasy about something. "Shelly," he greeted her, wondering what had brought her to his place.

"Dare," she said returning the greeting in what he considered a slightly skittish voice. "May I come in and talk to you about something?"

He nodded and said, "Sure thing," before stepping aside to let her enter.

His gaze skimmed over her as she passed him, and he thought there was no way a woman could look better than this, dressed in something as simple as a pullover V-neck sweater and a long flowing skirt; especially if that skirt appeared to have been tailor-made just for her body. It flowed easily and fluidly down all her womanly curves.

He locked the door and turned to find her standing in the middle of his foyer as though she belonged in his house, every day and every night. "We can go into the living room if you like," he said, trying not to let it show just how much he had missed being alone with her.

"All right."

He led her toward the living room and asked, "Are you hungry? I just finished making a pot of chili."

"No, thanks, I'm not hungry."

"What about thirsty? Would you like something to drink?"

She smiled at him. "No, I don't want anything to drink. I'm fine."

He nodded. Yes, she was definitely fine. He didn't know another woman with a body quite like hers, and the memories of being inside that body made his hands feel damp. The room suddenly felt warmer than it should be.

He inhaled as he watched her take a seat on the sofa. He, in turn, took the chair across from her. Once she had gotten settled, he asked, "What is it you want to talk to me about, Shelly? Is something wrong with AJ?"

She shook her head. "Oh, no, everything with AJ is fine. I dropped him off at the Sears's house. I think he's excited about spending the weekend."

Dare nodded. He thought AJ was excited about spending the weekend as well. "If it's not about AJ then what do you want to talk about?"

His gaze held hers, and she hesitated only a moment before responding. "I paid a visit to Ms. Mamie today to check on her ankle. I'll be her home healthcare nurse for a while."

Dare nodded again, thinking there had to be more to her visit than to tell him that. "And?"

She hesitated again. "And she mentioned something that I found unbelievable, but I was concerned since it seems that a lot of the older women in this town think it's true."

He searched her features and detected more nervousness than before. "What do they think is true?"

Dare became concerned when seconds passed and Shelly didn't answer. Instead, she moved her gaze away from his to focus on some object on his coffee table. He frowned slightly. There had never been a time that Shelly had felt the need to be shy in his presence, so why was she now?

Standing, he crossed the room to sit next to her on the sofa. "All right, Shelly, what's this about? What do Ms. Mamie and her senior citizens' club think is true?"

Shelly swallowed deeply and took note of how close Dare was sitting next to her. Every time she took a breath she inhaled his hot male scent, a scent she had grown used to and one she would never tire of.

She breathed in and decided to come clean. Making light of the situation would probably make it easier, she thought, especially if he decided to laugh at something so absurd. She smiled slightly. "For some reason they think you're trying to woo me."

His gaze didn't flicker, but remained steadily on her face when he asked. "Woo you?"

She nodded. "Yes, you know—pursue me, court me."

Sitting so close to her, Dare could feel her tension. He also felt her uncertainty. "In other words," he said softly, "they think I'm trying to win you over, find favor in your eyes, in your heart and in your mind and break down your resistance."

Shelly nodded, although she didn't think Dare needed to break down her resistance since he had successfully done that a month or so ago. "Yes, that's it. That's what they believe. Isn't that silly?"

Dare shifted his position and draped his arms across the back of the sofa. He met Shelly's gaze, suddenly feeling hungry and greedy with an appetite that only she could appease. He studied her face for a little while longer, then calmly replied. "No, I don't think there's anything silly about it, Shelly. In fact, their assumptions are right on target."

She blinked once, twice, as the meaning of his words sank in. He watched as her eyebrows raised about as high as they could go, and then she said, "But why?"

Keeping his gaze fixed on hers, he asked, "Why what?"

"Why would you waste your time doing something like that?"

Dare drew in a deep breath. "Mainly because I don't consider it a waste of my time, Shelly. Other than winning my son's love and respect, winning your heart back is the most important thing I've ever had to do."

Shelly swallowed, and for the first time in weeks she felt a bubble of hope grow inside her. Her heart began beating rapidly against her ribs. Was Dare saying what she thought he was saying? There was only one way to find out. "Tell me why, Dare."

He leaned farther back against the sofa and smiled. His smile was so sexy, so enticing and so downright seductive that it almost took her breath away. "Because I wanted to prove to you that I knew the difference between having sex and making love. And I had the feeling that you were beginning to think I didn't know the difference, and that all those times we spent in your backyard on that blanket were about sex and had nothing to do with emotions. But emotions were what it was all about, Shelly, each and every time I took you into my arms those nights. I have never just had sex with you in my life. There has never been a time that I didn't make love to you. For us there will always be a difference."

Tears misted Shelly's eyes. He was so absolutely right. For them there would always be a difference. She had tried convincing herself that there wasn't a difference and that each time they made love it was about satisfying hormones and nothing more. But she'd only been fooling herself. She loved Dare. She had always loved him and would always love him.

"AJ made me realize what you might have been thinking when we spent time at the cabin together," Dare said, interrupting Shelly's thoughts.

"He told me what you had said about the possibility of me getting married one day, and I knew then what you must have been thinking to assume that you and AJ and I would never be a family."

Shelly nodded. "But we will be a family?" she asked quietly, wanting to reach out and touch Dare, just to make sure this entire episode was real and that she wasn't dreaming any of it.

"Yes, we will be a family, Shelly. I made a mistake ten years ago by letting you go, but I won't make the same mistake twice. I love you and I intend to spend the remainder of my days proving just how much." Sitting forward, his smile was tender and filled with warmth and love when he added, "That is, if you trust me enough to give me another chance."

Shelly reached out and cupped his jaw with her hands. She met the gaze of the man she had always loved and who would forever have her heart. "Are you sure that is what you want, Dare?"

"Yes, I haven't been more sure of anything in my life, Shelly, so make me the happiest man in the world. I love you. I always have and always will, and more than anything, I want you for my wife. Will you marry me?"

"Oh, Dare, I love you, too, and yes, I will marry you." She automatically went into his arms when he leaned forward and kissed her. His kiss started off gentle, but soon it began stoking a gnawing hunger that was seeping through both of their bodies and became hard and demanding. And then suddenly Dare broke the kiss as he stood and Shelly found herself lifted off the sofa and cradled close to his body.

While she slowly ran her lips along his jaw, the corners of his mouth and his neck, he took the stairs two at a time, his breath ragged, as he carried her to his bedroom. Once there, he placed her in the middle of his bed and began removing his shirt. Her mouth began watering as he exposed a hard-muscled chest. All the other times since she'd been back they had made love in the dark, and although she had felt his chest she hadn't actually seen it. At least not like this. It was daylight and she was seeing it all, the thatch of hair that covered his chest then tapered down into a thin line as it trailed lower to his...

She swallowed and realized that his hand had moved to the snap on his jeans. He slowly began taking them off. She swallowed again. Seeing him like this, in the light, a more mature and older Dare, made her see just how much his body had changed, just how much more physical, masculine and totally male he was.

And just how much she appreciated being the woman he wanted.

She watched as he reached into the nightstand next to the bed to retrieve a condom packet, and how he took the time to prepare himself to keep her safe. With that task done, he lifted his gaze and met hers. "I'd like other children, Shelly."

She smiled and said, "So would I, and I know for a fact that AJ doesn't like being an only child, so he would welcome a sister or brother as well."

Dare nodded, remembering the question AJ had asked about whether he wanted other children. He was glad to hear AJ would welcome the idea. Dare walked the few steps back over to the bed and, leaning down, he began removing every stitch of clothing from Shelly's body, almost unable to handle the rush of desire when he saw her exposed skin.

"You're beautiful, Shelly," he whispered breathlessly, smiling down at her when he had finished undressing her and she lay before him completely naked.

She returned his smile, glowing with his compliment. As he joined her in bed and took her into his arms, she knew that this was where she had always been meant to be.

Shelly felt the heat of desire warm her throat the moment Dare joined his mouth to hers, and all the love she had for him seeped through every part of her body as his kiss issued a promise she knew he would fulfill.

They hadn't made love in over a month so she wasn't surprised or shocked by the powerful emotions surging through her that only intensified with Dare's kiss. He wasn't just kissing her, he was using his tongue to stroke a need, deliver a promise and strip away any doubt that it was meant for them to be together.

Dare dragged his mouth from hers, his breath hard, shaky and harsh. "I need you now, baby," he said, reaching down and checking her readiness and finding her hot and wet. He settled his body over hers as fire licked through his veins, love flowed from his heart and a need to be joined with her drove everything within him.

He inhaled sharply as the tip of his erection pressed her wet and swollen flesh and it seemed that every part of his being was focused there, and when she opened her legs wider for him, arched her back, pushed her hips up and sank her nails deep in his shoulder blades, he couldn't help but groan and surge forward. The sensation of him filling her to the hilt only made him that much more hungry, greedy. And she was there with him all the way.

He thrust into her again and again, each stroke more hard and determined than the one before; the need to mate life sustaining, elemental, a necessity. And when he felt her thighs begin to quiver with the impact of her release, he followed her, right over the edge into oblivion. This woman who had given him a little Dare, who gave him more love than he rightly deserved would have his heart forever.

A shiver of awareness coursed down the length of Shelly's spine when Dare placed several kisses there. She opened her eyes and met his warm gaze.

"Do you know this is the first time we've made love in a bed since you've been back," he said huskily, as an amused smile touched his lips.

She tipped her head to the side and smiled. "Is that good or bad?"

His long fingers reached out and began skimming a path from her waist toward the center of her legs. "It's better." He leaned down and placed a kiss on her lips. "Stay with me tonight."

The heat shimmering in his eyes made her body feverish. With AJ spending the weekend away there was no problem with her staying with him. "Umm, what do I get if I stay?" She closed her eyes and sighed when his fingers touched her, caressed her, intent on a mission to drive her insane.

"Do you have to ask?" he rasped, his voice low and teasing against her lips.

"No, I don't," she replied in breathless anticipation.

She trembled as Dare began inflaming her body the same way he had inflamed her heart. They had endured a lot, but through it all their love had survived and for the first time since returning to College Park, she felt she had finally come home.

Epilogue

Shelly couldn't help but notice the frown on Dare's face. It was a frown directed at Storm, who had just kissed her on the lips.

"I thought I warned you about doing that, Storm," Dare said in a very irritated tone of voice.

"But I can get away with it today because she's the bride and any well-wisher can kiss a bride on her wedding day."

Dare raised a brow. "Are you also willing to kiss the groom?"

Now it was Storm who frowned. "Kiss you? Hell, no!"

Dare smiled. "Then I suggest you keep your lips off the bride," he said, bringing Shelly closer to his side. "And there's enough single women here for you to kiss so go try your lips on someone else."

Storm chuckled. "The only other woman I'd want to kiss is Tara and I'm not crazy enough to try it. You're all talk, but Thorn really *would* kill me."

Shelly chuckled at Storm's comment as her gaze went to the woman the brothers had labeled Thorn's challenge, Tara Matthews. She was standing across the room talking to Delaney. Shelly thought that Tara was strikingly beautiful in an awe-inspiring, simply breathtaking way, and she couldn't help noticing that most of the men at the reception, both young and old, were finding it hard to keep their eyes off her. Every man except for Thorn. He was merely standing alone on the other side of the room looking bored.

"How can the two of you think that Thorn is interested in Tara when he hasn't said anything to her at all, other than giving her a courtesy nod? And he's not paying her any attention."

Dare chuckled. "Oh, don't let that nonchalant look fool you. He's paying her plenty of attention, right down to her painted toenails. He's just doing a good job of pretending not to."

"Yeah," Storm chimed in, grinning. "And he's been brooding ever since Delaney mentioned at breakfast this morning that Tara is moving to Atlanta to finish up her residency at a hospital here. The fact that she'll be in such close proximity has Thorn sweating. The heat is on and he doesn't like it at all."

A short while later Dare and Shelly had a talk with their son. "It's almost time for us to leave for our cruise, AJ. We want you on your best behavior with Grandma and Grandpa Westmoreland."

"All right." AJ looked at his father with bright eyes.

"Dad, Uncle Chase and Uncle Storm said all of us are going fishing when you get back."

Dare smiled. He had news for his brothers. If they thought for one minute that he would prefer spending a weekend with them rather than somewhere in bed with his wife, they had another thought coming. "Oh, they did, did they?"

"Yes."

He nodded as he glanced over at his brothers who were talking to Tara—all of them except for Thorn. He also noted the Westmoreland cousins—brothers Jared, Durango, Spencer, Ian and Reggie—were standing in the group as well. The only one missing was Quade, and because of his covert activities for the government, there was no telling where that particular Westmoreland was or what he was doing at any given moment. "We'll talk about it when I get back," Dare said absently to AJ, wondering at the same time just where Thorn had gone off to. Although he didn't see him, he would bet any amount of money that he was somewhere close by with his eyes on Tara.

Dare shrugged. He was glad Tara was Thorn's challenge and not his. He then returned his full attention to his son. "When school is out for the holidays, your mom and I are thinking about taking you to Disney World."

"Wow!"

Dare chuckled. "I take it you'd like that?"

"Yes, I'd love it. I've been to Disneyland before but not Disney World and I've been wanting to go there."

"Good." Dare pulled Shelly into his arms after checking his watch. It was time for them to leave for the airport. They would be flying to Miami to board the cruise ship to St. Thomas. "And keep an eye on your uncles,

AJ, while I'm gone. They have a tendency to get a little rowdy when I'm not here to keep them in line."

AJ laughed. "Sure, Dad."

Dare clutched AJ's shoulder and pulled him closer. "Thanks. I knew that I could count on you."

He breathed in deeply as he gathered his family close. With Shelly on one side and AJ on the other, he felt intensely happy on this day, his wedding day, and hoped that each of his brothers and cousins would one day find this same happiness. It was well worth all the time and effort he had put into it.

When he met Shelly's gaze one side of his mouth tilted into a hopelessly I-love-you-so-much smile, and the one she returned said likewise. And Dare knew in his heart that he was a very happy man.

His mission had been accomplished. He had won the hearts of his son and of the woman that he loved.

* * * * *

We hope you enjoyed reading

DELANEY'S DESERT SHEIKH

and

A LITTLE DARE

by *New York Times* bestselling author

BRENDA JACKSON

If you liked these stories, then you will love
Harlequin Desire.

You want to leave behind the everyday!
Harlequin Desire stories feature sexy, romantic heroes
who have it all: wealth, status, incredible good looks…
everything but the right woman. Add some secrets,
maybe a scandal, and start turning pages!